I0593730

Book of YESHUA

The Voice for Truth in a World of Lies

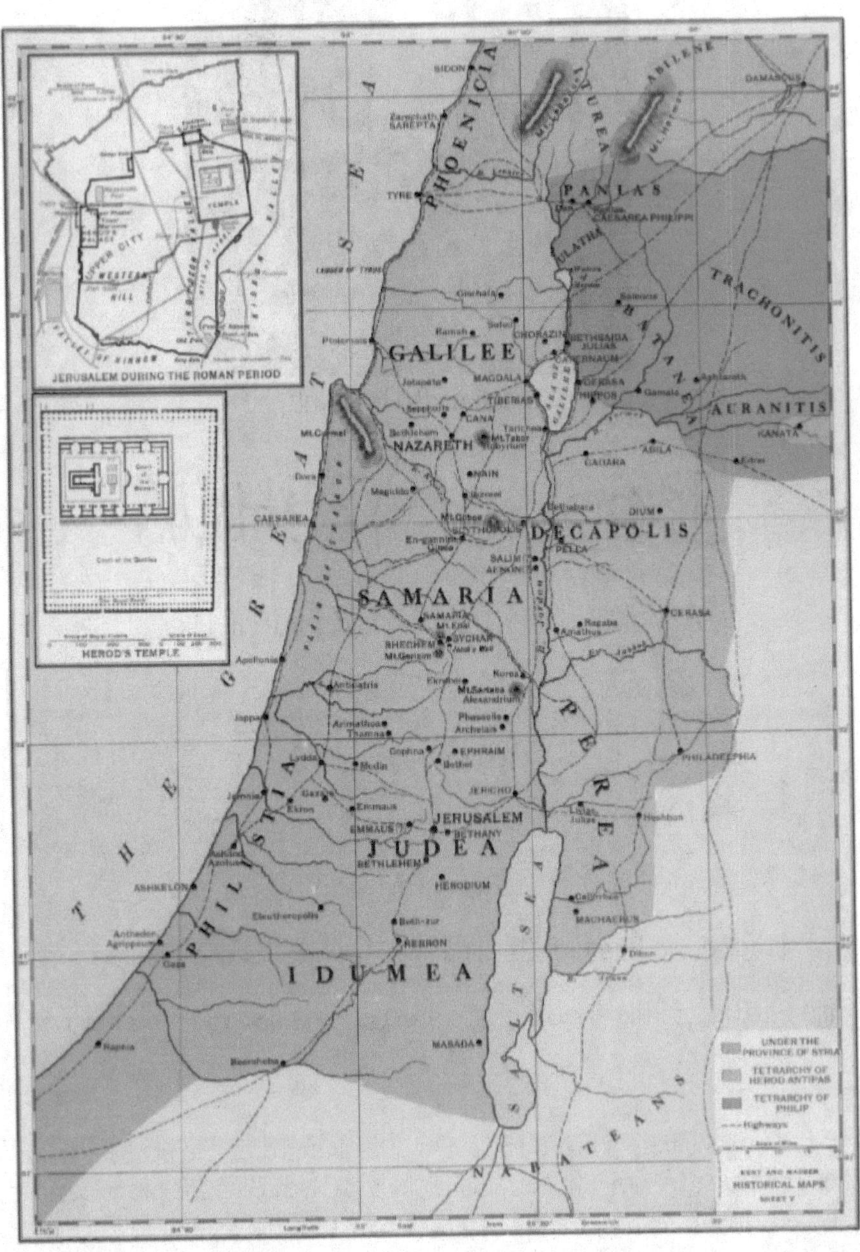

Map of Ancient Judea
Library of Congress

Author: Ecallaw Leachim
Cover Art: Dimce Stojanovski

Rembrandt Portrayal

Book of YESHUA

A Voice for Truth in a World of Lies

Imagine: You are in Ancient Judea

Imagine: You can understand the language

Imagine: You can follow in the footsteps of Yeshua

Imagine: Walking with the great prophet and hearing his words

This retelling of the ancient gospels will change how you see everything.

In this remarkable and lyric book, the author explores the possibility of what the true story of the Messiah might be. Given that the practices and beliefs of the historic Jesus fitted closely with the Essene faith, that little known path of Judaism from the area where the Dead Sea Scrolls were found, we reconsider the world through that lens.

Book of Yeshua

"The Spirit of the Lord God is upon me, Because the Lord has anointed me to bring good news to the afflicted; He has sent me to bind up the brokenhearted, to proclaim liberty to captives and freedom to prisoners." Isaiah 61:1

Author Forward: The Geography of Ancient Judea

Understanding the geography of Ancient Judea is important. Did you ever wonder why Jesus mentioned Samaritans over and over? He used them to emphasize the virtues of kindness, compassion, and acceptance of others, but why the Samaritans? Well, imagine if Mexico extended up between Arizona and California and you needed their approval to travel between those states! Imagine the resentment you would feel regarding those damn Mexicans. Samaria was squarely between Galilee and Judea - You had to pay a tax to go through it.

The only free path from Galilee to Jerusalem was down the River Jordan, and when you look at the 3D map you also see the obvious barrier that Samaria posed to those wishing to trade throughout the region. When we grasp that Samaria was a competing country we can also perhaps understand what Jesus truly meant about accepting others.

It takes the same materials and the same effort to build a wall as it does a bridge. The difference between the two is our level of acceptance of others. When we accept another, as they are, we build a bridge.

I am fully aware there are many who will not be able to accept this version of the Jesus story. Some may feel their beliefs are turned upside down and will wish to reject everything in this book out-of-hand. The whole notion of this work is NOT to diminish your faith. It is to give you thoughts and concepts to help make you a better Christian, a better Jew, a better follower of Islam, a better Buddhist, or Hindu - I write with the intention of helping your world, and your life, to be better.

Perhaps it will help to understand that Jesus was not a Christian, he was a Jew - an Essene Jew. Essenes were seen as little better than Samaritans, yet Jesus was able to bridge the gap and give out a message for the whole world. Here I give you a very different narrative of Jesus.

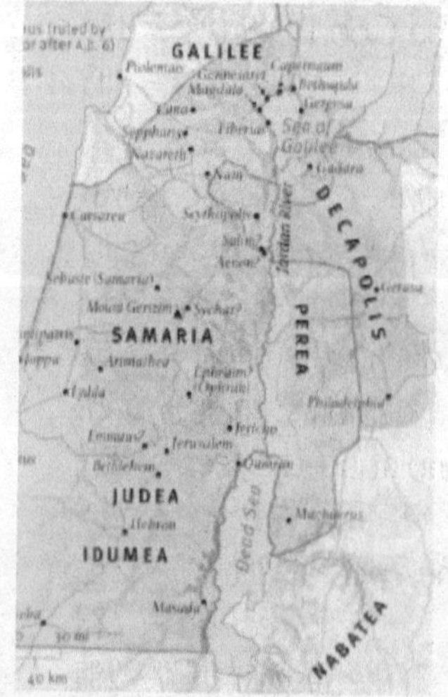

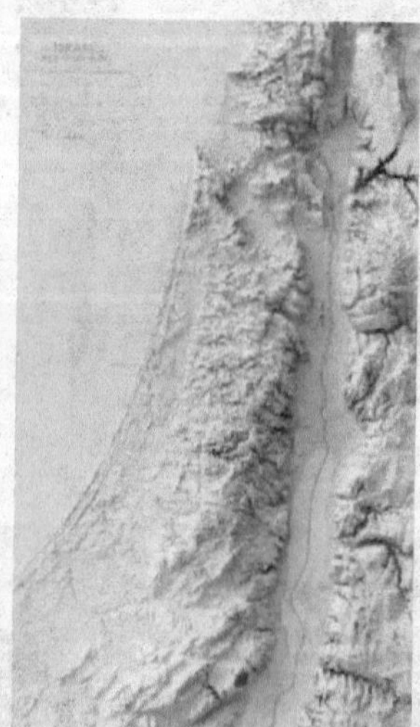

Other Books by this Author:

Available on Amazon

Psychic Nazi Hunter
(The Extraordinary Biography of Alan Wood-Thomas)

End of Times Trilogy (Sci Fi)
Eat Your Fill - Eat Your Religion - Eat Your God

The Book of Number Trilogy (Mantic Science)
Workbook - Interpretations - Practitioner Guide

Jemimiah Versus the Grabblesnatch (Fiction - Myth)

The Divinity Dice Series (Mantic Science)
Decimal Dice - Divinity Dice - Book of Aspects - Pythagorean Patterns

Ratology: Way of the Un-Dammed (Non-Fiction)

Ratology II: Who Gives a Rats? (Non-Fiction)

Fragments of the Mirror (Short Stories)

Witch Hunter and other stories (Short Stories)

Water: More Precious than Gold (Non-Fiction)

The Borringbar War (3 Day Auto Biography)

Hello Planet Earth (Short Stories - Modern Myth)

Rome Too / Rome Tree / Rome Tor (Parody)

Parables of Geoff (Biography)

The Wand (Fantasy)

Wolves of Planet Hope (Sci Fi)

Planet Aqua (Sci Fi)

Secrets of Delphi (Novel)

Hunters of the Mist (Sci-Fi)

The Birth of a Religion

At the end of days for Ancient Judea, six main groups created the state of conflict that led to its demise. Six sets of people, each with their own agendas, each with little idea how their actions would precipitate a war yet, because of this, from these ruins a extraordinary new religion arose.

The story starts with the Baptist, the first Jewish prophet in four hundred years, though there had been many pretenders. He emerged from the desert telling all to prepare for the accounting. He declared that liberation was at hand. He preached you must cleanse your soul of sin for the Messiah was coming. When he saw his cousin Yeshua, he declared this was the one.

Six points of conflict, overlaid like the Star of David. First, the Romans: Judea was an important staging point in the control of North Africa. The Romans wanted order in the country, and they wanted their tax. Into this play of power was cast Pontius Pilate. He was promoted by Lucious Sejanus, who had taken over the reins of the Roman empire. Pilate was sent to Judea specifically to secure Roman authority and break the power of the second group, the Sadducee.

Second, the Sadducee: These were the rich and privileged sons descended from Aaron. They controlled the Temple and a good deal of the finances for the country. These were Greek speakers who largely formed the diplomatic communication between Judea and the Roman Governor.

Third, the Pharisee: These were the observers of the law and were responsible for the day to day running of Judea. They conflicted with the Sadducee on many points of faith, and when the Temple was destroyed they became the precursors of the Rabbinical form of Judaism we see today.

Forth, the Zealots: These were to become the Sicarii, (Iscariot) the assassins who set Judea on the path to ruin by openly opposing Rome. They were, as the word describes, zealots for a Judea free of Romans.

Fifth, The Tetrarchs: These were the Sons of Herod the Great, the Temple builder. Here we deal with Herod Antipas, the man who beheaded the Baptist. He created the city of Tiberias on the sea of Galilee.

Sixth, the Essene: The writers of the Dead Sea Scrolls, a very early form of Judaism that lived on the Qumran. These were a people reliant on subsistence farming and known to share all they have with their community. They opposed animal sacrifice, drank no alcoholic wine, and lived apart from the other Jews. Yeshua was an Essene, as was the Baptist, and the Magdalene.

Everything centers in and around the seventh element - the Temple in Jerusalem. Rebuilt by Herod the Great with the approval of Caesar, it became a vast resource of money and hope for Judea. Now we read how the machinations of all these groups grind together like ill fitting cogs to form the remarkable tale of politics and schemes that became the birth place of Christianity.

Prelude:
The Year the Calendar was Reformed

It is 708 Ab urbe condita (46 BC)
The Year of the Consulship of Caesar and Lepidus.

Julius Caesar looked at the documents presented. Such a simple thing, you might have thought, reforming a broken calendar. But Bracius was right, if Rome wanted to have this accepted by all the various tribes and interests throughout the Empire, common sense was not enough. It would have to be timed to match an unquestionably auspicious occasion. The grey-blue eyes surveyed the evidence with the usual cool calculation. Creation of the Julian calendar had many hurdles to jump. He glanced sanguinely at his advisers, "445 days is a very long year."

A harrowed looking Sosigenes, nervous at being in the presence of one of the great Patricians of Rome, just nodded. "For this one year, Caesar. Smaller changes will be made after this, but we can adjust the calendar slowly until the planetary alignment forty six years from now."

A small detail, one of the thousands of reforms Caesar had set his mind to, but important. The Roman world needed consistency and the existing lunar calendar was responsible for too many military errors. Proper planning needed accuracy of time and date - a thing not possible with the current insanity. Caesar barely paid attention to the scholar, looking instead to Marcus Vipsanius Agrippa, "So, we will officially start the new date, which will be the Year One, in forty six years. How will the Gauls view this matter?"

Agrippa laughed, "They will hate us, of course. But they believe in the stars as much, if not more, than the Egyptians and Macedonians. If anything can work to setting up a single calendar across the empire, what the scholars propose with the planets aligning seems to make sense. Not that I care, I prefer a sword to politics, as you know."

"If a soldier can see the sense in it, the people will as well," Caesar replied, in that clipped, impersonal tone that indicated the decision was made. "This will be the last of the years of confusion."

He looked once more at the astrologer, "You can say with absolute certainty that the planets will align in this year?"

"I can say this with absolute certainty, Caesar," the man bowed.

"By the Gods I hate people who bow," he snorted to the Greek. But quietly he laughed to himself, "You know they will presume Rome lined up the stars to set the date for the new calendar. One more brick of organization in the great edifice of Rome!"

Bracius coughed, "Ah, Herod's delegate for Judea asked if you had yet decided on rebuilding the Temple and the city walls in Jerusalem."

"Hyrcanus and his Jews saved our arses in Alexandria, Bracius. Herod Antipater and his son need to be kept onside, so grant approval to rebuild the city defenses and the Temple, plus remove the excess taxes Pompey put on them. Control of North Africa wraps around the control of Judea, so let's support our friend in Jerusalem and reward him for choosing the right side. In fact, we will give him Roman Citizenship."

Agrippa noted, "They stand to make a lot of money out of their Temple Tax. Every man over age twenty has to pay it, just half a shekel, but it adds up. We should get a slice of that."

Caesar looked into the distance, "It is bad luck to take money from temples, Agrippa. We have had too many instances of greed overtaking religious propriety here in Rome already. Leave him the tax, I presume he will use it to rebuild the city, and it is important to have a client who is favorable to Rome sitting in Jerusalem. It is our Eastern flank and strategically, key to the whole region and the spice trade."

The great man felt something stirring in the desert province. The Jews were like the Greeks - they were everywhere, in administration, in business, teaching in the schools. He felt it in his bones, having them compliant and supporting Rome was important.

Position of Judea in the Roman Empire in 44 BC
It was an essential base for the trade routes to the East

Pontius Pilate

A Prefect for Judea

The Introduction of Pilate

It is 779 Ab urbe condita. (26AD)
Year of the Consulship of Lentulus and Sabinus.

Marcus Pontius Pilatus smiled broadly. His bet had paid off, supporting a snake as he had. Since Tiberius had come to power, the Equestrians were the rising order, and none had risen higher than the man who had turned the Praetorian Guard into his personal army. And here it was, his reward from Sejanus, written inside the sealed note - In days his sponsor would stand before the Senate, and Pilate would receive the prefecture of Judea. All he needed now were his final orders before departure.

Pilate took the trip across to the Palatine, to the home of Lucius Aelius Sejanus. He was received at the door by a Greek and taken to a private room - no windows, in a quiet part of the house. Shortly after Sejanus arrived, beaming and welcoming. He orders his servant to fetch wine, and indicates for Pilate to relax on one of the sofas.

Their rich brocade, stitched with purple thread, was a sure sign of the wealth and influence his sponsor had amassed under Tiberius. "The Emperor is well?" Pilate asked as a courtesy. A servant poured a wine and set it onto the finely decorated citrus wood table, with a jug of water beside it for him to dilute to his taste. He looked at the expensive inlay, a table worthy of Caesar himself. Despite the humble beginnings of its owner, the room dripped with wealth. Every inch shouted it, from the fine mosaics to the casual, confident air of the man who virtually ran Rome.

"As to be expected," Sejanus replied with little enthusiasm. "Judea, Pontius - you understand your job?"

Pilate inclined his head. "Ensure order, collect the tax, and break the power of the priests, by whatever means necessary."

"That damn province has always been trouble and will always be this while those bloodsuckers are given free rein. Provoke them, Pontius, needle them, anger them, cause them to riot - but never enough to force the Legate from Syria to have to come down. What I want is report after report of how you were able to pacify a region that refused to pay taxes, or that you found a weapons cache of potential rebels. You will be provided a sufficient guard, enough to maintain a strong presence, but be sure to hire in Samaritans, as well as any other outsiders whose very presence beside you will be an affront to the priests." Sejanus started to pace. His hatred of the Jews was well-known and now he had worked into a position to strike at their heart.

"I want you to start killing their religion, piece by piece. Turn the people away from the priests in any way you can. Isolate them, create divisions between Pharisee, Zealot, and Sadducee. Breed distrust in every area of their faith, but support Herod. Always remember, the priests who run the Temple are the source of all trouble in Judea, and represent a curse we must resolve."

"What about the Essenes? From what I have read, they live in groups outside of main towns, which is usually a point of rebellion."

"They don't count," Sejanus snorted. "Their only interest is finding a Messiah and writing up the history of every damn Jewish prophet. They are pacifists, and do not eat meat or conduct sacrifices to the Gods. They don't even drink proper wine!"

Pilate understood the general reason for him being there, but he was concerned because he knew the Senate had other clients they preferred to take over Judea. Sejanus had insisted on his own candidate, which meant rich people were going to lose money. This could make the position very temporary and you needed time to amass the returns to justify the effort. "You jumping me into the spot like this will be creating more than a few enemies. Should I expect a knife from anyone in particular?"

"You are MY client - Those who expected to get money out of the Jews know the risk of angering me. I will send you with a personal note of introduction to Herod Antipas and the other administrators, also his brother is another titular King over there at the moment. Don't worry about Rome - While I am here, as long as you do your job, you are safe.

"Your main enemy is the High Priest, Caiaphas. The Sadducee have all the money and they support him. The Sanhedrin is in his pocket and that one man, along with his father-in-law, Annas, now control most of the economy in Judea. They are the ones who are stealing our taxes. They will also be the ones organizing any assassins, and any rebellions."

Pilate had studied the desert state. Everything about it smelled of arguments and trouble, "Is it true that Gratis appointed him? Why would he have picked such a problem?"

"Gratis fired any High Priest that did not commit to his will. I would presume Caiaphas made the right noises and paid off competitors. Plus, Caiaphas' father-in-law had also been High Priest, so the man had sufficient connections to make all the bribes stick. If Herod was not so politically weak and ineffective, you could have used him to manipulate the Sanhedrin, but he is too Roman and they all hate him."

"They say this Herod Antipas, son of Herod the Great, built a city over a graveyard, knowing no Jew would enter it, then made it his capital?"

"It is true," laughed Sejanus, showing for the first time something other than grim determination. "His father built the Temple only Jews could enter, so he build a city they could not! You will like him, I knew him through my father - he was educated in Rome and speaks the language better than any barbarian I have known. He prefers Rome to Judea, which is why I trust him.

"He caused an enormous argument over there with that city, calling it Tiberias, of all names. Tiberius sucked it up like the doddery old fool he is - But you have to give it to Herod, it cemented his position in Rome, though at the cost of the local priests now hating him with a passion. However, despite the vaunted title of Tetrarch of the Jews, Herod has no real power. He has money, but no real wealth, and a lot of enemies. Even so, he will ensure you are protected, and I advise you to meet with him, make him a friend, and use his local knowledge. It will make your job much easier."

"The Syrian Legate, Lucius Aelius Lamia - He has no love for me. Any sort of trouble will be seen as an opportunity to march his armies down and rub my nose in it." Pilate warned.

"You will soon have no concern about anyone interfering in our little task in Judea," Sejanus responded. "Everywhere in the Empire, where ever there is trouble, and in every province where the taxes are being siphoned off, you will find either a Greek or a Jew behind it. The difference is that the Greeks don't hate us and are quite happy being subject to Rome. The Jews hate us, universally, and refuse to be Romanized. They think they are better than us, that their God is better than our Gods, and every night they pray to that God to get rid of us."

"And what happens then? Do they get to run things? Is that what they want?" Pilate was curious.

Sejanus snorted, "By the Gods, all they want is THEIR God to rule. Bringing down Rome would be proof their God is better, and no, they have no plans to improve anything, to build anything, or to improve society in any way. They live in the past and follow the rules laid down a thousand years ago. They are completely insane with their religion. For one example, they desperately needed a Temple, it is everything to them - Yet they made it hell for the first Herod to build one because having anyone around who is not Jewish offends their holy purity. The problem was, they were crap builders who didn't know how to make it! Herod had to train up a thousand priests to become masons to construct the central part, their holy of holies, because in THAT area only priests are allowed. They are fanatics, stupid, idiotic fanatics who are not even allowed to use dressed stone, because that isn't pure either."

Pilate said nothing. Everyone knew how much Sejanus hated the Jews, now he was beginning to understand why. "So we know you don't care so much for Jews, but from what you are saying, the priests are the real problem?"

Sejanus poured a little wine, watering it done significantly, for he was no Cato. "Let me put it this way, if you were playing with the other kids wherever it was you grew up, and you said to them, *'I am better than you, I am Chosen by God!'* what do you think will happen?"

"I get the crap kicked out of me is what happens," Pilate laughed.

"All their priests do is tell their people they are better than everyone else, that THEY are the chosen ones, and that their God is better than all the other Gods. There is no religion in the Empire that is so unbelievably arrogant. We run the place, yet OUR Gods are wrong. Our oracles are false, and our right to rule in Judea is non-existent. The reason? Because our temples and priests are all false - How DARE they!"

Put that way, Pilate saw how the priests were openly insulting Rome and the Emperor. "Lucius Sejanus, you are the First Man of Rome. Anything you order I will do. If you want me to rub their noses in it at every opportunity, I will. If you want me to flog their High Priest in public, I will. But let us be clear on specifically what you want, how you want it done, and when you want it done by."

The man just nodded. "First, start breaking down the powers of the Sanhedrin. This means ruining the reputation of the elite, which is a group called the Sadducee. Start taking away their rights to do anything. You have to make them look weak and ineffectual in the eyes of the people. Anyone who supports them, find a reason to tax them. If some group is favored by them, tax them. If for any reason one of them fails to pay their taxes, humiliate them in public.

"The key to this is grasping how the two main groups, the Pharisee and the Sadducee, detest and despise each other. So find ways to set them at each other's throats. A word in that ear, a whisper in the opponents, you know the story. When I get *complete* authority (he paused) to act, I will put my OWN High Priest into that precious Temples of theirs and start instructing the people to obey Rome. I want an end to this nuisance."

Pilate just nodded. He had heard the rumors, Tiberius was old and no longer had a grip on power like he used to. The new man was before him. It was a matter of playing your dice well, doing your job, and you will rise with him. "You must be very busy and I have taken up too much of your time already, Lucius. Thank you for your trust, you can be assured you will get exactly what you want out of Judea. When do you need me there?"

"Let your staff pack your house, just take a boat and get to Jerusalem. I have a Parabellum already in place, which will fund everything you need for this coming year. Remember, squeeze the damn priests till they squeal - Step on their toes, make them angry, because this will tell me who their protectors are. They are paying HUGE bribes to Senators here, and they will write to their clients demanding action. I will then take delight in looking puzzled as to why good Roman senators are busying themselves with the affairs of a desert province of no great account. This is the real job, shaking the snakes from the tree, it is not just about organizing Judea to be more compliant. I don't care how many you have to crucify, just break the power of the priests and stamp Roman authority all over that place"

The future Prefect for Judea bowed his acknowledgment and left, making his way to the house of a merchant captain he knew, to organize the next ship. He smiled to himself - Being given such an important province, with total authority - He knew the score - keep Sejanus happy and he could do whatever he wanted. After that, the Senate was the only force that could remove him, and the way to keep the Senate happy was to ensure that order was kept and that Judea paid her taxes. This was the opportunity of a lifetime! He felt it in his bones, he was going to make a name for himself over there.

Lucius Aelius Sejanus

The Story Begins with a Story ...

The Angels of Truth, Justice, and Wisdom

It is year 781 Ab urbe condita, (28AD)
The Year of the Consulship of Silanus and Nerva.

Rome was of little importance to those living in the quiet backwater of Judea that was Azzah. (Now modern day Gaza) The hum of life was mundane in that part of the world and precious little of interest came over the horizon other than the Sun and Moon.

In the fields beyond a small village, a man sits in an abandoned hut, weaving threads from the flax he had harvested from the roadsides. Outside and around his shack, a gaggle of children were begging, as they always did, for a story from him. He laughed, he was happy to pass the time speaking to the little ones. "Today, I will tell you the tale of two very bad children!"

They laughed, that had their ears. As they grew quiet to listen, he smiled and began his story.

There was a peaceful town with a wealthy landowner. He was the local lord, and the land he owned was prosperous and bountiful. However, there was a problem. The man had two children, a youth and his sister, who acted with impunity to the law. The pair took what they wanted from local fairs, saying it was tax. The boy would bring his friends to the tavern and drink all night without paying the innkeeper a shekel. Many times the father was beseeched for coin to pay for the goods his children has taken from the people, until he could bear it no more, and insisted they stop. He sent them to a mountain village, calling them troublemakers, which greatly appeased the community.

Yet away from the stern presence of their father, the two became even wilder. There was nothing of worth to be had in the little village where they were sent, but there was a very attractive girl the youth took a fancy to. But she refused him. However, he would have none of her protests and raped the poor soul, who went home in tears to her father.

The children of the rich man were not to know that this father of the girl was a holy man and when he heard this terrible tale, he beseeched the Angel of Truth to come down, and determine if his daughter spoke from her heart. He knew well how the passions of youth could drive a Soul and needed to know if she spoke from guilt. She ran from the house, hating him for not believing her.

Alas, she ran into the path of the sister, who asked why she wept so. The girl was very foolish and did not realize she spoke to the sister of the man who raped her. She explained that her father will bring the Angel of Truth to test her story of rape, she who had never lied in her life.

Well, the sister was not so foolish. She knew if the girl was tested her story would be proved, which meant that the guilt and its sentence of death would then fall upon her brother. This was a thing she could not bear, so she cut the throat of that innocent child, and went to see the Angel of Truth herself.

He stood in the clearing and assumed the girl coming to him was the one sent by her father. *'Your father sent you here?'* he enquired.

"Yes," she responded, happily speaking the truth.

The Angel warned. *"You must now speak only the truth, for if you lie to me, you will burn with the fires of hell and die where you stand. Tell me, were you raped by the youth as you told your father?"*

The girl laughs, and says honestly and openly, "*I was not raped by that youth!*'"

"You admit you lied to your father?"

"I often have lied to my father," she said earnestly.

What could the Angel do? She did not burn in the fires of hell, so she spoke the truth. This meant there was no need to confront the youth, to test him, so he left.

The girl laughed, she had saved her brother and fooled an angel all at the same time. The thought brought her delight. She laughed once more and went to find him to tell the tale of her cleverness.

But our story continues, for the father, distraught at his daughter running away, had followed her. He finds her dead body lying on the ground with her throat cut. He wails to the heavens for the Angel of Justice to come and deal with this terrible crime. He knew now his daughter had spoken the truth and presumed the boy had killed her to save his own life.

The Angel of Justice comes to earth, and finds the boy, laughing with his sister over some private joke. He says, "I am the Angel of Justice. You must answer my questions earnestly about the murder of an innocent child. If found guilty, your eternal soul shall be sent to hell."

The girl steps forward, she had fooled one Angel already this day, why not a second? "I will speak for my brother and will say only the truth."

The Angel of Justice looks at the girl, "A young girl claimed she was raped by your sibling. Now she is dead. Did your brother murder her?"

The sister stands before judgment and boldly says, "He did not murder the girl. I cannot say who did, but I can say absolutely that my brother played no part in the crime of murder!"

The Angel of Justice is confused. He can sense the guilt, yet when he weighs the heart of the sister, he finds she speaks the truth. He weighs the heart of the youth and finds no murder in there. There is no more to be done, so he too leaves the guilty pair unpunished.

The father has watched the trial and despairs. SOMEONE has murdered his poor child. SOMEONE must be guilty. He prays for the wisdom to understand and by doing so calls the Angel of Wisdom to Earth. He comes down and stands before all three of them.

The sister is perplexed. How can she fool the all-seeing eyes of the Angel of Wisdom? How can she save her brother, how can she save herself? In her shame, she realizes that she cannot trick this Angel with clever words, so she says nothing. Her brother also begins to see what he has done, and how his fate cannot be avoided, so he too stands, saying nothing.

Of course, the Angel of Wisdom cannot be tricked by fine words and cleverness. He sees through all deceit and lies and knows how his poor brothers were fooled. Yet, he also sees how the brother and his sister say nothing to incriminate themselves. Why are they silent? He looks into their hearts and sees the remorse. Yes, it is merely remorse for their guilt, and not for their act - but wisdom knows, this is how a soul starts on the road to purity. He knows it is possible for this pair to find redemption.

The Angel now looks to the tortured soul of the poor father, and sighs. He is weeping, tearing his hair out with the pain he suffers. The Angel nods slowly, saying, "Your daughter is now at peace in the arms of the Lord. What else do you need of the Gods?"

The father wails, "I want Justice! I want the hurt in my heart to be healed! I want my daughter back beside me!"

The Angel nods wisely and strikes the man down, right there in front of the shocked faces of the sister and the brother. He says, "So now he is with his daughter. The hurt in his heart is healed. What say you of this, children of sin?"

Shaking in fear, the boy sees the truth. His actions caused his sister to protect him and by doing so kill the girl. Her actions caused the father such grief that he called down the Angel that in turn struck him down. It was his fault, it was his burden, and he would spend all of eternity in hell. You cannot hide from the face of God. He looks at his sister, "My actions caused this, Angel of Wisdom. Take me to hell and let me pay the price, but spare my sister for she acted only to save me."

"No," she cries, "Take me, spare my brother. I killed the girl, I deceived the Angels. I am the one who deserves hell!"

The Angel of Wisdom smiles his crooked smile, the path to redemption will be long for this pair, but they have put their first step to it. However, words fly easily from a fearful heart, their new-found selflessness must be tested. "Your punishment is to care for the family of this man. You will take his wife and her remaining children back to your father's house, there you will treat them as honored guests and care for them as if they were your own family. Should you fail in this duty I place upon you, you will indeed spend an eternity in suffering."

And so the Angel of Wisdom leaves the children of the rich man, knowing that the Truth has been told, Justice has been served, and that Wisdom shall at last prevail.

There is a pause, the children look puzzled at this strange tale they have been told. Finally, a boy pipes up, "But how can this be justice? The man and his innocent daughter are dead, and the guilty are set free?"

"Ah," laughs the man weaving the flax, "So it would seem to human eyes. We always want revenge for the wrongs done to us and believe that justice will provide this. But true justice is a divine gift. True justice hides within the will of the Gods - and what they wish for each person is that he or she finds their purpose in this game of life. What we believe to be right or wrong is like an ant deciding what the world should be. The Gods live high in the sky and see across time. This means their understanding of truth, justice, and wisdom is far greater than ours."

A girl chimes in, "But they get away with it. You can't kill someone or harm them and get away with it!"

The man smiles broadly. These little souls are yet to see how the world works, how the children of the rich never face the law in the same way as the children of the poor. "You think they escaped justice? Consider that every day the brother and sister, these children of the rich man, are humbled by the evidence of their crime, the family of the dead father and daughter. Every day they must face the truth of what they did. Every morning when they awake, they know they must repair some of the harm done, or face far worse for themselves. How can this be anything but justice served?"

"But the poor girl and her father! They are DEAD!" the little girl insists.

"And suffering no more pain. There is but one certainty in this world, little one: No one gets out of here alive!" the man laughs. The children twitter on like little birds for a while, then slowly make their way back to the families as dinner time is drawing close and bellies must be fed.

The GATHERER of the FLAX

Each day on the highway the man could be seen collecting the flax. It grew wild by the roadside, and in the ditches and valleys nearby. This meant a man could survive where chance, in the form of traveling carts spilling seed, had cast her harvest. For the vagabond, it sufficed as an existence, for you could pluck the coarse plants that grew on the untenured lands, then spread them out to dry in the sun.

Each night he would take the dried flax from his gathering, then ripple it through a comb made of nails, to separate the fiber, then ret it, allowing nature to compost the useless bulk, leaving only the fiber.

Then it must be beaten, then hackled, before it can be spun. Then you weave it into rope or sell the raw fiber to the local weaver to make linen.

Some might have praised this soul for his industry, but this was a harsh land and such thing as praise and kindness were scarce. Collecting flax was the habit of children and his activity was seen as akin to scavenging. This was a creature on the edge of society and the man was considered low. A slave faired better, for the most part.

Yet there was something about this stranger that stirred you. The rough hands, the sun-hardened face, these things all working men shared, but not that distant stare, that foreign, alien gaze. It made you feel uncomfortable. Sensible people kept their distance, for he was an outsider, a nobody with no opening to the world of society. In our modern world, he would be like the lunatic on the bus, the alcoholic in the gutter, or the eccentric.

Obviously, no decent person wasted breath on this type of wastrel. "Turn the other cheek," the mothers would say to each other if his presence were brought up at either the well or market. In Ancient Judea, this meant to ostracize, to have no dealings with the person. But still, the presence of this outsider clung to the air in a haunting way. Some of the women swore he stared at them, even in their dreams. It was clear he was to be avoided. Someone said he was not even a proper Jew, but one of the Essene sect. (Those stupid people who lived on nothing but dust in the Qumran)

He was an outcast, untouchable, to be ignored. But did this appear to concern the man? Not at all, it seemed. He went right on as he had for months with his lowly business of gathering the wild flax. Turning it to thread, then winding it to be sold as rope. Each sunrise found him gathering, and each evening he was in the abandoned hut on the edge of the village, weaving his rope.

Of course, the men would have spoken to him as would all men that shared a beer, but he did not frequent the betting pools or taverns, or their gambling dens. This man had little discourse with anyone bar the children. Indeed, few but the gossips gave him even a passing thought as he scavenged in the wilderness.

Yet of course it was very different with the children. Gathering the flax, as they would be doing as well to earn a coin, the children saw him often. They loved to speak with him, and he was often seen laughing with them. They came to know and like him, for whatever the man was to the adults, to the children he was the most wonderful storyteller who always had a tale of amazing places and far-off lands for any and all who had an ear to listen.

"Tell us of the time you met the bandits at that merchant town!" One would call.

"Oh, that story is days old, children," he would say, laughing at their bright open eyes. "There are so many more to tell. What about a story about the COBRA? The amazing snake that flattens its head when it is about to strike!" His hand would mimic a cobra about to strike. The mouths would open, the eyes light up, and the ears would be straining to hear every single word. And so each day the tales were told, and every story became another adventure for the children. And there is nothing children love more than extraordinary tales with incredible creatures in some far-off land.

Naturally, the children did not tell their mothers about this. Little ones are wise in their way, and they know how mothers are too quick to say "You cannot do this! The man is a stranger and may be dangerous. You must stay away." But of course, as time went by the ripples spread out through the humdrum of village existence, and one mother after another saw how many children seemed to follow the visitor about. Strangers are not safe. One word of fear invariably breeds many and soon enough the women were up in arms at the dangerous evil that had crept into their midst.

ooo0000ooo

The matter was brought to the fore on the day the Roman Aedile came to town, on his regular route supervising the granaries, checking the weights, and collecting the taxes.

This may have been a rough desert to most, but the South of Judea had its charms. Only yesterday the Roman was enjoying a bath in some small seaside village on the Azzah coast. The prostitutes were friendly, and the town had not presumed the antipathy a Roman normally would meet in this backwater of the Empire. He supposed they wanted the coin a tourist might bring more than they hated the tax they must pay.

But today, on his normal circuit of tax collection, his carriage and retinue arrived at a dustbowl of empty dreams and angry women, complaining of a vagrant who made their life a misery. He had apparently insulted their God with the vile stories he would tell their children. The magistrate knew, you have to hear their troubles, and offer them either reason or justice, or else extracting the tax would be a much harder task.

"So tell me, what stories does this man speak that cause you so much pain?" Though he had not yet seen his fourth decade, Antipata's face was already lined with woes and worldly cares. As a Jew, he should be grateful for his Roman citizenship, but that piece of good fortune his marriage had brought him had to be paid for in service to the Empire. Even so, he knew he should put in for a transfer to some other place, as he had come to hate and despise these petty creatures before him.

A shrill creature pipes up, her whining voice no doubt a constant irritation for her poor husband, if his reaction to it was to judge. She had small, mean eyes, an unattractive face, with an inexpensive linen Chilton covering her. The headscarf had no adornment, so typical of the dull creatures that lived in the desert. "He speaks to them of GODS, not Yahweh, but of GODS. How dare he speaks of Gods like he were some Greek!"

"He must be stopped!" they shouted. The women had already called out to the village elder. The gaggle of angry women was like a horde of wasps descending, so the local elder wisely avoided the issue and merely agreed with the women. Then he said, “It seems like a legal matter to me!” Thus he side-stepped having to deal with things and sent them off with their plaint to the visiting Roman.

This was why they had descended on the Aedile without warning. The Roman, already bored with his day in this provincial outpost, had no mind to deal with anything but his business, and to get to the next town. He did not want his mid-morning repast disturbed by a vexatious clutch of women baying for blood at his door, but knew how collecting taxes from aggravated peasants was much harder than getting them from reasonable ones. So he went to see what the trouble was.

"The stranger is polluting our children's minds!" they caterwauled. "He tells them of incredible journeys, unbelievable tales, so much so that their hearts are stolen and they grow idle." The women muttered their approval of their mutual disapproval to each other, as they all agreed upon the evil in their midst. Naturally, the Aedile simply wondered how he could best get rid of this troublesome tribe of gossip-struck women.

He could pass them on to no one else, so he was forced to suffer their muttering and curses, or have trouble with the taxes and see bad reports written about him to the governor. Besides, he dreamed of becoming a proper magistrate and after that, who knows? Attending to these village disputes was good practice for his future dreams, so he took charge of proceedings by asking careful, deliberate questions about the matter. It soon became clear that the man broke no law, nor had he interfered in any way with the normal processes of village life. Roman Law had not been crossed, so the Roman declared that the problem was not his, thinking this would put an end to the matter.

"He breaks no rule, women. By your own admission, all he does is tell your children stories. Why, a storyteller we all are at some time! Further: He makes no trespass gathering flax on untenured lands. It is his right as a citizen to do so. Therefore I have no ruling except that you, yourselves, must take your own children in hand, and allow this man as much right as you would give any citizen."

Done. No nasty reports to the governor. He had the matter neatly dealt with.

The village women turned away, but they were greatly displeased. In their minds the stranger had grown to be a greater threat, and now they were all fairly certain it was Belial himself in their midst! After many hours of nagging, their husbands were forced to act. With their women folk pushing them, they went up to the Roman to further their wives' plaint. The hapless husbands spoke. "We have ordered our children not to talk to him," they cried out as instructed by their women, "but still they do so. We say to not speak or listen to this man, and yet he speaks to them still! He draws them in. They are bewitched by this devil!"

The Roman lifted his voice over their wailing. "SILENCE!" he roared. "Roman Law is very clear, and though you people barely deserve it, answer me these simple questions. Tell me: Does this man go out of his way to talk with these children? Does he seek them out?" he questioned the crowd.

Consternation broke out amongst those present. The rabble muttered, comparing notes that might incriminate the accused. Finally one spoke out, a wizened old crone. "He does not seek out the children, but by some dark force, he draws them to him against the wishes of the parents. We claim this as grounds for witchcraft, for our children were well behaved before this man came here." This brought a rousing murmur of approval. The Roman saw a thatch of nodding heads.

"But as you yourselves have stated: The children sought him out long before you forbade them to see him! I can hardly see this as a claim of some dark wizardry. Rather, it is one of disobedient children." The Roman spoke carefully and reasonably, knowing how easily he might anger the rabble before him. Villagers are like dogs howling at the moon. There is no reason for it, but you can't explain that to a dog! If you want some peace you have to silence them, and that means feeding them in some way. He decided to act, to soothe their consternation before it rose up like a snake to strike outside of the law.

He had seen it a hundred times. Crowds begin to turn towards that ugly shade of prejudice, which then turns into the mob authority fears. And a mob they were becoming. Men and women were now shouting accusations about the man, threatening that unless justice was done by the court, it would be done otherwise. The Roman saw they would have to be appeased, and so he arranged a hearing for the following day, sending word to the man and demanding his appearance.

He sighed. He wanted to be out of this godforsaken place, do his rounds, and get back to the relative civility of Jerusalem with his reports. But hearing of a riot the day after he left town would look bad to the governor, so he stayed. Pilate was not a man you wanted to annoy.

ooo0000ooo

Such excitement! A real Roman court to be held in their little village! The taverns were rumbling with the whispers all night and the women went visiting each other, nattering like geese, setting forth their case and confirming their own stories to each other. Satisfied they had found enough guilt to incriminate the interloper, the one who had disturbed their otherwise peaceful existence, they finally went to bed.

The sun shone brightly the next morning and with the cattle lowing in the pasture surrounding the town, the Roman called the day to order. Wearing his gown of office, he sat on a makeshift Chair of Judgment and signaled for the day's event to begin. He had the chair placed into the open arena in the village square, covered by a portico of fabric. In this way, he would show how open-handed he was going to be, but he also appeased the women with an air of importance.

The two bored soldiers that escorted him around the province were placed behind him, to make the matter look serious, and to protect him in case this lot turned into an angry mob. These were dull-eyed men, near retirement, who enjoyed sneering at the crowd and fingering their swords as a continual reminder that order must be kept.

And then the accused walks into their midst. The crowd stirred, and a few names were called, but the Roman held up his hand for silence and maintained order.

A large crowd of curiosity seekers had gathered to see the man. Indeed, the fellow now held an air of mystery as he stepped out from the shadows of inconsequence into the appointed place for trial. Though he was most often ignored, he was well known to all by the passing acquaintance of eye contact. He smiled at the Roman, laughing at the way it had all become quite the spectacle.

Somehow, the vagabond had managed to gather clean clothes and made his appearance to the court well-washed with beard trimmed. He went over to his appointed place, a small seat near to the makeshift dais.

Despite his washed apparel and trimmed beard, the obvious effects of the years of outdoor living showed in his nails and hands. The rough, tanned face spoke of many seasons under the sun. Lines were cast into his features like ruts on a well-worn road. He sat there impassively, hardened hands linked calmly in his lap. Despite the gawking and muttering all around him, his composure was completely unruffled.

The Roman was impressed. He was like every other working man except for the details. These were in the way he sat, and the graceful manner in which he moved. There was nothing awkward about his presence, and certainly, there seemed no sense of being intimidated by the crowd. Most of all, he had exceptionally clear, blue eyes. These were eyes undulled by circumstance, bright and alert, clearly untouched by the monotony of daily life and the tedium of humdrum affairs. It was more than his confident appearance, this one had an air of indifference that set him apart. At least, it seemed that way.

It was just this type of thing that the Roman looked for when judging a man's worth. As an educated man, sent out into the dirt and grime of local politics as most were forced to do if they wanted to climb the ladder, he despised the grubby and petty minds of all who surrounded him - but he did his duty out here in the dust, to get a better position.

Despite this, he found in himself a curious fascination about the fellow being brought before him.

Against the backdrop of so many village minds wrapped up in a cattle-like world of subsistence, here was a strength, a sense of presence that this would-be judge recognized. So it was that the accused man stood out. The Roman saw something that, in other circumstances, he might have wished to have known more of. But it was not to be at this moment, nor in this place.

"You." the Roman called, indicating for the man to step forward. "You have been accused of misleading the children of this village, causing them to dream and thus neglect their duties. These people say you are employing witchcraft to do so. How do you answer this claim?"

The man stood up, and unclasping his hands he spread his arms with a shrug and said, "How can I detain the children," he answered. "They are like the birds that come and go from the tree. I do not hold them, nor cause them to dream. I simply answer questions they would ask. I tell them stories, I tell them of where I have been and what I have seen."

The surrounding crowd ruffled like a peacock ready to display its wares. The Roman, aware of the mindlessness of uncontrolled men, took the proceedings in hand with the full weight of his judicial manner. "That is not sufficient. What questions do they ask? And what answers do you give?" he demanded.

The man shrugged once more. "The children will ask things like why the birds sing, why the rivers run, why is the sky blue?"

"And what do you reply?"

"I say simple things. That the birds sing because they love life and wish to add a little beauty to this world. I say the rivers run because they know that idleness in the sun causes them to become useless like a stagnant pond. I say the sky is blue because it is different from the green of trees and grass. That the Lord God made it that way so when people were of a different color, or type, or richer, or poorer, that they could be proud of their difference, as this is how God made them."

"See!" a woman from the crowd called out. "He fills their heads with empty nonsense, dreams, and imaginings. The children listen to this more than they listen to their parents, and we can't get them to obey us at all." The crowd murmured its agreement.

The Magistrate called them to order, asking further of the man, "You speak of different races. Have you traveled? Have you worked as a merchant?"

"Traveled? Yes, most surely. I have traveled past Egypt, Your Honor, to the land Alexander failed to conquer. I have traveled to the far ends of this planet and seen much, but I did not do this as a merchant. I traveled with them, but my purpose was for spiritual study."

The magistrate felt a wrenching in the very bones of his heart. By the Gods! Beyond Egypt! How he had longed to travel to Egypt, to see the wonders he had read of there, to visit the places Plato and the old ones had spoken of. But of course, none of this showed in his face. "You appear to have no trade. How do you survive?"

"I have a trade, Your Honor. I am a carpenter, and in the past, I served the merchant sailors with repairs to their ships, which gave me free passage, and I paid for my tuition at various schools with my work. But my tools were stolen coming back to these lands, so now I earn a few shekels gathering the flax. I knit the flax into rope or sell the fiber and trade this for food."

The weight of how a man can be so wronged with judgments made according to his appearance settled like a depression on the judge. A carpenter! A mere CARPENTER had taken his tools of trade and had journeyed freely to the far horizons. Astonishing!

Here he was, a learned man of significant means, trapped as an Aedile, and compelled by duty to remain at his post. His sense of imprisonment in this miserable dustbowl of a village increased with every word this man before him spoke.

Of course, none of this showed in his face. Yet did he detect a twinkle of amusement in this man's eye? Did this lowly fellow who stood before him realize what was running through his mind? He looked more closely and realized with a shock that this rough carpenter understood.

Somehow, this uneducated man had stared right into his heart, and for all the world the Roman fought to hold back a deep tear forming in his heart that wanted to well up in his eye. He mentally forced himself to snap back to his job and the matter before him.

"It is clear," stated the Roman, "that you are not a burden on the public good, for you do support yourself. It is also clear to me that you mean no evil intention to the children of this village."

The Magistrate paused to let the words sink in, but before the crowd could erupt in fury he continued. He looked at them all and stared down their anger, "But I ask you, what right have you to take children away from their duties and the way of life their parents intend for them?"

This cleverness brought a rousing murmur of agreement from the villagers. All admired the way this Roman had so tactfully dealt with the problem.

"What right has the bird to sing?" the man replied. "I simply say what I will, the children decide to listen. How does this draw them from their parents?"

The Roman once more looked deep into the man's eyes, understanding for a moment a little of the pain hidden therein. This pain, this separation, it was his pain as well. It was everything he had suffered in life, yet more. This man's pain shone like a golden coin in the depths of a lonely ocean. The Roman was taken with a wish that he could somehow reach in and take it, hold it, treasure it for himself.

Egypt! What a journey, and even beyond, the fellow had said. What he could learn from this stranger if they had but the time. Yet he also wanted to despise him, to prove to him that the cost of his freedom was too high. He wanted to take that secret coin from this sad-faced fellow, so that he might hand it back, saying, "Look! Here is the cost of your truth!" But he could not. Instead, he drew the man aside from the villagers and spoke quietly.

"I see in you, friend, a deeper wisdom. But this wisdom hurts the small minds of this place. They cannot contain it. You, by your simple words, have brought joy to the hearts of the children of this town, but when they seek to share this with their parents, the brightness of their smiles hurts their mother's eyes."

Then it struck the Roman. Could it be that this man was quite possibly educated like himself? "Can you read, and have you read Plato?" The vagabond nodded his agreement.

The Roman was shocked. This man was far more than a carpenter. He could have a position in any court. He could READ, he had traveled beyond Egypt! Why was he here? Why would anyone choose to live here in this miserable, god-forsaken place?

However, the crowd was beginning to rumble. "Then remember the cave! The eyes of parents who have lived in the darkness and ignorance of tradition cannot accept the change their children bring them. The children seek to bring home some joy, and the parents fear that this very joy will break the bonds that are both their curse and their security. They fear for themselves, and their children, for they fear what will happen because of change. Further: They hate you for causing this trouble in their lives, and when I leave, they will kill you."

Drawing himself upright, beginning to understand more clearly the pain buried in this man's heart, the Roman continued. "No matter my decision (He nodded towards the villagers) these people will harm you if you remain. Understand, if you can, that I by law cannot send you away but I can, as a man, say that the swan does not lie down with the carrion.

The jackals see no difference between a live swan and a dead rat, and would happily tear either apart in ignorance and hunger."

"And so I would say, as a man, for your own sake and this village's continued peace even though it be the peace of night, I say that you must go, though it pains me that I shall not know you."

The man gazed at the distant mountains, nodding his ragged head in understanding. "I thank you for your kindness," he said, taking the Roman's hand, and gazing deeply into the man's heart as he did so. "I can see you are a patient shepherd. I wish you well with your flock."

With this parting comment, he sighs. Yes, he had to leave, knowing that THIS is what he wanted to avoid. Knowing that every step would take him to a far greater danger, and a far, far more evil world. He got up and started walking.

"Wait." the Roman called, realizing a sudden, unexplained sense of loss. "I do not even know your name!"

The man turned, his tender eyes lit with a love born of hardship and a thousand, thousand insights into the nature of man. "Yeshua," he answered, "of Nazareth." Thus he turned and left behind another town, another placc. Hc now knew where he must go, and what he must do. He tied his meager belongings into a carry bag and headed to the Qumran. Towards his future wife and the destiny that he could no longer avoid.

The Qumran

His journey from the East was coming to a close. The Qumran lay ahead, with the olive groves and gardens, an oasis in the desert. Soon he would be in the house of his mother, out of the insufferable heat, and regaling his brothers and sisters with the wonders he had seen. They would sit there, eyes open in astonishment at what he had found. Finally, the journey brought him to the plateau and home to his desert people.

More importantly, soon he would speak with the Chosen One, the Zadoc. He would test his visions and listen to the wisdom of the old man - the same one that had sent him to the East so many years ago. He loved the dry air and the clarity of this place and was very glad to be back. Yeshua had no need for Jerusalem, all the madness and greed, but he would need to go there like his brother, looking for work. But first, his path was to his mother's! Still, he lingered for a moment at one of the byways - for the farm of the Magdalene's father, now a monk on the plateau, lay to his left.

He had seen her in his visions, many times. They were betrothed as children, the shiddukhin had been performed and now he felt a need to see her. He decided against tradition, he would go there first, speak with her, the daughter of Manaemus. Trekking past the barley and wheat he smiled, the crop was good. An excellent sign. As he approached the household, the old man looked up from the fields and saw the desert-bitten young man walking in, "Ho!" he called.

"Manaemus," Yeshua answered.

He came close, squinting with his old eyes. "I know that voice - Yeshua? Are you returned?"

"Yes, old man. Your eyes might be failing, but your ears are true." he laughed. "Come closer and you will see."

And the old man saw, it was true! "Yeshua! How wonderful, you have been away so long. You have come to see her?"

"I have old man. I came here before my own mother."

Manaemus nods in understanding, "She is in Jerusalem speaking to the other Jews of the Zadoc. I tell her to leave it alone, but she says they need to hear the Word - I cannot stop her. As you know, she is a firebrand that one. "

Yeshua nods, "Dangerous business. You must worry about her."

"I worry for the poor fools who try and stop her!" he laughs. "But it is true, I far prefer her here, studying her scrolls like she were a priest. It is so good to see you, Yeshua. Did you wish for some rye beer and bread?"

"I will break bread with my family first, old man, though I thank you for the kind offer. The Zadoc will know where she is staying in the city?"

"Of course, Yeshua. But I can tell you now, she stays at your brother's house! It is good to see you, for however weak my eyes might be, it is the vision in my heart that rejoices. It is good that you go to see the Zadoc, please give my thanks to him and my love to your mother. Ah, you will not have heard, but your father, he has passed."

"He came to speak with me in India - it is the reason I started back."

India! The old man was visibly shocked. So far away! He had heard words from traders who had been there, the boy had gone to the edge of the world! But he said nothing - this one was marked by destiny. "You took the invitation the Sages gave Joseph at your birth?"

"That and more, old man. That and more. Your wife is well?"

"She is, and will see me out!" the old man laughs, "When you are done on the plateau, please visit our community in Magdala and speak to us of your journeys and what you have seen, Yeshua. You know how our people love a good story."

Yeshua had a distant look, but smiled and nodded.

Manaemus knew that look, that searching for something beyond. The boy had always possessed it - the child was connected to spirit, the whole village knew. He and that wayward daughter of his, and mad cousin John, they all lived in other worlds and barely seemed to be part of the common way. "God speed, Yeshua."

ooo0000ooo

Mary howled with delight. She had felt him in dreams, but to see her son in the doorway brought her heart to song. It had not found a reason for joy since her husband had passed. Such a wonder he was, so much older, so lean and hardened by the sun - *The child of angels*, she had said when he was born. "He is the Prophecy!" said the Parsi sages who had visited that stable where he had come into this world. The star that had burned so brightly in the sky to announce his birth now seemed to be within his eyes - so bright and clear, possessing a love only a mother could understand.

"So long had it been, Yeshua, so long. Come, come inside out of the heat, and I will send word to you brothers. We must celebrate your return!"

He sat in the quiet of the family home as his mother spoke to a village boy, telling him to run and fetch his siblings. It was so good to be back, to be with his people, to feel the bond of his brothers and sisters of the faith.

Simon was the first to arrive from the fields near to the Dead Sea, his cart loaded with reeds from the springs down there. "I felt your presence, brother," he called out as he carted the reeds into the threshing shed, where they would be turned into papyrus. Yeshua helped him unload, enjoying once more the simple tasks that meant so much to his people.

He did not have to ask, Simon knew his mind. "Mother took the loss with peace in her heart, but every day she looks so sad," he sighed. "This is the happiest I have seen her this year, I know she worried about what might become of her firstborn."

"I spoke with Joseph in dreams," Yeshua offered. "I could feel his concern for her, it was why I returned, that and the omens that spoke of my time."

"We did nothing with father's workshop, as now it is yours and we supposed at some point you would return. We locked up the tools and any valuable things some wandering thief might want at the house of the scribes, so go by there with a wheelbarrow on your way."

"You are supposing I will stay, Simon?"

"It is hoped you will stay. The community would be very happy to have a carpenter of Joseph's stature back with us." The last of the reeds were in the storage shed and soaking in tubs, to be softened and made ready to be turned to papyrus.

Yeshua laughed, "One might have thought that as he was always in Jerusalem working for gold, he may not have been so warmly regarded!"

Simon smiled, "He gave us much more than gold as his tithe, he gave us respect. You know what the Sadducee think of we sad desert dwellers, but Joseph's exceptional work gave them pause to consider otherwise. Our uncle, the tin merchant, he sits on the Sanhedrin now, you know."

"The other Joseph? Really, well that is a step up for our people!"

"He sits as a Pharisee, but everyone knows. It is a small mark of respect, but they still refuse to accept the words of Enoch." Simon sighed.

Yeshua nodded, an old story of prejudice. "And many other words that are written here, my brother. They will not accept that the divine utterance can flow through the soul of a pure spirit in the present day because they no longer even know what a pure spirit is. The desert cleanses us of sin and allows the light of God to shine through, but even so, it is right that this be tested. Does Gamaliel still sit with us in the living?"

"He does, brother, the Lord be praised for his wisdom in keeping such a one amongst us. He supports Joseph in many ways, but of late he has been distracted by the Zealots. As a Pharisee, he must oversee the proper observance of the law, and on every street corner there is another Messiah standing up, proclaiming the Lord has spoken to him and given him the mission of getting rid of the Romans. The problem is that the new Governor has stripped the court of its power to put these false priests to the sword. Only the Romans can authorize a death penalty now, but when the Sanhedrin sends over a false Messiah, Pilate finds the whole thing amusing and pretty much lets them back out onto the streets. Disavowing their authority, as he does, means the Zealots now have no threat of capital punishment to hold them in check."

Everyone knew that Tiberius was living in Capri and that a Knight of the Empire had risen to effectively run the whole show. "I hear this Sejanus that appointed Pilate hates Jews." Yeshua was not interested in politics, but hatred was a disease that caused many deaths.

Simon grunted, "He does, and Pilate has clearly been put here to cause trouble. What follows from this, who can say? We are well to be here on the plateau, out of sight of Rome and Jerusalem. James keeps us up to date with the gossip of the city, so we should have a warning before trouble arrives at our door. But enough of what might be, Mother will have supper prepared and be dying to hear of your travels."

ooo0000ooo

His sisters were as keen as the rest of the village to have words of his journey. Soon after he returned with Simon, they and the rest of the people started to arrive, and Mary had to serve tea and sweetmeats on the terrace, there not being sufficient room inside. They all brought something to share, as was the custom, and soon a feast was to be had! As the moon rose dusty red over the horizon, Yeshua was like a jester before the court, telling tales of far-off places and the strange people that lived there.

"It is true, there is a religion where the men paint themselves with mud and walk naked by the rivers, giving prophecy for any who care to pay them. And it is also true that in India they have many, many Gods - at least as many as the Romans. Yet what I found remarkable was how so many there shared our vision, of how man comes again and again to this world to perfect themselves, and how eating the flesh of the beasts is undesirable. We are not alone in our beliefs."

Someone calls out about elephants, "Yes, those beasts that Hannibal rode to Rome. In India, they use them everywhere. They can lift trees with their NOSES!" Everyone laughs at the absurdity. Yeshua smiled, it was good to be back. It was a small, cloistered world, but so familiar and welcoming after so long living amongst the strange.

"Yet this is not the most amazing thing. Listen my people, in a town called Goa, a trading port, a Pharisee lived. Here I witnessed a true miracle, he took me in and gave me free board, in return for news of how things fared here. He heard how Joseph used to make Temple Furniture, and he wanted some things made. Despite me being an Essene, I was made welcome!"

Someone announced, "Now THERE is a true miracle!"

Yeshua smiled, "I suppose the distance between him and the Indian culture was further than between himself and myself. Or perhaps living amongst so many people who follow much the same laws of life as we do adjusted his view."

"I can't believe it!" his sister squealed. "You lived with a PHARISEE!" and the laughter from this made the absurdity of a beast who lifted trees with his nose seem almost ordinary.

The questions were many: Smiths asked about how iron was worked, farmers asked about how they grew crops, scribes asked about the language they used. Everyone was fascinated by how, in such a far-off country, things were not so very different. And after the questions, the gossip began, who was seeing who, what was happening where, the stuff of village life, as essential to it as the bread they ate. He sat back and watched the people all chatting away, happy in each other's company, and all this gave a rosy glow of love to the face of his mother. It pleased him deeply.

He did not say how he had brought gifts for all, tools, weapons, everything the people here would delight in. So many gifts, for he had made substantial money in India. He had to hire a carrier at the port to take everything to James in Jerusalem. But brigands attacked, and all was lost, including the gold he had stored for his marriage, most likely the only thing they wanted - but nothing was left, not even the life of the poor carrier. They found his body close to Jerusalem.

He missed the tools and the ease by which he could make a living. Having no money he started by foot to the Qumran, stopping at that little village. Sitting in the desert, weaving the flax, he heard the voice of God so clearly that he was compelled to stop and listen. This was when he knew, all the theft meant was that he was free of his past, that his only work now was God's work.

He had no idea how to go about it and he had first thought to go to the Temple. As the son of Joseph, he could easily regain his father's business. Such a temptation, to fall back to the past, to live off the society he could no longer abide. He may as well turn stones into bread as try to get sustenance from those dead souls called priests.

He knew God was sending a message with the loss of his tools and possessions. He was being told it did not matter, they were not needed. He must not bow to the Snake who whispered how he could have an easy life.

But knowing you have a mission and knowing what that mission might be are two very different things. Tomorrow was a day that required little beyond some work around the house in the morning and sorting out his father's workshop in the afternoon. When the day-to-day matters were cleared, he would go to see the Zadoc for advice, though he admitted to some surprise that the old man still lived. He was old when Yeshua was a child!

The Puzzle

The day dawned bright and clear, finding Yeshua already up with a wheelbarrow full of tools he had collected from the Scriptorium. The day began early in the desert and already he had a commission from the monks. Soon the simple structure built by his father, a shed annexed to a cave, came into view.

Yeshua stood in the familiar workshop. So long ago his family had moved to the Qumran, with Joseph setting down roots and creating this joinery. He remembered clearly that day when he was but a boy, playing around the smelting furnace where his father used to fashion hinges and handles. His mother had gone to chide him for being so near the fire, but Joseph held her back, looking Yeshua in the eye, saying, "Let the Spirit guide the child as it will, Mary. Life will teach us, either way, its truth."

He had a fascination with fire, the way the flames licked and absorbed all that came into contact with them. As a boy he used to create 'brands' from the scrap metal lying about the workshop. Using old tools of his father, he would heat it, and beat it into pleasing shapes. Occasionally Joseph would see what he did and smile, saying it was good. Of course, all he was doing was encouraging the boy to take up tools and by the time of his tenth year, he was already earnestly at work helping in the workshop.

The younger children showed no such interest, but Yeshua loved it. His father showed him simple things, like how to shape the leg of a table, how to do a miter join, all things that made Joseph seem like a God to him. He had asked about the cast-off wood, for the large square block that you started with had most of it taken away in the process of creation. His father had laughed, "It is how life shapes us all, and as much as we cling to what we were, in the process of becoming useful all the useless parts must be sloughed off. The true waste would be in not shaping the wood to become a thing of beauty."

He supposed this turn of words by his father was where he got his lyric sense of storytelling. But Joseph was no gentle shepherd, he was brusque and authoritarian, and everything must be done precisely as laid out. The forms for making the furniture were ages old, and he brooked no sense of invention nor any flight of fancy. As a child, he chaffed at the restraints, but now Yeshua supposed this also was a lesson in how things must be formed. To survive in this world, away from the kindness of the Qumran, you had to deal with bad-tempered, authoritarian men at every turn.

Over the years he learned how to choose the right wood for the right task. He knew how to select the direction of the cut according to the grain and temperament of the material he had to work with. "It is like people," his father had explained. "You cannot make a man who is made for working with numbers into the shape of a shepherd. We all have our nature, we all have our destiny. We must embrace the shape of what the Lord has fashioned in our hearts if we are to achieve this."

And yet, for a man so entrenched in tradition, so unyielding of nature, when he found his boy speaking with the Rabbi at the temple in Jerusalem, standing there in the Court of the Women arguing points of faith, he just laughed. No child of a carpenter should have been standing there like that, arguing with priests, but his father found it hugely funny.

And when Mary wanted to punish him for insolence, he stopped her. "They are idiots and a child proved it!" But later he said privately, "I am proud you stood up and spoke your heart, boy. But never forget, a Sadducee is a snake in human clothes. They will praise you only to laugh when you fall off the pedestal they put you on. They will say they love you, only to steal the clothes off your back. And if you show them a shekel, the only thought in their mind is how to get it from you." A tear formed in Yeshua's eye, such a wise, simple man was Joseph.

It was now many years since he had stood in this place, where he had said farewell to the father that raised him, both knowing they may never see each other again. But Joseph always knew, the quest for truth tugged at his boy's heart. He knew that this child would never be content living the calm, peaceful life of the woodworker.

He took a broom and started to clear the debris and dust from the floor and benches, wiping away the years of neglect. He had already seen the elder at the scriptorium, asking if anything was needed. He suspected the old man asked for a desk and chair more to ensure he was kept busy more than him needing anything, but it meant he could make his contribution and not be a burden, so Yeshua happily agreed.

The forms used to make legs were always kept in the tool cabinet, so when the workshop was made ready for work, he went over and selected the shapes needed for the job. Then he went to the cool storeroom set into the cave at the back of the workshop. You need dry, stable air to prevent the wood from twisting, and from the racks he pulled down the mahogany for the legs and found some rare fruitwood he could fashion into a top.

That was when it caught his eye, at the back of the storeroom where the most expensive woods were kept, the small puzzle box he made that designated the end of his apprenticeship. He smiled and pulled it out - amazing, his father had kept it all these years. To prove you were capable, an apprentice needed to create a mystery, something made of wood that looked like one thing, but using hidden levers could be switched to magically take another form.

He had created what looked like a simple square wooden block, but when you pressed a particular point at the base, it lifted the top, which when twisted released a side that moved out an inch. Then you twisted that and all sides were released, revealing the carved gearing and an 'exploded box'. Twist it back the other way, and it all shut up, forming the apparent solid block of wood once more.

He had spent months on that little showpiece of his ability, months. It took quite some time for Joseph to find the hidden release trigger, and open the puzzle. At the end, his father just grunted, saying, "Acceptable." This was high praise from one such as he. The fact he kept it all these years, safe in the safest place of his workshop, spoke of the true love he had for his child and of how well he had been taught.

Yeshua had no idea how wonderful a carpenter his father was until he traveled. Everywhere was slipshod work, poor craftsmanship, and badly finished surfaces. It meant he had an easy time finding employment, gaining a passage on a ship, or trading his skills for whatever he needed. You never know you have been trained by a master until you see the world and compare your skills to another's.

"Good enough is neither enough nor good," Joseph used to say, over and over. "Look about you, see the perfect forms of nature, how everything interlocks seamlessly. God is the master craftsman. If we are to dream of happiness in this life or the next, we must seek to emulate the greatest master. To do less is to fall prey to the whispers inside us. Our work must be superb, the very best we can achieve, not because we want praise from others, but because we go to sleep every night knowing we have worshipped God in the only way he values! The truest prayer to our creator is a job done to the best of our ability."

Joseph was one of the best furniture makers in Jerusalem. Because of his work in the Synagogues, it meant he did business with a lot of wealthy Jews. He was always in demand for the cabinetry and tables for their homes, and Yeshua supposed he had made quite a bit of money. Certainly enough to buy a tract of land beside the Jordan for the reeds Simon would harvest, and a house in Jerusalem for James and the family, but Joseph himself had little need for anything, bar the ability to buy the finest woods and the best tools.

Well, enough of daydreams. Yeshua set the formwork over the square timbers, marked his lines, and taking the bow saw he started with the cuts he would shortly chisel away to form the graceful lines of the table and chair legs. Having prepped all the legs, humming to himself, he worked through the day till evening. Tomorrow he would finish them, then start to work forming up the fruitwood tops for the furniture. He looked critically at the work so far, nodding to himself - Joseph would have found it acceptable.

How sorely he was tempted at his father's workshop, for he loved carving those simple things for the scriptorium. He truly enjoyed being a carpenter, a master of his trade. This place meant he could have everything, his family, a business, and an income to support the Qumran. It was a pure life, a life of goodness. How could the Lord not want this for him?

But he knew - a thin, high wind was blowing a different tune to his heart. He must see the Zadoc once the furniture is done, hear what wisdom the Lord whispers to his spiritual guide, and from this distill his purpose.

The Scriptorium

The walled compound looked almost like a fortress, as indeed it once had been. Now it fought for truth, recording the word of God with a mission for peace. There were many desks and many scribes, writing down with meticulous care their translation from the ancient texts.

Yeshua had arrived with a cart and a few men came to help him unload the desk and chairs he had made. The lead scribe looked at what was presented with admiration. "You have a fine eye, son of Joseph. Your father could not have done better. The inlay work is superb, and the fruitwood top magnificent."

"Joseph had forms and stencils already made. This makes the work go much faster. You are pleased then?"

"My boy, it is such a pleasure to have you back, that even if you had come with an unvarnished stick I would be pleased!" The old man had been a scribe here for all of Yeshua's life, and well before. Like all the scribes, they remained unmarried, living here together like monks. It was seen as necessary for the purity of the written work, that a man has but one thought: *What is the Lord's desire?*

In truth, it was a pleasant ideal. But they were human and he knew carping, bitterness, jealousy, and other evils crept in. It was a constant battle with devils from the desert, the monks would say, and perhaps it was. But for Yeshua, you cannot divorce yourself from life and expect to find balance. A life without intimacy is a life of solitude that grows into depression and misery unless one can bind absolutely to the Lord and find your true heart in him. He supposed their lifestyle forced the decision, for there was but one way to escape the trials of being human, to find the door within to the divine.

When a monk found this door, the words of the Lord would come through him. He would be visited by a prophet, or maybe he would dream walk to that soul, it was hard to say. But it was clear that the writing took on a different texture, the Peshar and the Raz would combine, as they would say, joined to take on a unique existence.

"Father, the Sadducee in the Temple has little regard for all you do. They detest the fact that you write of Angels and the wheel of life where man comes, again and again, to refresh his spirit, seeking to achieve perfection. You and those who came before you have been doing this work for two hundred years, but all the other Jews do is find fault. How do you keep your spirits up?"

Reading his mind for his true question, the old priest laughed, saying, "Weights and measures, Yeshua. We are like the ones who keep the merchants honest, checking their scales, and ensuring they give fair exchange in their business. Each day we weigh the words and find their right measure. The written form of God's truth is precarious and fragile, easily swayed by the breeze of opinion. Here we work to have the correct form, one that has clarity and truth working together. And when the grace of the Lord falls upon us, we commit this to a scroll."

"You do not care that after all your work on Enoch that it is still refused entry to the written record of the Temple?"

"We care greatly, my son. We weep over the refusal to admit the first prophet. We suffer when the words of our beginnings are ignored. But we know, the Lord has his time and his ways. Our pride must not interfere with the task we are given. But what is refused forms a mirror of truth. Because we are here, because we submit at each ecumenical cycle the words of the prophet, the Sadducees refusal of OUR work also stops them from changing the written word to suit their ends. So yes, we suffer, yet we know our purpose is more than the writing of scrolls. The Essene are a constant reminder to the elite in Jerusalem that the pure spirit of the original tribes still beats in the desert. We live here in the silence. The isolation harbors the heart of our people and the presence of the Zadoc ensures that it keeps beating."

Yeshua sat with the chief scribe in silence while they took tea. The other scribes looked up on occasions, smiled, then went back to the scrolls they were deciphering. "Checks and balances," he finally whispered, nodding. "I understand old man, the work is more than what we see before us. The weight of your effort is not just the scrolls you place into the caves, it is that this weight of knowledge you bring holds the tongue of the defiler in check."

He had to admit his thoughts in the past had been that these old men wasted their lives, writing words no one will ever hear or speak. The Essene came from the earliest roots of the house of Israel. They believed THEY had carried the role of High Priest, springing forth from the house of Enoch.

The monk smiled. "As you see is as you see. We contemplatives do not carry the world on our shoulders, Yeshua. Politics, money, power, ownership of land, murdering poor animals to satiate the blood lust of a cruel God, none of this exists in the orbit of our vision. All my little word soldiers here (he nods to the scribes) work with the sole aim of doing as the Lord wills, as best they can. We listen for his voice, and we write his words. This is our existence and we treasure each moment of it.

"Of course, sitting here in the Qumran I am given the luxury of consideration. I can see how the Essene faith challenges the Sadducee and Pharisee. I know how they hold us in low esteem and consider our beliefs absurd. But it is not my part to change them, it is the Lords. He will do as he sees fit."

"My brother James is quite active in the politics," Yeshua laughed.

"Your brother carries the burden of argument for our people, all our people, not just for the Qumran. He does a fine job and gives shelter to many Essenes needing a place to rest when doing business in the city. He serves the Lord in his way. But for us here in the scriptorium, our vision is confined to the words of the Lord and the purity of his scripture. We record the truths of our people, not the lies of priests or politicians, or the needs of business. The world of argument and politics is empty to us, we do not want this lack of truth written across our hearts."

"They see the Qumran as the place that lacks everything, including intelligent life." Yeshua jested.

The old scribe just smiled, "I had a vision, Yeshua. I saw you whipping a pit of vipers and driving them from the Temple, calling out 'IMPURE' as you did so." He paused a long moment, "You are going to see the Zadoc?"

"I go to seek his guidance this very day," Yeshua answered. There was little point in asking about the vision, the old scribe would just shake his head. He had said all he would say of it.

The old man nodded and embraced a farewell with the young Rabbi. As the boy who was now a man left to see the high priest, the scribe called out, "They use weights and measures in the Court of the Gentiles, do they not?" Then he shut the door to the desert heat and went back to his business.

Yeshua wondered about that puzzle as he made his way to the cave of the Zadoc. He remembered the money lenders in the courtyard. As a child, his father had joked about the irony of the house of God being the place of bribes, theft, and dishonor. It was common knowledge that the money changers were practicing usury, lending at exorbitant interest to those who can least afford it. He laughed, that wily old scribe saying he had no interest in politics, yet pointing out the greatest political thorn in the side of the Judaic people. The money changers paid the Sadducee for the right to their spot in the courtyard, and who knows what else transpired in secret.

Around the temple was a small city of its own, with rooms, cafes, everything you needed to live. But no common people were made welcome there, a point Herod Antipas had made sure to emphasize with him GIVING land to the poor in his new city. Such thoughts only highlighted the impossible divisions running through the heart of the Jews. How, if at all, could these seams of discontent be made whole?

He knew in his bones he was called back for a reason, a purpose. He had truly thought that Kashmir was his home for this life. It was such a happy place, it filled his heart with delight. There you could have an open discussion with the Sadhu of the various faiths. There was a complete lack of ridicule from the priests with the disparate arguments the people had. Nowhere had he found such an acceptance of different faiths along with an open-hearted inquiry into the nature of the Lord. Plus they had advanced knowledge of healing, which they shared willingly.

An entire society that permitted complete religious freedom, especially in the flower of India, Kashmir. All the wealthy families would spend their summer there, where it was mild and cool, and always they wanted work done. These people respected good work and paid handsomely for it, so in all, that place was heaven itself for Yeshua.

But when Joseph called in the dream state and said he was needed, without saying exactly why, Yeshua knew. Whatever his purpose, it could only be fulfilled here in Judea. His hope was that the Lord would speak through the Zadoc. He had seen this happen in the past, where the High Priest became the spiritual guardian and spoke with his voice. He prayed to the Lord as he walked and begged for his light to shine upon the path he must take.

Archeological remains of what is believed to have been the Scriptorium in the Qumran

The Turtle and the Fish

Zadoc looked at the boy who was now a man. He had listened closely to his dreams, heard of what Yeshua hoped to achieve, and he felt concerned. The spiritual leader of the Essene remembered well the boy's father telling him of the time Yeshua had been compelled to speak to the priests in Jerusalem Temple- who knew why, but the spirit was in him and needed to be given voice. Now he wished to speak of the spiritual truths to everyone, including gentiles. It was a dangerous thing.

"You know, the Essene has been content to sit here, to capture the dreams and record them, to study the ancient texts and translate them. This is our task and in this work, we are left well enough alone, but this is because we do not seek to press our truths on any but our own. I do not question WHY you wish to give voice to the teachings, but you know we are as similar to other Jews as a turtle is to a fish. Yes, we all swim in the same ocean, but beyond that, there is no connection between the Essene, the Sadducee, or the Pharisee. We would be closer to the mad Zealots than those who run Judea! You will be as welcome in their schools as a pig is in their synagogue."

The Zadoc, high priest to the Essene, had known Yeshua since his earliest years. His name was forgotten, a symbol of his rebirth as the Master. If any knew what name he was born to, and called it out, he would not hear it. This man was at the center of what it meant to be an Essene. This priest looked deeply at the boy and wondered, why?

Yeshua's mother was a staunch supporter of the faith, his father was a steadfast worker who kept his workshop amongst the faithful, though it would have been far easier to move everything to Jerusalem. Why was he breaking with tradition? "I see your heart is set, may I ask why?"

Yeshua looked to the horizon, "I traveled far, Master. I looked for truth in every corner of the world, under every stone on my path, and in the hearts of all I met. Everywhere, except in the heart of children, I met loneliness and desperation. The message I give now is very simple, very clear; unless we become as little children we cannot enter into the kingdom of the Lord within us."

The priest sighed, it was true. The entire reason for the separation of the Essene here on the plateau was to preserve the angelic heart. Their way of life, their beliefs, their very purpose in life defied the laws and traditions of the other Jews. "The Sadducee run the Temple, and all they desire is money and prestige. The Pharisee run the streets, and all they desire is the observance of the Law. The Zealots are the only ones who might listen, but they are crazy and dangerous. Who is there to hear and understand? You would do better going to Rome."

"Master, I have not yet taken the ritual of death and rebirth as yourself, and I cannot speak for the wisdom of my path, but I know it is before me. I know it is hard, but in amongst the sea of suffering, there will be a few who might have ears for my voice. My thoughts are to train a small group in our ways, to draw them from the confinement of tradition and belief so I might release them into the freedom of truth. I ask for your blessings in this."

"This is like saying you can take a fish and turn it into a dove!"

Yeshua laughed, "All have the wings of freedom in their heart, master. You yourself taught me this as a child. We just need to let go of the weights, the traditions, and the fear, and we will rise up into the ether."

"Oh we all know what Socrates spoke of, and we also know what happened to him. But despite the truth of history, it was not the Greeks that killed the philosopher, it was his pride that drove him to the grave. He was offered release, freedom to live and breathe, but in his pride he stayed in Athens, claiming that by avoiding death he would insult all he believed. So you must ask, is it pride that drives your truth, Yeshua?"

"I would hope it is not, Master. On the journey here, all my worldly goods were stolen. I knew God was speaking but I could not hear his voice. So I stopped in the Azzah deserts to cleanse and prepare. There I found an intense peace and after my forty days, after dealing with my demons, I found a small abandoned house near a village. It had a communal well and I harvested wild flax and wove it to provide food. Despite my sudden abject poverty, I felt incredibly free, I felt wealthy, and I felt Spirit move within like never before. This was when the children came, laughing and singing, a joy of joys in my life. All they wanted were stories and I had such a wealth of stories to share.

"They were a delight, but the happiness and carefree ways of the children caused a darkness on the face of their parents. I saw their pain, their stubborn ways, their sense of loss, their fear - it was written across their faces, and I knew, soon they would write those same messages of lack and loss onto the hearts of their children. Soon they would wrap those bright, shining souls in the shadows of their small world. But what could I do? Steal the children and bring them here? I stayed to give them a little light and therein I was amazed, for every ounce of light I gave a pound of wisdom was returned to me. I felt so blessed by the gifts of love and truth that I received in their presence.

"That was when the Roman came to the village, a kind man, a wise man in his way. He gently explained that my presence would drive the parents to murder me and he asked me to leave that place - not ordered, not commanded, he asked. *A Roman asked.* This affected me deeply and I found an understanding and compassion I had never expected. Who was more cruel, the parents who would trap their children in the darkness and fear of tradition, or these new men who simply wanted their world to be ordered?"

Zadoc laughed, "So you found you preferred ROMANS to Jews?"

"He was no longer a Roman to me, Master. I saw in him a man, a man struggling to escape the trap of his upbringing. This was a man who knew he was trapped and desperately wanted to be free. I knew we had found understanding between us, a bridge between hearts. I also knew that such a man had the ability to become free, given the right insight, given the right path."

The Master sat there in deep thought. Long moments of silence streamed through his heart as he sat awaiting the wisdom. "Miracles have always followed you, Yeshua. The power of the Lord flows through you like no other I know or have known. Your father knew, that was why he kept you close, made you work hard, and made you into the craftsman you are. His unrelenting discipline I felt was too severe, but when I questioned this he said to me such profound words that I saw the truth. He said: *The wild spirit of freedom will burn down the house it resides in. It must be tamed. It must be contained in the hearth and trained to serve the household."*

Yeshua smiled, yes, that was Joseph. He stood and poured some tea for his Master, feeling the love as a tear escaped from the old man's face. After a time, the master spoke, "We all loved him, even those who hated his ways, going down to the city as he did. But we all loved him. Well, it seems now that his son is also set on going to the city!"

"Zadoc, my father carved beauty out of ordinary wood. My carpentry is to carve souls out of the beliefs in which they are trapped. With the right guidance, a man can take the shape of truth just as rough wood can take the shape of a chair."

"I understand Yeshua, you do not care if you deal with a Jew, or a Gentile, or even a Roman. You do not care about the religion or the race or the color of their beliefs, you only care to release the child within. I understand the path you seek and I cannot stop you from this task given to you by the Lord, but take care. You have my blessings."

"Thank you, my Master."

"And Yeshua, when you get to Jerusalem take Mary under the wing and pull her from the streets. She argues our faith in public squares, as is anyone's right, but she is stirring up anger. The Jews in Jerusalem have no interest in our ways. The Pharisee want to believe this is but one life, and on Judgement, they will arise from the ground. Our truth of Soul coming again and again until it is refined and perfect is an anathema to them. Our disdain for eating flesh and making sacrifices of beasts goes against their Law, and we are hated for this. And if that were not bad enough, our communal life of sharing everything is detested by the Sadducee. Our disdain for money makes us fools in their eyes. This was WHY we turned from Turtle to Tortoise and made our way from the sea of Jews up to this dry plateau. Yes, the air is good for storing the parchments, but it was also because distance stopped the abrasion between our faiths." Zadoc looked at his disciple and smiled. "Marry her, Yeshua."

"Not altogether my choice, Zadoc. I am not as pretty as I was!" They both laughed. "I spoke with her father coming up here. He is still mindful of the marriage contract but we both know, Mary is not one to be confined to another's will."

The old man smiled and sent her blessings. He sat there for some time in silence, looking for the guidance of the Lord, reaching into the mist to see what shape would emerge.

A vision came to the old man. He saw a single flame reaching into the house of Judea, and lighting a candle. Then that candle was taken, and it lit another one, and another one until the room was full of light. Now he understood. "I see the light you wish to share, Yeshua. To start a fire in the heart you just need but a spark of truth. Yet as Joseph warned, if that spark escapes, it can burn the whole house down. I understand you wish only to provide a path to freedom for Souls trapped in darkness, but I warn you, keep moving. Do not settle in any one place, rather go from town to town. That Roman you met, he showed you the truth of this world."

Yeshua was silent. He knew well his teacher's truth and how it would flow unimpeded through his consciousness. These rare moments were what he missed most on his travels, and the old man did not disappoint. The presence of the Spirit entered his soul, and his age fell away. Zadoc suddenly flared up as the wisdom of the Lord took him.

"Law, what is it? A construct of man to corral the various forces of life. The Laws of Moses are for social peace and well-being, necessary tools to shape society. They tamed wild Jews and made them obedient servants. The Pharisee see themselves as protectors of this law. They cherish the minutia of their intent and look closely at the individual letters of each law, yet they utterly fail to grasp the purpose and meaning of why they were given. This was to tame the wild Jew.

"But the spirit-filled man has little need for earthly laws. He does not break them, but neither does he yield his sovereignty. He is directed by the Lord to do the Lord's work, which is the refining of soul to become the perfect instrument. Truth and purpose guide him as he fills the heart and soul with their meaning. Without fear, he casts the seeds of his wisdom amongst the people. This is the prophet, the bringer of change, the changer of law and custom. He takes the message of love and writes it onto the heart of all who would listen. He is the light, he is the way, he is the truth. He is a storm that breaks through the darkness. He is a light that breaks through the storm.

"He follows only the law of love, the same law by which man was fashioned. He follows the path of compassion, the same path that man walked when he entered Eden. He follows the truth in his heart, the same burning heart that is taken from the furnace and fashioned by the blows of life until it is perfect and pure.

"This act of pure freedom defies the laws of man. There are no boundaries, there are no penalties, there is no controlling such a one. The man of law fears this man of God, for if God's truth is revealed in the heart of all, laws become useless. If all follow the dictates of spirit, authority no longer has a voice or a purpose. The man of law will hate the man of God even as the man of God finds compassion and understanding for the man of law. This is the way of things."

There is a long pause, Zadoc gathers the breath of spirit to him. He is in trance, reaching to the inner worlds for the truth that wants to flow out from the hidden recess of the spiritual forces residing in the Noumena. Another voice emerges, one known to Yeshua, the voice of the father. "There are but two laws, Yeshua. If a man follows these, there is nothing else that is needed. The First: Love God. The Second: Love thy Neighbor as thyself."

A few moments later, Zadoc opened his eyes and looked to Yeshua, "Did the Lord speak?"

Yeshua bowed his head, knowing what acceptance of this service would mean. "The Lord has spoken, Zadoc. He said: *There are but two laws. If a man follows these, there is nothing else that is needed. The First: Love God. The Second: Love thy Neighbor as thyself.*"

The priest had a tear in his eye as he shook his head, "You must confirm the gift with your cousin John. He is a true prophet, a follower of the old ways, and is baptizing people by the Dead Sea. There you will receive clear guidance from one already walking the path you wish to tread."

As he made his way back from the lonely cave of the Master, Yeshua knew the mission had begun. Just as Moses had received the laws for HIS time, so too had he been chosen to receive the laws for THIS moment. It was all so clear to him, this pure illumination. In this warring world, there could be no peace until these principles were obeyed. A man that loves his neighbor will protect his community against wrong. A man that loves God will protect his heart against sin.

It was such pure common sense that even a blind Pharisee could see it!

Zadoc had spoken with the voice of God, it was his time. He had been given the Laws, his task was to share this with all who would listen. But, how? First, to see the Baptist as he had been directed, then - who knows? The breath of spirit blows in worlds unseen, he must trust that it will come and guide him.

Meeting the Baptist

The ride down on the cart was a luxury for Yeshua. He had worn out many sandals in his journey and was unused to comfort. The joy of his brother's presence made it even more pleasant, as they chatted about this and that, nothing and everything. It took him to the carefree days of youth, the odd wrestling match to prove that the young brother was not quite a man, the verbal sparring over some prophet's intent, and the shared disinterest in studying in the scriptorium.

"You didn't follow down the road our brother James took, being involved in the Jerusalem community, supporting the inclusion of texts, and all the religious stuff. Was I the cause of that?" Yeshua asked.

"Possibly, the truth is, I find my best truth cutting reeds. I am as close to God as my heartbeat, there on the land my father bought me. I truly find contentment, my brother, in this uncomplicated way. Mother has found me a wife, did you know? I will meet her soon enough, she comes from the community in Petra."

"I trust it will go well. Though I wonder, how do you imagine a city girl will cope with a boring reed cutter?" Yeshua jested, prodding his brother in the ribs.

"Take care brother, I am more than your match in wrestling now. With all this work hauling reeds, likely your better. Truth is, I have no idea of marriage, women, or what I am meant to do." Simon sighed.

"Oh, I think you know what to do!" Yeshua was laughing now, seeing the discomfit on his brother's face. "But as far as marriage goes, you have two options. She will accept you as you are or she will want to change you. Pray for the first. Mother is good with the details of these arrangements, and the dowry should help build a house for you both. And Simon, I know how tight you are with a shekel - Don't be a fool and move your wife in with our mother."

Simon seemed surprised, "Why not? There is room, it is as good a house as any."

"Ah, well maybe I returned in time to save your marriage before you doom it with your laziness and penny-pinching. You truly do not understand women. Our mother is the kindest soul you could meet, but it is HER house, HER ways. Which is right and true, I obey and am happy to live with this. But your wife will want HER house where HER rules will be obeyed. It is the instinct of women to rule the roost where they sit. And if you are wise, you will build the house near to your reeds, where you can come home for midday and work on making babies."

Simon seemed deeply shocked, "I had never thought of this. I presume life just carried on. You are saying I have to upend everything, change my entire existence? Maybe marriage is not worth the effort."

"You are too comfortable, brother. It dulls your wits."

"I suppose I get a lecture now?" Simon snorted.

"Lord, forgive him his youth!" Yeshua laughed. "No, the last thing I wish to do is to lecture anyone on the right and the wrong. Perhaps I did lecture you when I was young. I apologize for putting the tedious burden of my wisdom on your shoulder, but just as you do not understand women, back then I did not understand myself. The truth is, I feel the way you have chosen to live your life IS wise, Simon. Contentment is a jewel, but at what point does it change to complacency? Imagine a songbird seeing the morning sun and saying, *'oh well, another day!'* Or the fox looking at the eggs in the henhouse and saying, *'I will come back tomorrow for those'.*

"What a good wife will do is beat some sense into you, telling you to work harder because she wants some cloth for a new dress, or that the roof needs fixing. A good woman will keep you on your toes and save you from the curse of complacency!" Yeshua was doubled over in laughter with the look on his brother's face.

"Well, now you are making marriage out to look just awful. But I note, you haven't been rushing to the side of the Magdalene. Maybe your words are echoes for yourself to hear!"

Yeshua smiled, "The gears on the threshing machine that beats your reeds are driven by your donkey. Imagine how much extra work you would have to do without him? A good wife will make your task easier, but it has a cost. She must be stabled and well fed! You will understand when you meet your future bride, how the gears of life mesh only to useful purpose with your opposite. Trust me on this - Build a house for her, build a life with her that is separate from your past, and watch how your good fortune multiplies."

"I thought you weren't giving sermons anymore?"

"Lectures, no. But I still offer open-hearted advice. We can so easily fall into the ruts of the road we travel every day, but a good wife will look for new roads, new ways. It shakes us up from our sleepwalking. You will do this, build her a house? The workshop is there to make the furniture, and my wedding gift is the wood you need for this."

Simon just nodded. "I can see the sense of it. I am so used to being the youngest that I am used to being told what to do, but I understand, you are telling me to put away the things of childhood. I will build the house, I already have the mud and straw at hand for the walls and roof. We have cow dung a plenty for the floors, and that wood in father's workshop will make beds, tables, and chairs. I can't imagine creating anything to your standards, but it will suffice. Thank you, brother."

The wagon rolled along the road, the amazing outlook unfolding with every turn of the vast expanse of the Dead Sea. Simon noted, "The Enoch thing, the scribes are all up in arms with this. It is all they are talking about lately."

Yeshua looked over and sighed. "I know we are supposed to care. I know the purpose of the Qumran is to protect the sacred texts. But I am like Joseph, as he fashioned furniture from wood, I fashion Souls from stories. The tales they write here on the plateau are all well and good, there is great wisdom in them, but a seed has to be placed in soil to grow - stuck in a scroll, it will never germinate, never become its potential. Enoch? That prophet barely speaks to me and I am one who has faith in his word of the heavenly hosts! What chance does it have for acceptance with the Pharisee who denies this or the Sadducee who do not care? Enoch is a stubborn donkey that will never be useful to anyone."

Eventually, the road wound to the flats and Simon kindly took Yeshua to their cousin, John. He was there with a flock of followers, for he was generally considered to be the next Zadoc. Here, those who wished to join the community would come for baptism and lessons, for no soul was allowed to become one of the brothers until they understood and practiced the principles. Which was much harder than most guessed, not eating meat after a lifetime of it was difficult. Sharing all you have is extraordinarily difficult for those who come from a world of ownership. Accepting that we return again and again to this world until we are purified, this defies what most were taught on their mother's knee.

The mind wanted to rebel, but the peace of the Qumran, the well-being and good health of those who lived there, and the general happiness on the face of the Essene, this was hard to argue against. Plus the brothers accepted criminals and thieves, which was like accepting a leper into your midst for the rest of the Jews. Yet, time and again it was proved, for once the peace of the Lord settled in the heart and your needs were met, the desire to take from another departed.

Spirit was alive and well in the Qumran, entering a man's heart and turning his face to God. This was all a man needed, along with a community that supported this. Anger departed, the fury of existence petered out, and the quiet acceptance of the day itself being sufficient entered your Soul. But first, they had to survive John! No easy task.

The man was a giant by the local standards, well over six feet, and built like a small mountain. There he was, half drowning people and calling it baptism. Asking them questions, demanding truthful answers, and with any hint of a lie - down they go! It was very effective in ensuring the next person spoke only the truth.

"How have you wronged the Lord!" he would shout in their face.

"I, er, I did not observe the Sabbath!" the helpless fellow called out, hoping it was sufficient.

"LIE!" shouted John. "Let the water of God enter you, by your soul or by your nose, it doesn't matter to me! You have come to be purified and purified you will be!" And down they went, into the water, and were soon struggling for air.

At the last moment, he pulled them up, "And how have you wronged the Lord!" he would shout into their faces.

Eventually, they would admit they were a thief, running from the courts, or that their wife had cast them out for infidelity, or any of a thousand sins. And as they spoke the truth, a light came into the face of the Baptist, a smile would come to his lips. He knew the truth had arrived in their soul and he would cheer, with a huge, "Praise the Lord, another confesses his sins!" This confused the poor souls utterly. They thought it was what they were ashamed of, but here the Baptist cheered, praising them. He put them under one more time, saying, "Now you are ready to be free of your past and be cleaned of sin. This is a day of celebration. Go to the scribes and learn of our ways."

Again and again, as Yeshua watched, he saw men confess the evil in their hearts as John drove the forces of darkness from them with his relentless pursuit of the truth. Patiently he waited his turn as the line of petitioners came up to the great teacher. The divine madness had taken him for all the Baptist saw was the fallen one before him, and his determination to drive out the evil that had taken over their heart.

"Guilt and Shame will not open your heart to the Angels," he shouted at some hapless fellow. "They are coins used to pay the devil, not the Lord. What will you DO to restore your family's faith in you? What will you DO to recompense those you stole from? It is what you DO that redeems you, not your pathetic groveling."

The man breaks down, "I know, I know. I will make restitution, I will offer to repay as I can the loss. I will admit to my family what I have done."

Down he goes, washed in the waters of the spring that flowed into the Dead Sea, and when he comes up, John says, "Don't be stupid. If you tell them you are a thief they will cut off your hand. You can work here and we will find a way to repay your debt. Go see the scribe and he will give you the guidelines of what is required."

It was then he saw Yeshua, there in line with all the sinners come for redemption. "No no nooo," he cried, "I am the one who should stand in YOUR line, Cousin." and he walks through the waist-high water to embrace Joseph's firstborn. "He said you would return, just before he passed. He said you would be here, and here you are! Baptisms are done for the day," he hollered to the rest.

Yeshua would have none of it, "This is God's work, Cousin. These men are possessed by ghosts of their past that need to be cast out. Today is the day, as I too have ghosts that need casting from my heart."

John just nodded, "Then tell me what burden is keeping you from God!" he demanded.

"I fear I am not sufficient for the task I am given," Yeshua admits. "In my youth, I had no doubt. I had only certainty. God's flaming sword was in my hand, and I would cleave through injustice, through falsehood, through pretense. Now, all I want is to whisper the truth, and even whispering is loud to my ears. All I wish is that the current of love I feel will just flow to you, fill you, relieve you of your burdens. I have no desire to change you, to make you better - all I desire to do is share this love, and let the love do what it will. But this is a harsh world, it is not enough."

John looked into Yeshua's eyes. "I see the voice of the Lord in you. What were you told?"

"I saw the Zadoc. He moved into utterance. I was given two laws: Love God, and Love thy neighbor as thyself"

John's eyes light up with understanding, "I see. A terrible burden, or is it? Yeshua, look at the sea this river runs into, you cannot save anything in there, it is already dead. No fish survives in those waters, just as no soul survives in a dead church. Your sin is pride. It does not matter if you are good enough, you have been chosen. The Lord will give you strength, wisdom, and charity enough to do his work." With this, he pushes Yeshua under the water and holds him, shouting, " The Lord has not sent you to save the fish in a dead ocean, but to find the still living ones who would have drowned there without his word in their hearts."

Finally he pulls him up to breath, declaring to all who watched in amazement, "This man has the task of giving the laws of Love. The Law of Moses was God's voice calling the lost tribes to gather, but we are called now to a higher place, to God itself! This god within our hearts knows only the Law of Spirit, which is the Power of Love. Love is God in action. Love is God made real. Just as a man must be baptized to awaken to the truth, Soul must be drowned in Love if it is to grasp God."

And the spirit entered into Yeshua and awoke in his heart like a flame. With new eyes, the prophet let go of his fears and understood that his voice, his words, his love, they were nothing. There is only Love - Love that the Father flows through him, reaching out to all who have ears for his silent whisper. The curtain is parted, his heart is awoken and the journey is revealed. This was his trial and his blessing, his final step on the destiny he was born to fulfill. Sensing the change, the Baptist pulled him from the water,

Yeshua first gasped for air, understanding how vital life was to the living, then sighed, knowing what lay ahead. "Zadoc gave his blessing, and now I ask it of you."

"You have my blessing, now stay with me while we finish our business here, and we will go eat."

But with two masters present, the energy shifted. Now it was not just the men who came up, it was also the women who had been idly watching. They came in pairs, in groups, and they stood before the Baptist shouting out their crimes, asking to be washed clean of their past. John no longer had the fervent, driving energy, but just greeted each man and woman as a child of God.

Together, Yeshua and he spoke the words of release to a hundred or more. The scribes had never been so busy and were addressing people in groups, explaining the laws of the Essene. Explaining WHY they did not sacrifice animals to God, and why the only worthy sacrifice was the release of the sin within, which granted you purity of soul.

And after the sun fell low in the sky, glowing red in the dust, John came from the waters and showed to the people the tethered goat. He spoke to the hapless creature, "You will release the sins of these people. Do not fear, you will be blessed in the heavens for what you do." He spoke the ancient words of penance and placed the sins of the people upon its shoulders. But he did not slaughter the goat as so many had expected, he let it go!

He kicks it so it runs away into the desert, declaring to the people. "This goat now bears your sins. It goes into the desert, where the beast Azazel waits for him. He wants the taste of your evil on his lips. He will take your sin and devour it. But he takes not just YOUR sin, he takes all the crimes and evil doing of all who came before you. We have fed the beast so that he shall no longer stalk you. Know you are freed from his grasp, know you are a new born child on the road to God!"

The people cheered as the goat ran off into the twilight.

ooo0000ooo

Later that evening, as John sat with Yeshua at a table of feasting, with food provided by those who came into the wilderness for the forgiveness of their sins, he laughed, "The look on your face when you thought I was going to sacrifice the goat! That was priceless."

Yeshua smiled, "You had me wondering how far you have strayed from the Essene ways."

"It is theatre, but important theatre. These people, they EXPECT sacrifice. Without it they are pretty damn certain God will be deaf to their plea, so I provide a sacrifice of sorts. The goat will probably live a pleasant and long life, but that isn't the point. These people believe there are Djins out there in the desert waiting to consume their souls and by releasing the goat to the Devil, it lets their fears go with it. It is the fear that controls them, and the release of fear is the secret," he explained.

Yeshua looked at his plate of stew, full of desert herbs and root vegetables. He broke the bread, ceremonially handing a piece to John, to symbolize the start of the meal, and together they bowed their heads to bless the food and thank the Lord for his providence. "It works," Yeshua noted. "You can see it in their eyes, they believe their sins were being taken away to feed the hungry beast. Is this ALL theatre, then?"

John grinned, "You felt it, didn't you? I knew you would. While it may start with theatre, once the heart is invested the play comes alive and the actors are no longer acting. There is the hard shell we have to break through, Yeshua. The theatre takes them through their fear. It is all fear, fear of what others will think, fear of God, of the Devil, fear is a cocoon that wraps their heart and prevents the love of the Lord from entering into their life. By drowning them as I do, they have to face their fear, the ultimate fear - that they might drown. And you can feel it, you know when they let go. Because they physically let go, and just accept that they will die."

"I saw that, the men thrashed about like madmen but you just kept holding them down. I am not sure I could do that, being a third your size and all!" he laughs. They both laugh.

"But it WORKS Yeshua. It WORKS - the Lord DOES enter into their hearts. I just live in his presence, I feel it in me, I know it is with me, and he instructs me what to do and say with every sinner. The Lord wants these sins cleansed so that his people can become more like the true soul he fashioned them from. We are all good at heart, no baby is born angry. No baby wants to steal another man's wife. No baby wants to kill another in jealousy and rage. This is all stuff we take on, that we LEARN, and so I teach them to drop it. That is all, just drop it and let the Lord in." He slurped down the stew and broke some more bread, handing a piece to Yeshua, contemplating and eating before continuing.

"But on the Essene thing, you know my thoughts. They are good people, but what do they DO? Sitting up there, writing the stories, I am sure it is all part of the great plan, but it is not for me. I can accept so much of what they hold as true because it makes sense, I send people to the communities because it makes sense - It works both ways: the sinners need a support network to help get them through the change, and the communities need strong hands. We are all part of the great wheel, but it is the journey, not the wheel that matters. I follow the way, I observe the wisdom of Zadoc, but I take my own path at the same time."

Yeshua said nothing, however, John echoed much of his thinking. Since taking his leave of his mother early that morning, he knew in his bones, he would not be returning to the Qumran. His heart told him to speak, "I feel a heaviness and a sense of loss, Cousin. I know I shall never return to the Qumran to live, it is not my way. I do not want to be a carpenter shaping wood, as my father did. I am a carpenter made to shape souls and I have seen this in what you do. I was deeply moved."

"Then join me! You saw how much easier it was when you stood by my side. You saw how the WOMEN started coming up, I guess it is your pretty face, but the women always stand back. They are afraid of me, but not you. We doubled the number of souls set free today, Cousin. I feel like a solo singer has found a harmony, and the song is so much greater for it." He looked hard at his Cousin. He knew it as soon as he saw him standing there, he was the ONE.

"It felt good, out there in the water with you. I felt the love of the Lord flowing through, reaching out, touching each soul. You were like my father, teaching me to carve wood," Yeshua joked.

John considered for a moment. "I am based in Galilee, in Herod's new city, mostly because I got given a decent piece of land, but also because the priests do not bother me or my family as they won't go near the place. There is plenty of room for one more. We will spend most of our time out of the cities in the rivers, baptizing, always close to Essene communities where the people can go after their conversion. I always keep moving from place to place because otherwise the local authorities take too much interest in mad Jews playing Messiah."

Yeshua looked with interest. This seemed the right course. "It was what Zadoc said, that giving out the message would mean always moving.

But I thought you lived in the wilderness, ate locusts and honey, and wore camel hair shirts? A settled family man is not what I expected."

"What do you call traipsing around all over the river Jordan if not living in the damn wilderness? I did survive in the mountains as a boy, mostly to get away from my insane father. If you wonder why I detest the Pharisee and Sadducee so much, he is the reason. People starved near us, he was happy to let them. I refused to live under his roof. Now, it helps to be seen as a wild, untamed madman."

"The Zadoc said you were the first true prophet in four hundred years, I always thought you would be the one to follow his shadow?" Yeshua dipped the last of his bread and broke off more for his cousin and himself.

John laughs, "He said that? And I thought it was you! Maybe we will share the job, sitting up on the Qumran, doing nothing."

Yeshua shook his head, "He is the heart of all the communities, you know this. But no, I can't see myself growing old up on the plateau."

John smiled his crooked smile, "I am not likely to grow old, Yeshua. I stir the pot too much, and the priests hate me. You have to understand, joining the traveling baptism show, it will make you a marked man as well. Which is why I have made a practice of living every day as if it were my last! So the music is playing, we have eaten, we have spoken, it is time for us to dance!"

Hours flew past as the music flowed like the wine of the Essenes, a pure juice from the local fruits. The traditional dances were many, the laughter was great, and the community of souls felt the love of the Lord reach down and touch them. As it has done for centuries, the bonding of dance and song united hearts and fulfilled the need for friendship.

By the end of the evening, as people made their way to whatever amounted to a bed for themselves, Yeshua sat in the moonlight with his cousin. "I will come with you to Galilee. In truth, this is the most joy and freedom I have felt since I started on my journey. In your presence I have truly come home."

"You ARE home cousin. You have not yet met my wife, but she will like you. We may be as kings out here in the wilderness, but all husbands are sheep once tied back to the folds of their shepherd! She is the heart of my life, as is only right. Sometimes I almost feel bad about being out here enjoying myself so much!"

"Liar!" declared Yeshua in the voice John used when baptizing. They both laughed, full of the spirit of the evening and the gentle friendship of a shared fate.

ooo0000ooo

As the morning rays spread to warm the air, the camp was up and moving to the next baptism, a few miles upriver of where they were on the Jordan, towards Galilee. There a more traditional lustration bath awaited them, and as they arrived they found a small crowd had gathered, already hearing of the new Messiah that had joined with the Baptist. "Seems you already have new friends," joked John.

The day progressed as more and more people came to confess their sins and receive Baptism, until finally, Yeshua asked what had been on his heart, "How many stay?"

John laughed, "Let me put it this way, I often meet old friends who come every time I am in the area. Whether they hold to the Lord or wander is not my concern, but that they come means they are looking for better than what they have. But as you ask, perhaps two out of a hundred go to the local commune and become part of the society, the odd one joins me in the call to duty, but for most, they try, but it is too much of a break from their traditional ways. They visit their mother at Passover who insists on the sheep being killed and all partaking of the flesh. That is when they stay home, but I like to believe something of their life has changed for the better."

Then he got more serious, "The real problem is the people are not free, we are under the yoke of the Roman. The oppressors do not care if we live or die, only that we pay taxes, and swear allegiance to Caesar. I hate the bastards, as you know, but there are things we can learn from them. In some ways Romans are far better than us, they organize every step of their journey and all sides of society are embraced in some way. Every child grows up knowing their part and their options. Every army knows the order of leadership. Every aspect of their life is defined, and Romans have the curious benefit of choosing the God they want. The drunk follows Dionysus, and feels no guilt for his drinking. The soldier follows Mars, and has no guilt for war and death. The lover follows Venus and suffers no shame bedding the wife of his friend. But here, the rules are fixed, the law is settled, and if you suffer any flaw you are condemned.

"This is where we can help. By offering the people a release from their guilt, they are better able to pick up and start over. They are one step closer to becoming organized. And if they start over many times, this too is part of the path they walk. I don't expect or look for perfection, Yeshua, and I very much doubt that the good Lord does either."

"You know it is not the whole truth, John. Every sin meets its payment, while forgiveness of guilt, while it helps us carry on, does not absolve us of the consequences. The scales must be balanced."

"Must they? How much payment is made to the temples, to the Romans, to the dark shadows of money lenders? How much is stolen from the people by their king or their priest? It is not for me to determine the fate of an individual, I just lift them out of their misery and set them on the road of the righteous. God sorts the rest. But think of it, one people, Yeshua, one path, one focus - the Romans cannot resist the will of the single-minded nation. By relieving the people of their guilt, by creating brotherhood, we give them a door to freedom." John waved for the next one to come forward.

Inner freedom, thought Yeshua. He said nothing, John was a believer in a free Jewish state, but what did it matter who ruled in the external world? The only thing of importance was the inner rulership by the father. This was the only truth, the everlasting glory that is the sublimation of the human will into the will of the divine. The God-directed man was an immutable force for good, both in this realm and all realms.

Whatever the difference in their beliefs, they worked well together, John demanding the truth, Yeshua offering a kind heart and a helping hand. Many found more than salvation that day, many were touched by the healing hand of God. This was new to John, that infirm men were able to walk after their baptism. Some even said that their eyesight improved, and were joyous.

"That is you," John said. "I had a few healings, but this is different."

"I do nothing but bless them," said Yeshua. "The Lord comes and takes pity on their suffering, and any healing is due to his grace, not mine."

"Even so, it's good for business. Nothing brings people forward more than the desire to be healed, so keep doing whatever you do!"

And so it continued, traveling from point to point up the River, coming closer to Galilee, until the day before the Sabbath when they took the tables and tents up to Tiberias, Herod's shining and new city on the Sea of Galilee, to make ready to spend the following day at John's farm.

ooo0000ooo

The tracks by the Jordan were well defined and flat, easily negotiated on the night of a full moon such as this. You could smell the bright moisture of Galilee long before you saw it, and as they approached in the moonlight, the sparkling diamonds the silver orb cast over the inland sea were entrancing. "The Sadducee ridiculed Herod for building his city here," John noted cryptically. "I mean, what on earth would anyone do with all this arable land and fresh water?"

"Built over a graveyard, was the plaint, no?" Yeshua laughed.

"The dead are dead. Are they scared of the ghosts they don't believe in? I could never accept the flat lie my father lived, his blunt rejection of anything spiritual. The Temple and his precious rituals were his only interest. If you reject an afterlife, what is the point of this one? What purpose do their mindless offerings and sacrifices serve? The Pharisee with their noses in the books of law are little better. Hypocrites who all do what Rome tells them. Herod may be a Roman, but he understands the people and their needs, and at least does something of use."

"You know I have no idea about politics, John. I truly have no interest in the games men play with other men - only the game of catching God has my interest. These last six days, living and working with you, this is where my joy is."

"And long may it be so, Yeshua. But consider if the Sadducee got their claws into our show, what we do here would be called heresy. Casting out sin, that is the same as proclaiming yourself a Messiah! Talking about higher realms, of Angels, of Djins, all this is forbidden. So often did I hear the never-ending complaints from my father about how the villagers of Cana were such fools, and how wise the masters who ran the Temple were. I hated him and could never understand why he married an Essene. I still don't. Yet, now I thank my father every day for grinding my nose in his beliefs. He is the one who drove me into the mountains, where I found God awaiting me with open arms. Up to that point, you could not believe how jealous I was of those who had a happy family, whereas I was a leper in my own house - rejected as surely as my face and arms were covered in sores." John laughed, but his voice always had an edge of harshness when speaking of his father.

"The sea is no less beautiful than what I remember, coming up here with Joseph. He would often then go on to Jerusalem, when he would call in to see Elizabeth, bringing small gifts from Mary. Your father was never there, so I never met him. From what you say, that was a blessing. When did he pass away?" Yeshua asked.

"Not so long as I care to remember, some years ago. I have been up to Cana only twice to see her since he passed, I know I should visit more often, but the work of the Lord does not pause. There is a wedding there in a couple of weeks, one of the relatives I barely know. I will take the time to visit then."

"Mother told me of it, she is going to visit her sister, so perhaps I can come along?"

"Please, I need the distraction. I cannot tell you how little I love the place I was raised, nor the incredible smallness of the minds that live there." At which point the party arrived at a shed at the edge of Tiberias, where John instructed the storing of the baggage and the donkeys. "Let the men finish this, my house is just up the way.

ooo0000ooo

John's house was as simple and plain as he was, though much more than a peasant hut of a single room. This house was built in the Roman fashion, with rooms facing onto a courtyard that had a covering trellis entwined with grape vines. All was made from simple mud brick, but charming and cool. His wife Martha, kept it clean and added some small touches of cloth or flowers to soften the clay walls.

She greeted them warmly and had a stew ready, with fresh baked bread and juice from the grapes. They sat in the courtyard with some children shyly peeking around corners at the stranger. "I tend not to let the followers in here, it might cause them to think I live in luxury, which in truth, I do! I bless Herod every day, despite his half-Roman ways, but at least he is sticking it to the priests and sharing his bounty with the poor. He GAVE us this land, the only qualification I had to provide was poverty!" John the Baptist laughed, "And by God weren't we well qualified, Martha!"

As a good wife, she just smiled and said nothing. Yeshua remained surprised: Children? A wife? A house in a lovely town? It was not exactly the image of the wild man in the desert living off locusts, but as he said, the image was good for the work he did. "You always had God, dear cousin. Your faith has brought you his blessings and I am happy for you."

He wanted to ask Martha how she felt about her husband being away all the time, but even as the thought passed his nose he could see there was nothing but happiness in this household. She seemed to understand he did God's work and had no complaints. His mind briefly saw Mary, always in trouble, always pushing for truth, always demanding one step more. She was in a relentless pursuit of fairness for all and privilege for none. How would she accept a man wandering about baptizing strangers? In that moment he knew, she would not be sitting at home like Martha.

"I have promised the Zadoc to go to Jerusalem and take Mary under my wing. He says I should marry her, but I have no home, no place for her."

John roared with laughter, "And you think I had a bean to count when I married this soul? A good woman cares for one thing, her man, and following on from this care, her children. This house fell from the blue into our laps, or at least the land did. But I have a lot of followers, and we knocked up the house in a week."

"So you think I should give up my freedom and settle down?"

"That is a nonsense that people speak. Freedom without purpose is like the Jordan flowing into the Dead Sea. Saying marriage is a chain and that freedom is running around, drinking, playing dice all night, these are foolish words. I am never happier sitting here with my family, perhaps because family was something I barely had. It was all I ever wanted. I met Martha here while baptizing. She stood by all day, watching me and my madness. At the end of it, she served me food, saying nothing as she always does.

"That was it, she knew she was to be my wife and she just waited till I understood it. She served me every evening for months until the Lord opened my eyes. I asked her why she followed the baggage train, serving me every night. She said nothing, just smiled. Finally it dawned on me, as I was the servant of the Lord, she wanted to serve me. How foolish that I did not see the Lord had sent me a wife. We were married the next day. So Yeshua, it is not about what we have, but what we give that makes a marriage. I give to God, she gives to me, and God is born in our hearts through our service. This is the wheel, and it is all we need."

They ate their soup in peace, Martha quietly preparing some tea for them, saying nothing the whole time. Yeshua wondered if she even wanted to speak, and then supposed his presence made her shy. Perhaps it would be wise to see what houses were open to him in the area.

"You seem to get on with the fisherman?" John noted as they sat in the moonlight, watching the sea sparkle with diamonds cast off from her light.

"Peter? I find him interesting. How can a man can seek God so earnestly, yet insist he isn't?"

"All he wants to do is argue with me," John laughed.

"The same, but I fashion his complaints into questions that become buckets he must fill with answers, and he seems to like it."

John nodded, "Peter and the crew of his boat are Baptists in name only. They are good men, but not part of my close team. Why don't you look after them, get the feel of dealing with these fishermen of Galilee?

They are stubborn, opinionated, argumentative, everything a follower of God is not supposed to be, but if someone could spend more time with them, I think a diamond could be found in the rough stones of their thinking."

"You want to tie me down with disciples?" Yeshua laughed.

"I love the work," John explained. "But you need men who will tout for you, speak to people, generate interest. There is no shortage of people needing to be baptized, and you can train them to help with the work itself."

"I saw that," Yeshua noted. "The men look after most of the people, and seem to know the right ones to send to you."

"The Lord opens the eyes and ears of the devoted Soul. I get told when a man is ready, the only question is if he understands and accepts God's grace. That takes time, and I feel you could work with the fishermen on Peter's boat, and make something of them."

"I have been impressed at how well everything runs. Where does the money to pay for it come from?" Yeshua asked.

"The whole show works because many hands are helping out. I don't want to think of this as a business, but in some ways it is. It is the Lord's business, but you have seen the small army I move. It takes people to organize the many things to pack, cooks to prepare food, people to get food, and we always have to feed the baptized. It is expensive and while the Lord provides it is generally paid for by way of tithes and donations. Some of the rich people who have taken baptism feel they are not going to hell if they give the Baptist some cash. I don't refuse, my principles are that they must pay in Herod's coins, though. My view is that we are a Temple and that the images of false prophets must not be erected, and Herod was smart enough not to put his head on his coins."

There was silence for some time as both men absorbed the beauty of the sea and the harmony of each other's company. "Yeshua," said John eventually, "you fit in well. The men like you, and I like you. God has sent you to me for a reason. I know you have studied your whole life for this mission of yours, but fruit does not spring perfect from the tree - it grows to its final form. I am going to suggest that you stay, help out, be part of the circus."

ooo0000ooo

In the morning the whole family and Yeshua went to Sabbath Prayers. On this day they traveled to the Synagogue in Magdala, at John's urging, for he wished to meet the mother of Mary. Stone-covered roads, well-kept gardens, and a fishing fleet at rest showed how prosperous the city had become during the reign of Herod Antipas. The Synagogue itself was a fine structure with superb mosaics on the floors. John was popular and welcomed warmly by most. Some stood off, and when Yeshua asked, "Sometimes my abrasive nature is used to finish the stones of rough men and they take it amiss. Pay no heed, here I have selected a reading for you."

Yeshua looks at the scroll, Isaiah 61, and glances up at John. John merely pushes him forward. Having been introduced by the celebrity of John, silence fell, waiting for this new man to speak. Yeshua paused for some moments over the words, he knew WHY John had selected this for him, and why he had selected Magdala, where he was well known as the betrothed of the Magdalene. It was virtually his home town, his mother was there so often. He began, "The Spirit of the Lord is upon me because God has anointed me to bring good news to the poor… to bind up the broken-hearted. God has sent me to proclaim release to the captives and recovery of sight to the blind, (he skips the vengeance of the Lord, and goes to a later part of the scroll) to let the oppressed go free, to proclaim the year of the Lord's favor."

It appeared to be a direct affront to one of the men John had evidently upset. "You?" he snorted. "A carpenter and an ESSENE? God has anointed YOU? John pretends you are his Messiah, I say you are a false prophet!"

Yeshua said nothing in response, other than to announce the reading was finished. "Today this scripture has been fulfilled in your hearing."

There was a great rumbling of discontent. John was a trouble maker, and he was bringing his Messiah nonsense here, on the Sabbath. Those who opposed his ministry quickly rose up, saying, "A false prophet! He needs to be stoned!"

But when they went to grab Yeshua, he was not to be seen. John roared with laughter, for he knew what his boy could do. His wife grabbed his arm, "He cannot be seen by those men, yet we see him as plain as day. How can this be?"

"Woman, I say to you, those with the eyes to see truth will see truth. Those with eyes of hatred cannot see such a one as he, who has not hate or bitterness in his heart. Miracles, they follow Yeshua around like a lost puppy."

"Husband, can it be? He is truly come?" Martha was in awe. She liked him right away, a simple, unassuming soul who understood her shyness. But this, a prophet doing miracles in front of her eyes, just as John had said. She hugged him close.

He delighted in her warmth. "Let my words say nothing more than what you have witnessed."

ooo0000ooo

Later that day at the house of the Magdalene, her mother was laughing about the events that morning. "You cannot believe how offended those angry men are, shouting that a devil has come to their midst and must be found. They went completely crazy when they couldn't find you, Yeshua. How did you do that?"

He just smiled at the mother of his betrothed. "I do nothing but embrace the Lord. It seems that when he embraces me in return I am hidden from the sight of vexatious souls. It is a secret taught in India, to be wholly possessed by the Lord. They call it Samadhi but in truth, it is just love and trust in the guidance of the Lord."

"My dear daughter would do to learn it," she laughed.

"Still causing trouble?" Yeshua laughed in return. They all knew what a fire brand she was.

"She knows you are back, I am surprised she did not return from your brothers house. But yes, still stirring the pot of those stale and foolish men. She remains offended that she can take no post in a synagogue and lets them know by debating them better than any man." Martha sighed, "But she cannot vanish like you. Joseph, our friend at the Temple, has had her acquitted more than once for proselytizing the Essene way."

"Well, you saw how they chased after me and I was speaking properly in a Synagogue. I suppose she is speaking of the Essene faith in public view?"

John laughed, "And criticizing them to their faces, calling them false and vain. But when they seek to argue scripture, she is so much smarter than them that they get a little like what you saw today. Having a prophet on a street corner is bad enough, but a WOMAN? "

Martha begged him, "Please, Yeshua, go to Jerusalem and speak with her. I am very worried."

"We have a wedding to attend, but at Passover I will observe the rites and speak in the Temple. She stays with my brother, so I am sure we will meet."

John said, "If you don't have a coin, I can provide one!"

(Note: Formal proposal of *marriage* in Ancient Judea can be made with a coin or gift exchanged)

The Wedding at Cana

The Essene community at Cana was not particularly large and was intermingled with all the faiths present in the town. Mary's aunt (whom she called her sister) had lived there since the purge of Herod the Great, in a large house of stone as befits the wife of a wealthy man. John despised the place, calling it impure, despite the fact he emerged from precisely this. After all their walking they took the cart, chatting amiably as they left behind the work of baptism for a few days.

"You do not appear overly happy to be seeing your mother?" Yeshua quizzed, hoping to break through his gloom.

John just grunted. "I don't know why she stays, I have made it clear she is welcome to live with myself and Martha. It is a far better town than Cana."

Yeshua laughed, "I am sure she finds marble floors and stone walls objectionable and a misery, plus all the friends she made over the decades, that must be an annoyance as well." he jested.

"I will never understand why she married him." was all he answered.

The wheel found new ruts as the road took a turn up to the plateau where the wedding was to be held. Eventually, Yeshua spoke, "You know what sort of man you were in the wilderness, full of anger, spite, and venom. Hating the world, hating the false priests. But you found your purpose, and everything turned on this pivot. I know you still hate the priests, or at least what they stand for, but you are not the same man now as you were then. I saw you at home, content, at peace, held in the arms of devotion.

"Consider then that the man your mother met and married was your opposite. He was content with his lot, his father was wealthy, and he followed in his footsteps as a priest of the Sadducee. He probably imagined he was following God's will, and then he met Elizabeth - Despite her being an Essene, he felt a deep connection. He chose love over what would be seen as his duty. I am sure he was happy and content as you are now, at first.

"Now, go forward a few years. Your mother finally falls pregnant, much later than what would have been expected. My mother arrives to help her because Elizabeth has no one. She is alone in a house near Jerusalem. She sees her husband only rarely, and then the death of the infants is ordered by Herod.

"Elizabeth must move quickly, her mother had died, and she has inherited the house in Cana, where friends and others of her faith live that will say nothing of her child. So she moves to a place of safety, instructing the servants she left behind to tell the soldiers traveling from house to house that she and the boy have already died from fever. They then go to the Temple, quiz your father, demanding to know what has happened. The truth was, he simply did not know. He could guess what happened, but it was his son, so he says nothing. HIS father sees his opportunity, and bribes the inquisitor to say his son has died under torture. The marriage is technically at an end.

"Perhaps his father had already been carping at him to fulfill his Temple duties, whispering in his ear to stop playing around with that idiot woman of a wife that he chose. I am only guessing, but we know the Sadducee, they have no scruples. I imagine the grandfather found a nice pretty thing for your father to sleep with in Jerusalem, a bribe to keep him close. He could see his son slipping away, and so he does whatever he can to hold him to the Saducee faith." Yeshua paused, letting this thought slip in. As he spoke, he felt he was watching the show unfold. He had practiced this as a child, being able to walk into the world of another to better understand them.

"And what happens? Your father falls in love with this willing accomplice of your grandfather, no doubt being paid well for her service, and finding the job rather pleasant. He is being wound into the web by the spiders of doubt and soon he looks at your mother with nothing but contempt. That hoar understands him so much better and does whatever he wants her to.

"He now has a position on the Sanhedrin, he is a man of means - his father has ensured his acceptance into the world of wealth and privilege. Yet, despite what the world believes, that his wife and child are dead, he knows he is still married, so by the law he cannot divorce. He now grows angry with his choice and sees his father's wisdom. Why did he marry outside his faith? It brings him nothing but pain, and the proof of this pain is that little bastard son who asks too many questions. You did ask too many questions, didn't you?"

John looked at him, shaking his head. "How do you know these things? I have not spoken to a soul about what I knew, or the reason why I left. I found garments, beautiful satin, and silk from the Orient, incredibly expensive, and I was so curious. Mother would never be seen in such indolent luxury, so I asked who they were for." John laughed, "And I asked him in front of my mother! My God, the fury and rage he unleashed. He beat me black and blue, and when my mother stepped between myself and the stick, he beat her. I threw a chair at him, to stop him, and he turned on me.

"He had become a mad bull, and I was a red rag for it to charge. And he did charge, he ran at me, screaming. I ran, he took off after me, pursuing me for an hour before his legs gave out and he collapsed in the mountains around the town. I didn't stop. I hated him so much that I knew if I turned around, I would have taken a rock and killed him."

John was silent for quite some time. "I went completely mad in the mountains, Yeshua - completely mad. Time had no meaning, night and day were as nothing. Cold and heat did not touch me. My clothes were torn, I didn't care. My hair grew long and I lived like an animal. I did live off locusts and wild honey, and whatever I could find, but I ate through habit, not because I was hungry. It was only that I could see muscles wasting away that I took food. Water was not difficult, I knew the springs and places to wash, I mean, I guess I wasn't completely mad. But in the clarity of the desert, the ways of society, the mindless repetition of habit that formed the lives of everyone I knew, all this grew transparent.

"I grew transparent, and when I stopped hating, which took quite some time, truth was revealed. I came to a clear and simple understanding that 'I' was as transparent to God as the people were to me. I made the decision, I would never hide from the gaze of the Lord. All I wanted was to be seen by God, as I was, for what I was. I lost all shame, Yeshua, I didn't care what people thought of me, only that God could see my soul and that my soul be pure. All I wanted was to be transparent to the will of the divine, to let it flow through, to guide my every step.

"Then one day, some years later, I can't say for certain, I was in one of the desert baths, cleansing my soul and body, completely naked by now because my clothes had gone by the way. I heard weeping. I followed the sound and an old man was there. I didn't know him but he was racked with pain and suffering. I asked him what the problem was, well, didn't I scare him! I frightened the devil right out of him, I reckon, because he stopped sobbing and just gasped. Probably thought it was Azazel himself standing there, naked, my beard and hair long, more a beast than a man."

He paused for a long time, feeling the rocking movement of the cart as it shifted around over the bumps, pulled by the mule up the hill. "That was when the Lord entered my heart, Yeshua. I knew, I knew with absolute certainty that this man had committed a terrible crime. I demanded of him the truth, *'What did you do?'* I shouted at him. He was scared, he must have truly believed I was a demon about to devour him, and at that moment he broke, he admitted everything.

"He had raped his daughter, and worse, in his shame, he killed her, and carted her body out into the mountains. That was when I came across him, for the madness had left, and he realized what he had done. He did not know what to do. I dragged him, physically dragged him while he screamed and shouted, over to the lustration pool, and plunged him in it. It was an instinct, Yeshua.

"My old self wanted to chastise him, to punish him, to judge him, but the person I had become just wanted to know what had brought a man to such a place. I plunged him under the water, demanding to know WHY. I wanted him to tell me why he did it, and after a few dunkings and near drownings, he broke down and told me. His wife would have nothing to do with him, she would not send him to her sisters, and she left him to suffer without relief. In his mind, the love for his daughter turned to passion, and he imagined she felt it as well - He didn't even realize he was raping her. He had gone mad, but when he came to his senses, seeing her weeping, understanding what he had done and how he would be punished, he panicked and struck her. One blow and she was dead.

"He didn't mean it consciously, but the devil within him knew exactly what it was doing. That voice of Satan was whispering for years, telling him to pluck the fruit, and finally, he gave in to it. He was sobbing, begging forgiveness. What can you do? I told him I can't forgive anything - Only God can forgive, but I did tell him that Satan had left his heart. Of all things, a village goat had come up for water, so I placed my hands on it, and looking at the man, I told him his guilt had passed to my hands through the will of God, and that now I would place this burden on the goat, and send it out to be eaten by devils.

"Well, you know the routine. The thing is, it worked. He stopped sobbing and declared me a prophet of the Lord, saying he could feel Satan had indeed left his heart. He made his way back to his village and I thought that was the end of it, but no - he returned the next day, calling out for the prophet of God. He brought food and drink, and some clothes. That was the start of the journey and he became my first disciple, which I didn't want, but he insisted on following me, saying he could never face his wife for what he had done.

"He was the one who sought out and brought to me that sinners who needed to be baptized as he had been, to be released from their fear and self-loathing. And when they came, the spirit of the Lord entered into me, and I knew what had to be done." John had finished his tale.

"Clothes hey?" Yeshua smiled at the thought, mere pieces of cloth had lit the fuse that ignited the prophet. "Are you ready to forgive your father yet?"

John smiled happily, saying, "He can burn in the Hell he doesn't believe in."

Yeshua laughed, "Well, maybe so, but are YOU ready to forgive him?"

John looked at him directly, a strange haunted look as the light dawned, "Only God can forgive. You are right, it is not my place to judge or to forgive. Very well then, I release him and I release my hatred. Do you want to baptize me now?"

"You can baptize yourself, the point is that you let go of the dog that bites you. John, my beloved cousin, it is ALL God's will. We can all see another clearly because we are not trapped in their skull. I see easily that without your father being as he was, you would not be what you are. You know this, you preach this, you speak of acceptance over and over and while I know you have accepted the situation and moved past it, I am not so certain you have accepted the guilt you feel. It is just a picture in the back of the mind, but because of this, a little part of the past still owns you."

"It's a good reminder not to be a prick," he snorted back.

ooo0000ooo

Despite the gruff demeanor he usually showed, John was remarkably pleasant at the wedding, saying hello to village folk he had not seen in many years, almost appearing to be civil and happy. He never enjoyed the charade of pleasantries, yet he was trying not to make a fuss for the sake of his mother. Then someone made the mistake of talking about the Romans.

John arced up, as always, his legendary temper barely in check. "Would you sit down to play a game of dice with a person when you KNOW they have loaded the dice in their favor? You would be a FOOL, a complete FOOL to do so. That is what you are doing trading with the Romans. They make all the rules, and all the rules are in their favor. All that a Roman has to do is claim you under weighed something, and BAM - into prison you go.

"You now have to prove your innocence. They have to prove nothing. Their arrogance, their strutting, their absurd claims to rule the world, it is sand in the eyes of the true believers."

The couple to be married were oblivious to the small ruckus at the back of the courtyard where the wedding ceremony was underway. They were young, looking forward to a life together, and had no care for politics or right or wrongs. Yeshua liked them, good people. More to the point, it had been a month since his return, and seeing the siblings and his mother was a welcome break from the constant work of renewal.

"How goes it with John?" his mother asked, the question in her voice asking how he was coping with his temper, now on display in the back of the hubbub of wedding guests.

"I find him most agreeable company. I steer clear of mentioning Romans or Priests, of course. He told me a lot about this place and his father on the way up, your sister did not have an easy marriage." Yeshua knew that Elizabeth was his mother's aunt, but they had grown up together in the Essene community at Magdala. They were as close as sisters.

"She did not, this is true. When I sat with her in the last months of her pregnancy, Zac was not to be seen. When he did turn up, it was only briefly. He had no interest in the boy at all, didn't send him to be educated, and didn't even bother turning up for his Bah Mitzvah. Zachariah was about for a year when John was fourteen but that ended with the child running away. I barely said three words to the man during his entire marriage to my sister." Mary sighed.

At this point, his great-aunt arrives. She was old now, very old. "Yeshua, so good to see you. I hear you have been helping John with the Baptisms. Not that HE tells me anything, of course, but I do get told. Some bad news though, they have run out of wine."

The wedding had been going for days now, and far more people had turned up than were expected. "Real wine, or the Essene wine?" Yeshua asked. His community made their concoction from dried fruits, quite lovely but it had no alcohol. It was believed the blessing made it part of the essence of God, and that drinking it brought clarity and purpose while opposing this, alcohol created dullness and confusion and therefore was not of the Lord.

"It is an Essene wedding, what do you think?" Elizabeth laughed.

"Can you sort that out, Yeshua?" his mother asked, an odd smile on her face.

What exactly she had in mind, Yeshua was not sure, but he supposed she was asking him to make the cordial extracted from the remnants in the pot. You could get a little more out of the bottom of the pot by adding a mix of dried grapes and citrines. He went over to where the water and wine were stored to see what was up. He looked in the empty wine ones and saw that there was a good remnant of herbs and spices left, along with the overly tangy slops at the bottom. He asked if they had dried grapes and citrus. The fellow that he supposed was looking after things said he did, and went to fetch them. "Bring some honey, as well as some fragrant herbs and a mortar and pestle!"

Which the man did. In a few moments, Yeshua had ground some of the herbs from the base, added the citrine juice, and then worked the raisins in with the grinding stone, turning it to a fine paste. Next the honey, some more herbs, and a little boiled water. Finally, he tipped the mix into a pot and got some fellow to pick up one of the water ones. While they poured, he stirred it into his cordial.

Soon it was ready, but Essene wine is nothing until it is blessed, and so when all prepared, he placed his hands on either side of the vessel and spoke the words of blessing. He said them to himself, feeling the presence of the Lord as he did so. He felt the pain of his aunt, the pain of John his cousin, the isolation they must have felt here. He asked the Lord to heal, to uplift, to bring a greater understanding into the hearts of all. It was his true desire, that people be released from the imprisonment of sin, and set free to sit at the foot of the Lord.

Then he felt it, that peculiar sense of something, he could not describe. This is what happened when the healings occurred. It started at the top of his head, a tingling, and it flowed down through him, and out his hands. This time, it flowed into the wine had had just made - he felt it strongly, that the Lord was blessing this day and these people.

And then it passed. He signaled for the fellow who brought over all the fruits and herbs that it was ready and he might serve the fresh wine, and then it happened. As the wine touched the lips, he could see the spirit flowing through. Their faces took on a light as their eyes glowed, and the father of the groom called out in delight. "Normally they serve the best stuff first, but this is magnificent!"

In the background, Mary smiled. She knew he was special - from the very first breath he took, he was special. He came over and sat with her as libations were poured and the ceremonies for long life and good fortune were spoken. "What happened?" she asked.

"The Lord spoke through me," Yeshua was not sure what this was, but happy it had brought such great joy and happiness. Even John had become friendly and gregarious. Elizabeth looked not long for this world, however. "How does my aunt fare, mother?"

"She is well in her heart. Her life is content for she knows that through the trials she has given the world a prophet - what more could a soul want, what could make a mother happier than this?" She smiled with so much love and pride and hugged her oldest boy, her little miracle. "I saw the Angel Gabrielle the night John was born, and again the day you were conceived. I just knew in my heart you two were part of the same journey."

"I am grateful for all John has given me, mother, I truly am. But he wants so many things I have no interest in, getting rid of the Romans for one. I have seen whole countries run by one petty despot after another. In India, if a Sultan dislikes the way you look, he can have you killed for no reason. He is accountable to no one. Even in a country where they know all must pay God for their crimes, where all accept they will return to earth again and again until they find perfection, still there are brigands and thieves and no shortage of pride ruing the hearts of ruthless men.

"In truth, the Romans look reasonable and cultured compared to so many others. The ones I find cruel and indifferent are the Sadducee, our own people. They would be far worse if given their chance, and without the Romans, this is what we would have." Yeshua looked over, "I am sorry mother, I know you have no interest in such things."

She smiled, "As long as children are fed, families are housed, the rains are kind, and my village is secure, then my heart is light. What men do is their business. I am grateful I had a husband who was kind and the fact he was prosperous was a wonderful bonus, but it was his kindness I cherished. He thought as you did, the Romans are the lesser of evils we might face. He did some work for them on occasions, you know, and they always paid for good work, unlike the priests who constantly tried to shirk their debts."

They chatted as mother and son will do over the small details of life for many hours and it was well into the evening before people made for their own homes. Men came over, full of cheer, asking if Yeshua had a recipe for that wonderful brew. Children were laughing and playing with no parents sending them to bed. Eventually, mother and son worked their way back to the house of Elizabeth, lit candles, and sang the songs of blessing for the day before retiring to sleep.

ooo0000ooo

But sleep for some is when their day truly starts. In the peace of the village, Yeshua slipped easily from the body that carried his spirit and walked amongst the shadows and wishes of the people. This was why he could see so clearly into a person's heart - for he saw their true spirit. Once a Soul experienced the illumination of dream walking, there were no more barriers between individuals.

Here his work began. A man is carrying pain over the loss of a beloved child, he calls to him and asks of the child's name. Then, following the trail of love between them, finds her where she dwells with the Lord. He takes him to her, so he can see she is well and loved. His heart will be eased by the morning, even if he cannot recall the dream visit.

Zadoc once explained this dream life was the world of the Moon, and that the physical world is an outer reflection of this inner place. An aware teacher will reach out and do his work here, knowing his love will flow through into the lives of those he touches, "But do not expect them to remember, there is a veil of forgetfulness drawn by the mind when they wake."

He had once thought the Essene alone knew of this, but in his travels, he found many teachers who understood the ways of dreams and how you can use them to uplift. He first went to see the Magi in Persia and was welcomed. They consciously taught students how to leave their bodies and travel in the inner worlds, but it was their knowledge of healing that was of the greatest benefit to him. He had already started this practice of healing with some of the followers of John, relieving them of worms and other injurious afflictions.

The dreamscape was like a mirror of the physical, but far easier to bend. Imagination ruled here, all you need do is open the heart and imagine the greatest of gifts flowing through to all, and the will of the Lord would be revealed to you. He knew when it came, for it was presaged with a fine, biting wind, like the single note of a flute. Then light would form, and the teacher appeared. So much he had been given in this state, so much wisdom, so much love, that it filled him to the rim of his cup. How could he do anything but love all around him? Life was beauty that flowed out from the secret font within.

But this freedom only highlighted the tragedy of man. So many could not access their highest self because of the traps and conditions into which their seeds of thought had been planted. People were so caught up in convention, ruled by tradition, by their self-limiting beliefs. These were the walls that defined man's limitations - It was why people felt so alone in the outer world. He saw the fear that controlled the heart of man, forcing him to build a house into which each man had locked himself. Yet, if you unlocked the door and invited him to step outside, that soul would hate you.

That is the nature of the self-created prison. He spent years seeking to understand this and the only explanation he ever came to was fear. Their whole world was based on fear in some way, which opposed his world of love. "Oil and water," the Zadoc was now beside him, speaking to his student. "You offer them the living water but their sin repels it, like an oil-stained cloth, the sinful self rejects the water of life. The person doesn't even know why, but they are repelled by purity."

It came to him then, the meaning. The Zadoc had said it many times, *Oil and water do not mix.* In the dream he looked at Yeshua, "The offering of water and wine to the seasons is a reflection of this ancient understanding. Hosanna Rabah, the people cry, praying that the rains will come."

As always with the teachings of the master, he gave you a riddle to solve. How was the Rite of Libation practiced in the Temple, which was the mixing of water and wine poured over the altar, connected to this sense of people rejecting love? What was the thread that stitched together these notions? And in that thought he understood the simplicity of the ancient practice: *Through the acceptance of difference, the difference within us is united.* A man that loves his wife without hesitation, loves the Lord. A child that respects his elder, respects the Lord. A mother that teaches her child the ways of the Lord learns of the Lord already in her heart.

And the opposite is also true. A man that strikes his wife, strikes his own heart, making it deaf to the word of God. A child who hates his parent plants a harvest of bitter fruit he will eat later in life. A mother that neglects her duty in teaching a child the word of God will have a child without ethics that will leave her without support in old age. It was all the Wheel of Becoming, the Awagawan of the Indian priests. They called it karma, the rolling out of personal reality according to the images a person holds in their mind and heart.

Oil and Water. The two do not mix. The Spiritual and the Physical, how do you lessen the belief that they are opposites?

How to change this, how do you shift a person from the path of doom to the ways of righteousness that leads a soul to the door of heaven? The Zadoc never said things directly but gave a person images and questions. The mind will accept a story and nurse a question while it rejects a sermon. The mind will follow the heart on the journey of dreams you weave before it.

Stories went past the criticism and doubt, so Yeshua told people stories. The oil of sin stains the mind and the beauty of soul within can not get past it. The heart that is trapped cannot travel into the delight of the Lord. But give them a good story and it brought out the child within, the part that existed before all the poisons of the world afflicted them. By following the breadcrumbs of dreams that he laid, people could leave the labyrinth of confusion and find the light of day.

But this miracle with the wine, this was different. He was happy for the wedding feast that it happened, but the Lord had always been a cat on silent feet, moving like a whisper through him. This was different, this was a powerful force he could feel, an ancient thing he had no name for.

At that point, his cousin John walked into his world, "Yeshua, wake up. You are the chosen one. It will soon be your time."

Yeshua sat bolt upright from where his body had been sleeping. His breathing was ragged, his heart beating hard against his ribs, and a sweat had formed on his brow. He knew the scent of fear, the sense of repulsion. He must let it go, he must listen only to the Lord and the silent voice of his truth. He asked for a sign, "If this is truth, if this is my time, I need a sign, dear Lord. Show me your ways, show me your path that I might walk it knowing this is your will."

And in the back of his thoughts, the voice of Zadoc, *"Oil and water, they do not mix."*

ooo0000ooo

"That was a pretty damn impressive show yesterday, with the wine," John laughed, slapping his cousin on the back. "It was like baptizing people on the inside, even I felt it. Hello, I didn't even hate the Romans for a bit. I felt such an incredible release, nice trick. Can you do that again?"

Yeshua shook his head, "It is not me, John. It is never ME. I am just wood being fashioned by the chisel of the Lord."

"Yeah, maybe, but can you do it again?"

"I don't know, possibly." Then he looked hard at his cousin, "John, you KNOW we cannot control the gift Spirit brings. It flows where it will, carving the river of truth for all. The notion that I am in charge of anything is madness. I stumble from moment to moment and the ONLY thing that holds me up is the love of the Lord in my heart."

"You seem out of sorts, what is up?" John was curious about this strange spirit flowing through his cousin. He seemed different this morning as they made their way back down to the work of baptism.

"Zadoc spoke to me last night. I was wondering how to best give the love of the Lord, he said, *Water and Oil do not mix.* The spiritual truths and the material reality oppose each other. How can I bring the love of the Lord into this world, we both know it will be rejected. You have found your way, I need to find mine."

John looked at the road ahead. "If a person who knew nothing was standing by the road and saw us, what would they see? He would see two men being led by a mule. But if that person had som`e understanding of how things worked, they would understand that the Mule is being controlled by the two men. Yet how true is this? The mule doesn't care, it just does what it does, following the path before it."

"You are doing MY thing now?" Yeshua laughed. But he got the message, HOW we see is more important than WHAT we see.

"The path will be made clear, cousin. I am just grateful I have a mule and a cousin and that we can share this beautiful day." John laughed.

Yeshua smiled, John was rarely so carefree and happy. He began to understand that the wine the Lord brought forth through his hand really DID have a punch.

John had a question, "What I am thinking is this - how did you manage to communicate when you traveled? You went to Persia, India, God knows where else - I know they have different languages. How did you cope?"

Yeshua sighed, "It can be difficult, but you learn a few key words, like bread and you make a gesture to your mouth. People get the idea. You need to know the words for Good Morning, and Thank You, to start the ball rolling. Plus you need the word for the sort of work you do, which can be trickier than it seems. To this end, I created miniatures of the tables and chairs, and other furniture, so people got a clear idea of what I could do, and after that everyone understands trade.

"Goa was where I got lucky, finding the Pharisee trader there. He spoke the main language and made it much easier for me. Yes, he got a cut of the work he organized me to do, but I was looked after and was able to meet some remarkable teachers. They do dream walking there as well, and talk of the many layers of heaven. Mind you, they have a God for everything, it is confusing. Even so, our idea there is one God that flows through everything they accepted. They have a saying, roughly translated, *'The One flows into the many to reflow back into the One'*."

"I like that," said John.

"I did not get around the whole country, but there was a place called Kashmir, high in the mountains - mountains that make what we have here look like anthills - It was the home of the Lord and the opposite of what we have here. It was green, cold, with water everywhere."

"That's the thing, isn't it? We start out in life not knowing a language, but we pick it up soon enough." John explained, "Everything we start, we start not knowing anything, but soon enough, we pick it up. I had no idea, out there in the desert, and the Lord brought me a sinner and planted the notion of baptizing him in my head. You will sort it out, the Tower of Babel is not a curse, it is a learning experience."

Long moments of thought followed the wheels as they turned over bumps and through ruts. "Crazy you got so far away from this land of ashes, yet came back."

"It was Joseph. He dream walked to me in that far-off place, saying it was my time to return. I saw my mother heartbroken, it was not possible for me to stay, even though at the time I believed I had found my true home. By the way, your mother looked happy."

"They are both saints. I barely see her, yet never a hint of recrimination from her lips."

"But you send her food and money, more than I did for Mary!" Yeshua laughs.

"I have plenty of food and what use do I have for money? It is no big thing, just a courtesy. Your mother needed neither, the Qumran is good to her people."

At that moment, the dream walking returned and the thought came to him: *A mother that neglects her duty in teaching a child the word of God will have a child without ethics that will leave her without support in old age.*

Little else was said on the journey back to Galilee.

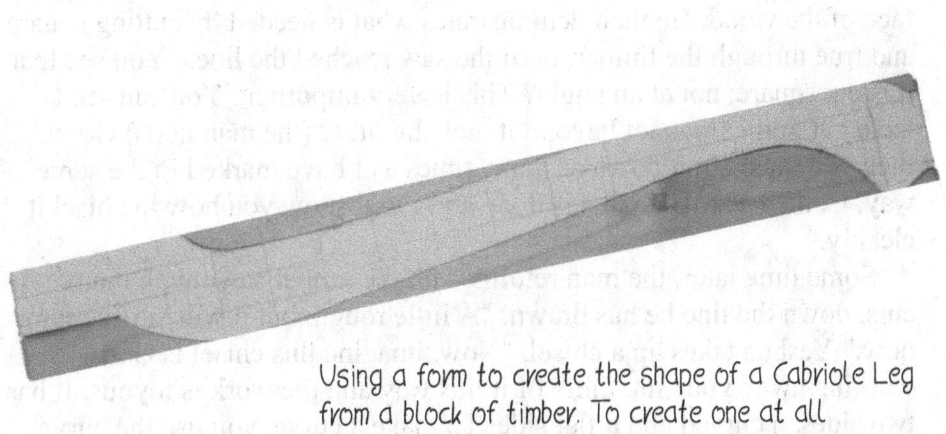

Using a form to create the shape of a Cabriole Leg from a block of timber. To create one at all requires a competent tradesman, to make one without a form is proof of a Master Carpenter.

How to Shape Wood

Jacob, a member of the entourage that followed the Baptist, just looked blankly at the raw timber, not knowing where to start. He had wanted to make a table for his mother, imagining it was a fairly simple thing, but with the raw materials in hand, he did not know where to start. Which was why he had picked up the pieces and gone to see Yeshua.

Seeing the hapless fellow with his tools and wood standing there, it was hard not to laugh. There were chipping marks on the blanks where he had started to shape things, but it was disorganized and clumsy. Yeshua sat him down, saying, "The father gives us tasks like shaping wood because in this process we shape ourselves to be better chisels for his hammer. Jacob, you cannot start a project without drawing the plan. Only a fool builds a house by just throwing bricks on top of each other. I will show you the secret we carpenters use, which is what you must do."

Yeshua took a carpenters pencil picked up one of the pieces of wood that were to be the legs, and drew a simple, elegant line. A curve that started at one end and finished on the other. "First we must create the pleasing form. Once we have carved one, we use this as a form to give the shape to the wood on the other legs. See this line? (the man nods) You take your saw, and you cut square to this line. You need many cuts, I will mark the wood to make it easy for you."

Yeshua draws a series of straight lines, very close together, across the face of the wood. He then demonstrates what is needed by cutting square and true through the timber, until the saw reached the line. "You see that it is cut square, not at an angle? This is very important. You can see I have cut to the line, not beyond it, not shy of it? (the man nods) Good, then you must cut it down as many times as I have marked in the same way. Come back when this is done and I will show you how to chisel it cleanly."

Some time later, the man returns with the timber sawn with many cuts, down the line he has drawn. "A little rough, but it will suffice for now." Yeshua takes up a chisel, "Now, imagine this chisel is God working away your sin, think of it this way and the work is joyous. It has two sides, a curved and a flat side. To make a curve, you use the curve, and likewise for planing flat surfaces." He takes the chisel and starts to chip away the slices of wood. "You see how the form now reveals itself, take this and carve as carefully as you can, taking care not to cut below the line."

The fire was burning low by the time he returned, it was a fairly decent attempt. The shape of the leg on one side is now revealed. "You see my friend? You now have one face of one leg appearing." The flowing curve of the wood was graceful. "The Lord chips away our dross and reveals the beauty within, so despite this being merely a leg, it is also God's work. Let me finish this leg for you, so we have a form by which to shape the rest. It is important to get this first part right, for all follows on from it."

The man, who had labored for hours over getting it to the barely formed state it was in, looked in wonder as the carpenter took hammer and chisel, whittled away at the imperfections, and formed up a smooth, perfect curve. "Now take the roughing stone and smooth this until it feels like a woman's skin. I will draw the line on the other side for you to do the same with saw and chisel. We will look at the other pieces tomorrow."

One of John's disciples, the fisherman Peter, had watched the whole process and marveled, "You make it seem so easy. That poor fellow has no idea at all and will spend all week on making a table, where you would have it done in hours."

"Time and patience, Peter. You shape what you have with time and patience. The Lord is the master carpenter, but have you ever wondered why he lets us stumble along trying to grasp his will? Would it not be easier, as he is so much better at this, to just shape each man and woman as he wished them to be?

Peter looks somewhat askance, trying to grasp what he is being told. "Do you mean, why do we have Romans here?"

Yeshua laughs, "No, I am not the Baptist. My thoughts are not wrapped around priests or Romans nor is my life dedicated to removing either from this world. No, I am asking you why God allows all this imperfection. He is God, this can be the Garden of Eden with merely his wish. Why is it a garden of weeds and trials?"

Peter was not good at riddle. "Well, Eve took from the tree of Knowledge. Then Adam did, that is why."

Yeshua laughs heartily, "Dry words in a book. Have you ever considered that God put the Tree there KNOWING Eve would take the fruit? He knows all, surely he knew what she would decide?"

Peter was uncomfortable with all this thinking, "Well, I suppose."

"And it was the Tree of Knowledge of Good and Evil! Why would God want man to stay ignorant of right and wrong? And why would he let a fallen angel in to his garden to pervert the innocent?"

"That sounds like blasphemy!" Peter says, worried he is on shaky ground.

"I showed that man how to make a leg, surely this is the same as eating fruit from the Tree of Knowledge. Was I doing an evil thing? Am I Satan?"

Peter made up his mind, "No, you were helping him with a gift for his mother. This cannot be evil. But I don't understand."

"I should call you Petra, the rock. But just as the master carpenter will shape the wood, so too will the master sculptor shape the stone. Look in your heart, Peter, for truth. Look in your heart to see the true shape of things. The Lord reveals to us the most basic of truths, such as the line we must cut to. The rest we must work through in our own time, slowly coming to understand how we might best form ourselves to the line drawn by the Lord.

"He takes the rough blocks of wood that are the foolish men like myself and yourself, and over the years he shows us how to shape our world to be more pleasing. We come to this place, again and again, to learn the art of fashioning the self to a more perfect state. I could have taken that man's wood and made him a table, but of what benefit would this be to him? His mother would have a better table to cover with a cloth, but what she truly wants is her son's love, what he truly wants is the acceptance of his mother." Peter still looked puzzled.

Yeshua laughs again, "Peter! THIS is why it was evil for Eve to pluck from the Tree of Knowledge. She had not earned it, she had not fought for it, she had not taken the time and the patience to learn her craft. This is what evil whispers to us, '*Just take it now!*' What were Adam and his wife doing there anyway? Sitting around in the sun? Do you think the Lord intended for his creation to be idle wastrels? Of course the Lord understood Eve's heart, of course he knew what she would do, how she would tempt Adam - All this he knew, just as he knew man would have to make this journey to earth over and over until he learned the ways of the master craftsman."

Peter scoffed, "That Essene stuff again?"

Yeshua smiled, "Tell me this: How can you find a benefit from the Tree of Knowledge without the ability to USE this in some way? Knowledge without skill and the ability to apply it is useless. This is why I don't make his table for him. Instead, I offer him a fragment of truth, a seed of wisdom, and from this he can create his own Eden. God did not PUNISH man by sending him from the Garden, just as I did not punish that man by sending him away to make his table. God set us free to find out own perfection. The father must let his children find their way in the world, knowing they will suffer, knowing they will hurt, but knowing this is needed for them to become whole."

"I am just a fisherman, Yeshua. I don't have fine words like you. I have not traveled the length and breadth of the world like you, and while what you speak of sounds wonderful and important, it goes past my ears like a cool mountain breeze." Peter was still stitching the nets as they had spoken, and he continued to do so, practiced hands working with the fibers.

Yeshua liked his stubborn honesty. Even if he understood, he would not admit it! "You need help with the nets?"

"What, and slow me down? No thank you."

Over the next few days, the man making the table made a few more appearances, Yeshua gave him a few more tips, and soon enough he had a rough table ready to give to his mother. He beamed with delight as he showed off his finished product, a perfectly serviceable little table that will last many years.

Glowing with pride he left to see his mother in a nearby village. Peter had his boat in dock and was bringing fish ashore for the market, and his tithe for the Baptists as well. "He is a happy man, Yeshua. But I don't think he can quit laboring and take up carpentry just yet," he laughed.

"Not in this life, Peter. But perhaps the next, maybe?" Yeshua asked, baiting the fisherman.

He laughed, "You Essenes and your beliefs. I swear you were put here to annoy the Sadducee and Pharisee. How did we all come to be in the same religion anyway? It seems to me that our people are opposed to each other even more than they are to the Romans."

"Harmony comes from different notes working together, Peter - Not from everyone singing the same song."

"What do your people do, anyway? Are they all just sitting up there writing up the words of the Prophets? I mean, I get that the Baptist sends up thieves and criminals to be reformed, but my mother is certain this is a secret plan to build an army to attack the Romans."

"Not the people of the Qumran, Peter. They would not willingly kill anything, even a Roman. But because the Romans know the Essene are essentially peaceful and only interested in the works of the Lord, they leave the Qumran alone. Yes, we pay our taxes to the Aediles as they come through, and of course people complain. But the fact is, BECAUSE we have little money, BECAUSE we have few worldly goods, this is WHY we are left in peace. The wheel, Peter, the wheel of life. If you use it to make a glorious chariot, bedecked with gold and silver, drawn by magnificent horses, then you have to spend your time and energy defending it from thieves and brigands.

"Having nothing, they have everything. No one does without, for all share what they have. No one is beating at the walls of our fortress, for we have no walls, no fortress. Anyone can walk into the Qumran and take what they want, but there is so little to take they don't bother to come. Yet everyone has plenty of food, everyone has water, so we all have fruit trees and gardens." Yeshua explained.

"But you don't eat meat. How can a man do hard work without meat to sustain him?" he argued.

"You have seen the Baptist? He is the size of my father. We have a smith up on the plateau that makes them look the size of a child. The people are perfectly healthy, happy, and strong eating eggs, herbs, and bread. Plus, because the chickens are used only for eggs, we need fewer chickens. Because our sheep are used only for their wool, we need fewer sheep. Less to feed, less to care for and it is so much cheaper!" Yeshua laughed because THAT was the argument that would win over Peter.

"Yes, this may be so, but what of MY profession? A man like myself would starve if he were an Essene."

"This would seem to be true, yet my father made a great deal of money selling furniture to rich Jews. He made Temple furniture as well, and not as a donation. One does not have to eat a fish to be a fisherman, does he?"

"Now I know you are crazy. Who would catch a fish and not eat it? And the Baptist, I thought he was Essene as well, he happily eats what I give them. They all do!"

"Technically, John is a Sadducee. His mother is Essene, so I guess he gets to choose what he wants to be. I do not argue the Qumran is perfect, far from it. Some people do not honor the pledge as completely as they might, but the community lists do work, overall. Most are content to live within the laws of the list."

"That is another thing, your people do not obey the Law of Moses. You seem to have your own law entirely, which is why the Pharisee hate you so much. The Sadducee hate you for your notions of man returning to earth over and over till he finds perfection, and your dedication to poverty they find abhorrent."

"Do I seem poor to you, Peter?"

That caused him to stop and think, "No, Yeshua - You are the richest man I have ever met. You have nothing, yet you walk like you own this world. You have no home, yet you are at ease and comfortable wherever you go. Plus, I cannot understand it, while everything about you is true and kind, you have a hardness deep inside. I respect that, and I am not sure why."

Yeshua smiled, all these months and Peter is finally beginning to grasp the truth. "I am a fisher of men, Peter. I draw them up from the depths of ignorance, where they lay drowning under the waters of convention, and I bring them to the brightness of this day. I cast my net into the depths of despair and draw up those who are lost. I set their feet upon the true path where my father can breathe his spirit into their hearts, to inspire them to become all they can be."

"But the miracles, all the healings. This is new. John helped so many, he helped me find my feet after the death of my brothers. I am eternally grateful to him which is why I give him my tithe - better he than the local priests. But blind men are walking away with sight, how do you do this?" Peter looks at Yeshua, finally asking the question that has been plaguing him for months. "In other words, I am asking if this man before me is the Messiah?"

Yeshua laughs out loud, "Oh Peter, do not confuse me with the father. The Lord heals, not I. I am but the vessel that contains his gift, and who it flows to, how it flows, that it is HIS work, not mine. And there is no secret, there is no mystery, it is love. All I have in my heart is love. When I see a downtrodden soul, all I feel for them is love. When I see a lost soul, all I feel in my heart is love. I am not here to judge, I am not worthy to judge another. I am a carpenter who found love and allowed this to rule my heart. And yes, I am now the richest man in the world because of this.

"But Peter, this wealth of love is unlimited. The Lord has a boundless supply, he is willing to give it to all, but so often only the broken can find it. The Lord is like this lake before us, we have to bow down low to receive its eternal waters."

Peter is determined to get a straight answer. "John tells everyone you are the Messiah, that you are the one who will free Jerusalem from the yoke of oppression. Does he speak the truth?"

"My cousin speaks truth as he sees it. But tomorrow, if he sees differently, he will speak a different truth. You cannot decide what is true on the words or beliefs of another, my fish-smelling friend. You have to look inside your OWN heart, see with your OWN eyes, decide with your OWN mind what is truth." While he could see the fisherman just wanted a simple answer, how do you explain there IS no simple answer? All men are Messiahs. All men can change the world and uplift their brothers, but you cannot say this to a soul locked into their past, trapped by their beliefs, and their ingrained ways of living.

"Perhaps a story will answer in a way words alone cannot?" By this time a group had gathered, as always happened when Yeshua began to speak. People flocked to his words like bees to a hive. He looked at the eager faces of the people and began.

"I will give you a riddle. Imagine Peter's boat sailed under the water, and he cast his net up to catch the stars." he started.

"But he would drown," said an incredulous voice.

"Imagine he has a bubble surrounding his boat, and that it stays beneath the water."

Another voice chimed in, "But it would bob to the surface!"

"Imagine then he has a boat, surrounded by a bubble, but that he had the hull filled with lead that keeps him under the water. Can we see this?" Yeshua laughed, he loved these argumentative followers of John. They all seemed to murmur that this was an acceptable place to start.

"Good, now we are agreed, let me say that a long time ago, there were a people that called our physical world the 'Marine Planes'. They believed we swam in this physical world in the same way as fish swim in the ocean. Now, let us imagine we are on Peter's boat, deep in the water, surrounded by our bubble, held down by the lead in our keel. Our greatest fear arrives, a terrible monster of the deep comes up, and goes BUMP BUMP BUMP against our bubble. What do we do?"

"We sail away! Or we get swords to defeat it!" one calls out.

"But you are deep under the water, and if that bubble breaks, you all drown. There is no wind in your bubble, how can you sail away? How can you escape, how can you attack the monster?"

"You throw the lead in the keel overboard, that way you rise to the top!"

Yeshua laughs, "There you have it! The simple answer and the best so far."

"But that can't be true. If you threw out the lead it would fall through the bubble and it would burst, and we would all drown." a different voice calls out.

A good deal of muttering ensues as each man tries to solve the riddle, and soon people are shouting and arguing. Yeshua holds up his hand, they grow silent. "Let me give you a clue, the name of the monster is 'Change'."

This puzzles them, until Peter laughs. "I see, you make a friend of Change. You bring him close and you try to encourage him to take you up out of the ocean."

"Almost Peter, almost there. The first part is correct, we make a friend of what we fear. But have you forgotten, the Lord made Change, just as he made you? When we WELCOME Change into our life, it breathes a new spirit into our boat. That breath of spirit enlarges the bubble, and we rise naturally to the top. Once we are there, what do we do?"

Voices shouted out, "Drop the lead overboard!"

"And what does THAT do?"

Peter laughs, "It bursts the bubble and we float free on the surface."

Yeshua becomes serious, "This is truth. Change will come, we either welcome it and live, or fight it and die. We can avoid change, but eventually it will come, and we will have to choose."

The crowd murmured, another good story! They loved this new guy, he was far more entertaining than the Baptist. As they departed Peter looked at Yeshua, "You were talking about the Romans?"

"I was talking about life, Peter." Yeshua paused, he rarely spoke directly, mostly because there was little point as truth and wisdom flowed too quickly over the brim of a shallow cup. "Each of us lives in a bubble of our society, our beliefs, our fears, and our doubts. This is our protection from the world. The Essene live in a bubble on their plateau and are happy enough, but change will come, sooner rather than later. The Sadducee, they live in THEIR bubble, as do the Pharisee, and the Zealot. All will soon face the great monster of change. Even the Romans will have their time. Eventually, change comes and the walls we have built to protect our city fall. This is the way of things, it is always the way."

"John would not like this way of thinking," advised Peter.

"Which is why I say it to you, not him. I have no secrets, Peter. I am with the Lord, the Lord is with me, and we have no secrets from each other. I can open my heart knowing that he will walk in like a cat on silent feet and that his claws will be used to protect me, that his teeth will fight injustice brought against me. I live in change, Peter. I do not need to defend or fight change, I just need to accept it."

The unspoken question in the heart of Yeshua need not be given breath just now, but he could feel it beneath the surface. Since his baptism, the sleeping cat of love had awoken in his heart, and it was fierce in its hunger for truth and freedom. The Lord was using him to bring the change, and the Lord would tear down all walls presented to him.

Including his own.

As the fisherman made his boat ready for the next day, Yeshua went into the soft desert near Galilee with a prayer on his lips, "Lord, they will be done here as it is in Heaven. Give me your truth as my daily bread so that I will not sin with my ignorance. Show me your path. Lead me not into temptation, deliver me from evil, and forgive me if I trespass against you."

As he came back to this world he had come to, as the glamor of love that flowed from Spirit radiated out as it would, he understood a silent message was being written in his heart. His time working with the Baptist was coming to a close. His own journey must soon begin.

A house had come up at Capernaum, on the shore of Galilee. It was time he made his way there.

John the Baptist preaching, by Rembrandt

How to Catch God

The morning was bright on that day as the men at Capernaum enjoyed the fruits and breads laid for their breakfast. Yeshua came down to see them, eyes distant from his contemplations. They knew this look now, he had been traveling to far-off lands, places they could not go. "A story, Master!" they cried.

He looked at their faces, they held such simple happiness that it cheered his heart. "Very well, I will teach you how to catch the Lord!"

There was a fisherman! (The men all laugh) *He went out onto the sea of Galilee without a net.* (They laugh at the absurdity of this) *He had decided that he was the greatest fisherman of all time and that he was about to catch a fish with just his hands!* (they rolled about in laughter) *So he dove down, but every time a fish came by, he was too slow. It escaped him. But he was a stubborn man, and he truly believed he could catch a fish without anything but his wits and skill.*

Day after day he went out, jumping into the cold waters, and catching nothing. That other fishermen were casting nets meant nothing to him, that they brought up many fish was a thing he was blind to. They all laughed behind his back, telling each other what a fool this man was, but he was deaf to what anyone said. He was completely focused on the single task before him, and then it happened! A fish swam past and somehow he managed to catch it.

He looked at his prize with joy and pride, saying, "At last I have you!"

To his vast surprise, the fish turned to look at him, and asked in surprise, "You have ME?" And with this, the fish took to the deepest part of the ocean. But the fisherman would not give up so easily - he had battled for a long time to catch this fish and he was not letting it go. Down he went, still holding to his catch, down until that water turned black and icy cold, but still he held to his prize.

When at last when it reached the bottom, the fish saw the man still held on and laughed, "You do not have me, fisherman - I have YOU!"

This was when the madness left, this was when the fisherman realized how foolish he had been, wanting this fish so much had brought him to his end. "Oh, at last my eyes are open," he said. Finally he let go, and his consciousness faded to black. But when he awoke it was in a land of milk and honey, with many friends surrounding him, welcoming him home.

"Have I died?" he asked.

The people laughed. "Does this look like death to you?" they asked.

The men looked eager, what was the extraordinary ending to this tale? But Yeshua just smiled and walked away down the foreshore, towards the Greek side of the sea. His close disciples were curious and followed. John, always the questioner, asked, "The fish is the Lord, Master? You are telling us that to catch the Lord we have to die?"

Yeshua looked at the man, "Every day you must die for the Lord. You cannot hold onto both his presence and the things of this world, so you must choose. Every hour and every minute you must lay down your life as you know it, and sacrifice it to the Lord."

Peter muttered, "I wish you would make all this a little more appealing. Hard to get people to listen when all we get is a riddle."

Yeshua went up and knocked his head with his knuckles, "Yes, it is hard to get people to listen when their head is full of thickness and doubt and problems. This is why you must let it all go, your fears, your blindness, even your thoughts."

Then he looked to the distance saying, "Let us sail to the healing baths at Bethsaida."

This was much easier than riddles: Peter rigged the boat, and inside a few minutes, they were underway, catching a favorable wind for the few miles they had to go. Yeshua had said little, only that they needed to get to the healing baths there. Once the breeze caught up the sails and the disciples were settled, Yeshua asked if they wanted a story. Of course, they all did.

There was a man who disagreed with his father as a child. He did not like the constraints and disciplines placed upon him, nor the strict rules of behavior demanded of him. He wanted to play with the other children, but his father bade him stay home and learn his craft, which was shipbuilding.

The child believed that all his father wanted was an extra pair of hands. He was the one providing the labor and doing so without payment. He became bitter and resentful, but the father ignored him. Shave this staff, cut this pole, weave this linen, make this rope, all day long, one task after another. This went on for years without let up, until finally the boy ran away from home and from his family.

He did not run far, he went across the lake to Tiberias and found a shipbuilder who took him on and paid him wages. He was still working as hard, if not harder than he had for his father, but now he was getting a wage. It was marvelous for he could spend the night in taverns, talking and having a good time with new friends. He hated his father even more, thinking how all this had been kept from him.

This went on for some years, the boy working harder than he ever had, but he was paid for his labor. The man who employed him was happy, for the youth did excellent work with all he was given to do. In fact, he was a better craftsman than the man who owned the business, though the man never mentioned this for the boy would ask for more wages.

The lad stayed at the man's house, paying rent, and ate the food provided, for a reasonable fee. This went on for some years before the boy finally realized - he had nothing for the time he spent at that man's workshop. This is when he understood his employer's work was not as proficient as his father's. Slowly he came to see that he had no future in the house of this man, he needed to start his own business - But with what?

He had no money to buy tools, he had no shed to build boats, neither had he the wits to understand how he had everything he needed at his family house, or if he did, he was too proud to admit it. As a result he felt a growing rage and fury inside. He began to complain how life had given him a poor deal. Bitterness became his best friend, resentfulness his wife, and self-pity the air he breathed.

Even the man he worked for became annoyed, having this morose and unhappy creature about all day and all night. It was his wife who complained about the ungrateful wretch who never gave thanks for his food or lodging, and finally the man had enough and terminated his service.

So the boy went to another boat builder, but of course, that man asked the former master why the lad had left, and when told, was not interested in employing the boy. And so it went, from one builder to the next, until there were none left to ask, and the child became hungry and cold as the evening descended.

A long dark night fell on him, and he cried out his woes to the Moon, who listened with serenity and peace. In his dreams, she came and whispered to him, "Why do you struggle? Go home and ask forgiveness of your father, and the blessing of your mother."

The boy woke with tears in his eyes and took a boat across the lake to see the father he had ignored for many years. There he found the one he once hated, but now his eyes saw a different man. Where a cold and indifferent soul forced him to work, now a warm smile and a welcome greeted him. Where a harsh taskmaster had forced him to do his bidding, now a kind old man asked if he wanted some tea.

Seeing the error of his ways, the boy wept and asked forgiveness from his father. But the father just laughed, "What is there to forgive my boy?"

"I thought evil of you, father. I thought you made me work too hard and used me for your own gain!"

"Did you? Well, this is often how boys think of their father, my son."

"I felt I was being ignored, that my thoughts were not welcome, and I hated you!"

"Did you? Well, I thought this of my own father for a time."

The child is perplexed, all that anger he had towards his father, all the hard tasks he was put to, he truly believed the man to be a monster. But he now seemed such a kind and gentle soul. The father saw his confusion, and laughed, "My father once told me, when I returned in a similar way that you do now, that he was also surprised at how much his father had improved between his youth and his adulthood."

The old man looked up at the child who had now grown to a strong, strapping fellow, and laughed. His boy had returned! "One day I suppose you will marry and have children. Then you will understand, your job as a father is to teach your children how to follow the laws of society and to be able to support themselves. The job of the child is to learn to love their parents. Now, come and help me with this mast, for an extra pair of hands makes the whole task so much easier."

And so the child returned home, willingly helping his father for the simple benefit of a place to live and food to eat, and in doing so found both gratitude and love where once there had been resentment and hatred.

Every man in that boat knew this story, for it had in some way been their own. Mathew asked, "Are you speaking of the Lord as the father?"

Yeshua smiled, "The Lord, our father, asks nothing of us but that we do his bidding. It is his task to shape us into the vessel that contains the truth he wishes to share. It is our task to learn to love him, despite all the struggles we must go through to learn what we must."

Peter smiled, at last an easy-to-understand story that didn't tax his brain. "I hated my father, with a passion. I wanted him dead and I wanted me free, but then my wish came true - He died, but my brothers also died, and I was washed up with the boat onto the shore. It was only when repairing it that I understood; he had given me all the skills needed to survive. I knew how to do what was needed to get the boat back on the sea, how to sew the nets, how to do everything. I can never forgive him for beating my mother, but I did learn to think of him with more gratitude than hate."

Yeshua looked at him, "I say to you, you CHOSE your parents, you CHOSE this life, and you chose it for what you need to learn. When you learn to love your parent, what you are truly doing is repairing the boat of self that leaks out fear, hatred, and poison into the water in which it sails. So too, as we learn to love the Lord, our leaking boat is healed."

They had reached the dock, and tied off, ready for the walk up to the town the Romans now called Julias. Soon they came to the healing baths at Bethsaida, and the Master took his bag of potions and utensils, and sat with the people, giving them advice and assistance in their healing.

As always, people would come to talk to the disciples, "Is it true, a blind man was healed by this Soul?" and so on, all were curious as to the miracles that followed in the wake of this teacher. When asked how it was done, the disciples confessed they had no idea, but that Yeshua always attributed any healing to his father, the Lord in Paradise.

And then the people asked, "Can you Baptize us?" for this is what the last prophet did, forgive them their sins and set them closer to the Lord.

Peter considered this reasonable, and went to ask Yeshua about this, who just looked up and asked, "What is in your heart?"

"I wish for them to be free of fear, and to find the presence of the Lord," he stammered back, realizing for the first time a sense of his mission.

"Then do as the Lord instructs you, Peter. You have my blessing."

And so it was that where Yeshua went, the disciples started to initiate people into the path of the Lord by giving them the baptism by water. They would take the people into the water, and as they were blessed, they would teach them what their master had given, *"You are soul, a divine spark of the Lord that lives within your heart. This spark of god cannot be harmed, hurt, or pierced in any way. It is eternal, and as you come into a deeper understanding of this as your true self, the things of this world will hold less importance to you. As you understand the teachings of the master, you will start to dwell in the high places of the Lord. And you will come to know that all of this world, everything that exists, is here because the Lord wills it. You exist because the Lord loves you."*

A small number of baptisms turned into dozens, which in time became hundreds, all of whom would sit after their baptism as one of the disciples outlined the credo of the Master, which was how to find inner grace by offering mercy, kindness, and respect to all.

Last of all, they were taught the Lord's Prayer.

On their way back to Capernaum, the moon was full, and the water still. You could see the dancing ladder the moonlight cast upon the waters, moving like a snake, entrancing all who gazed at it. Yeshua spoke, "The light of the moon is upon the water and it points always to the source. This is like the good deeds we do each day, they are not the Lord, but they point people to where the Lord resides, high in the heavens."

Mathew asked, "How can we reach the Lord, master? The gulf between heaven and earth is great, how do we leap and grasp the divinity?"

"The Lord is as close as your heartbeat, Mathew. He is not up in the sky, he is within. There is no leap to make, just allow the Lord to bring you to him. Just as our sails fill with the breath of wind to take us home, the whisper of spirit will speak to you, fill you with its power, and guide you to port. To FIND the Lord is a matter of faith, in yourself, in the boat on which you travel, in your fellows, and in the wind of truth the Lord sends to all of good heart.

"But finding the Lord is not knowing the Lord. I can find the Temple, but unless I am permitted into the heart of the holy, I cannot truly know it. Only those pure in spirit will be given admittance to the knowledge of the Lord, only those who have suffered the trials of fire where the dross of this world has been burnt from them can know the Lord. For he is the smallest thing, a speck of dust you would overlook unless your whole house was clean. THEN you can know him. Which is why I say, rejoice when men slander you, reject you and call you what they will. They do the Lord's work in sloughing off all vestiges of pride.

"And further, merely knowing the Lord does not let you sit at his right hand. Knowledge is not wisdom and without wisdom, your tongue will speak foolishness and the Lord shall not abide with a foolish man. Therefore I say to practice silence in your heart, for only in silence can you hear the wisdom the Lord will whisper. Wisdom brings us silence in our dealings with others, for wisdom knows that with careless words you can bind yourself to invisible contracts. Know that careless words are a prayer to a false God, the God of Money, of Desire, of Hate. The fool will pray to the world for what he can get, not to the Lord for what he might give.

"Wisdom teaches us to give all our thoughts, all our dreams, all our hopes and wishes to the Lord, and ask HIM to do with them what he will. Only when we give all we have, all we are, all we hope to be, without thought of reward, will we have found the wisdom that will allow us to sit at his right hand. But remember, wisdom is deaf and blind without virtue.

"If a man is lost and asks of me the way, if I have wisdom I can direct his path. But will the man hear? Most are lost in a jangle of thoughts rattling about in their heads, and any words you offer are like echoes, insubstantial and hard to catch. But a man filled with virtue can see this raucous noise in another and understand what the person needs is peace and virtue, not wisdom. For in finding virtue he had to master these same thoughts and feelings.

"A man filled with virtue is a still, certain, point of truth. The Greeks call this the Omphalos, the belly button of the world. Such a man has traveled the paths of this world and others, and knows all ways to truth, for virtue is the path of truth. He sees with kindness and speaks with wisdom. He hears the din, but knows the harmony. He understands the lie, but speaks only truth. He has faith. knowledge, and wisdom, but he practices only love."

Yeshua looked at the glass-eyed men before him, the cup was not yet deep enough to contain all he would give, but in time, they would understand. "Finally, brothers, as is stated in the Torah, whatever is true, whatever is honorable, whatever is just, whatever is pure, whatever is lovely, whatever is commendable, if there is any excellence, if there is anything worthy of praise, think about these things. In other words, if you wish to catch the Moon in your net, cast only virtue into the air, and be amazed at what it will find."

All were as if asleep by this time, save Peter who was guiding the boat into dock. "You put them to work, for once, Yeshua. They are all tired out, it seems!" he joked. But he knew, for he had seen, that the power of the Lord moved through this one, and silenced the hearts and minds of those who would love him, carrying them off into other worlds. He had been hard-pressed himself to stay in the present moment.

And it came to pass that day after day, Yeshua went to the towns and villages around Galilee, and healed the sick while his chosen few baptized and educated the people in the ways of the Lord.

Transparent Before The Lord

Some of the disciples had walked with Yeshua that day as he traveled to the Greek side of the lake. In due course they came to the outskirts of a small village, where the humdrum of life carried on as it did.

Yeshua looked at the mother nursing her child, the soft gentle expression of love, one giving life to another, while the bay received with complete trust. "All seek this circle of trust. Men desire a woman, a woman desires a child, the child desires to live. Each wants to be close to the object of their wants and needs, but with this comes the fear it will be lost. Only the little child in its mother's arms has no fear, for the child lives only in this moment.

"The Lord is like a small child, trusting we will love him, so feed him, care for him. For if we do not, the child leaves this place and goes back to its eternal home. It does not blame or weep, or curse, it just fades back to the place of becoming, leaving this world as it is. But feed the Lord with love, kindness, and compassion, and the child grows strong.

"The Lord is here now, as close as our heartbeat. All we need do is love and cherish him, and the seed of love will grow. When you look into the eyes of a woman and see the Lord, all other desire will fall away. When a woman looks into the eyes of a man and sees only the Lord, nothing else will matter to her. If you want true intimacy, a true connection with your brothers, see the Lord in everyone you meet.

"If you do not, then the Lord will eventually leave your heart, and you will be left barren, shamed, and bereft of grace. But you cannot hurt the Lord by not recognizing him, only yourself. He is eternal and cannot be harmed by arrow or sling, or false word, or false heart. Can you imagine such a world where not one person sees the Lord? It is a lonely place. People are wandering in the dark, unable to reach out and touch one another.

"In this state of loss, men lose their humanity and forget the presence of the Lord. They become beasts that must be fenced lest they run amok in the village. This is the purpose of the Law, to restrain the beast within." He paused, considering his next words.

"Which is why I say to you, resist not evil. For if you see evil in another, you are not seeing the Lord in them. If you feel hatred or fear, you are closing the door to the whisper of spirit and its guidance. If you seek to destroy evil the only thing you will harm is yourself."

"But Yeshua, if a man seeks to harm my family, I must defend them. How can I see the Lord in my enemy? How can I see the Lord in a man I must kill for my family to live?" Mark was blunt. He may as well have said: *Nice words but how do they work in the real world?*

"If you seek to see the Lord in all, you will also see when the Lord has left. A man vacant of love is not a man, but a beast, and there is no evil in putting down a beast that threatens your family. But remember that a beast is not evil; it is hungry, or it is blind, or it is foolish. I say to you, when we defend what we love with love rather than hate, we become a greater threat to evil than any sword."

"When you find the man of constant love in your heart, you will find certainty in your all actions. When you find that permanent self, that voice that has always been within you, you will find love in its most personal, intimate place." Yeshua paused for a moment, gazing out over the wheat field before them as they walked the Sea of Galilee.

"Each grain in that sea of wheat before us is like a soul before the Lord. In its inherent goodness lies the promise of a greater tomorrow. Each grain that is properly nurtured can become a field of grain over time, or it can be ground into flour to become bread. What causes the farmer to choose which seed to keep and which to turn to dust?"

Mark smiled, "He chooses the tallest, strongest plants, the ones that stand out from the crop."

"I say to you, what makes a man stand tall in the eyes of the Lord is his virtue and his kindness. But what draws the Lord to his side is his love. A man of love is the seed that is kept close, to become the source of a greater crop for the Lord." He paused, then added, "But in all the Lord must first separate the chaff from the grain. As he tosses you up so that you may separate the good and useful grain from the useless chaff, you have a choice. Are you the chaff that gets blown in the wind, or the grain that is harvested by the Lord?"

Yeshua looked down the path to a well, where women were drawing water. And past this, to the shining Greek city of Hippos. To their right, the sea stretched away, a scene of peace that enveloped them. He was surprised when Thomas was the one who spoke, he rarely said anything.

"Master, surely the fate of either is not what most would aspire to. I do not want to be ground up and made into bread, nor do I like the idea of becoming chaff tossed by the wind. Do we not have some greater future than this?"

Yeshua looked for some time, waiting for the Lord to speak. "Thomas, this world is a millwheel for God. It will never be anything but the endless cycle of learning until we come to the perfection of the Lord.

Your question is how do we come into the Lord's Grace, how do we grow past the millwheel of becoming, the Awagawan?"

Yeshua was intent on the disciple, in a way Thomas rarely saw. He looked about him, to see if the Master was talking to someone else, but all the fellows that traveled with them had fallen asleep. He was surprised, for at that moment there was only he and the Master. His gaze poured into his heart like an ocean into a cup. Yeshua smiled, "This physical world is a poor reflection of the inner worlds. We have a self here in this world, but we also have a self that lives in the higher planes. When you are initiated into the path of truth, the higher and lower self is united. This is the time to focus on purity. When you become pure, you become a lens the light of God will use to enter this place, to bring an end to darkness."

He paused, "Only when we serve life, with all our heart and mind, are we set free. If you wish to grow past the endless churning of lifetimes, be of service to the Lord. You may imagine he doesn't need you. After all, it is the Lord, all things can be made in the blink of his eye. But we ARE needed. The heart of man is guarded, and the song of the celestial angels does not reach his ears. We have the gift of language and can form the song of the Lord into a shape our brothers can understand, but this is pure and unsullied only if we are transparent to his divine will. And so your real question is how do we become transparent?"

Thomas said nothing, could say nothing. He was transfixed by the power of the Lord, flowing through his chosen instrument. He saw this clearly, the light and sound pouring through the vessel of Yeshua.

The teacher continued, "To be clear as a still, perfect pond, to have no contamination to obscure the light, this is the goal of the Godman. How do we reach this? It depends on how much you need the Lord. Are you as the drowning man needing air? Will you give up everything for sake of one sweet breath of life? THIS is how we become transparent to the Lord. When we have nothing else but him in our heart, when he is the air we breathe, the food that sustains, the heart that beats, then we are transparent to the Lord.

"When you are transparent to the divine father, you are a vehicle of his love. As you open your heart, he can reach through and open the heart of all that touch you, and then the next, and the next, until all of creation is a song of love. When the Lord is our heartbeat, we gain incredible strength and purpose. We can lift whole nations as easily as we can lift up our brother. Those who have found this transparency can now raise the spirit of those who have fallen into slumber and forgotten the Lord."

With these words, the others began to stir, and Yeshua made his way further down the lake.

Thomas followed, wondering what the words meant, and why were they for him alone?

ooo0000ooo

They called by the house of a farmer. He bade them welcome and made no demands, giving them bread and water as hospitality obliged, but he also laid out fruits and nuts and such delicacies as you might find on the tables of the rich. The master and disciples ate with an appreciation of the gift, and at length, Yeshua asked the farmer, "How long have you tilled these lands?"

"Since I was a child, I have helped my father, as my father helped his. I am the seventh generation on this land," he answered.

Yeshua smiled, a man who was content with his lot was a boon to the Lord. He gazed over the well-tilled fields and carefully managed vines, thinking how some of the priests spoke against self-interest and how a man must lean only on the Lord. If this were the case, they would go hungry, for the farmers would sit and contemplate all day rather than maintain their holdings.

"I come from the Qumran," Yeshua mentioned, "Where our farmers work as a collective, under the law known as the Way. All contribute to the well-being of each other, all share the task of planting and harvesting, and each takes what they need to feed their families. Do the local people assist each other in such things as well?"

The farmer nodded, "They do indeed. No man can do all that is needed, and we each rely on the other for support in the planting and harvest. But what I grow on my lands is mine, save the tax demanded."

At this point, a poorly looking child came out of the home and went up to Yeshua. "Who is this, Daddy," he asked.

"Do not be rude, my son. A visitor, that is all," he replied.

"He came to me in my dream and said I will soon be well," the child said.

The man looked distraught, for the child looked near to death, being pale and malnourished. Yeshua smiled and reached into his bag. "The child has been infected with worms. Give him these herbs and he will begin to recover in three days." Yeshua then looked at the father, "Be not aggrieved, the child will be well, but while I know the customs in this area are Greek and not Jewish, I would suggest that this affliction came from the meat of the pig. Feed the child only bread and fruits, and give him a tea made of these herbs four times a day."

The man looked at the visitor strangely, "You are a doctor? You came here as a simple man, I feel I have dishonored you with such poor fare."

Yeshua laughed, "You honor me by allowing me to serve. If you must give an offering, offer a prayer to my father, the Lord in Paradise. Give thanks that he brought us to your door. Your child will be well. Peace upon your household, old man."

And with this, Yeshua departed the house and made his way back to Capernaum.

Mathew was greatly puzzled, "We came all this way to see a sick child? Why did the father not bring him to you at your house?"

Yeshua looked at him, "You understand nothing, even though your eyes see everything. Do you suppose the Lord tells me, *'go here for a child is sick'* or *'go there for a woman is depressed and needs council'*? The Lord guides my steps without words, and without reason I obey."

Thomas said nothing, as always, but he considered the words the Master had given him: *When you are transparent to the divine father, you are a vehicle of his love.* The child had dreamed of the Master before seeing him, before even knowing he existed, and he knew his voice. The apostle felt humbled yet again to witness the small miracles that surrounded this man.

The Magdala Boat mosaic showed a typical fishing boat of the era. It carried a sail and room for four oarsmen. They were made from cedar planks and were exceptionally strong. Thanks to the Madain Project for the image.

The Miracle of Sharing

Praise waiteth for thee, O God, in Sion: and unto thee shall the vow be performed. O thou that hearest prayer, unto thee shall all flesh come. Iniquities prevail against me: as for our transgressions, thou shalt purge them away.
Blessed is the man whom thou choosest, and causest to approach unto thee, that he may dwell in thy courts: we shall be satisfied with the goodness of thy house, even of thy holy temple.
Psalm 65

The seas of Capernaum were rough and choppy, and Peter put the boat into a small harbor to avoid the squall of anger nature had brought with her. "She is going to get worse before she gets better," he shouted above the winds as they heaved to the dock, strapping the boat into the calm water.

Yeshua had gone with them this day of harvest celebrations, leaving behind many throngs of people who had gathered to hear his words, looking for healing or some miracle. Where they had docked, an old woman who had lost her husband in those waters saw them, and though not knowing who it was, bade them rest in her courtyard till the storm passed. Simon, Mathew, Peter, and John were with their master that day as he gratefully accepted her offer. She brought out tea and bread for them, offered with warmth and happiness, for though she was poor, she was lonely and loved the rough company of the fisherman.

Peter asked, "You do not fear the gossip of your neighbors, old woman, bringing men into your house?"

She laughed, "Into my courtyard? Let them gossip. No man pursues me anymore, not that I am unhappy about this. Soon I will be with my husband in Paradise."

Mathew was curious, "You are so sure he awaits you there?"

"Oh, he had flares of anger, and would suffer trouble in his heart, but it was always for some injustice done another. I was happy enough to comfort him, and I never had any hint of his anger directed towards me. He was as good a man that ever lived and if he is not in Paradise, then no one is. You are Simon Peter, yes? You would have known him, Josephus, from Hippos."

Peter nodded, "As a boy. He has been gone some thirty years woman. I knew him but in passing, my father, as you would know, was not so friendly and not so careful in his distribution of anger."

She smiled, "It is good to see you, Peter, all of you. Be at rest here for as long as you must. There is water, with olive oil and bread. I have no beer, but suffice as you need." She went to go inside, for her world was made happy with the good deed, and seeing those strong men there brought joy to her heart, feeling she was closer to her man.

Yeshua stopped her with a question, "Old woman, I have a riddle for you. Would you like to hear?"

She turned, the fellow seemed familiar. "Ask away, though I doubt I will have an answer!" she laughed.

"There were two men, one had suffered terrible burns to his body. Bandaged and unable to care for himself he lay in bed, in pain and unable to move. His brother came to see him, dripping cold soup into his mouth to sustain him, feeling the awful suffering. Day after day he visited, but his good deed afflicted him. He slowly went mad with grief, sitting there, unable to even touch the burned hand of his brother. Tell me, of the two, who was the most ill?"

"Does it matter?" the old woman asked. "They both suffer."

"This is true, but when they pass away, as they must, how does the Angel of Death judge which one is worthy of Paradise?"

"To be free of the suffering is Paradise, no Angel can judge the worth of freedom," she answered.

Yeshua smiled, "I hear and listen to the wisdom of age!" Then he did a thing the disciples had never before seen, he stood and bowed to the old soul. As he did so, the wind ceased and calm came upon the waters.

As they got underway, Simon asked, "If she married a Greek, why doesn't she live at Hippos? The couple would have had a hard time of it here. Maybe she came back after he died?"

Peter shrugged, "My father was incredibly rude at the best of times, but he was blatantly rude to her husband. I had not even remembered his name until today, but I do recall how my father turned his cheek when the fellow was in the same port, and would not even trade at the merchants the man sold his fish to. But that was the way of it, the Greeks had their people, we had ours."

The political tension between the Hebrew and "Greek" side of the sea had decreased since Herod created his new city. The trade it brought for all on the lake made most of them rich enough to ignore their differences, and the influx of Gentiles into Tiberias and surrounding areas was so great that holding animosity to them was pointless.

The Sea of Galilee was now one large, cosmopolitan center of many tribes, both near and far. The money Herod Antipas had poured into that place brought artisans and craftsmen from all over, and more than a few stayed for the mild climate, inexpensive accommodations, and the generous nature of the King. All about farms had sprung up, and vineyards stretching up the slopes surrounding the lake were now common. The roads from Tiberias to get goods to ports on the Mediterranean were good, and the place was becoming a tourist destination for the more adventurous Romans.

Yeshua asked a question of them as they sailed back to Capernaum, "Why do people gather at the Synagogues and the Temple?"

The disciples looked at each other, Mathew suggested, "They wish to be better people, to become holy, and such places encourage this."

"So you say we can collect holiness, like going to the river with a bucket, gathering up water to take to your home?" Yeshua asked again.

Peter laughed, "When you put it like that ..."

Yeshua continued, "And what then do you do with your bucket of holy water? Dole it out to your children, splash it on the door to protect from evil spirits? Perhaps you just leave it there on the mantle above the fire, hoping it will make your house holy?"

James understood, "This is why we are on the sea, all those people back at the house, wanting a miracle, they sent us away with their constant clamouring."

Yeshua looked at the men, they were starting to grow wiser. "What if they found the Cup of Harvest, the bottomless, fathomless cup from which all bounty comes? Surely if you took that to the temple it would take in so many blessings, that when you carried it back to your village you will have enough to fill the hearts of all?"

They laugh at such an absurd notion, Peter knows it is about something, but what? Yeshua's riddles seemed to get more obtuse. "Are you saying there is no point to the Synagogues and the Temple?"

"What is the point of taking a thimble to the river of God? People seek to collect wisdom, love, holiness, so many things, but the depth of their heart is as a thimble. If they catch a drop they cherish it, clutch it to their hearts like a precious gift, whereupon it dies. I say to you, the weight of tradition sits happily in that cup of possession, but the living water must flow if it is to keep living. It cannot be held or owned.

"Our hearts must be like the Cup of Harvest, the bounty of nature herself pouring through us in a never ending font of kindness and generosity. Our love cannot be like a well that we draw from only as we need to sup on it, it must be a river, endless and giving to all who come to your bank. This is the nature of the Lord, it is the nature of our Soul, to love without question, to give without thought of reward, to share all we are, knowing that the light we spread will take root in the hearts of those who are ready, and will gather a harvest of love as those seeds ripen."

The shore near Bethsaida was approaching, where they would celebrate the feast of harvest. Yeshua saw many had come, and smiled.

ooo0000ooo

The boat came to the wharf for the day of harvest, an ancient rite of the Essene people shared by many in the old world. Peter's youngest surviving brothers, Andrew and Phillip, had gone to the Essene community there and brought the sacred Fish Loaves to the harbor for the ceremony. Why this had to be so, the master had explained before they landed, was that this bread was made from living grains, sprouted to their peak, and raised in a slow oven without the addition of yeast.

This special loaf was made to celebrate the end of harvest and the bountiful nature of the Lord. They all knew of the ceremonial loaves, cast into the shape of a large, round fish. Most of the men had eaten some in their youth as they scarpered around the various homes on the feasts days, looking for morsels. The Essene were always generous to the children with hungry bellies, and their bread was so tasty.

But to their dismay, the disciples saw that the people, having heard of this feast day, had turned up in droves from the places around Capernaum. "How are we to celebrate the feast now?" they asked.

Yeshua was undaunted, and stepped from the boat to greet the brothers of Peter. They had radiant smiles, whether for him or their beloved oldest brother, who could say? But they were happy and opened the basket they were carrying to show off the Essene bread they had brought down from Julius for this day. Peter came up, embraced them, but asked his Master, "What do we do now? There is not enough to go around all these people."

Yeshua smiled, saying nothing, but took the basket to the unhewn stone table set in place by the sea for this type of offering. The disciples and many others crowded round, wondering what the teacher would speak of that day, hungry for his words of wisdom. In a high, clear voice, he announced, "In the tradition of my people, all who come must partake in the celebration of summer, and the gift of life so freely offered by the Lord." He then offered up the loaves to the heavens, speaking some ancient words. He then broke the loaves and gave each of the disciples a section, including Peter's little brothers. They stood by the table with their half a loaf, breaking off a tiny bit to give to those who had come.

John, who had not been on the water but had come from the Capernaum house, had been followed by the crowd to this place. He shook his head, "Master, this will feed no one!"

Yeshua smiled, "Would it pain you so much to not eat for a day, John? This gift we offer to the Lord as the Lord offers his gifts to us, do you understand?"

And so the men do as instructed, breaking off the tiniest bit of loaf, to ensure there was something for everyone. And the people as they approach accept it, smiling as they see the truth, that though the prophet had little it was freely shared. As they passed by the makeshift altar, each gave a little of their own food as offering to the Lord of Summer, nodding to the Master their thanks.

Yeshua declared the feast of harvest and spoke the words of bounty. He praised the Lord who brought the seeds out of their slumber. He praised the sun and the wind and the waters from the Heavens. He praised the men of the harvest, and the bakers that made the bread.

"Lord of salvation, whose voice stills the angry sea as it does the angry heart, thank you for the rain which you share from the eternal river, which brings us the wheat and corn, which softens the hard ground and makes it ripe. This bread symbolizes your goodness, we gather around it to thank you. Because of you, the pastures are clothed with flocks, the valleys dressed in grain, and all sing for joy because of your presence."

And by the end of the celebration, a large amount of food was found on the table. Yeshua spoke, "You have come for words of wisdom, but I say to you, a greater truth has come from YOUR hearts this day. In seeking a higher path you took a grain offered by us and returned, by way of thanks, a multitude of offerings to the altar of the Lord. This is the miracle of sharing given us by the Lord, that a tiny seed of love planted in the heart of a good soul will grow into the Tree of Life.

"This is the truest harvest of the Lord. This sacred tree was never hidden, it's seed was placed into your heart, so that in the journey from Eden all you need do was look inside to find the Kingdom of the Lord and the gift of life he offers. But for this seed to grow, you cannot hide it in fear. You must water it with kindness, fertilize it with Love, and allow in the breath of Spirit to give it air and light.

"No tree grew in a dark room, no faith became strong in isolation. As you have come together to give thanks for the harvest on this day, so must you come to yourself every sunrise and sunset, to give thanks to the

Lord. Share with him your love, your loss, your fears, and he will give you the water of life."

And the people were happy, each feeling the warmth and love of each other as they all experienced the Miracle of Sharing.

With this the disciples went to the home of an Essene who lived there, to offer them some of the gifts given so freely, but to the astonishment of the disciples, they all still had half a fish loaf! "How can this be? "Master," Peter asked in amazement, "We gave out this loaf to all those people, yet we still have what you gave us!"

Yeshua smiled, "The real Miracle of this day was that selfish people shared, Peter. Our small gift brought the Lord into their heart, and made it possible for the people to come to a new place within, where love may now take root and grow, pushing out the small, mean-minded spirit of lack they inherited from their forefathers."

He did not labor the point, but smiled as the old couple took them in with warmth and good cheer, thanking him for blessing their house. And the disciples saw the love and brotherhood of the Essene people in their hearts, and understood perhaps a little of why their master had brought them here this day. But all they could talk about was how they still had half a loaf of bread to eat!

ooo0000ooo

Later that day, back at the house there were far fewer people hanging about, for many from that days ceremony had gone up to Julius for the evening celebrations. Peter asked Yeshua, "What was that about the Tree of Life not being hidden? I thought that was the whole thing about being cast out of Eden, that we lost it."

Yeshua looked at him, "There was a man who stood guard at the house of love. Each morning people would come with empty cups, wanting them to be filled, and he gave each a small portion, enough to survive that day. It did not matter what you came with, a bucket or a spoon, each got the same, small portion.

"This went on for a hundred years, the guard giving out his small portion from the house of love, until the people learned, just bring a spoon. Accept the tiny morsel you are given and expect no more."

Peter laughed, "You are talking about the priests at the Temple, aren't you?"

Yeshua ignored the comment. "Who gave the guard authority to stand there? The Lord? I say to you, walk through the door of the House of Love and take your fill. Soon enough you will learn you must share the bounty, for if you do not, you will burst and that love will be the death of you. That guard at the gate took his place there centuries ago because people could not share what they were freely given. The small offering he gives is enough for them to survive, but never enough to flourish. But this day I have shown you the way past that guard, I have shown you how you can be a part of the Tree of Life itself, for this IS the House of Love.

"If you are to grow in wisdom, faith, and love, you must give what wisdom, faith, and love you have in your heart to your fellows. But you must also be like the guard and know when a person has had their fill. Does this make you a judge? No, the Lord will whisper 'enough' when it is enough. Trust the Lord within, Peter, for he will guide you more surely than my stories when I am gone."

Yeshua retired to his contemplations of the evening, saying no more. Peter went to his brothers, who had joined them now, and hugged each one with all his heart. He felt the truth of the words flow through him and the love of his brothers flow back. But something also burned, the way he said 'when I am gone'.

Annas (left) & Caiaphas (right) painted by James Tissot. This work shows the rich clothes and scheming nature both were perceived as having in Victorian England.

The Sanhedrin

Caiaphas had arrived, as always, at the temple precinct before the first rays of dawn touched her gold and white walls. He met with the small enclave of his most trusted associates in the Gentile's courtyard, speaking in the open as if they had nothing to hide. In this way, he could meet and talk with his Roman spies without suspicion. You could even exchange money in this court without offending the Lord, which was convenient, for you could offer and accept bribes through your proxies and you didn't have to cart gold or silver about the city

The first rule, his father-in-law had always said, was never to appear cloistered. "Never cause the guests to sneeze!" was his joking reference to the Romans.

If you have to beat the dust from a rug, you don't do it in the house. Out here, in the open, people could come and air their differences. If judged as sufficient, their plea would be presented in the Hall of Stones, half in and half out of the sacred temple itself. In this way, the Sanhedrin could meet and deal with both Jews and non-Jews. Mostly these were territorial disputes or questions of inheritance, day-to-day matters which took the burden of law from the shoulders of the invaders.

But the real business was conducted in the small rooms behind the Hall of Hewn Stone. As the first rays of dawn lit the sky, his priests started hearing the matters of the day and organizing the people for their hearing. In the hubbub, the High Priest and entourage went into the Temple and away from any ears that might be in Roman pay.

They went to the Hall of Wood, to put on their vestments, freshly laundered and purified. Caiaphas opened with the great problem of the Roman governor. "Pilate is a monster, we all know he was sent to cause trouble, but with Sejanus backing him up, there is nothing we can do. I have contacted everyone I know in Rome, no one will lift a finger."

"He has defiled our most sacred space, our temple, with images of Tiberius," Joseph of Arimathea protested. He had spoken on behalf of the Essenes long and loud on the subject. "And he used GENTILES to hang them when no Jew would have dared. Surely there is someone in Rome who will stand up for the rights of religion?"

Caiaphas sighed, "Pilate is a pain, but he is not a fool. If he had nailed up anyone or anything other than our most beloved Emperor we would have a case, but Tiberius was good to the Jews. If we claim religious rights over the hanging of his image we reject the only friend we have in

Rome. But you are correct, I will enquire as to who might be traveling to Capri, and see if we can bring a plaint to him privately. Even then, who can say what he might do - we all know he lets Sejanus run free."

Privately, most in the room felt the same way about Joseph as they felt about the portraits. He didn't belong in the sacred precinct because Essenes did not observe the law with sacrifices, a thing which disturbed both the Pharisee and Sadducee blood. But in his consolidation of power, the High Priest had bent many scruples and cut deals with people he would have preferred to have left outside his door.

"I must also stress Enoch and the need for his inclusion into the Torah," Joseph had reiterated his claim so often it was annoying. "NOT including this prophet is as bad as allowing the inclusion of a Roman in our sacred house."

Bilibus spoke, "You have your opportunity to present your prophet during the normal liturgical cycle, Joseph. You know this, and have already done so many times."

"Enoch is not OUR prophet," Joseph protested. "He is the first prophet, one of our most important messengers, a chosen of the Lord, the great grandfather of Noah! The Essene scribes have written his story and merely want his presence spoken of in the synagogue."

Bilibus and all present had heard the arguments, many times. "And when the Sanhedrin agree with you, you can dance your victory in front of any one of his seven archangels. But to the business of the Romans and what to do about Pilate."

Joseph added nothing further, knowing how the Sadducee didn't believe in Angels at all. Even the Pharisee only had two, and to admit Enoch meant a complete readjustment of all their teaching. He knew why they refused, but it didn't alter the truth of the matter, that one of the most venerable of prophets was ignored.

It was Jonas, the patriarch of Azzah who spoke. "I was speaking with a retired soldier from Syria, an Assyrian who gained citizenship but who got tired of waiting for his land. He was essentially a sword for sale and I had need of his services. When I was paying him, he made a passing comment about how the Syrian Legate hates Pilate. It struck me then, if we can cause enough trouble he will be compelled to act and bring his troops down here. If so, it will go badly for Pilate."

"You are a sly old dog, Jonas!" Caiaphas was grinning from ear to ear. "I have a connection with the smugglers who could be used. They are being hard pushed by the Romans and their leader came to see me. He is a reasonable man, he hates Romans, and he wants to build a small army to spill their blood. It will cost quite a bit of money, but I feel it is well worth it."

Joseph laughed, "Ridiculous! You would invite the Legate and his army here? That is madness. Even if you killed every Roman in the city, inside weeks we would have ten times that number beating down every door in the city to find and kill the guilty. And as we are Jews, we are automatically guilty."

"My thoughts precisely," agreed Caiaphas, surprisingly. "We can't get rid of the Romans, but we may be able to rid ourselves of Pilate. Jonas has provided the answer, ENOUGH trouble so that the Syrian army is needed, that is all. This makes Pilate looks incompetent, so the Senate votes him out, despite the support of Sejanus. I will talk to my man and start organizing weapons and training. But it will cost gentlemen - How much can we afford to tip in?"

And so discussion on the raising of finances was brought about. Caiaphas had, of course, handed Jonas the information to pass it on. He was already in discussion with Barabas the Zealot, organizing him to make weapons and recruit men. Annas supported him in this, for they intended to make Pilate pay dearly for their suffering by chewing on his good name, a piece at a time. It would be death by a thousand cuts.

oooo000oooo

As head of the Pharisee, Nicodemus had no love for the Sadducee leader. He and his people sat off on a bench in the courtyard of the women, discussing this latest plan of Caiaphas. With him was the venerable Gamaliel and his protégé, Saul, along with Joseph the Essene lover. "You need to stop pushing the Enoch business, Joseph. It distracts from the real order of business and weakens our voice. I remind you that you are a Pharisee. You must be seen to no longer be supporting the desert people, even though you married one. Our real problem right now is Caiaphas and Annas cooking up this game to annoy Pilate. It can easily go off in our faces and WE will be the ones to suffer, not the Greek lovers."

Gamaliel sighed, "We cannot command a man not to follow his conscious, Nicodemus. If Joseph feels strongly about Enoch, his voice must echo his heart. He has a valid point, but so does the Sanhedrin. After all, what does a batch of astrological calculations have to do with the spiritual purpose of the Temple and the people of God? Enoch as read in the liturgical cycle is a flawed document. But aside from this, yes, we all know Caiaphas is up to his tricks, and yes it could backfire -

but Pilate must be blocked in some way. I do not support a war with the Romans, because we will lose. We must block Pilate but it is not our role to organize the shedding of blood, unless it is as a sacrifice to the Lord, according to the law."

Nicodemus laughed, "But in the meantime, our dear High Priest has his hands out for more money. I say let his Sadducee friends pay for his little plot. When it all blows up in his face, as it will, we can honestly hold our hands up and say it wasn't us!"

Joseph said nothing, just stared at the multi-colored marble tiles, cut into the points of the compass and demonstrating the finest work of any tradesmen throughout the Empire. He thought of how Herod brought in craftsmen from across the world, despite the protestation of this same Sanhedrin, but had to promise to train one thousand priests to do the work in the holiest of holies, where only priests were allowed. It was absurd how they objected to having their damn temple built, but equally absurd was how they ignored one of the founding fathers of the true faith. However, Joseph understood the game. "Caiaphas is supported by Annas. He will get the money for his rebellion."

Saul spoke. Despite his junior status, he was the chosen of the patriarch and in small enclaves with his people his voice carried weight. "We cannot support the shedding of blood. We cannot support an open rebellion. Caiaphas is wanting money to arm rebels, is he mad? Does he believe Pilate will see this as anything but what it is? No one likes the Romans here, we all know why Pilate does what he does, but this plan of the Sadducee is stupid. The Syrian Legate, if he comes, will butcher thousands of Jews, then plunder all the gold he can find, and in the end, there is no guarantee we will be rid of Pilate."

"What do you suggest?" Gamaliel asked as if he didn't already know.

"I say a better plan is to keep Pilate busy trying a hundred cases a month. As he stripped from us the power to execute false prophets, let us make that work for us. We have hundreds of Zealot Messiahs out there in the streets, the vast majority of which we have been ignoring for decades. All we have to do is enforce the letter of the law, try them here, and find them guilty - but now HE has to hear the matter, as it is a capital crime."

Nicodemus laughed. "Brilliant Saul! Two birds with one stone, I like it. More to the point, it falls to the Pharisee to enforce the law, so we can advise Caiaphas that we have a more trustworthy plan to make Pilate's life a misery. Killing off a Messiah in public always triggers a riot by his followers, and when he has had enough of this ongoing trouble we can start negotiating a better deal."

They parted ways to go about their daily business.

Walking back to his house, Gamaliel was quietly pleased. "Saul my boy, we have turned the sour note of sedition into the sweet wine of purity. These would-be prophets on every street corner are eroding the true faith, distracting the people with their wild prophecies. With Nicodemus now onside we can break up this rabble of fakes. I want you to organize not just rounding them up, I also need a team of scribes well versed in the law to take them to task out there in the streets. I want these Messiahs publicly humiliated before we try them.

"We also need to get facts by which to crucify them. The majority of their claims are facetious babble, but these claims have to be recorded and used in their trial. Set up a team of inquisitors, to quiz them, and collect eyewitness accounts of their assertions. Do not use professional priests, nor anyone connected to us, just scribes well versed in law who can write down what the pretenders claim and report this to the courts."

As they reached his doorway, Saul bowed to the Elder, who asked him, "How is your father? I meant to ask earlier, but we got a little busy."

"He is well, as is my mother. He is talking about a post in Turkey. He is tired of working for Pilate, so I will need to find accommodations if he goes."

Gamaliel sighed, "No, you should go with them. Organize my scribes for me, I can instruct them and sort out the testimony. Your parents will need your strong arms and your support. Plus, it is good for a young man to see the world, not stay cooped up with us old priests talking politics."

Whipping the Money Changers at the Temple

Clearing the Temple

Early in the morning he came again into the temple, and all the people came unto him; and he sat down, and taught them. And the scribes and the Pharisees bring a woman taken in adultery; and having set her in the midst, they say unto him, Teacher, this woman hath been taken in adultery, in the very act.

Now in the law Moses commanded us to stone such: what then sayest thou of her? And this they said, trying him, that they might have [whereof] to accuse him. But Jesus stooped down, and with his finger wrote on the ground. But when they continued asking him, he lifted up himself, and said unto them, He that is without sin among you, let him first cast a stone at her. And again he stooped down, and with his finger wrote on the ground.

And they, when they heard it, went out one by one, beginning from the eldest, [even] unto the last: and Jesus was left alone, and the woman, where she was, in the midst. And Jesus lifted up himself, and said unto her, Woman, where are they? did no man condemn thee? And she said, No man, Lord. And Jesus said, Neither do I condemn thee: go thy way; from henceforth sin no more. *John 8:3-10*

They came to the Temple in the fading light of the day, when all but the guards had gone home. Yeshua stood there in the Court of the Gentiles, his face showing disgust at the filth and excrement left by the careless ones who made a living off the faithful. And with the filth came rats and creatures of darkness, feasting on the cast-off scraps.

The air carried the scent of blood from the sacrifices, making the place more like a butcher shop than the house of the Lord. He said nothing, but his silence spoke loud. Peter could see the fury in his eyes. To himself, all that was about him, the tables, the cages, all this was just normal, the effect of the day-to-day Temple business. It was accepted only because it was kept in the external court while the holiest of holies remained pure.

Yeshua spoke of his distaste. "The Sadducee will not touch a corpse, saying it will defile them. They will not deal with anyone impure, yet in the courtyard of the Temple, the house they are charged with maintaining, all we find is defilement and greed. This here, this is the symbol of all that is wrong here in Judea."

Some disciple spoke up, "Surely the Romans are a greater defilement?"

Yeshua barely looked at him, "You will not find filth like this in the home of any Roman of note, but this is not the point. It is the hypocrisy of these priests, to pretend they are pure when they allow this sort of insult in the house of the Lord. They say to the people how they support the written law of the Torah, yet they allow the image of a Greek God to be dropped into their treasury as a Temple tax."

"They say the Temple is for the chosen," said Peter. "Maybe so, but I have made the journey many times for Passover, and it seems to me the rich ones tend to be the preferred Chosen!" he laughed. It was a standard joke about the two-faced nature of the Sadducee.

Simon noted, "We all know the money lenders are used by the Sadducee. As long as they keep it out of sight, most don't care."

Another laughed, "Their laws of purity mean nothing. It's a show they put on."

Yeshua said nothing. He turned and made his way from the Temple to the house of James. There, along with many relatives, he and his people would be made welcome in readiness for Passover.

ooo0000ooo

James smiled broadly, "Welcome to the house, brother, and all your friends as well. Please enter and be at ease. There is tea, refreshments, bread, and soup for all. I am glad you brought bedding because we have none spare with all these visitors. Blessed be the path you walk."

Yeshua hugged him, "And may the path be true for all. Has it truly been eleven years since we last met? You look older, but not necessarily wiser, brother," he jested.

James smiled, said in jest but true. "There is much complication to life here, Yeshua. I do not doubt I have aged. It is all plots and gossip, who did what to whom and when. It gains not one inch on the true path, yet we must deal with it. We protect the community and now we Essenes have a voice in the Sanhedrin, so in this way it is greatly improved since you left. Not to say we have achieved all we must, but the Essene are accepted for readings at the Temple now. But this is dull, and your life has been fascinating and extraordinary compared to ours. When you are rested we would love to hear a little of your travels. Good to see you back, Yeshua."

"Mary is here?"

"She is meant to be here, but you know that one. Out arguing with the Pharisee and Zealots. We have had to pull her out of the fire on more than one occasion, men do not like being bested in logic by a woman!" they both laugh.

"I would have thought she would have targeted the Pharisee?"

"Too easy, she says. There is so little logic in any of their beliefs that it is like beating up a child. Debating with them is mostly just prodding them to anger, then asking where the love of the Lord is."

Yeshua nodded, indicating for his people to relax and have some food and drink, explaining, "Bread and wine is always plentiful at Passover in this house. The whole of the Qumran supports us here. It is the unofficial Essene embassy, created by my father, and now run by my brother." He said little to respond to the talk of Mary, he felt she was walking into a pit of vipers, and that he would need a bronze snake to draw them out. It would wait for the present, tomorrow he would teach at the Temple and he felt in his bones he would be challenged.

"You are working with the Baptist, Yeshua?" James asked.

"I am, brother. He is a powerful force for good in the land. He has cast off the burden of sin for many thousands of souls, and he preaches a return to the values of the forefathers."

"This may be so, but he is also telling everyone you are the Messiah, and the people talk of miracles and with it the Messiah who will end the occupation?" James was curious what his brother had to say. It was dangerous to stand out like this.

"John says many things, and has many passionate beliefs, but he seems disappointed that I do not particularly care about the Romans." Yeshua smiled.

"He was at the Temple earlier, on the stones of Solomon, shouting like a madman that Herod has lost his way, and that the marriage to the wife of his brother is sacrilege. People came for baptism and were turned away by his followers. This is a very unwise course to follow."

Yeshua nodded, gravely. "It is indeed an unwise course, one I tried to dissuade him from. He seems possessed by this curse. It is why we came to Passover by different paths."

"This is sad news, I had hoped you could have spoken to him and got him to lower the tone. It will not be tolerated, to speak against the King like he is doing. In the country it raises but a murmur - here it calls up the very hounds of hell." James sighed.

"That is precisely what he wants. He creates clarity through confrontation. I have seen him batter down the resistance of many a man through his demands for truth. What is more, they do give in to the force in him, and they do repent. Perhaps this is his way to get a personal audience with Herod?"

James laughs, "I am fairly certain this is what will happen, though he will be wearing jewelry made of iron chains for the court he would talk in. But enough of the problems, let us celebrate your return and hear what wonders you have seen."

And the evening passed with many oohs, and ahhs, even from his disciples, for Yeshua spoke of the great building called the Pyramids, and the Sphinx, of the River Nile that made the Jordan look like a trickle. And the fabulous library at Alexandria, full of scrolls from all over the world. And the Doctors of Egypt who had many and marvelous cures for ailments, including certain types of blindness. Yeshua produced a curious fine dirt, "This is dried clay, and when a person has a cloudiness over the eyes, when mixed with a healing aloe, this draws out the affliction."

There seemed no end to the wonders he had seen and the things he had learned, and he spoke of these things and more until the early hours of the morning. When finally people made to their beds, Peter sat with him, gazing at the night sky, "Are the stars the same in India, Master?"

"They rise and fall at different times, but they are the same constellations in the same order. The Egyptians explain this as proof that we live on a vast ball that travels around the sun."

Peter shook his head, too many wonders had filled his thoughts and another puzzle was too much for his tired brain. "Your fascination with all things never fades, Yeshua, while I am but a dull and boring fisherman who struggles to learn a new knot when shown one. Our world being a ball, and having it run around the sun, this is one step too far for an old man."

Yeshua laughed, glad of the company. He had not wanted to say too much to his brother James earlier about the Baptist, but everyone had noted how driven John had become over Herod's actions. He was now obsessed and any public speaking he did was now almost exclusively on the subject of the King, and how wrong he was. "Let us send our love to the Baptist, Peter."

The fisherman grunted, "Another thing I am not particularly good at."

ooo0000ooo

Yeshua arrived at the Temple early, to speak his parables. The place still stank, but he found a spot near the courtyard of the Women, where a gentile could still attend. His reputation had grown, not just as a miracle worker and healer, but as a man who told fabulous stories. It was a raucous place with crowds already swelling in the courtyards, with both tourists and Jews side by side, celebrating this holy time.

As was his way, as a Rabbi he taught through his stories and asked questions of petitioners that allowed them to reveal their truth to themselves. He was in the middle of this when a covered woman was brought up to him by some Pharisee. They asked Yeshua what they must do with her.

"She is accused of adultery, Rabbi, and bearing false witness. Should she be stoned, in accordance with the Law of Moses?"

Though she was completely covered, Yeshua knew that attitude and who was being hidden from him. He acted surprised, "You say adultery as if you were present and watching?"

One of the men coughed, "Well, not specifically. She speaks flagrantly in the streets with men, and they follow her about. We have many witnesses. And she speaks of beliefs not in accord with the Law of Moses. It disobeys the law and she must be punished, yes?"

A cold fury arose in the eyes of Yeshua. Such false men as these, seeking to test the word of the Lord. He started winding the cords of rope into a whip, attaching it to a short pole, then snapping it in the air to test it, and to scare the men. When he was ready, he spoke, "Only those who are pure can administer judgment, is this correct, according to Law?"

Another man, feeling uncomfortable at seeing the whip being flexed, stammered, "Ah, this is the law."

"So, first you lied to me, saying this woman was an adulteress, and now you admit you made this claim without evidence? Where are the guilty men, the ones she supposedly slept with? You know the law, all parties are subject to the punishment, so where are they? I see them not. And yet NOW you ask for stoning, which means your real claim is that she is proselytizing a false faith. Is THIS the judgment you are seeking to have determined? Is THIS why you are asking for an innocent soul to be stoned?" There was a distinct sense of threat in his words, and the Pharisee trembled. It was not what they had expected.

Seeing their silence as proof, Yeshua offered the answer. "Well, I have a solution for you. If any amongst you here has not sinned, then you must now pick up the first stone." He made the statement a question, with the looming threat of the whip behind it. He stared with fury at these liars before him, and they understood exactly what he meant to do.

The leader amongst the Pharisee looked at the others and indicated for them to leave. But he said, "You are Yeshua, son of Joseph, the carpenter who made much of the furniture for this Temple."

Yeshua laughed a brittle laugh, "You do not know my father, as you do not know me. You come here, asking me to judge the flesh, but I judge no man or woman. The Lord my Father is the Judge, and that he speaks through me is proof of his light. All who follow me walk in this light of truth, but you who come here, you know nothing of the father, nothing of the light. I say to you, those who live in the whispers of darkness, cannot know me. You cannot know where I come from or where I go, for you have not the light to see, nor the wisdom to understand."

The old man could say nothing, for he saw their trap was revealed, and he understood the truth, that they had truly lied in the house of the Lord. He left, berated and chastised. Nicodemus will not be pleased, they were only meant to stop these would-be Messiahs from preaching in the Temple. He left like a beaten dog, leaving the woman standing there. Yeshua indicated for his disciples to remove the covering. There stood Mary, not particularly happy as being treated like cattle, herded about. "Where are your accusers?" he asked her.

Mary then smiled, saying, "There are none, unless it is you?"

Yeshua shook his head, "I understand the fury that drives you, woman, for it is in me now." With this, he calls over Peter and the other disciples telling them to quietly go about as if interested in buying cattle for sacrifice, "Make them parade the animal to ensure it is worthy, then we will show this nest of vipers the reward for their avarice and greed. When I am done, I will meet you on the Mount of Olives."

And they went off as requested, acting as buyers of the cattle. Mary smiled, "Good to see you. Not quite the milksop youth living in the clouds that you once were, Yeshua."

He sighed, "As I have hardened, woman, so must you soften." With these words, he reached out, and taking her hand, placed one of Herod's coins into her palm.

The Magdalene looked at the gift of love, not quite knowing what to say. He had been away so long that she was certain he would not return. Yet, here he is, seeking to honor the pledge they made as children. "I will not marry for duty or custom," she said plainly, making her heart known.

Yeshua spoke with equal truth, "You wouldn't marry to save your own skin, woman. You know you are loved, you know how we have spoken in the inner worlds, and you know why I have returned. Do you accept the coin?"

A tear escaped her eye. Mary bowed her head as she had never done before. He not only loved her, he had saved her, and he accepted her. "I accept this gift of love, Raboni."

"Then go back to my brother's house, but first stay and watch, for I have business here that will put happiness back into your heart," and with this, Yeshua flexed the cord had woven, and went into the fray of money changers and temple offerings, and shouted as he whipped them, "This is a house of prayer, and you have turned it into a den of thieves. Get out!" And he whipped the cattle, now free of their binding, and they ran headlong into the tables spilling the merchandise and all the goods that were being hawked. The beasts ran towards any exit they could find, and in their dumb panic, ran over many of the sacrifices, freeing cages, and setting doves, chickens, and pigeons free.

People scattered in all directions, squawking and fretting like chickens out of their coups. And the disciples were wroth to laugh, for fear of what would happen to them, and instead made ready themselves to retreat to that place of the graveyards and olives that lay past the East Gate.

Some of the merchants gathered themselves, and picked up stones and whatever they could arm themselves with, and went looking for the madman who attacked, but they could find him not. Even as Yeshua rampaged through the last of their tables, causing their business to scatter, with people grabbing what coins they could as they fell, even then they could not find him in the madness.

Mary laughed, watching the scene unfold, nodding happily to herself. Finally, a man she could truly respect. For love was not enough, love came and went like the breeze, but with respect the seeds of love were bedded in deep soil that every season would spring afresh with fruits and flowers.

ooo0000ooo

And watching all this was Nicodemus and Caiaphas, one angry, one laughing. "That will make a mess of the finances for this Passover for you, Joseph ben Caiaphas."

He snapped back, "I am the high priest when I wear these robes!"

"Indeed, Kohan Gadol. I made the mistake of being too intimate, and thinking you might share in the humor of this day." Nicodemus was loving this. His man had already come and given a brief essay on what had just transpired. This was the first Messiah he might come to like!

Caiaphas stormed off, ordering the staff to clean up this mess. However, the temple offerings were all but gone, as were most of the money changers, because they were chasing people who were walking away with their coin.

Joseph of Arimathea came up, "Satisfied now?" It had been a dangerous line to walk, setting up Yeshua like that, but he had warned them that Joseph's son was unlike any that had come before.

"He speaks of the Father as if he were the son of the Lord himself. That seems somewhat arrogant. However, he walked around that little trap better than I expected, and I have to say, he isn't wrong about the filth out there in the courtyard." Nicodemus responded.

"In the Essene faith they are all the children of the Lord, Nicodemus. It is second nature for them to think of the Lord as their heavenly father. They also believe in and practice being one with the Lord. Their High Priest will speak with his voice, on occasions, they believe."

"Most of the Essenes I have met were somewhat more subdued." he snorted.

Joseph laughed, "You met his father and his cousin, were they subdued?"

"Fair point, Joseph. But no, I am not yet satisfied. Even so, I have heard of the miracles and have now just seen one. I know he does not preach against the Romans like his fool cousin, but I am not convinced. Can you organize a meeting so I might speak with him directly?"

Joseph sighed, "Of course, as you will. I shall endeavor to assist as I can. Are you going to seek judgment against our boy for what transpired today?"

"Not today, but if he keeps turning up it will be another story. I have to admit, all this was quite amusing. People will be talking about it all over the holy city by the evening, but Caiaphas will take it personally. I imagine he is even now heading over to talk with Pilate while he is in town, to complain."

"Perhaps we should have a representative there as well?"

"True, we must make sure Pilate hears the whole story. I will go."

ooo0000ooo

Pilate found huge amusement at the ranting of the high priest demanding action against rebels who disrupt the sacred holiday of Passover. "He trashed the whole place!" Caiaphas exclaimed, incensed at the ruination of the Temple celebrations.

"A terrible shame," Pilate said with a straight face, but he could not hide the merriment in his eyes.

"You hate us, don't you? You are here to make my life a misery!" Caiaphas sniped.

"Well," Pilate nestled his hands together in his lap, a sign of infinite patience, "I hate no man, not even the High Priest of the Temple when he comes and moans about things that are entirely HIS business. However, you have to admit, this Yeshua fellow made quite the point. We all know the money changers are money lenders, handing out loans at exorbitant interest, which is technically against the Law of Moses, or is that not correct?"

At this point, a slightly flustered Nicodemus was granted admittance to the anteroom where the two were talking. "Good day to you, Governor."

"You here to complain as well, Nicodemus?" Pilate's voice was slightly bored.

"Not at all, your eminence. I am here merely as the representative of the Pharisee in what is a religious matter that is ideally dealt with according to the law. We all want peace in the streets, and I am concerned the righteous anger of my brother might jeopardize this."

"One of your people ran amok in the Temple grounds, whipping approved agents, scattering the cattle used for sacrifice, causing a lot of damage and costing a lot of money. Caiaphas here wants him dead, what do you want?"

"My Lord Pilate, I want nothing but the peace of Jerusalem and to uphold her laws. And on THAT point, our rabble-rouser was technically upholding Hebraic law. He is a preacher of some small renown, a friend of John the Baptist, and he is correct - the image on the Temple coins is in truth against the law, so unless Caiaphas here chooses to use Herod's coins, which have no face upon them, he is technically in breach of the covenant."

"Which reminds me, did you like those lovely images of Tiberias I gave you?" Pilate smiled.

Caiaphas flinched, he was not used to getting wound up like this in public. Nicodemus merely smiled, "He is a friend to our people, my Lord. How could we not welcome a friend into our midst - If ONLY he would convert to our faith!"

Pilate laughed out loud. "At least you two are entertaining. The Temple guards report that the man appeared to take nothing, just shouted at the money changers, calling them curs, and whipping them out the door. One man, one whip, against all of them and they just ran? I should charge your money changers with cowardice."

"It is our fault, your eminence," explained Nicodemus. "As you know, our task is to round up the false prophets, try them, and if found guilty, send them over to you, so you can set them free. But this one cleverly escaped our trap. I believe we may have upset him. But to ameliorate the situation and ensure it never happens again, I am presently organizing to meet with this Yeshua, the son of one of our best temple carpenters."

Pilate smiled, "There you have it, Caiaphas, one of your own is taking care of the situation. You know, like YOU should have done? So, was there anything else?"

Caiaphas asked, "Why are there Roman guards overlooking the Temple if they will do nothing to protect the people?"

Pilate shrugged, "You are mistaken. Our soldiers protect the interests of Rome. I cannot see our interests have been interfered with and it seems to me that you and yours have the matter well in hand. And on that point, given that your money changers are money lenders, a thing directly opposing the tenants of your faith, maybe they deserved a good whipping? Let me know if any were missed, and I can arrange it."

The High Priest bowed, and moved backward, out of the Governor's orbit. He was on his way back to the Temple before his scowl became self-evident. He carped at some lieutenant that accompanied him, and they stormed back to the mess the carpenter left.

"Nicodemus?" Pilate wondered why the other was still here.

"Your most gracious Proconsul (A term used to remind Pilate he served on a year-to-year tenure) while I admire and respect the order you have brought to this city, the inspections of houses without warning is unsettling to the people. It puts them on edge, never knowing if they are going to be accused of something. If you feel there is some conspiracy, surely you know my people enough by now to understand we accept your tenure and offer no ill will towards Rome. Indeed, we pray for the well-being of the Emperor every day. Perhaps if you suspect a Pharisee is involved in some plot, then you might send an arbiter to my house and I can make quiet inquiries?"

"The sewers are running red from weapons manufacture and you want me to play nice? Of course, if you happen to know who is involved, there might be room for discussion?" Pilate leans forward.

Nicodemus comes up and whispers, "It is a Zealot called Barabas. He does not just want to rid the city of Romans, but of Sadducee and Pharisee as well. He is mad but well financed."

"How do I recognize such a one or his followers?" A name is something, but not enough.

"They all carry small, sickle-shaped knives of eight inches - sufficient to penetrate the body and strike an organ, ensuring death. I myself cannot go about the city without bodyguards now, they are truly insane."

Pilate looked at the man for some time, this was useful information. "Choose a representative and I will give him free access here in Rome and at my main residence. If there is anything regarding your people that is significant, he can be your eyes and ears." Pilate gave what was a fairly large concession to the Pharisee, a clue that he understood who was really behind the plot.

"Simon Joseph of Arimathea, a tin merchant who has much to do with the Romans here and in Briton. He is trusted by us, and as his well-being is based on your well-being, you can trust him."

Pilate mocked the Pharisee then, saying the words of this new Messiah, proving he had ears everywhere, "Go and sin no more!"

Nicodemus smiled tightly and departed, going to the appointed place Joseph had arranged where he would meet with the carpenter's son.

ooo0000ooo

They met beside the graveyard at the Mount of Olives. Nicodemus smiled to himself, *fair call* he thought. The Rabbi is addressing the power imbalance, for as a member of the Sanhedrin, his own person could not enter that graveyard, while the humble preacher could walk everywhere freely.

Yeshua stood there calmly, not affected by the situation, a thing Nicodemus also admired. He had to know why Joseph supported this fellow so wholeheartedly. He says he knew this one was special when, at the age of becoming, he addressed the priests of the Temple, and argued their claims to dust. A mere child defeating the minds of his betters.

He had to admit, how he got the Magdalene out from the shadows of the trap set for him was impressive. Yet the man speaks of the Lord as HIS father, as if he is the chosen one incarnate: The one who will set the world to rights and bring in the golden age of peace. This the Pharisee found impossible to accept. But better the devil you know.

"Thank you for seeing me. As is obvious, I come without a guard, on terms of peace."

"My Uncle tells me you can be trusted. What is it you want?" Yeshua was to the point.

"My son, it is clear that you are what you say, a man of God. Many attest to the miracles that surround you. It is also clear that you do not argue against the Romans, or seek to usurp their position. I do not dispute any of this, nor do I curse you for what you have done in the Temple. In many ways, I agree with you, what is there is not according to the Law."

"Miracles, you say? I am the son of my father, Pharisee. He is with me, and in me. It is only from him that miracles and blessings flow, not I. What is it you want?" Yeshua knew a snake when he saw one, but this one worked with his Uncle and had helped the Essene.

"John called you the Messiah, many believe him. I want to know how it is that any man could make this claim and expect it to be believed? The Messiah will bring an end to pain and suffering, and the world will come to know peace. This doesn't seem to marry to a fellow with a whip driving the money changers out of the Temple grounds."

"Your tongue is split, Nicodemus. You speak of Law, yet you cannot even speak the language in which it is written. My people in the Qumran DO speak the ancient words, they DO read the texts as they were intended, and they translate this to the common tongue. Yet you refuse to admit they have validity." Yeshua stated what was obvious, that the Pharisee had lost much of the knowledge of what was written, and decided law on their understanding of it through translations.

"Believe me, I have been told this many times, Yeshua. Your uncle makes sure of that. But you can hardly call me a snake for standing up for my people?" Nicodemus had learned the most important thing in negotiation was to never take personal offense.

"If I had called you a snake, I would be calling you a fallen Angel, one who had known the father yet walked away. But you know not the Father."

Was that a backhanded compliment? Seemed like a subtle insult. "Then tell me, how can I know the Father?"

"Only that a man be born of water and of Spirit can they come to the foot of the Lord. Once born into the light you will hear the voice of God, often as the thin, biting sound of the wind, or as the keen, high note of a flute, and it will guide you. You do not know from where it comes, or where it goes, but only those born of Spirit can hear it. Trapped here in the snares of this world, you cannot reach this place, and you cannot know the guidance of the Lord."

"But how can a man be born of a woman and born of spirit? How could I be born twice? I do not understand."

"You are a teacher of Israel, and you do not understand even this, the most basic of truths? You call a convert to Judaism a newborn, so how can you ask this?" Yeshua snorted, the man was feigning ignorance as a ploy. "Enough of games. You must enter into God for God to enter your heart. Just as a child must enter this physical world to be born of the physical, so must Soul enter the spiritual worlds to be born of the Lord. Embedded in your heart is the spark of the Lord, but you must fan it to a fire, and that fire must consume all you believe yourself to be. You must burn your past to ashes before you will be released in heaven."

Nicodemus rested against a tree, this one was not easily caught up in rhetoric. But in what he said he was touting the basic precepts of the Essene faith, which he already knew. "The real question I am here to ask you is if you are going to be beating the Money Lenders out of the Temple grounds on a regular basis, because the Romans will be forced to act if you do."

"I do only as the father wills."

"Yeshua, let me be blunt. How can you be so certain what the father wills? Many men claim they are being spoken to by angels of the Lord, many go mad, many are lost in their dreams. I truly wish to know how it can be that you carry such certainty. And I am not being clever, Yeshua. I saw how you became invisible to your pursuers, I watched it happen, so I can believe you are in some sort of connection with the Lord. What I cannot understand is how you can KNOW this, for many men know many things, but precious few are correct in what they presume."

"Can you tell me how a bird knows how to sing? It does what it does. But I will ask you a question and test your wisdom. There is an ancient riddle, a butterfly is in the sky and it looks down on a caterpillar. It seems so familiar, and it remembers something but it is not sure, so it alights beside the creature and asks, *'How can you move all those legs at the same time and not fall over?'* The caterpillar is confused, and looking back, falls over." Yeshua just looks at the Pharisee.

Nicodemus is a man born of study, of long hours contemplating and understanding every nuance of the writings of his people. It was true, he did not read ancient Hebraic and that he relied on translations. Was this man saying the translations were the butterfly that emerged from the cocoon of the past and to NOT look back? Or was he saying HE was a butterfly, and Nicodemus was a caterpillar, struggling to understand? "I truly wish to understand, Yeshua. But I don't."

"You are like a caterpillar looking at a butterfly and asking how it can fly into the heavens above."

Ah, the carpenter's son IS saying he is better than the Pharisee. "I am trying to be your friend, Yeshua. Caiaphas wants you dead, I convinced Pilate that this was not necessary and that I would talk with you. So I ask: Do you think that your father's will is done? Now the point is well made, will you leave the Temple in peace?"

"Everyone who does evil hates the light, and will not come into the light for fear that their deeds will be exposed. But whoever lives by the truth comes into the light, so that it may be seen plainly that what they have done has been done in the sight of God. I am a light, Pharisee. Wherever I walk this light casts knives into the darkness, but I throw no weapons, I cast no aspersions. The Lord acts through me as he will, and the Son of the Lord will not disobey the father or do anything to stop the rightful wrath or path of the Lord."

Nicodemus got the message. Now it was time for HIS message, "Well, son of Joseph the carpenter, you have made your view clear. I believe I have made the view from my side of things clear. I may be a mere caterpillar in your eyes, but I take it as a compliment that I might achieve the status of your butterfly at some point. The reality here is that the Sadducee hate you, we do not. I guess you are saying that it is up to your father, I suppose, as to what happens next?"

Yeshua nodded, it was as best as he might expect from one such as he. "The savior of our faith could have easily been Judas Maccabee, or Herod rebuilding the Temple, but I tell you, I do not come to save you from yourself. I come as light to show the light within you, for only through this light of revelation can a man become as the Father and act with his will."

They parted ways, Nicodemus knowing that there was more to come from this one. What he had just said directly opposed the priests, and because of this, they would fight him tooth and nail. But the words of this Yeshua echoed the thoughts of his people to some degree. The question was, in what direction would this river flow? He felt in his bones that this Rabbi had the power to turn the tide of affairs away from the Sadducee, but how high would the flood rise?

And whose side was he on?

Judas Maccabeus, Jewish guerrilla leader who defended his country from invasion by the Seleucid king Antiochus IV Epiphanes, preventing the imposition of Hellenism upon Judaea, and preserving the Jewish religion. The way he succeeded was by creating a treaty with Rome. Image by Gustave Doré.

Part Two

The First Years of the Ministry

Beatitudes

Blessed are the poor who are rich in spirit: for theirs is the kingdom of heaven.

Blessed are those who lack arrogance: for they shall possess the land.

Blessed are they that mourn in earnest loss: for they shall be comforted.

Blessed are they that hunger and thirst after justice: for they shall have their fill.

Blessed are the merciful: for they shall obtain mercy.

Blessed are the pure of heart: for they shall see God.

Blessed are the peacemakers: for they shall be called children of God.

Blessed are they that suffer persecution for justice' sake: for theirs is the kingdom of heaven.

Blessed are you when they shall revile you, and persecute you, and speak all that is evil against you, untruly, for my sake: Be glad and rejoice, for your reward is very great in heaven.

Capernaum

The house at Capernaum was large and gracious. Since the arrest of the Baptist, most of the followers and disciples had come to the North of the Sea of Galilee, to the house of Yeshua at Capernaum. They worried that the King saw them as troublemakers now. Yeshua sighed, they had little need to fear, everyone knew Herod liked the Baptist for he disrupted the priests and broke up their ways.

Herod had not even brought down the man's house on the land he himself had given him. It was a telling sign, but at the same time he also knew, John would not bend. The King had married the wife of his brother, divorcing his own, and the unrelenting fury the Baptist felt when this was made known was the reason for his imprisonment.

Political pronouncements proved time and again to be the death of prophets. All John had to do was the work of the Lord, but he felt that if corruption existed so blatantly at the top, it was a river that could only flow down to the bottom. He envisaged a world where men carelessly threw away old, faithful wives for younger prettier ones - and such a world was a harvest for the devil. He stopped baptizing, stopped everything, and started preaching openly against Herod and his ways.

While all good men agreed with him, few would say so openly, lest soldiers turn up on their door and the wrath of the king would fall upon them. It was foolishness, but Yeshua knew what had driven the prophet mad, what had driven the boy out into the wilderness. The casting off of the old wife for a new one was the cause of all his pain. Little could be done now, other than pick up the pieces and carry on with the work.

By now, many of John's close disciples had been taught the ways of the Lord in Baptism. They had caught the holy fire and many came to experience the blessing of the divine wisdom as they practiced the cleansing of sin. Only now, Yeshua was in charge, not a thing he particularly wanted. He was sitting at the dock gazing at the sea when his friend Peter sailed up, still paying his tithe, no doubt.

"Yeshua," he called, "Good to see you. How goes the brotherhood?"

"With sadness, Peter, but they continue. I fear John's obstinacy, we all do, but we carry on in the trust of the Lord."

Peter starts unloading fish for the people of John, laughing, "Ha, I am not so worried. Herod likes him. Eventually, he will let him go, when all the drama has settled down and people get used to Herodias. You can't blame him for wanting such a pretty thing and at least this one is Jewish."

"You are not concerned about him divorcing his former wife, and breaking with Jewish law and tradition?" Yeshua is curious, and he finds the voice of the common man far more enlightening than the priests.

"I would like nothing better than to unload my burden called a wife, Yeshua. I don't wish to offend, but she is an ungrateful harpy who, if she accidentally drowned, would not cause me a moment of distress. Why do you think I spend so long out on this sea? Why do you think I spend my time here, with you and all the other followers of John? This is joy for me; friends, company, and good conversation. My house is cold and desolate, so no, I do not curse him or call him names. I consider him lucky! Herod is rich, he doesn't need to play by the rules. I wish his example would be followed, and men like myself could settle their debt of marriage and move on to a happier place." Peter was gruffer than usual.

Yeshua guessed he must have had a terrible argument before setting out from home. The law was unforgiving in Judea, though divorce was technically permitted, it was greatly frowned upon. A man could place a GET on the shoulders of his wife, and the parting could then proceed according to law, but it was generally seen that the man had failed and was unworthy. Plus he had to return the dowry. What the King had done was something else, Herod had not just married the wife of his brother, he was flaunting his careless disregard of Hebraic tradition, daring the High Priest to say something. Caiaphas and the Sanhedrin would have been forced to denounce the union, but instead, John stepped up and took all the limelight of protest away from the priests. It ruined what was most likely been a clever plan for Herod to rid himself of the High Priest.

In many ways, Yeshua understood both Herod and Pilate. He wanted the power of the priests broken as much as they did, but John would not listen and insisted on a crusade for the sanctity of marriage. The people were like Peter, so often stuck in a loveless union, unable to free their hearts and unburden their woes to their bitter, judgemental spouses. What is the point of marriage if all it engenders is hatred? If a man places a GET onto his wife, he must settle their dowry in her favor, and few men can afford such a luxury - so they are trapped.

Yet opposing this was John's view. He believes if you allowed the devil to roam free in a man's heart, if you allow lascivious behavior and careless regard for the sanctity of vows undertaken, then all of society will degenerate. This was also true.

Joining the Peshar with the Raz, the spiritual understanding and the facts of scripture, this was the quest of the scribes on the Qumran. It was why he told stories and gave no judgements. Men confronted by facts degenerated into opinion and argument but when these same facts were written into a story, they did not lock horns with ethics, with right and wrong. The listeners suspended their doubt with fascination, and in that small opening, the soft, gentle steps of the Lord could enter their heart, and bring the Peshar, the understanding.

"There was a house, a large, beautiful home by a lake, but the people who owned it had left. A man and his sister, wandering vagrants, came across the empty home with the doors open and wood for the fire. They could see no purpose in passing by this gift of the Lord, so they stepped in, bathed in the bath, combed their hair with the combs they found, and washed their clothes - But it was not done to walk around naked, so of course, they put on the clothes they found in the cupboards there.

"They stayed a goodly length of time, getting fish from the water, taking herbs and vegetables from the garden, while generally tending to the house where things had become overgrown, and cleaning where the dust had fallen. They planted more vegetables, trimmed and watered the trees, treating the house as if it were their own. And then, one day they moved on, continuing their travels, leaving the home much as they had found it." Yeshua looked at Peter with a question.

"Another riddle, Yeshua? What can I say, you pose no question."

"Do I not? Surely the brother and sister must be caught and punished, living in another's house, eating their food, yes?"

"If they were caught there, yes, but they did no harm. And who could charge them, anyway? The owners were not there." Peter found this parable a bit odd.

"Well, the people come home, and at first, nothing is amiss. Then the wife notices the logs for the fire, they are in a slightly different order than when they left. The husband notices the gardens are well kept, and they should be overgrown. The daughter notices the floors have no dust on them. The son sees that the boat has had some repairs. They all join at supper that evening, telling their stories. Finally, the husband realizes someone had been living there when they were gone!

"He is outraged, and goes to the local magistrate the following day, and demands he find the interlopers and charge them." Yeshua smiles at Peter, "And what do you think the Magistrate did?"

"Well, he would be forced to act, to find the brother and sister and charge them for trespass."

"Of course, but first he must ask who it was, the trespassers must be identified. However, the man who brings the plaint says he has no idea. So what does the Magistrate do now?"

"He asks about the village, others would have seen the pair, and can identify them."

Yeshua laughs, "This is very true, and he does, but all the people of the village say they presumed the brother and sister were friends of the owners. They did not know who it was, did not speak with them, and had no names to give. So now what does the Magistrate do?"

Peter scratches his head. He has no idea where this is going, nor can he think of what the fellow could do next. "I have no idea, seems that the trespassers have gotten away with it."

Yeshua finds this so funny, he is laughing out loud. "Well then, many years pass, and the brother and sister get ill and die. They go in front of the Lord, who asks if they have sin to confess. They do not, they see themselves as blameless, even though all their lives they found empty homes and lived there for a time. Here is the question, Peter - What shall the Lord do?"

Peter is truly puzzled. "This is an excellent riddle, Yeshua. He can hardly punish souls who in their hearts are blameless of sin, yet they have broken the law. I do not know what the Lord would decide, can you tell me?"

"First, can you tell me what has been taken from the owners of the house?"

Peter shrugs, "Well, nothing."

"Can you tell me what the brother and sister have done wrong if nothing has been taken?"

Again, Peter is completely puzzled, "Nothing at all, I guess."

"Well, this is not entirely true, for what the brother and sister have taken is time. They have taken time for themselves to enjoy their life, but there is no law against this, is there? The Lord cannot judge you for taking the time to enjoy your life, can he?"

Peter gives up, "No I don't suppose anyone lost anything, and really, everyone gained. The people came back to a house that needed no repair, so really the interlopers improved their lot. The brother and sister, they had a good life and did no harm. It is all good."

"Despite the letter of the law, it is all good - this is true," laughed Yeshua. "But what of the Magistrate? As chance will have it, he died at the same moment that the brother and sister did, and he was there hearing their story. Finally, he found his criminals! What did HE do?"

"It was the Lord's court, he has no power or authority there to do anything!" Peter exclaimed.

"Exactly true, Peter. More than speaking truth, you speak wisdom!"

The fisherman looked askance at the new prophet, the Messiah, John had told him. He was sure there was some deeper meaning to all of this, but it completely escaped him. Instead, he turned to the question in his own heart. "The Baptist was furious that you didn't denounce Herod as he had done - is this what this story is about?"

"Peter, imagine a woman has a donkey she does not love, but she found a horse she did, so she left the donkey and went riding on the horse. Would anyone decry this as evil?

"Well no, but she was not married to the donkey," he got the message, but still, there were things that were right, and things that were wrong.

"So, we have discovered that if a house is empty, and a person moves in, leaving it in the same or better order when they move out, no crime against the Lord is committed. We have decided that a woman is free to ride a donkey or a horse, as long as she is not married to it. But what if the marriage was like an empty house, someone had once lived there but had moved out? It was an empty place, useless and sad. But people came by who could use it, and both they and the house found peace and harmony. Is this wrong?"

"Well, yes it is!" Peter was defiant in his defense of the law.

"It may be to man, but is it to the Lord?"

The fisherman stood there, open-jawed. The obvious struck him with the force of lightning smashing a mast. "The Lord does not care for the Laws of Man." he was staggered by this realization, utterly staggered. He had never even considered such a notion before.

"There are but two eternal laws, Peter. *Love God,* and *love thy neighbor as thyself.* If a man, a family, or a nation, follow these two laws, then all other laws can be forgotten. There will be no trespass because a man who loves his neighbor would not seek to harm him. There would be no adultery because a man would not wish his brother to suffer while he took his wife. There would be no theft, no hatred driving a man to murder. There would be no magistrates, no courts, for people would commit no wrong." Yeshua looked to the fisherman, seeing if he could grasp the blunt truth.

"It sounds wonderful, but it is a pipe dream. I respect others, but I hate my wife because she makes my life a misery. I cannot love her because I detest her, I am sorry to say."

"And what if you lived next door? What if your wife had her house, her garden, her life, and you had only a nodding acquaintance with her - would you still hate her then?"

"Well, no. I suppose that would be different. I would be quite happy to leave her alone, and she would no doubt be much happier not having me about."

"By your own words, Peter, you have spoken the golden-hearted truth of love. By your own words, Peter, you have given yourself permission to follow the path of love. Can you not see what you have said?"

Another bolt of lightning struck the fisherman, opening his heart to the truth, "I don't have to be there. I can just move in here, where I love my life, and where I am loved. How could I have been so blind as to not see this?"

Yeshua nodded quietly. "Peter, soon this house will be empty of John's followers. He is asking them to choose between his way and mine. He believes I have done wrong, but he stands there like a magistrate before the Lord. I have no desire to overthrow the Romans, my only interest is in filling the empty house of the Lord with truth, love, and the joyous laughter of children who were once dour, sour, men.

"Before us, there is a house called Judea where the rulers have become empty of kindness. There used to be wise men sitting in the Temple, now there are craven, greedy creatures who only desire power. There used to be a wise King, but now there is one who plays the fool in order to anger the priests. There used to be a wise governor, but now there is a puppet controlled by strings from Rome. We must give the message of love, of freedom, of truth to the people. We must awaken in their hearts the remembrance of the Lord. I believe in my heart that you have been called to this, will you hear this call?"

Tears of release are in the fisherman's eyes. He has been released from the chains that imprisoned him. He can walk free, or he can return to the misery of his wife. "John said you were the Messiah, now he says you are not. I loved John with all my heart, (Peter shook his head with the distress) but it is you that I will follow. I have seen the miracles that chase after you like a stray dog looking for love. I have heard the wisdom of your teaching. But more than all of this, from your words, your love, I have felt the liberation in my heart, the giving up of hatred."

Yeshua embraced him, affirming his decision. "Tonight we celebrate. Come to the house of the Lord, it is empty and in need of care."

ooo0000ooo

Herod Antipas had sent his trusted advisor down to counsel the mad Baptist. Did he not understand how much Herod liked him? He got right up the nose of the Pharisee and Sadducee, and more importantly, was turning large numbers away from them. They had gotten on well, he had given him land, and why would anyone care about someone getting a divorce from a gentile? He didn't understand what this tirade was about.

Zachariah shrugged, "He is not amenable to reason, your Highness. He was ranting about the laws of God being cast aside for personal privilege, all the things he normally directed at the Sadducee he is now sending towards your good self. He is entirely mad."

"What do you think, he will settle down after a couple of months? I like him, other than this nonsense. He has gotten up Herodias' nose instead of annoying the priests at the Temple. It is so stupid!" Herod was walking in the sun, filtered by the grape vines over his courtyard.

His advisor looked upwards. Herod himself was insane, angering the Nabateans like this. He had said so at the time when he was consulted about divorcing Phasaelis. Tactfully he replied, "Madness can make us behave in strange ways, my king."

Herod was no fool, his advisor was telling him that he only had himself to blame. "I know, Zak. It **was** madness, I admit it, but the madness of love. Plus she is properly Jewish, and if I am to have any sort of legacy I have to be aligned with a Jewish bloodline. There will be no respect of my household until they start seeing I am a Jew."

Zachariah just sighed, "Master, my King, you have enormous respect. The people love you, so what does it matter what the Sadducee or Pharisee think? The fact that they hate you only brings you more love from the people."

"The damn people have no say in who runs things. THAT is determined by the Romans, so for them to have a decent ruler I have to remain in the good graces of Tiberius. To him I have to make it clear I am not part of the Jewish establishment, to the Sadducee I have to look like I am not a friend of Pilate. I am thinking my best hope is both Tiberius and Sejanus die and we get someone who will be our friend wearing the purple." Herod was thinking out loud, as he would do. The balcony where they stood looked out over the Sea of Galilee.

"That, my King, is betting on a race when you don't know who is riding the chariot or if they are pulled by camels. We have but one certainty. King Aretas will seek revenge for the insult you have slapped his face with."

"Oh, he won't step over the border and put himself at risk with Rome. Right now, the biggest issue is the Baptist and his preaching against me.

It looks bad that my people are stirring trouble and it needs to stop. How long before he runs out of steam down there?"

"Well, considering he has steadfastly and faithfully protested his hatred of Rome, the Pharisee, and the Sadducee for his entire life without faltering, I am not supposing he will change until you admit you made a mistake. Now, as you are never going to do that, I expect he will just continue." Zachariah was used to being blunt with his master.

"Visit him every day, take him fresh bread and fruit, make sure he has clean water for washing and let him have visitors. Let us see what a month or two of kindness will do to soften his heart, and let him keep his house. We can hold him here till the gossip fades and the public's interest moves on." In the distance Herod sees his stepdaughter, and calls her over, "Salome I have a small job for you, you like board games, yes? (she nods) We have the Baptist downstairs, can you place your beautiful smile on him and soften up his heart? Spend some time down there and keep him company."

She was a very beautiful girl, barely thirteen but already showing signs of perfection. She nods in agreement and goes down to see what this Baptist looked like. "If THAT creature can't weaken his resolve, nothing will!" Herod exclaimed, laughing.

As they were walking away from the house, into the surrounding vineyards, Herod said in a hushed tone to his advisor. "I have it on good advice that the Pharisee are very wary of some plan of Caiaphas. I need you in Jerusalem to make quiet investigations into what this might be, and let's see if we can't use this to get the law holders onto our side."

"You just broke one of their most basic laws on marriage, my King." Zachariah was astonished at the man's audacity.

"Did I? Marriage to a gentile carries nothing like the weight as the marriage to Royal Jewish blood. You might find this Nicodemus is an extremely practical man, and far more amenable to a quiet arrangement that benefits us both. The trick is in showing him how great a benefit we represent as leverage against the Sadducee."

ooo0000ooo

Moving down into the subterranean haunts of the Zealot fighters, the Sadducee priests were clothed as traders and common folk. They carried no gold, all those transactions were done in the Gentiles Court at the Temple. Instead, they carried the hopes and expectations of the High Priest to the curious ears of one most feared, Barabas.

"How goes the weapons manufacture?" asked the minor priest, concerned about his purity despite how Caiaphas had assured him God's work made you pure, no matter where you stepped. Just the smell here was certain to carry with him when he left, he could not face his wife in such a state.

Barabas laughed, he loved seeing the faces of these priests as they squirmed. "It goes well, priest. We already have many thousands of swords and shields, though we have to keep shifting the workshops as the Romans track the rust in the water and look for its source. I gather they are getting nervous."

"We are instructed to witness this," the priest said, bluntly doubting the outlaw's claim. The Temple had paid a small fortune to this rabble and Caiaphas wanted to ensure they were getting value for money.

"We do not keep all the weapons in one place, but I can show you the cache we have here. Barabas walked over to a few chests set onto wheels for transportation, and opened one of them, revealing many freshly minted swords. "This is difficult to hide, the smiths must have fire and fire creates smoke. The beating of the metal creates noise, so we need sentries and outposts everywhere to watch for the Romans."

One of the priests picks up a sword, made some awkward swings with it, taps it flat against a stone, listens for the ring, then puts it back. He looks at the other priest, who nods, saying, "They are very rough but sufficient for the task."

They pick up and leave, happy to be out of this den of ill-repute.

Once they are gone Barabas laughed, "They are such fools," he sneered at the burly man beside him. Anyone who understood weapons would know that what they picked up was a rubbish cast sword out of Egypt. He just beat some Hebraic prayers into them and sharpened them up. He made some more traditional weapons that he would show Caiaphas, but the bulk would be the cheapest he could get or ones he managed to steal.

In the meantime, he was using the priests' money to feed people, get them clothes, and generally place himself in good favor with the locals. It meant none would betray him, but also that mothers sent their sons down to build the army that would rid them of the Romans. That was the real job, taking teenage boys and training them to swing a weapon without hurting themselves.

The gall of Caiaphas, to presume he had the right to rule because some Roman governor made him High Priest. He thinks if he quashes the Pharisee he will be the one calling the shots, well he is in for a rude awakening. The Zealots have waited too long for power - it is their time.

ooo0000ooo

When [Yeshua] entered Capernaum, a centurion came to him, appealing to him and saying, "Lord, my servant is lying at home paralyzed, in terrible distress." And he said to him, "I will come and cure him." The centurion answered, "Lord, I am not worthy to have you come under my roof; but only speak the word, and my servant will be healed. For I also am a man under authority, with soldiers under me; and I say to one, 'Go,' and he goes, and to another, 'Come,' and he comes, and to my slave, 'Do this,' and the slave does it." When Yeshua heard him, he was amazed. And to the centurion, Yeshua said, "Go; let it be done for you according to your faith." And the servant was healed in that hour.

Mathew 8:5-13

Peter woke early, as usual, wondering about that strange experience. He could not call it a dream, the Centurion seemed to be there. Why would a leader of a Roman military unit call by on his own? Why would he act so humble? It was a thing that could never happen. As he made tea for those who would wake shortly, he was surprised to see Mathew already up. "Had the strangest dream," he said, "A centurion came to the house, talking about a paralyzed servant."

Peter was shocked but said nothing. Simon had overheard, "I had that dream as well. I thought it was completely mad, imagine, a Centurion turning up here!"

"I too had this dream. Did any of you hear of the address of the man?" Peter asked.

Andrew piped up, rubbing sleep from his eyes. "I had the same damn dream, can you believe? There is only one Centurion in this area, he lives in Tiberias and looks after the city. He is a Syrian who got his citizenship, knows Herod quite well I am told."

"We have fish to sell at Tiberias this morning. When we are there, I want to go by his house and ask one of the locals if there is anything to this strange, shared dream."

Yeshua was away in contemplation somewhere. But this was a detective story easily answered, they would go there and see how much of it was truth. The men were soon ready and prepared the rigging, they were good fellows, hard workers like his older brothers had been. To have lost them in a storm, well, this was always a risk on this dangerous sea - it was so shallow that strong winds could whip up huge waves that could swamp even a boat as large as his.

Only Peter survived, but one man cannot fish this sea, so he had taken on Simon, Mathew, and Andrew as crew. They worked with the cool efficiency of men who knew their trade, and shortly they were sailing to Herod's city, disposing of their catch to the local market traders. After sharing out the bounty, the men made their way to the quarter where many of the Romans lived.

There they asked a woman drawing from a well which house was the centurions. She pointed to a typical Roman villa, painted white and with paved stones around it. "The Centurion, did he have a servant who was unable to move?"

The woman looked surprised, "Why yes, he did, but no more. This morning the fellow was up and about as if he had never been ill. The fever passed overnight."

The four looked at each other with wonder, "How can it be?" they asked themselves.

Sailing back as they were setting the sails to come to the jetty, they saw Yeshua on the shore and waved to him. As they docked they came up to ask him what had happened. Peter spoke for all of them, "Master, we all had the same dream, that a Centurion came here and asked for his servant to be healed. And this day we went to his house, and a woman in the street told us that overnight, the servant in the house of the centurion had indeed been healed. How can this be? How can we see things in a dream that are real?"

Yeshua nodded, "Do you think this world is real?" he asked.

Peter laughed, "Well, I would hope so, else we are in a dream now and nothing is real!"

"So you say," said Yeshua, explaining nothing.

The men were puzzled, but set to preparing the boat as tomorrow was the Sabbath and it had to be strapped and tied in case some storm blew up. It was only a few moments, but when Peter looked up to ask another question, no one was there.

Andrew was the first to speak, "You think this is the 'dream walking' thing he talks about? I have had it since Yeshua joined with the Baptist - at night I wake to find myself in my parent's house, playing with my baby sisters that I miss so much. I swear it is as real there as we are here."

Peter said very little, but he too had similar experiences. He was no longer certain if Yeshua had said something to him in this world, or in the dream world. He had felt himself on uncertain ground this whole time, but this SHARED experience proved there was a reality to the illusions.

The news about John had shaken many of them and made them nervous. Then Peter laughed, as the obvious struck him. "Did we all just go to the city of Herod, then stand outside a Centurion's house, right when we are all fearful of what Herod will do next?"

Mathew also laughed, "I am not sure if we are courageous or stupid? We were all so curious that we forgot our fear!"

It was at this point that Yeshua did walk up to them, smiling. "Just as little children," he said.

Peter took another double take, how the hell did he turn up without them seeing him arrive? "Master, what was that dream about? We all shared it, we proved it was more than a dream."

"So you say," said the teacher. He almost left them hanging, but then he laughed, "Answers are a form of death, Peter. Questions create the curiosity that gives up the desire to know. And so we climb the obstacles between the unknown and ourselves and find what we will. What I will say is that there is more on heaven and earth than any one man, tribe, or nation can know. With the Lord, all things are possible."

Mathew had to know more, "Master, this dream tells us that the work you do here is but a small parcel of what you do elsewhere. I cannot imagine what it is like for you, do we look like ants in your sight?"

The Master laughed out loud, "I am the servant of the Lord. I do nothing but his bidding, and by doing his work his power flows into this world and uplifts the downtrodden, heals the sick, and gives sight to the blind. I am the smallest grain of sand on a beach of wonder, just as you are grains of sand. Brothers in spirit we are, and the breath of the Lord unites us, but I will tell you the secret if you have ears to hear?"

The men all lean forward expectantly. Yeshua smiles, holding up his thumbs. "For most, this thumb is reality, and that thumb is the dream." He starts to draw his thumbs together, "The spiritual seeker starts to discover who and what they are, and the dream and the reality start to merge, to become one." His thumbs come together as one.

"But the world distracts. Our fears and our troubles pull us from this point of awareness," the two thumbs separate again. "But the one who is with the Lord, who had the Lord within him directing his path, (the thumbs come back together) then his dream and his reality are one and the same. His wish is now the wish of the Lord. His dream is the dream of the Lord. And I say to you, learn well what I teach. Take fully to heart what I give. As you come into the fullness of Spirit, as you come into union with your most pure self, what miracles you see in my presence, you shall do, and more."

All four are mesmerized by the thumbs before them, they can see nothing else. Then a squall hits the boat, and they look to see if it is properly tied. But when they look back a moment later, Yeshua is not to be found. Simon was the one that spoke all their feelings, "Do you ever get the feeling we have sailed into an ocean way bigger than our boat?" They all laugh, but even as they do, all wonder what on earth this morning was about.

When they get back to the house, where Phillip and James greet them, saying, "We all shared the most extraordinary dream last night!"

ooo0000ooo

Caiaphas was overjoyed. "We got the main bastard," he laughed, welcoming his people to the palace of the High Priest. The finest of wine was poured in the courtyard for his guests, and many sweetmeats and choice cuts were offered on open platters.

It was a twofold win, the first being the obvious removal of one of the worst troublemakers. Hard to imagine that a rude dog like the Baptist could have come from their ranks, but there you had it - finally he overstepped the mark AND he saved him the trouble of a head-to-head conflict with Herod.

It had been tricky business, you cannot have a King ignoring the Law of Moses without the priests saying something in public, and the repercussions of that would have been very bad. Herod and Pilate were both plotting the downfall of the Sadducee, and if you openly attacked an agent of Rome, as Herod was, you made yourself an easy mark. He could be removed from his position and accused of treason. That was the whole problem, the Romans held sway over their existence.

But then that delightful idiot stepped up and took all the flak. Now all Caiaphas had to do was nod knowingly, say that John was indeed a prophet, and decry the unfairness of it all to Pilate. And if anyone asks him directly what he thinks, he can fairly say, "Those who quote the Law of Moses are imprisoned in this land!" Thus he attacks both the Romans and Herod, but says nothing to incriminate the Sadducee specifically.

He comes out to the courtyard with his wife and children, smiling broadly, and offering up a toast, "This is for the Baptist who took the sins of Herod onto his back like his fabled goats. May he rot in Herod's prison!"

The cheer went up. All were relieved, because they knew Herod had laid a trap for them, knowing the Sadducee would have to openly declare his marriage a travesty, which would cause riots in the streets, which in turn would force Pilate to imprison the instigators of the trouble. But because of the Baptist's obstinacy, now their worst critic had become their savior!

The marble floors and granite columns were ostentatious displays of wealth all on their own, but the High Priest had imported dancers from Egypt, and fine delicacies from as far afield as Persia for this evening of celebration. It had been a month of trepidation, waiting for the axe to fall, but Caiaphas had masterfully sailed around the rocks of destruction and not only kept his position, but he had also improved their strength against the Romans.

Herod's plan had failed, and NOW there were now rumblings of war on the horizon from the divorced girl's father. This would occupy Herod completely for his very survival was at stake. Best of all, word was to hand how Sejanus had played the October Horse in Rome, and his head had rolled down the Senate stairs! This meant Tiberius was back and because of this, Pilate was in fear of recall, or worse.

So BOTH the enemies of the Sadducee had been neutered, and the annoying Baptist was taking the heat. It didn't get much better than this. "We WON people!" Caiaphas boldly declared. "Proof that the Lord is with us is self-evident this day!"

ooo0000ooo

Pilate sat up, watching the moon coming to full in the sky, sitting with his wife. Despite the miserable nature of the people, Judea was quite a beautiful place. However, the death of his sponsor was certain to cause ripples here in Jerusalem. They had just received the news, but what it meant for them here in Judea was not yet certain.

Claudia knew when he was deep in thought, just as she always knew the right time to ask a question of him. "I liked Sejanus, he was rough and crude, but he was good to us. What will his death mean for us, darling?" she asked.

"I am not certain, my love. But I am no friend to Tiberius - we are going to have to play a careful game if we are to avoid some Legate turning up and ordering us back to Rome. Not that I would mind being back in Rome, just not traveling back in chains, and ending up flying from the Tarquin rocks." he half-joked.

"You have been following orders. If Tiberius punishes all who followed the orders of Sejanus, there will be no one left running anything across the entire empire," she suggested.

"True, but when did this stop a vindictive old man who wants to wreak havoc? We have a weakened garrison and no friends in Rome. We must take precautions and make no wrong steps. The first is that you and the children can not appear in public. The way the Jews are at the moment, you could end up with an arrow in your back and we will have a full-scale war on our hands. Even in Caesarea, we must take great care, for we hold on to power here by a thread."

Pilate sighed before continuing. "There is open revolt being planned, my spies all say it, and if this happens the Syrian Legate will be on our door and we will be held responsible for poor management of the Province. If so, our efforts here will amount to nought."

They both knew what that meant, seizure of property and public humiliation. Pilate could even be expelled from Rome. "Well Darling, no one walks the tightrope as well as you do. I have every confidence in your ability and I will make sure the children understand. I presume they are to no longer have any Jewish friends over?"

Pilate was surprised, "They have Jewish friends?"

Claudia laughed, "Yes my dear, they do. Mostly from the business class."

"We cannot show fear, let them have their friends over, just no going out to markets or public places. Tiberius is old. With luck, he will be dead soon and the next one will be a little friendlier to us."

What excellent fools
Religion makes of men!

Sejanus - His Fall
Ben Johnson 1603

The Boat

The news had arrived as a thunder clap, striking fear into the heart of many. The Baptist was dead! He would walk up and down the Jordan no more. His wife was now a widow, his children orphans, all because he spoke his mind.

Over the last year, there had been many and varied disputes in the camp of John, but always his voice would roar out to silence them. Always his presence was there to calm the raging sea of anger that could erupt. But John was no more - his death at the hands of Herod was unthinkable, the shock of his passing unforgivable. Yet Yeshua had said nothing, and acted as if nothing had happened, which angered John's followers even more.

He did not hide from them. The man just went about his business, ignoring the pleas and demands of the headless chickens running around in a panic. But then it came to blows, with the followers of John attacking the followers of Yeshua. It was then Yeshua roared out in a voice Peter had never heard, a voice of absolute authority.

"SILENCE!" it demanded.

Peter swore flames came from the man, as his eye burned. Surely this was the Messiah, surely now he would draw the Sword of Righteousness from the heavens and smite those false prophets. And in his mind, he DID see the sword, flaming blue. In his thoughts, Yeshua held the sword at the heart of every man there, all at the same time. He saw the ones that were full of hate and fear push themselves onto it, but they did not die. Yeshua did not move.

This carried on for a short time, but finally, people fell into the stillness of Yeshua. Like awkward children caught stealing biscuits, they stood there, eyes downcast. He said nothing. For long minutes only thoughts echoed around the house. "Still your hearts," he spoke almost in a whisper. "The Lord shall not receive an angry Soul. That man shall sit outside his door until forgiveness and kindness enters his heart and he is once more worthy of truth."

Berated, the men started to sit, to consider, and to weep. Their master was no more, beheaded by Herod. "Know this, the Lord has received John in glory, in celebration. Do not despair, for he walks within us, his laughter is here now, in our hearts. In life, he was a giant, physically and spiritually, and there will be no other like him. Do I shed a tear? Yes, but that tear evaporates from my cheek and ascends to the heavens. My tears baptize his memory and cherish his presence amongst us."

His voice picks up strength, "The Lord gave him to us as a gift. Cherish that, hold it in your heart. As John makes his way to the eternal throne of the Lord, walk with him, do not leave him behind. Go with him in Spirit, be with him in your hearts. Do not abandon him now, and do not blame the world for his passing, for he knew what he did. He understood the nest of vipers he walked amongst, and he blessed them, even as their poison took his life. For John knows, this world is a shadow of the next. John knows, the light of our sun is a candle to the light of the Lord, and now, for him, there is no more darkness. Rejoice in his freedom, even as you shed tears for your loss."

"But what will we do now?" a plaintive voice begs. There is a murmur of fear, for they have no sense of what is to come, or even if they are safe from Herod.

Yeshua looks over to Peter and nods. Peter tells them what he had found out. "I dropped some fish to Martha yesterday. Zachariah, the confidant of Herod, had visited her, saying her house will be left and she will even be paid a stipend so she can live without further suffering. I believe we are safe from Herod taking action against us, plus from what I was told, the King was tricked into it by his wife. She is indeed pure Jewish blood, controlling her man through whiles."

There is a muttering amongst the followers, Yeshua then speaks. "The followers of John can keep doing what they are doing with the blessings of Herod. I will not be leading you, for I will baptize only with the Spirit. So, those who wish to follow John's ways may depart this house and return to his warehouse near Tiberias, where you can choose a new leader."

This was a shock, most presumed Yeshua would take up where the Baptist had left off. "But who will lead us?" one stocky fellow asked.

Yeshua said with absolute certainty, "In the ways of the Essene, when the Zadoc passes from this world, and the next is to take his place, we spend two weeks in contemplation, asking the Lord for guidance. If the chosen passes the trial of death, he becomes our new High Priest. To be fair, most Essenes thought John would be the next Zadoc. Just as they must recount their ways, so too must you. The Lord will find his way into your heart and whisper who this shall be.

"For some, this is our last day together as brothers of the same house. Tomorrow, some of you will follow the ways of the Baptist, as is your right and your truth. Trust that the Lord will guide your decision.

"And if the Lord bids you to depart, know we are eternal cousins, born of the same blood, born of the same father, our Lord in heaven, but living in separate houses. This will be your first choice, which house will you call your own? To help you choose, I will say that in THIS house, the baptism by water will be replaced with baptism through the holy fire of the Lord. I will not stay by the River Jordan, but travel across this land, reaching those souls that the Lord has put in my path."

"But the miracles, they were bringing the people for baptism," one of the followers exclaimed, shocked by this abrupt parting of the ways.

"The Lord performs the healing, the Lord uplifts the spirit, not I. This is your choice, your leader has died, I am telling you I will not follow the same path, this is all. You are free to choose a new leader or to follow me. But I will not be performing the baptisms for the forgiveness of sin, nor casting sin into a goat and sending it into the wilderness." Yeshua stands, "For now, I go to contemplate my time with John and all he has done for me. Do not ask me what you should do, ask the Lord within. Do not ask me what road you should travel, ask the Lord within."

He gets up, takes some bread, olive oil, and water from the kitchen, and a blanket, nodding to Peter as he goes outside. Peter does the same, he has something he must say to his master, and now seems to be the time. "I go to speak with the Lord on the Mount behind us, Peter. I will speak tomorrow of the path I will tread to all who wish to hear, so bring all who follow me with you."

"Yeshua, I will do as you ask, but before you go, there is something I must say." *It is like catching a bird,* Peter thought. He was already away, transported by the chariots of the Angels to wherever it was he went.

Yeshua just looked with that distant expression, coming back only because he was asked. "Master, I have arranged to sell my boat. I have settled with my wife on agreeable terms, not with divorce, as that would humiliate her. After speaking with you, I understood, there is still love between us, but we are now oil and water. She knows and accepts this, and there are sufficient funds for her and the children. The rest I will use helping you with your message, the Lord has spoken to me and told me to leave everything and follow you. I will obey his word."

There is a tear in Yeshua's eye. This harsh, hard, uncompromising fisherman that had a heart of stone has been melted by the grace of the Lord. If such a one can receive the wisdom of Spirit, what better omen could he have on this day, the start of his true ministry? "We all follow the path the Lord sets before us, Peter. We are like the sails of your boat, while he is our rudder. We are taken by the wind of his will to the place of his choosing."

Peter felt awkward, foolish, and stupid. But he had heard the call, and despite his mind telling him what an idiot he was, all he knew in his heart is that he needed to hear more of what this man called Yeshua had to say. "I will bring the followers up the mountain in the morning, Master."

ooo0000ooo

A great deal of discussion was being had by those who believed in either John or Yeshua. Up to this point, they had presumed they were all the same tribe, but a division had been rising for some time, with many not knowing what to do. "I felt when Yeshua threw all the money changers out of the Gentiles Court that John would have changed his tune. Let's face it, not even John would outrightly challenge the authority of Caiaphas in so blunt a way. I felt Yeshua WAS the Messiah, the one who would throw out the Romans like he did the corrupt lenders. We all know they are corrupt, but to practice that corruption in the house of the Lord, what more could we say?"

Another chimed in, "But Yeshua has said, again and again, he doesn't CARE about the Romans. His only interest is saving the soul of the individual. John is the one who was going to get the bastards off our back, John was going to lead us to the true path. Yeshua cannot be the Messiah if he is not going to deal with the Romans. I am not disputing he is a good man, but I am with John. We cannot have a pure state of Israel with corrupt leadership. I want the Romans gone, I want Herod gone, I want the Sadducee out of the Temple, and good men put in their place."

And so it went, Peter shook his head, there were no answers to their arguments. He had heard the wisdom of his master, get rid of everyone who is corrupt, and what have you got left? People who will slowly become corrupted by the whispers of evil because they do not have the love of the Lord as their guide.

After an hour of pointless quoting of scripture, arguing on points of right and wrong, and who had the better path, Peter stood. He felt the power of the Lord within him, he had made his decision, and he was a follower of Yeshua. "Listen up you lot, you are going round in circles. Talking will provide no answers, arguing will give no result but argument. I lived with a nagging wife for twenty years, I don't want to be nagged ever again, and you lot are sounding like a nagging wife to me."

Each man understood exactly what Peter was saying. This is why everyone liked him, he was blunt and to the point. "I have made peace with my wife. I want peace to live here, not fury, not anger, not pain and suffering - I had that for years. You have a decision to make, a hard decision for most, as it was for me. I loved John, I loved him with all my heart. He was a great man, the best of us, the wisest of us, and now he is dead. Before he died, I had decided to follow Yeshua, because his words spoke to me in a way that opened my heart to the Lord. The question is this, not who am I going to follow, but in what house do I feel my heart more open? That is it, there is nothing else. And believe me, I feel like a complete fool - I am leaving everything behind, my livelihood, my family, even my good name, but the Lord spoke to me, and I know who I must follow.

"Now stop arguing, and start asking yourself what it is that your heart is telling you. I spoke with Yeshua just before, he said he will be speaking tomorrow on the Mount. If you think you want to follow his path, come with me in the morning and hear what he has to say. If you are not interested, then maybe the Lord is telling you to follow John. I don't know what is right for you, I only know what is right for me.

"So everyone, piss off out of here, come back tomorrow before dawn, and those who want to listen to Yeshua come with me. The rest, do what you want, but no more arguing, or I will take a stick to the lot of you like Yeshua did to the money lenders!" And then Peter laughed, "But wasn't that a hoot! Watching those slimly little toads scurrying away and those gutless priests squawking like crows on a fence."

The men laughed, they all loved sticking it up the establishment. Peter continued, "But this is not why I follow Yeshua, yeah? It is fun but that's not why. It is because when he speaks to me in those riddles of his, some door opens inside my head and I see things in a way I had never seen them. We have seen the miracles, we all know he says it isn't him, but they don't happen without him around. But THAT is not why I follow Yeshua. It is the love on the faces of the people he touches, he does something no one else does, he opens the heart.

"I was afraid of that when I first met him. I fought it, I didn't want to be exposed, to be shown as I was. I hated the feeling of him seeing through me like I was glass, but when I got past that, it dawned on me - No one had ever bothered before. Not one person in my life BOTHERED to see me. Not my wife, not my kids, not my parents, no one. He SEES me, and because he sees me, I can begin to see myself, and admittedly, sometimes I don't like what I see.

"But then he tells me, this can change. I can change. And you know what, I believe him, and what he says is a REAL miracle happens, I change. You know he calls me a rock? Reckons I am as thick as the bricks I used to build my house. He is right, I am an idiot. I am a nobody, but when he is around, I feel I am someone that matters. And I like that. But you people, make your mind up. I am telling you my mind not to change yours, but to let you know you are not alone in confusion and doubt.

"The Lord spoke to me, and if he will speak to an ignorant fisherman full of hate and spite and anger, then maybe he will take the time to talk to you. See you tomorrow if you are coming up the Mountain." Peter left them to it, and went to his boat, to sit on her, to feel the gentle waves shifting her. This was his one true friend for so long. He remembered how he had worked so hard, surviving the brutality of his father, working to gain his favor so that he inherited it when he died. But then he died, along with his brothers, in the fateful storm, leaving him the boat. The pair of them, they had survived storms and loneliness, and now they were to part ways. Talk about making a choice.

ooo0000ooo

The day dawned clear and bright, the hint of frost fled as the sun crept over the hills surrounding Galilee. The sky was a peculiar blue, almost a hint of purple, with long feathers for clouds. To Peter's surprise, a lot of people had turned up, far more than he had expected. Perhaps it was in the thousands? If it was a haul of fish, he would count it, but certainly, more than the village held. They had come from all over, partly he supposed because this was some way to honor the Baptist, partly because they wanted to know what the new guy was going to say.

Everyone had heard how he whipped the money lenders out of the Temple, no one liked them, and no one liked the Sadducee they supported. But Yeshua did this and walked away, proving the Lord was with him. The stirring of the people's heart was a great force that day, and many souls had gathered to hear this Messiah speak.

Peter had the chosen with him, and many of John's followers had also come, deciding to see for themselves what the one ordained by their former Master had to say. They all knew John's message, be pure of heart and the Lord will send us the one who will rid the world of evil. Was this the one he spoke of?

On the Mount, Yeshua had arrived in the hour after dawn. He had been deep in communication with the Lord but now his eyes came back to this physical world and he saw that many had come. He took a spot where he could see the people, near to where Peter has set up a day camp. He smiled, his friend and follower had brought tents, with food and wine for his people, expecting a long day, no doubt.

Peter came over and asked, "I have a small pavilion for you, Master, should you wish?" Yeshua nodded, not ready to speak, for the Lord was still subsuming his fear and doubts. This day he would tell his people what the mission would be. As Peter and his friends set up fabric on poles to shield the master from the sun, Yeshua asked himself, *"What can I give them, Lord? What can I say that will lead their hearts to you?"*

GRACE, whispered in the wind. And there the truth arrived, he knew the people needed to hear what qualities they must have to sit in the Grace of the Lord. He looked at the followers of his cousin, deeply sorrowed, deeply concerned, and his heart went out to them.

"You are the salt of the Earth. But John spoke of what happens when a man becomes lost in worldly pursuits, he loses his essence. Their salt becomes tasteless and the Lord will overlook them when choosing what to place on his table."

He points to Hippos in the distance, "I say to you, each one of you, that you are the light in this world. Just as that town built on a hill cannot be hidden you must let your light shine. Do you light a lamp and put it under a bowl? No, we put it on its stand, and it gives light to everyone in the house. In the same way, let your light shine before others, that they may see your good heart. By your example, you will show them the path to the Lord Father in heaven. Even in hard times, this light will shine from the pure heart, a candle in the darkness to lead your brother home.

"For those who mourn in earnest loss, be comforted. The sorrows and travails of this world no longer afflict my cousin, the Baptist. He walks with the Lord, no doubt shouting at those knocking on the gates of paradise to repent!" The men smiled, shedding a tear, but also laughing silently. It was true, he is probably up there dowsing people, demanding they tell him the truth. "He is with you still, be comforted. His presence is in your heart and in your Soul, be comforted. Know he is still here, that what he gave and what he taught you is alive within your heart. Be comforted. No man who has lived an earnest life, a life dedicated to the Lord and to his truth, will suffer the torments of loss and pain. They are set free in the bosom of the Lord, so be comforted, and do as he did." Yeshua looked to the next jewel the Lord wished to share and he saw it in the kind heart of Peter.

"Blessed are those who lack arrogance. Those who have nothing to defend, nothing to say, these are the ones who hear the voice of the Lord. The din of worldly haste and the pretense of believing you are better than your fellows because you possess wealth, or wisdom, does not touch the humble heart. The practice of *prautes (Greek word that meant freedom through a lack of self-interest in your external world, a lack of pride)* will shed your burdens, and you shall walk this land as if you are in Eden, with all the fruits of wisdom and truth a gift to you from the Lord."

Then he thought of John, the deprivation of his time in the desert, the total loss of all things of this world to the point even his own life had no value to him. "And most blessed are the poor who are yet rich in spirit. A man who has nothing but God has everything, and more. A man who has nothing but the presence of the Lord walks even now in Paradise. His trials became the gift of divine wisdom and all his sufferings are but the steps he took into the heart of the Lord."

All the followers of John were openly weeping now, a torrent of loss poured from their hearts. They knew Yeshua spoke of their Master, they felt it in their hearts. Yeshua smiled and continued, "The Lord welcomes all who hunger and thirst after justice. They shall arrive at his banquet of love and be fed his grace until they are grace themselves."

"I promise you, all of you, this simple truth. Those who are pure of heart shall see the Lord in all his glory. Those who clean not just their bodies, but their eternal soul, and wash it each day in forgiveness of those who have trespassed against them, they will know the Lord, and the Lord will know them.

"For mercy is the way of the Lord. And I say to you, act with mercy, act with kindness, act with acceptance of another's fault, and the Lord will visit the Temple within your heart. He will take up residence and guide you. So act knowing that the Lord is with you, moving through you, being the light that guides you, and know that Mercy is the purest offering you can place at his feet. Mercy and kindness are the prayers our Lord listens for and hears most keenly.

"Do this and you will find in your heart a depth of peace that cannot be shaken. Do this and the mercy of the Lord will flow through your veins and dwell in the heart of your being. And when the Lord's house is secure in your heart, then his generosity, his deep peace, will flow from you. Where there are harsh words, you will find soft. Where there is a clanging of swords, you will find a way to reconcile the hearts of the angry. I say to you, the peacemaker is the child of the Lord."

He looks once more to the followers of John. "But we all know this world. Those who love and care for their people are rarely given love and care in return. You have the Lord within as solace. Despite those who persecute you, who find fault in you, who despise you, and who revile your name with gossip and lies, forgive them. Know that the whispers that have taken over their mind and heart have separated them from the Lord. Do not allow them to drive you into their ranks of pettiness and misery, but stay with the Lord. If you can do this, the doorway to Paradise is open to you.

"There will come the day when you will bless them, you will understand their ignorance and know they acted not against you, but against the purity of your spirit. Their curses are like a dog howling at the Moon, it knows not why it must, only that it acts as some whisper inside tells it. But know this, a lesson in what is false can be as important as a truth you share. For there are many who witness and say nothing, and your peace, your inner strength, this shouts the name of the Lord to them. Your patience allows others to see and judge the path they wish to take. And that path of peace you follow, with grace and perseverance, leads you with absolute certainty to the doors of Paradise, wherein those Souls you instructed with your kindness, your wisdom, your humble acceptance, will all soon follow."

Yeshua let silence fall and sat in stillness with the Lord, asking what more he wanted said. He knew how the Zadoc felt when the Spirit of the Lord moved through him, and he awaited its presence. Instead, a whisper arose, a hissing snake that wanted to strike. A grain of fear wanted to sprout. He remembered the Egyptian who showed him the cobra and the words that were embedded on his heart that day.

The fellow had prodded the cobra, which reared up, its hood flattened to strike. "A snake is not cruel, it does not wish to harm you, it is reacting with fear. God gave it that fear. God gave it the fangs and poison to feed and protect itself, but God also gave you mastery over the serpent. He gave you the heart of love that can charm the beast." With this, he took out his pipe and played, while the snake watched in fascination. It fell into the calm radiating from the charmer, and the man took it, stroked it, and placed it upon his breast, saying, "When its fear is gone, it no longer desires to harm me."

Yeshua sees that he must speak of the snake in another's heart. "We have all met men who speak with a pious voice, but whose voice does nothing but gossip. We all know men who wear fine clothes, but their soul is dressed in darkness. Far worse, we have all met that man who pretends to love, but all he loves is himself. I say to you, if you dream of love, but do not act with love, you live in the paradise of the fool. I say to you, your actions must marry your good intentions if you are to walk the single road of truth. And the only action worthy of truth is love."

Thomas, the one who rarely spoke, asked, "Master, you have given us words, and I have seen by your miracles that you are with the Lord - but

I cannot do these things as you. How can I be this light you speak of? Tell me what I must do to earn the Lord's trust and presence!"

Yeshua smiled, "This is easy, Thomas. If you see a man who is hungry, feed him. If he is thirsty, give him water. If he is naked, clothe him. If he is wandering and lost, give him a place he can shelter from the world. If he is imprisoned, visit and console his heart. If he is sick, call and see how you can help the family. If he is dead, do not leave his body to the vultures, but bury him."

Thomas is still wanting more, "We saw John, berating people for their sins. Was this unkindness justified?"

"If a man is walking to Jerusalem, but his feet are taking him to Rome, is it wrong for you to correct his path and set him in the way he must go? Speak your truth to a sinner so that he may read the signs the Lord has already given him, and correct his path. If he is a fool, educate him as you can. If he has doubt, counsel him in righteousness. If he is sad and lost, comfort him with kindness. If he is in error and cannot see it, be patient. Let the Lord speak in his own time to his heart. If he has trespassed, forgive first then explain your boundary. No man ever found an answer to a dispute with an argument. But most of all, if the soul be walking in shadows or in light, pray for them. Give them your blessing and ask that the Lord show them his light."

Encouraged by the silent disciple, one of John’s speaks, "Master, the Baptist was clear, the King had broken the Law. John spoke openly against it, which cost him his life. Should we also speak against the wrongs we see?"

Yeshua is back in his youth, where he had gone to see the Parsi master, to ask this same question. He had traveled to Persia and even learned the language, needing to know his place and his purpose. He had asked about how one must address falsehood and wrongful actions, and the Master just laughed, "Change the world, will you? Perhaps you will, but unless you know your OWN path, your OWN truth, and know it with such strength and power that it cannot be shaken even by the most fierce gale of opinion against you, then fighting the world will only change YOU. It will then carry on with its vast river of deceit, and your trickle of honesty will not prevail."

He spent a decade pondering those words. This was when he came to understand that stories illuminated the heart and inspired goodness far more than criticism or harsh truth. What to say? The man was not ready for the words the Parsi Master had given him, or was he? "Resist not evil. There is a river of deceit that flows from the temple. I whipped some of the fish that swam in there, but did it change the river? No, it flows on unchanged. I did not act seeking to change the river, but to set up a light that people might see. Place your light of truth at your window, not to illuminate the night, but to give another wanting that light a path they can follow.

"I say to you, once enough people light up the night, that river of lies shall dry up and become barren. That false house shall fall, not by my hand, but by the hand of the Lord. Do not resist the evil in men, resist it within yourself. Do not raise your voice in anger, raise it in righteousness. Say what you must, speak your truth as you will, and if the Lord speaks with you he will bring about his truth, his wisdom, his power, in time.

"Know this, the Lord is not bound by the day or the hour. The Lord is not tied to the beliefs of the few, or the many. The Lord is not owned by the Laws he gave Moses. He moves in HIS way, in HIS time, and it is vanity to suppose we know better than him."

The man was shocked, he had expected this Messiah to say they must go out and continue the work of his teacher, "So do we do nothing? Do we now sit idly by while we await the Lord?"

"We do as we are taught to do. You cannot save the river flowing into the Dead Sea, it is doomed to die there. But you can save those who live by its banks. As you save one fish from drowning, soon you save a school, and in time an entire nation will be blessed by the waters of the Lord's grace."

The followers of John nodded to each other. This made sense. They had been taught to baptize and cleanse the sinners in the grace of the Lord. This they would continue. What Yeshua had said last night also made sense, they needed to vote for another leader, someone who could organize the day-to-day matters of their faith.

A Greek stood, "Master, I find great beauty in your words. But I am a Greek, my God is not your God. How do I know your heaven is the right house for my family?"

Yeshua laughed, "Indeed my friend, this is an ancient question. Does my being right make your ways wrong? I say to you, the Lord is greater than the religions that claim him."

The man was still standing, not sure if his question had been answered. Yeshua had gone distant, looking at some far-off place. He was now in Kashmir, speaking with a Sadhu, a man of power. He was asking how his belief in the One God fitted in with the general belief the people there had in many Gods. The man had said, "You have your Lord, his breath is your Spirit? Well, already you have two Gods. You have your snake in the garden, a fallen angel according to your wisdom. What is this but another God people might worship? The truth is that everything is God if you see God in it. I see this rock my foot rests on as a God. I feel the air I breathe, this also is God. I feel the days of my life are like dreams that pass, but if I were to remain in one single repeating day, then this would be my God. The pure love of creation flows through all things, and all things are blessed by it. From the heavens the rain falls, single drops that combine to form a river. From the ONE, to the many, all rivers flow back to the ONE. This is the wheel, the Awagawan."

How to say these words so that this man will understand? "My friend, if you went into a house where there was an African, a Roman, and a Greek sitting there, arguing over whose God or Gods were the most true, what would you say?"

The Greek was an educated man, as most Greeks were. "It would be pointless to say anything. That is the problem, everyone thinks their God is the right God."

It was indeed the problem, Yeshua smiled. "What if you sat them down, poured fine wine, and gave them a feast of delight to enjoy, what would happen to their argument?"

The Greek laughed, "It is hard to argue when your mouth is full of delight!"

"I say to you, whatever fills your heart with pure delight, that is the God within. I say to you, no child argues over God, yet God lives most truly in the heart of the innocent and pure. The Lord I speak of is that which dwells in the heart of the childlike soul, and all races, all people, all faiths share this truth. If you are to know the one, true God of all, be as a little child."

The man starts to weep. He had studied all his life, he was a scribe who understood many languages, visited many shrines, spoken with many priests, and yet in a simple stroke of a few words, this man has cut all his learning to pieces and revealed the truth. Yeshua indicates for Peter to take him in and the man follows, a humble lamb to the shepherd.

The Greek had inspired the words of the Lord to flow. "Religion is not faith nor faith a religion. A religious man without faith is an empty shell, echoing the words he has read. Yet a man of faith without religion is like a boat at sea without a rudder. Our religion is what gives us direction, but even if we have faith and religion, without the breath of the Lord filling our sails, we are becalmed and helpless. The Lord has placed us where we are for what we have to learn therein. What is right or what is wrong by the law - these are things that change from place to place, country to country. But the eternal truths of love, charity to all, and faith in one's heart, these laws are fixed, they are like stars in the sky.

"You may find moments of doubt with your faith, or your religion, but do not doubt the power of love, faith, and charity. This is the banquet wherein all souls find delight and harmony. If you have love, faith, and charity in your heart as your guiding light, you will harm no man, you will not steal, you will not injure another in any way. So what need have you of the laws of man? I say to you, all the laws can be spoken as two truths. Love the Lord, and love your neighbor as you love yourself."

Yeshua looked within to see if the Lord had more to say. The well was empty, the bucket had no more to give. He looked to the audience, to the eager eyes and ears, all wanting more. He felt the light of the Lord flow through, reaching out to touch them, to embrace them, to hold them like the child they truly were.

He finished with his favorite prayer. "Lord, they will be done here as it is in Heaven. Give me your truth as my daily bread so that I will not sin with my ignorance. Show me your path. Lead me not into temptation, deliver me from evil, and forgive me if I trespass against you."

With this, he walked from the Mount, down to the house at Capernaum.

ooo0000ooo

Peter instructed his people to pack the tents and bring them to the storage shed near the house. He gathered the disciples, and they followed their Master in order to protect him, as the crowd had gotten up and trailed behind him, with people asking questions, and getting upset when there were no more answers. As he caught up to his Master, Yeshua said, "We will have no peace, go down and prepare the boat and we will go out onto the waters where they will not follow."

Peter looked at his master, and was about to argue that it was the Sabbath, but then he reasoned, they were not going out to work, and a man was allowed to travel a short distance and do what he would as long as it was in contemplation of the Lord. He instructed the men to protect Yeshua from any who grew angry in the crowd, and he and his brothers ran ahead to prepare the boat.

By the time the Master arrived, they were ready to launch, and had to be firm in who was allowed on board. For the people wanted more, like hungry dogs begging for scraps. The Master was clearly exhausted, not just from the day but the whole time they had spent in Jerusalem, and by the loss of his cousin. Peter felt it then, the sense of compassion for all things that the Master spoke of. A small part of him realized that seeing another's life through their eyes opened the heart to understanding.

They were soon away, a beautiful day, a perfect moment in a perfect world. All were contemplating the wisdom of their teacher, who lay in the back, snoring. He probably didn't even sleep last night, thought Peter. But all the stresses, all the worries, all the concerns were put behind them as his boat flew across the waters. Then, the fisherman in him broke through the carefree sailor, and whispered to look behind.

This was bad, a storm had gathered behind, coming from nowhere, flowing down the hill where Yeshua had given his talk. It was dark and foreboding, and he knew what that meant. He snapped James and Simon out of their happy day dream, "Look idiots, we have a storm about to fall on us!"

With practiced hands that ran around the boat, leaping over those who were sleeping soundly, tying off sails, and strengthening the stays on the masts - only just in time as the first squall whipped against the ship, driving it sideways. Peter flipped the rudder and turned the boat into the wind. This was bad, this was the sort of storm where his brothers died, for you had no purchase out there on the sea. The waves could pick up, and expose the bare bottom of the lake to his keel. If you were carried up on one, when the boat fell from the peak you could hit the sand.

The ship was strong, but it was the thumping that would throw men overboard, and they would drown. It had already started, huge vertical waves bearing down on their vessel and it took all his skill to position the boat to not fall sideways against them. That was certain death, if she rolled and took them all into the sea. Up they went, barely holding it into the wave. But it did not stop, up and up they went, a rogue wave had caught them and they were now flying in the air

At that moment of peril, Yeshua opened his eyes, and saw what was happening. He stood up, held his hands to the storm, and commanded it. "SILENCE!" he roared in a voice unlike any Peter had ever heard. The quiet, gentle shepherd was gone, and in its place stood a firebrand of power. The story teller vanished, and in his place stood a mighty sword that cleaved the world in two.

And as he spoke, the storm obeyed. The wind ceased, the waves abated, while the ship sailed effortlessly down the back of the wave that threatened to destroy them. The people on board looked at this man they had followed with fresh eyes. This was no meek shepherd protecting the flock, this was a man of power commanding the very elements to obey him, and they did.

With peace now restored, Yeshua said no more, and simply laid down and went back to sleep. Peter did not know what to make of this, a man who says he has not come to toss out the Romans but who can command the heavens themselves? It made no sense to him, but if he had doubts, this answered them.

Only the day before he had commanded the hearts of men to silence, and they obeyed. Now in that same unearthly voice he commanded the elements themselves. Was this man a God?

"We had better put into harbor," he said to Simon. The closest was his own house and the fiery wife he had just told he was leaving. It was not going to be pleasant, but another squall would sink them, which was possibly a little worse - possibly.

ooo0000ooo

As they hove to, his wife stood there with arms crossed, angry as always. He felt like an intruder in his own home when she was about. She called out before they could throw ropes, "You are here to apologize, or because of the storm?"

Peter thought of the words the master had spoken. He would seek to be humble rather than proud. He would seek to find harmony rather than argument. As they tied off, he went to his wife, "I hold no hate in my heart, woman. I wish it could be the same for you."

She just looked at him, this fool chasing after dreams. "I saw the storm, it hit you full on. I expected to be picking up pieces and bodies after it passed, for it threw you clear into the sky on that last wave. Then it was just gone - what happened?"

Peter had a tear in his eye, something he had never done before any woman, let alone his devil wife. He indicated the sleeping Yeshua, "He did. At the peak of it, he woke up, help up his hands and commanded it to silence. And the storm obeyed him. I have never seen anything like it."

She looked at him for long moments. He might be many things, but this man never lied, not knowingly at least. The tear had softened her heart, and she had witnessed the miracle herself, otherwise she would never have believed it. "I have been harsh with you, husband. For this I too offer an apology. I have no more hate in my heart towards you. But honestly, I am happier with you gone. If you must follow anyone, I suppose a person who can command the wind is better than most."

She went back to her house, but did not forbid his children from gathering around, hugging their father and listening to the amazing tale that brought them there.

The Wise Owner

Simon had read that God must be feared, which confused him. "Master, it is said in the scriptures that the fear of the Lord is the beginning of wisdom. I am confused, for you speak of the Lord as a kind shepherd who cares for his flock, why should the flock fear him?"

Yeshua looked over the table where they were eating their bread and soup and laughed at the young fellow. "It is a good question, one I asked myself when I was your age. Perhaps a story?"

The disciples applauded, for this was the part of the evening they enjoyed the most. And so Yeshua began:

A man owned a vineyard beside which a war between four kings was being fought. Each day, men would leave the battlefield and approach the owner for wine, saying they would pay when their King paid them, which would be at the end of the war. Now, the master of the vines spoke with the owner, saying, "Surely only one King will win, therefore three out of four of these men asking for wine will not pay!"

The problem was if the owner refused the men the wine, they would take it anyway, and possibly kill him and his staff. As it was not possible to move his vineyard away, the poor man had to find a solution, so he said to the various Captains of the Guard, "We must meet, all of you, under a truce, and discuss how I am to be paid."

Of course, the Captains of the Guard thought that was completely foolish, but the owner said, "If you do not meet and discuss how I will be paid, I am better off burning the vines, destroying my farm, and leaving - for surely if I give each one of your men wine, even if I do get paid it will be at best one-quarter of my cost, so I shall be ruined either way. Do you not see? It is not reasonable for people with an argument to carry it into the house of their neighbor, so I ask that you come here and resolve how this will end for me and my family."

One by one, the Captains of the four armies agreed to meet, and discuss how the vineyard owner should be paid, for they all knew that without wine, their troops would soon mutiny. The wise owner invites them into his home, offering each bread and oil, along with the best of his wine. Knowing the power of wine to help men talk, he guided the conversation to their own families, and how they must miss them.

One by one they spoke of their wives, their families, their home, and one by one each saw that the other Captain was just a man doing their job. When the Owner saw they had understood each other's hearts, he asked, "So why do your Kings not meet like this and enjoy fellowship? Are they not brothers? What is the argument that caused this war?"

One by one, the Captains admitted they did not know what the war was about, why they fought, or why their Kings did not get along. "Well then, perhaps you should invite them here, to meet my family, to have some wine, for surely I will not be paid unless there is some sort of agreement amongst you all, and after all, I am not part of your argument."

One by one, the Captains all agreed that this was indeed an excellent idea and that they would ask their King to come and meet at the vineyard as they had, and they all left best of friends, having enjoyed each other's company now that they understood the heart of their fellow soldiers.

The Kings were, of course, very confused. The war appeared to have stopped and they wondered why. This was when each of their captains explained that they believed the Kings should talk to each other, and at the very least, decide what this war was about. Well, of course, the four kings were brothers and they were arguing over the right to rule all of the lands held by their father before he died, and what could meeting a vineyard owner do to solve their problems? Nothing, they decided, but when they asked their Captains to start the war again, they shrugged their shoulders and explained that all their men had a family, friends, a house that needed caring for, and that before they would go back to fighting, they had to know what they were fighting for.

The Kings wanted to cut the heads off their Captains, but realized the soldiers would desert if they did. Far worse, now that the fighting had stopped all had their hands out for wages, as they had agreed to be paid at the end of the war. This was a quandary, and the four brothers agreed, they had to meet and resolve the problem of no one fighting their war.

Now, of course, each intended to kill the others and solve the problem that way, which was the real reason they agreed to the meeting. Each had a poison in their robes, which they intended to slip into the drink of their brothers when they had a chance. And so it was that the royal carriages all turn up to the vineyard, and were greeted by the owner, who thanked them for coming.

One by one they came into the room, which had no great table, just six lounges in the Roman fashion with a small table for their wine. Each were invited to sit at whatever one they chose, but not the richly decorated one clad in purple velvet. The Kings all laughed to themselves, knowing that the owner was putting himself above them, and that he intended to lord it over them by sitting in the best chair. Each in their hearts knew that when they won, because of his arrogance, this vineyard owner would die soon after.

The couches were all equally placed, in a circle facing each other, and all the same, except for the richly brocaded one they were not allowed to sit in. Grumbling about this inconvenience, each King chose a chair and glared at their brothers as they did the same. There was only silence in the room until the wise owner of the vineyard came in, but to their surprise, he did not sit on the expensive lounge but sat on one the same as their own.

He brought with him the finest of wine from his vineyard and offered the kings a fine silver cup, but on a small table before the richly decorated lounge, his servants placed a gold cup set with jewels. And now they began to wonder, was there some other King who wanted their lands? Was this a trap? They started planning on slipping their poison into the gold cup, and worried less about their brothers, who they could deal with later.

The vineyard owner began the proceedings by asking each of the Kings about their families. This they were happy to talk about, for they all had beautiful wives, cherished children, and a fine castle. And as they talked, each remembered the invitation they had gotten to their brothers' weddings, and the gifts they had given. One King, the oldest of the brothers, asked, "Those fine glass goblets I brought to your wedding, where are they now?

"Ah, brother, they have pride of place at my table and are only used when an honored guest arrives. But brother, the silverware I brought to your wedding, where is that now?"

The oldest smiled, "Truly, those were a fine gift. I keep them for special occasions for when my closest friends come to visit." And so each asked of the other of the gifts they had given over the years, almost forgetting that the fifth king had not yet arrived. They started to talk, remembering the times they had growing up, the pranks they pulled, the mother that loved them all, and they grew close once more. But still, that fifth King, where was he?

One of the brothers asked their host, "This mysterious fifth King, tell us about him, and why he is given pride of place amongst us?"

"Ah," the vineyard owner exclaimed, "that King as you can see is far greater than all of us. His Kingdom is enormous, his wealth unimaginable, and his power is beyond belief. His ships cast nets that

catch whales. His fruit trees bear pomegranates so huge it takes four men to carry a single one. His vineyards produce wine that makes the heart sing with joy. His grain fields are so rich they produce bread that a single slice will suffice a man for a week. I cannot speak enough praise of his power and majesty, for my hollow words are nothing compared to his wisdom and purity."

The four brothers are now confused, who could this be? And why was he here, if not to take all their lands and leave them as beggars? And they pretended to get up to embrace the other, each meeting in the middle of the room, whispering, "We are under threat brothers, this great King wants our lands! What can we do?"

Finally, after much discussion of how they might join forces, the oldest asked the owner of the vineyard, "And, ah, when does this King arrive?"

"Very soon," the owner of the vineyard explained, smiling warmly. "He was very keen to meet you all, for he knew your father."

This confused the brothers even more, and they all agreed that they had to leave before this King arrived for surely he would imprison them, and take their lands. "Well, we would love to meet him, but in the time we have been here we have mended our hearts and come to love each other once more, so our war is ended. Please explain to this King when he arrives that we are all unified in love and respect." For in this way, they hoped to put him off invading them, thinking he met a unified force, rather than armies weakened by war.

"I will explain this to him, my Kings. Thank you for coming."

As the Kings left in their fine carriages, his master of the vines came up and asked what had happened. The wise owner of the vineyard laughed, saying, "Fear of the Lord has brought peace to our lands."

The disciples loved this tale and laughed, but Simon creased his brow, "But surely the Kings were not fooled by this trick, and went to war again when they realized no great king was coming?"

Peter went to tell his younger brother to be quiet, but Yeshua held up his hand. This young one was closer to his heart than most. "So you think their fear of the greater King is what caused them to end their war?"

Simon looks at the master, "Well, that was what the story said, didn't it? I mean, we all get that the brocaded lounge was for the Lord, but brothers will fight as brothers do, and they will soon forget the lesson given by the vineyard owner."

"Do you still fight with your brother here?" Yeshua asked.

"Well, no," Simon was now feeling nervous, thinking he had overstepped some boundary.

"Why not, as you say, brothers fight as they do."

"Respect for your presence, master. I have no wish to fight with my brother for here there is only love."

Yeshua laughed, "You speak the truth, Simon. I say to you, those who are earnest and truthful in their dealings with others have no reason to fear judgment. The true problem was that the Kings had forgotten to respect each other. When they discovered respect they discovered love."

This simple message struck to the heart of all present and they were silent for a time, until Peter laughed, "Do you remember when you were pestering me over something you wanted and went on and on until I put your head under water and held you there till you tapped that you gave up?"

Simon laughed, "Yes, you were truly horrible to me."

Peter also laughed, "Well, I am sorry, but you did deserve it."

Simon looked up, saying, "You never laughed when I was growing up, Peter. You were always so serious. I had also heard tales of my father, and how harsh he was. I came to believe this is what made a man a man, and felt that happiness and laughter were a weakness. Life was a grey cloud for me until I saw you with Yeshua. It was the joy in your heart that led me here, brother, for now I saw a life worth living."

They went out to the moonlight together and spoke of the old times they shared, the things they thought, and the people they knew. There would be no war between them ever again.

The lake at Capernaum lapped the shore, singing the ancient song of peace to the night sky, welcoming the tides, the wind, and the echoing sounds of the night creatures to come and take what they needed from its depths.

Great multitudes followed Him – from Galilee, and from Decapolis, Jerusalem, Judea, and beyond the Jordan.

Matthew 4:25 NKJV

Healing the Soul

The men had made their way to the healing baths at Bethsaida, below the town where the river passed through. Yeshua regularly went there, teaching the people knowledge of herbs and cleansing of the body both within and without, he caring for the men, and Mary the Magdalene caring for the women.

With him were certain gourds that he filled with water and salts of various types. These were used in a manner the disciples at first found extraordinary and humorous, for he would take those suffering from particular diseases and tie them to a ladder strung between trees near the river bank. Then he would place the person on the ladder and invert them so that their hands touched the ground, but with feet tied in, they did not fall.

This is when the gourds were used to pour the salted waters into the poor soul via the passage normally used for the removal of waste. Then they would be tipped back up, and a gushing of foul fluid would come from them. This the master would often do three or more times, explaining that poison had been trapped within the body and needed to be washed out, "Just as you bathe to clean the outer body and purify it, so too must we bathe the inner body to purify it," he explained to the dubious patients.

Once the people saw how many began to be free of ailments, they came in great numbers to be washed clean. In a tented area not far away, Mary was doing the same. To her cleaved many of the wives of disciples and other women interested in healing, and to them she explained in more detail that worms and other creatures of evil can enter the body, and this was one way to flush them away. They both instructed the people in the cleansing herbs and the use of vinegars to clear the poisons and parasites of the body.

Many were also cured of blindness and praised the healing power of the Lord that came with these remarkable souls. And for those that needed healing of the Spirit, the disciples would take to the waters of the Jordan and baptize them to clear the sin from their hearts. But Peter noted not all were cleansed or made pure, and on this day when they had finished their business and were sailing back to Capernaum, he asked, "Master, what of those we could not help?"

Yeshua nodded, "Not all are ready, Peter. The reasons are many, but mostly it is the pictures locked in their minds that whisper to them they are unworthy. We can do much to alleviate suffering, but if a person is poisoned in spirit, they will call back that suffering no matter what another might do."

He paused, wondering if they were ready. "As you have seen, many times when I turn a person upside down, I will tap the Occipital and other areas of their spine. This is to release tension that has caught up there, and if that tension is created through misfortune or accident, then the body will release it. But if the tension is of the mind, if deep fears and doubts lurk in the heart, then it will return."

"The reason for this is clear, for no child has this concern. It is what we are taught, by family or society, and usually, it is a teaching of unworthiness. But also I say to you, some are controlled by a deeper malevolence, a wickedness. Many are but puppets under the control of a person in their household, or by a priest in their synagogue. They live in fear and fear is the doorway that allows in devils from the desert that poison the well of their being."

"Is there no cure for such things, Master?" Asked young Andrew. Still a boy in many ways, he soaked up all the master offered like a sponge.

"There is, but it will surprise you. Curiosity, such as you find in an ordinary cat, draws the spirit of adventure and this spirit can break all bonds wrapped around one person by another. This curiosity can come in the form of wondering what is in the next town or wondering if that girl might love you or being fascinated by some piece of scripture.

"Fascination with a thing outside yourself can lead you away from your problems and into a healing of the spirit and a repair of the breach that has broken your connection with the Lord."

Yeshua did not say it, but all those with him had started breaking with their past by using this power. "Curiosity will cause you to stand outside of your present beliefs, your traditions, which is what allows the light of the Lord to enter your heart. Curiosity is the easiest way to find truth."

Peter joked, "So be like little kittens, then?"

The men laughed, as did Yeshua. *"There was a man,"* he started with a story, causing them all to hush, *"a man of means. He had everything you could desire, a good wife, happy children, a fine house, and a healthy herd of sheep, but he felt something was missing. He did not know what, but every morning the feeling became stronger - something was missing!*

"He started looking behind doors, under carpets, in cupboards, but there was nothing. He went out and looked in forests, under stones,

behind barns, but nothing. His wife thought he must have gone mad, and ridiculed this strange person she met every day, but he paid her no heed. Instead, he would look under the plate his food was served on, inside the cup his wine was poured, something was missing.

"And then one day while he was out, he saw a fair maiden washing her hair in the river. His heart leaped, for in his joy he saw this is what was missing, and yet he felt such shame that it might be so. He said to himself, 'I have a good wife, a happy family, I should not even have eyes for anything but them!' yet his heart pulled him to the beautiful creature washing her hair, singing a lovely song, and being so carefree he felt his heart soar just listening to her.

"He wanted to go speak to her, to tell her of the joy she brought his heart, but he could not move. If he stepped forward, he was betraying all he had worked for and earned in this life. If he did not step forward he was betraying the pure joy his heart had finally found. This was a thing he could not go past, and so he stayed there, locked and frozen in limbo until he turned into a rock.

"His wife in due course wondered where her foolish husband had gone, but no matter how much she looked, she did not find him. 'That foolish man, looking for something he could never find!' she muttered to herself, as she herself spent all her days looking for something she could never find."

The men looked puzzled, but not Peter. He knew in his heart the master spoke of himself. "Was he cursed to remain a rock, then?" he asked.

"Well, so it would seem," said Yeshua, "but as it turns out that beautiful woman that sang like an angel WAS an angel. She took pity on that poor rock, and with tools of song and beauty, she sang to it night and day, and slowly the rock softened and took the form of a man once more."

"And did he go back to his wife?" asked the fisherman.

"Well, these things remain to be seen," laughed the master. "But healing takes many forms, and time takes its time. Who knows what will grow from the soil, but surely we know that when the seed within it is true, all that comes from it must also be true."

Soon they would be leaving Capernaum and traveling to the villages and regions away from the Jordan and Galilee. Mary had been assiduously gathering in the herbs and potions they would need to help the people, taking from their gardens and the gardens of the other Essenes. That night as they lay in the moonlight that shone into their room, she asked him, "Husband, how long does this last?"

At first, he said nothing. For many long minutes he contemplated, letting his spirit fly into the region of the future. "The hour is not close, beloved. Rest easy, but wheels turn within wheels, the wheat is being ground and refined as we speak."

"I know, husband, that your journey is to heal the soul and repair the breach between man and the Lord, but what about the women? How long must they be subject to the whim of their husband?"

He laughed and tickled her, and she fell back on the bed, laughing, "And so you accuse me of controlling you? I could only wish that were true!"

"You know what I mean," she said, kissing him gently.

"I do understand, my love. The woman will always be the light that draws the man to the Lord and if she is imprisoned, so is her man. As you speak with them and open their hearts they shine, but the darkness over their husband's heart does not want this light. No matter what we do, say, or give, this will not change. But as the tide lifts one boat, it lifts all, so we must be the incoming tide of goodwill and peace, and trust that the Lord will lift all who are not tied to the shore."

They rested in each other's arms as the moon came over the sea below them. It was a picture of peace and harmony. Mary spoke after some time, "You know what I like about you, Yeshua?"

"My incredible wealth?" he joked.

She laughed, "Obviously that, but of far more value to me, more than any spiritual or worldly wealth you bring to our table, you listen with your heart to what I say. No woman could want for more."

She snuggled in to her man, feeling the comfort and warmth of his heart beat as she placed her cheek on his chest. She felt a small chuckle, "What do you find so funny, husband?"

Yeshua gave a small sigh, "You know, when we were children I was horribly in love with you. You cannot imagine the joy I felt when our parents agreed to our union, what, we were six or seven years?"

"You were six, I was seven," Mary said. "So are you saying you are no longer horribly in love with me?" She poked his ribs.

"Ow! No, I do NOT love a rib poker, and you have always been a rib poker." He laughed as he saw her eyes squint, the punch was next. "But no my love, I am no longer IN love with you. Being in love is a dream, a lovely dream, but it is lacks substance and floats away on the changing tide. What I have is a permanent truth. You are the star in my sky, and the cup of my heart is full to the brim with your light…"

She punched him, but smiled. That was sufficient.

The Wild Bird

The birds flew past, chirping as they stopped by a tree to watch the small band. One came down for crumbs that had fallen to the ground, nervously approaching the place where humans sat, it quickly took the offering and flew back to the tree. The owner of the house where they sat also had a bird, a parrot that would sit on his shoulder and say the word, "Welcome!" to you if you gave it a crumb.

Mathew joked, "Do you suppose the wild birds are jealous of this tame one? Or is it the other way round?"

Yeshua said nothing and just held out his hand with a crumb on it, and closed his eyes in praise of the Lord. A small baby bird must have mistaken his arm for the branch of a tree for it alighted there, and took the crumb. It sat for a moment, looking at those watching it on the table, and those watching it from the tree. It hopped off soon enough and went back to its fellows.

The teacher was not there, he had left, to a time and place far away. He was at the cave of the mad woman, the one so many of the children feared for she had a sharp beak into their business and would pry at their thoughts. She was a wise woman, an oracle, beaten and abused in her youth for she had no family to protect her.

Like John, she had spent much time in the wilderness but unlike him, she had made a home on the Qumran, where she was accepted for what she was, and cared for. It didn't stop her speaking out against the evil she saw in a person's soul, for gratitude was not her gift, nor happiness her reward. Instead, she was a wild bird that the other birds knew and loved. They came to her cave docile as the parrot on their host's shoulder.

She was his first lesson in love. He took up food and drink to her every day, at his mother's insistence. She never said thank you, just looked at him. He would go back and ask why his mother remained so kind to such an ungrateful soul, and she would smile, saying, "We who have nothing can only follow the voice of the Lord". It took him many years to understand - his mother was not just saying SHE followed the voice, but that the mad woman did as well.

Their host was beaming, he was proud to have such a teacher in his house, and begged for a story that this prophet was so famous for. Yeshua looked at the man, not with unkind eyes, but with clarity. "The bird on your shoulder, have you clipped his wing?"

"Of course," the host was a little puzzled.

"Then he must still yearn for freedom, is this why?"

"Ah, no - but birds will fly off, and he may become lost."

"And what then?

The host is truly confused, he had expected a story not an inquisition. "Is this the story?"

"I say to you, the Lord cares not if you come to him wild, or tamed. If you are happy or sad, rich or poor, generous or selfish, fat or thin, brave or fearful, none of this matters to the Lord. He will receive all who come, whether it is for the spiritual food he offers, or the wisdom they wish to take, or the possibilities his power might give. The Lord accepts all who come to him with the same welcome, but only those pure of heart find sustenance at his table. Only those without judgment find freedom in his heart. Only those who have suffered find solace at his door.

"The rest are like crows in the market, arguing over scraps, pushing aside others to get what they need. Yet the Lord welcomes those as he does all birds that fly and all fish that swim. All of his creation is welcomed when they return. But only a few stay."

"I knew a woman, rejected by society, beaten and abused. She lived in a cave and my mother bade me feed her. She never said thank you, never one word of gratitude came from her lips, yet the wild birds would flock to her presence. Often she was feeding them the very food my mother have given her, but when I complained, my mother just smiled. One day she said to me the words that opened my heart and allowed me to see the mad woman with the eyes of the Lord. She said: *A wild bird with a wing so clipped that it is broken does not know how to say thank you, but if she doesn't bite you, that IS her thanks.*"

The birds around them seemed to sing more loudly as if rejoicing in the words. Yeshua did not then offer thanks to the master of the house for his hospitality, instead, he got up and left with no further word. Peter nodded his thanks, and the others stood and followed, leaving the man in shock as to what had happened.

It was some time before Yeshua spoke, "The Lord receives all. He asks not for thanks, expects no words of wisdom, nor wishes for you to bow before him. Many come and go at his door, like wild birds feeding on scraps." He paused to look at each and every one of them, "But I say to you, be warned, for if you give all of your heart to the Lord, all of your Soul, he will consume it in fire and fury. The Lord will eat all your impurity, all your sin, all your misgiving, all your fear, leaving only the pure bones of his creation behind."

He walked quickly off up to the mountain, and the disciples knew not to follow. One of the followers half-joked, "Doesn't seem to make the effort all that worthwhile!"

The others looked at him, "What?" he demanded. "Let's face it if you take the words as spoken, we are mad to be following him. Yeshua was so rude to that poor man, and that sort of thing can lead to a lot fewer invitations!"

Finally, the light of understanding lit up Peter's heart, "I get it now, the man wanted to trade his hospitality for a good story. So Yeshua gave him a story, but no thanks, for this is not what the bargain was." He laughs out loud, "I felt so bad just walking out. I so much wanted to say something, to apologize for the master's rudeness, but that was what the story was about! He had served a mad woman through his childhood with no word of thanks. That man should have been grateful he didn't do a Baptist on him, and plunge him underwater demanding he repent his sins."

The disciples laughed, however, that one disciple who spoke did not. He had judged Yeshua as unworthy, and presumed Peter was justifying his faith, in order to keep everyone there. That man left that day, never to return. In this way, he fulfilled the truth of the story.

ooo0000ooo

It was around this time that one called Judas Iscariot arrived. He was a Zealot, working for the underground, with a keen desire to rid Judea of the Roman presence. It was during the second Passover of Yeshua's mission that he came to the household of James, asking about this so-called Messiah. James had laughed and sent him out to the kitchen, saying the disciples were preparing food for the evening, and that he should go talk to them.

He did and he found the followers of the prophet around a very large preparation table in the kitchen at the back of the house. But no lamb did he find, "Where is your sacrificial lamb?" he asked.

Simon explained, "Our master does not touch the flesh of a dead animal, he is an Essene. Nor does he sacrifice creatures to the Lord."

"But this is against the law? Why do the Pharisee not bring him to trial?" Judas was astonished. This was a blatant breach of a household obligation at the most crucial time of the year.

Mathew laughed, "Brother, I say to you that the Pharisee appear to like Yeshua. You heard how he whipped the money changers out of the temple last year, yes? Well, that appeared to make Nicodemus happy, but apart from that, Yeshua is Essene, and their tradition is different from ours. He eats no flesh, he drinks no fermented wine, and believes all of us are the children of the Lord. In deference to his beliefs, this is a thing we mostly follow, though I have seen a few sneak out and grab a bit of lamb now and then!" the others laughed, for it was true.

"Why do you follow him, because he is as the Baptist claimed, the Messiah?"

Peter looked at the others, "I and several here were disciples of John. It is true, he said Yeshua was the new Messiah, but this is not why I follow him. His words touch my heart, but this is not why I follow him. His miracles are everywhere he goes, but this is not why I follow him."

Judas snorted, "Well, then why do you follow him?"

Peter laughed, "Because the Lord in my heart told me this is the one, and because I have no heart to be anywhere else but here."

Iscariot was a follower of Barabas, the rebel that struck against Rome and caused much strife to those who aided Romans. "My master and teacher is Barabas. He has no miracles other than he has avoided capture all these years. He says the Messiah that comes will rid Judea of her enemies, and he was a great admirer of your Baptist."

Thomas, the one who rarely spoke, said but few words, "It is easy to follow a dead man's path, we all go to the grave in time."

"The people say your man is the Messiah. Is this true? Is he the one who will rid us of Rome and bring about peace?" Judas demanded.

At this point, Yeshua walked in to see how preparations were going. He looked over to Judas, smiled as he would, but said nothing. Judas did not know what to say, or what to do. He felt a lightness enter his heart, a gladness he had not known before. This man's smile lit up his world, and he knew not why. "Who are you, are you the Messiah?"

Yeshua laughed, "Everyone is a child of the Lord, Judas Iscariot, follower of Barabas. Even the Romans you so hate are the Lord's children. So tell me, what would you do with a misbehaving child, if you were the Lord?"

The words were so simple, he should have laughed at the stupidity of it, but he couldn't. The sense of it was too terrible, too clear. "I would beat them till they behaved," he said, feeling he got his point across.

"And what if that child were a Roman who cleaned your house, set your dinner, and washed your clothes? Would you beat him then?"

Judas snorted, "Of course not, but the Romans here are hardly like this!"

"Are they not?" Yeshua asked. "Surely some Romans are good and obedient children, else they have a Lord called an Emperor who would beat them, and cast them out of his house."

Judas seemed very confused by this strange man. He had presumed everyone hated the Romans, surely all the people he knew hated them. "Are you saying you are happy for the Romans to be here?"

Yeshua responded with a question, "Are you saying the Lord did not put them here? For if he didn't then I would object strongly, but I am not so certain this is the case."

The mind of this new fellow was spinning. This upended everything he had ever believed, his whole reason for existence had been to rid Judea of the evil that had come into her midst. Yeshua smiled and continued. "Or are you saying you would prefer the Sadducee to be running things? You are a Zealot, yes? Then you must have seen how Pilate has stopped them killing your people for breaching the laws that the Sadducee have set against you, yes?"

Judas stammered, "Well, this is true. The Sadducee are indeed as bad as the Roman, and we would better off being rid of them as well."

"Then why do you follow a man who is paid by these same priests?" The look of confusion on the face of the fellow was obvious, Yeshua softened, "Sit with us, Judas Iscariot, Zealot, hater of Rome. Share bread and ease your heart.

It was then it occurred to Judas, "How do you know my name?"

Yeshua said softly, "You do not remember speaking with me in your dreams? I know you Judas Iscariot, but it seems you do not know me."

This shocked the doubter greatly. Judas did not understand why tears were flowing from his eyes. Yes, he had dreams with this man, but they were just dreams. Yes, he had followed him around, with the crowds, and listened to what he had to say, but these were just dreams. It was why he came, to understand why he kept having these strange and unwelcome dreams. But this man knew things he had said to no one, the type of dreams he had. Perhaps there was truth to him being the Messiah? He stayed, and he listened.

It was not long before the master spoke, "My father made this table, you know. It was much larger than any other preparation table, and he was asked why. I was with him at the time he bought this house, and he said: *Many will come to this place needing rest and respite. This is to be a home for the Essene here in Jerusalem, for they can now come to Passover knowing there is a house that respects their ways*."

The clatter of tools as vegetables were cut, and the smell of bread baking, it was comforting and friendly. But Judas was puzzled, "You have no women doing this work, how is this so? And I see your men carry water to and from the household?"

Yeshua smiled that smile of understanding, "In the Essene tradition, men do the work of the women. Many of my people are unmarried and so we have different ways of doing things. Just as our Passover is not the same as with the other Jews, our customs also differ."

"Does everyone who follows you have to convert to become an Essene then?" Judas was finding all this difference to be getting under his skin.

Peter laughed, "I am a fisherman without a fish, what teaching do I belong to?"

Despite his confusion, his lack of understanding, and the strangeness of these people, Judas stayed and found great peace in that household. The calm tide of brotherhood seeped into his soul, settling his anger and soothing his outraged heart. He stayed for their Passover, and the next day he stayed as well, and the next. It was not just the kindness of these people, not just their open acceptance, but the words Yeshua had mentioned in passing that the Sadducee funded Barabas.

That seemed crazy, Barabas used to laugh at the stupidity of the priests, openly saying they were the next on the block after the Romans. All knew Barabas was a great man, his words inspired many, but he was not kind nor caring. Judas stayed to know more of this brotherhood, plus they fed him! This meant he no longer had to risk his life on the streets, watching out for Romans chasing his former master.

Georg Lechner as Judas in the Oberammgau Passion Play

Walking in the Dream

Peter had a good haul of fish that day, soon they were leaving Capernaum, and before he sold the boat, he was trying to bring in as deep a reserve of funds as he could, so he was out fishing most days while the brothers sat at the feet of the master. He had no regret, they needed their time and he had already been given so much by Yeshua.

They had just returned from the second Passover in Jerusalem and had been joined by the new fellow who was so good with money and organization. He was no great fan of this Judas, but he had to admit, when it came to planning and getting everything sorted to go on a healing and teaching circuit, he was brilliant. The donkeys were packed, the food organized, grains made ready for baking, and the whole show ran like clockwork.

And a good thing, as well, for larger and larger crowds were turning up to hear the words of the Master. The program was simple, go to the local synagogue, read from the scriptures, then teach what they meant. "Uniting the Peshar and the Raz," the Master always said. From here the afflicted would ask for healing, and with the miracles the crowds grew.

As always, the master decried any claims of his divinity, saying he was but the messenger for the word of the Lord, but everyone knew that without him about the miracles weren't happening. Now it was time to go, for it was not just friendly faces who turned up now, but angry ones, demanding to know about some imagined breach of a law, or if this Yeshua was a false prophet

He felt sad, leaving this place that had seen so much harmony and contentment. All they had to do was what they had always done, take out the boat, sell the fish, then come home to the brothers and listen to what the master had to say that night. However, too many strangers were turning up out of the blue now, asking odd questions, testing this so-called Messiah. Yeshua said it was time to move, they needed to reach more people, to give them the light and love of the Lord.

The master had said all the trouble was coming from the priests, for they had not forgiven him for beating the cattle and disturbing the money changers, and that they needed to get moving. Peter sighed, he had been working long hours with the men and would have far preferred to stay by the sea, but it must be what it must be.

The fellows on the boat were all followers and had been working hard. All were tired, exhausted, and now that the day was almost done, he set course for Tiberias to get his catch to market. The day was warm, even in its closing, and as he set the sails he felt a deep tiredness. Tying off the rudder, he lay beside it and closed his eyes, as had all the others on board.

It must have been soon after that the huge storm arose, lightning and thunder roaring and crashing about them, charging the water with threat and danger. He awoke to find it dark, how could this be? And he woke to find the seas surging over the gunwales and crashing onto the deck. The boat was being twisted, up and down, and turned around by the rough seas.

Once more he was back as a youth, fighting that storm that killed his father and his older brothers. Fear seeped in, was it all to end so soon? He had only just found peace and happiness with the master, and even his wife was less bitter when he dropped in to give her some fish or coin. She almost was pleasant to him! Things had finally come good in his life, but he knew what sort of storms these were, places people died, and where ships were destroyed.

"Yeshua," he called out to the storm, "I am sorry, but it seems we will not have the funds from the sale of this boat as I had expected! I did not mean to fail you."

But then the tumult ceased, and across the water coming from Tiberias his master was walking, with a huge smile on his face, saying, "At the time you thought death had come to take you, you called my name, Peter. This is why you shall have eternal life."

And Peter woke with a start, to feel his boat bumping against the very wharf he had intended to sail to, with the merchant there laughing as he tied it off, seeing all the men waking from their slumber, "By the Gods, Peter, your boat knows these waters so well it sails itself to the dock!"

Peter smiled, how times had changed, now his main merchant was a Greek! His father would have died all over again if he knew. But what was that strange dream? As the men woke, they all laughed, all saying how they were in a huge storm, but that the Master had walked out to save them, then woke to find themselves at the dock!

They were amazed that they all had the same dream, and saw this as further proof of the divinity of their master. But Peter was starting to grow a little wisdom, and he knew: this was more than a dream, it was a premonition of what was to come.

Inheritance

The way they walked wove wound round the slopes, passing vineyards and houses that dressed the landscape in a pleasing order. The master was spending time with Luke, who had seemed perplexed about a matter of inheritance but he had not wanted to ask, for such things were below the spiritual perfection of Yeshua, or so he thought.

"Greed," said the master as they strolled aimlessly through the gardens, "is when a man has an orchard but wants all the fruit for himself. He will not share it with the birds, who he rushes out to attack should they land nearby. He will not share it with the neighbor unless the man makes a bargain that is to his advantage. And when the Aedile comes for tax, he will point to the trees and say it is a woe, but they produced nothing, and he has no tax to give - while he has bushels of fruit hiding in his basement. What do you imagine the opposite of greed might be?"

Luke understood well what Yeshua spoke of, he had dealt with it for many years as a man who assisted the Aedile, recording the worth of the individual farmers in his area. "You would imagine it is sharing, but I am guessing I am going to be surprised."

"Greed is building a wall for fear of what will be stolen from you, but surely this is not foolish, for men do steal from each other, for the heart of so many is ruled by greed. True greed is closing your eyes to the suffering of your neighbor, shutting your ears to his pleas for mercy, and barring your door to the Angel of Kindness. But what can cure a man of these evils?" Yeshua asked.

Luke started to get the notion this was about the problem he had not spoken of, his family that was at each other's throats for a better part of the inheritance from his father. A light dawned on him, "Agreement, Master. Finding harmony, finding a point where people can accept their lot."

"But this goes against the greedy heart," Yeshua said.

"This is why we have laws, to sort out the fair sharing of goods, is this what you mean?"

"Well, in an ideal world, but surely our laws do more to support the greed than cure it. The principle of law is that a man is expected to protect his own, and is that not the seed from which greed springs?"

"This is true, Yeshua. I suppose you might be talking about the Qumran, where everything is shared, where the law permits no ownership. Is poverty the cure for Greed, then?" Luke is perplexed. One generally presumed there was no cure for Greed, as it was such an ingrained thing in people.

"Do the people of the Qumran look poor?" Yeshua asked.

Luke had to admit, it was the opposite. They were well-fed, content, and happy with almost no argument from what he saw when traveling through with the Aedile. "They share everything, is this then the cure for Greed?"

"Surely a greedy man will just take from his neighbors, with no thought of fairness. Sharing would only feed such a one, surely?" The Master was almost laughing now at the confused face of his disciple.

"Master, I have no idea. That is my problem, how do I deal with greed?" Luke confessed what was in his heart, for he felt the need to protect his portion of his father's inheritance, for the sake of his family. But this meant putting himself against his brothers, a thing he found ugly and cruel, the opposite of what the master taught.

"Then perhaps we should ask in what story does a greedy man share? In what situation will he give freely, with no thought of what he must hold?"

Luke thought of his most avaricious youngest brother, the one who stood to get the least, and who protested the loudest. He had been to his house and seen how the fellow's heart softened when his daughter walked in. She was all of four years and he was helpless before her smile. "Little children have no thought of greed, they just want food and affection."

"NOW we come closer to the truth, for no man is born with greed. They have picked it up along the way, so surely now you have the answer?"

Luke heard it in his heart, "Let go!" the voice said. He sat with that thought as the sun beamed down, as the workers moved through the vineyards, as the clouds moved past. He knew then, in his own heart that sharp taste of greed lurked, let it go. He knew that in the hearts of his brothers, they did not see their demands as greed, but as fairness. Let it go. He saw the whole picture, how there was enough for all, let it go.

"You are saying I have to let it all go? How does this help my family?"

Yeshua laughed, "Luke, you let it go, and you give the matter to your solicitor. Losing your family over money is far worse than losing money, but this is because you are holding on to the problem. Let it go, give it to someone who understands and deals with these things. There is no answer to Greed, other than everything we have said. You need agreement, you need fairness, you need a heart open to sharing, but most of all you need to let it go. Greed is a poison that kills the heart of all who touch it, so let it go, free your heart, free yourself from its grasp."

The disciple almost had to laugh, it was so incredibly simple, he already had a solicitor who was looking after the matter. "I see it, master. I have hired a guard dog, but I am the one at the gate barking. I see it now."

And his heart felt the burden lift. And then he saw it, the cure for Greed, "It is trust!" he exclaimed.

The master nodded, "It is trust, Luke. In the Lord, in yourself, and in those you employ." There was a long pause as they walked, then the master added, "The spiritual solutions to the problems of our life do not come on the wings of angels, but the wings of angels come when we lay down our problems and offer them to the Lord."

This eased the heart of his disciple, for he saw that his lawyer must be trusted to deal with the matter. He must not carry the burden, not involve himself in the argument. It was only money, but he had hoped to use it to buy a house that would secure his old age.

To such a thought as he heard the master saying, almost to himself, "Foxes have holes, and birds of the air have nests; but the son of man has nowhere to lay his head."

Luke wondered at such a thought as they wandered slowly back to the house. Soon he knew they would be leaving, perhaps this is what Yeshua was talking about, no longer having a home base.

They walked towards the Capernaum house and found some of the others at work in the gardens, being ordered about by Mary, which made Yeshua laugh. "You see, Luke? Here they are hard at work harvesting our inheritance from the Summer. Our lady of the sun has graced us with warmth and rain enough to bless the vines and the soil with bounty. So too, our true nature needs no determination of this much or that much, of who is right and deserving or otherwise, for we live in the inheritance of the Lord, and upon us is bequeathed a wealth so great a thousand men would struggle to carry it.

"No, our laws are in place for the unwilling hearts, the unkind soul, and the foolish dreamer. The one who is industrious in the harvest of what the Lord brings is free of such things, for their action becomes their law. All actions that serve the many are free from the law, for by their intention they become consecrated to the Lord." Yeshua went in and helped the others with the harvest, as did Luke.

He still had questions running through his thoughts, yes, it made sense to put the matter to his lawyer, but why did it become necessary in the first place? "Master, what is the font of trouble in this world?"

Yeshua looked up and smiled, "Such an odd question from a man harvesting beans!" he joked. This made the others laugh, but it also brought their attention to his words. "Truly we might wonder in the darkness: Why has this trial been brought to me? Why must I bear it? Why has the Lord made me suffer? Yet in truth, most trouble we bear does not come from the Lord, but is created by ourselves, and by the walls we have put up against his presence. A story?"

They all cheered.

There was a man, a humble servant, who wished to further his part in life. He harvested the vines in the vineyard of a wealthy man, but the work was hard and his back sore, so he asked if he might learn how to press the grapes, which the Lord permitted. And so he happily drew the raw juices from the grapes, but still he was curious and asked if he might go further, and learn how to ferment their goodness into wine. Again, his Lord permitted this, and he spent many years in service of the wine master, learning his trade.

Then fate dealt him a blow, for a great drought came, driving all the local farms into hardship. The Lord who owned the vineyard fell into hard times and had to sell the lands to a merchant in town. The merchant had taken over many of the properties in the area and could hardly see the need for two wine masters, so the youngest was cast out. And in this way, our humble, obedient servant, who only sought to improve his lot, found himself in the dust outside the vineyard where he had worked his whole life. "Woe to me," he said to the heavens, "that I thought to become more than my lot. If I had stayed a humble picker I would still have employment and a place to live!"

And so he wandered, a beggar looking for scraps.

There the story appeared to end, which struck the disciples as strange.

Peter was very used to not understanding what Yeshua meant with his stories, but this one seemed to miss the mark. "Surely, now he had greater skills, he could have found employment elsewhere? It doesn't make sense he would become a beggar." The others had a nodding agreement with Peter, that he became a beggar seemed foolish.

Yeshua smiled for they had fallen into hands. "So you say, but rather than claim nonsense, why not ask what sense brought him to become a beggar?"

Peter paused, knowing he had been tricked, but not knowing quite how. "He didn't appreciate what he had been given, is that it?"

Yeshua said nothing.

"Maybe he was at heart lazy, this was why he wanted promotion, to get out of hard work?" said Simon.

Yeshua said nothing.

"Perhaps the Lord wanted him to become humble once more, perhaps he had developed too much pride?" John suggested.

Yeshua said nothing.

It was Thomas that laughed, saying, "Or maybe this is not the end of the tale?"

Yeshua smiled, and continued.

And so it was that the man who had taught him all he knew of wine making saw his student in the streets, begging for bread, and felt a great sympathy for him. He took him home, fed him, washed him, and gave him fresh clothes, then instructed his wife to care for him. For in his time teaching this fellow, he had come to think of the servant as his son.

And at first, the man was grateful. To show his gratitude he performed tasks around the house that the old man could no longer do. He repaired their roof, tilled their garden, cleared out the weeds, all things a good son would have done, and for a time all were happy. But then he got to thinking, for his skills as a winemaker truly exceeded that of the old man, and surely he should have been kept on, while this man who had so much could have retired.

After all, he was well provisioned, had a caring wife, and a happy home. It was no loss for the man to live there, and leave the servant he allowed to be cast out to do his work, so he suggested this to the old man one evening when they sat for supper. "Master," he said, "Let me bear the burden of your work for you. Allow me to care for you both, as repayment for all the kindness you have shown me."

"Thank you, my boy," the old man replied. "But though he is not here, I have my son who will follow after me. He lives many miles from here in another of the vineyards owned by our former master, and which the merchant also owns. He has said to me that while my position is secure, he expected my son will be able to carry on the task at both of the vineyards when it is time for my retirement. So while I find your offer appealing, it would not work for this reason."

And with this, the old man thought the matter settled. But it was not settled in the heart of the humble servant. In there bitterness began to take root, how he did all the work of the son, but received none of the payment. Why should he harvest their vegetables and fruits? Why should he repair their house? The old man's wife was no fool, and she noted the change in his attitude, and at length, she spoke to her husband. "He has grown mean and shiftless, husband," she explained. "He does nothing but eat our food, wear your clothes, and complain."

With sadness, the old man started to understand their time had come and they needed to part ways. He, too, was no fool and understood that from the moment he refused to offer the man to take over his role, the fellow's kind intentions had changed. He understood, and made careful suggestions that the fellow he brought into his house approach the merchant who had bought up all the lands about them, and see what work might be on offer. If he had work, he would feel much better about moving him on, for he had come to love this fellow, despite his moods.

But what the humble man heard was, "You are no longer my son!" and he felt great anger. Already he had served one master faithfully, and been cast aside. Now he served another faithfully, but was also cast aside. He felt murder in his heart, and his mind whispered to him that if the real son died, the old man would not be able to travel between the vineyards, and that if he approached the merchant then, he would attain his rightful place. After all, he had worked for it, he deserved it.

The next day, on the pretext of looking for work, he made his way to that vineyard, to see for himself the difficulty of the task. There, he was amazed! For it was beautifully run and the house provided by the owner was huge and lavish, worthy of a lord. He saw the vine master, checking the vats, so similar to the ones he had worked in. He checked the vines, so similar to the ones he had harvested. He then went and checked the fermenting hall, and there the humble man saw huge vats, many more than he had tended at his former masters.

Now you might have thought him seeing this large vineyard, much larger than he had worked in with the old man, and seeing it run by one man, he might have been given pause to think. A wise person would have seen that it was only with kindness that the former owner have elevated his position, for it would be obvious to all he was not needed there. If he had been wise, he would have seen that this man he planned to murder worked far harder than he did. If he had been wise he would have brought gratitude back to his heart, for the skills given freely to him, but he was not wise.

He sat there in the shadows waiting until the days work was done, when he knew the son of the old man would do his rounds of the vineyard. He nursed the knife he would use to plunge into that man's heart, never even thinking of how he would kill an innocent person. All he saw was him living in that fine house, making fine wine, and having a fine life. In such a position, he could even consider a wife and children, and in such a mind he dreamed all that day until the sky darkened.

At that point, Mary came out and seeing all the idle men, bristled and told them to stop listening to stories and to get their work done. Like obedient children, this is what they did, but whispered to the Master, "How does this story end?"

Yeshua said nothing, but as the day drew to a close and it was time for supper, he smiled. "You tell me how it ends!" he laughed. "Through this day you have nursed this story in your heart, like he nursed his story in his. What have you come to?"

Mathew laughed, "True enough. I was sitting there imagining he got run over by a cart as he stepped out, and had to meet the Lord and explain himself."

Peter laughed along with Mathew, "Well, I saw him committing the murder, but the merchant was wise, and would not hire him, knowing that in the former vineyard he did not work as hard as expected."

Mathew said, "Well, I had him about to commit the murder, then the light of understanding finally breaks through, and he begs forgiveness. Maybe the son offers him a position?"

It was Thomas who said, "The story is about misplaced passion and how it controls our thinking and actions. He could have chosen a different path, he had many options, but his passions determined his course."

Luke agreed, thinking of his own family, fiercely fighting for a piece of what they thought they should own. "I do not know the ending, but if we look at the beginning there is a clue - he was a humble man who turned to one with murder in his heart. True humility would not permit this, true humility would keep the heart pure."

Yeshua smiled broadly, "And so it is. If our humility is true, when the waves of life flow in, we remain unchanged. If we are raised in station, or lowered, nothing will change in our heart. That whisper that allows the desire to harm, or steal, or corrupt, into our heart cannot enter the door of a humble or grateful man."

Each was left to reflect on the times they were less than the ideal follower, and they understood this was true. For in those times, their humility and grace had been found wanting. But it was Luke that could see a step further into that story - the master was warning him, there was an aggrieved soul in his family feeling they deserved more. That was how it was with his stories, always another layer to peel back that revealed a deeper heart.

Healing the Lepers

They had been away from the sea at Galilee for some months, traveling through the towns, teaching at the synagogues, healing the body and repairing the faith of all that came. The circus of Yeshua was popular, with many coming from miles around to see the new preacher.

The troupe were walking through to a place of healing when they traveled past a deserted town, inhabited by lepers. While it was not done to go to these places, Yeshua felt something and decided to walk through. As he did that sense of the Lord passing through touched him, and he looked in the direction of some men leaning idly under a tree.

They called out for some money, or food, whatever the passing strangers might have. They rarely saw anyone going by and hoped for some sort of benefit.

The disciples, knowing that leprosy was a disease caused by gossip, wondered at the foolishness of the men, gossiping still even though they had been outcasts from society. But the Master acted as if he didn't hear their jibes at the expense of those men who were ill.

He walked over to them, knowing that the healing power of the Lord had awoken, and said, "Go seek your Rabbi and ask that he test you."

Now, this meant going to the local priest and sitting in isolation for a two-week period to see if your leprosy will leave. If your skin became healed you were seen to be healed of gossip and released. It seemed that one man followed the word of the passing stranger, a Samaritan, and after the allotted time passed, the priest pronounced him healed, so he could rejoin society.

Yet he was greatly fearful. For one, he was a hated Samaritan, and two, where would he go? He remembered the passing troupe and nervously asked a stranger who they might be and where they went. The man wrinkled his nose, he didn't want to talk to a Samaritan, but gave him directions of where the healing rabbi had gone, hoping that the man would leave. "They say he is the new Messiah," the man snorted. It was clear he doubted the truth of this.

But the healed man was fascinated, who else could have alleviated his misery? Finally, after a deal of searching, he found that wandering Rabbi and went to thank him. Yeshua remembered the fellow, and asked, "Only one of you? Were not ten men asked to see the Rabbi? Where are the other nine? Has no one returned to give glory to God except this foreigner?" He wasn't talking to the man, but to the disciples, asking of them what they imagined might have happened. When they appeared to have no answer, he then said to the Samaritan, "Stand up and go. Your faith has healed you."

John was curious, "But they were healed when you passed by? How could it be that his faith healed him?"

Yeshua looked at all of them, "To be cast from society, to be called a leper, is a cruel fate that marks the heart with a deep injury. Why did the other nine not go to see the Rabbi when they noticed their skin was healing? Fear is the reason. They feared they would be rejected once more, as they have been for years. But that one Samaritan had courage enough to rise above his fear. What we have just witnessed is the power of faith, to lift us when nothing else will."

Yeshua went back to his business, speaking with people, offering them advice on healing with certain herbs, but Thomas stood there and watched. He saw the kindness and patience of the master, dealing with people who were confused and ill, explaining the simple things they can do to help themselves. It was the love he gave that opened their hearts, that in turn opened their mind to hope. He sat by, doing small jobs to assist as he could, feeling as he did so the deep well of being that was an ocean around this teacher. Just sitting there he felt his heart heal.

Thomas had been a teacher of the doctrines, a son of a scribe, he was able to both read and write in a number of languages. He noted that the master advised fasting as the prelude to many cures, so when the day's work was done, he asked him, "Do you want us to fast? What diet should we observe?"

Yeshua laughed and said, "Fasting can be many things. For one, do not tell lies, and do not do what you hate. This will clear your mind and free your vision of what is, for all things are plain in the sight of heaven. Fasting with either the mind or the mouth is a way to clear unwanted thoughts and feeling from your heart. When you find this certain clarity there is nothing hidden from you that will not become manifest, nothing covered will remain without being uncovered."

Thomas gave that wry smile, the Master had told him much, and yet nothing at all. "There is soup waiting for us in the kitchen, would you like me to bring some to you, so you might sit in silence with the Lord?"

Yeshua shook his head, "I am always with the Lord, Thomas. Let us sit with the fellows."

When they came to the place where the food had been prepared, the men were chatting happily, and when they saw the Master they greeted him warmly, saying there was bread and soup for all.

As the master approached and sat, he gave them with an odd look, and asked, "Compare me to someone and tell me whom I am like."

Peter said to him, "You are like a righteous angel."

Matthew said to him, "You are like a wise philosopher."

But Thomas said to him, "Master, my mouth is wholly incapable of saying who you are like."

Yeshua looked into the distance, saying, "I am not your master. Because you have drunk the wine of wisdom, you have become intoxicated from the bubbling spring which I have measured out." And he took his portion and left for a quiet place, taking only Thomas with him.

In private he spoke, "The world of men is full of dreams and hopes and wishes and schemes and thoughts that come to no end. It is not wrong that men are happy in each other's company, but when the Lord is speaking, you must learn the fine line between what is man and what is divine. The light of the message can fill the heart until it overflows and spills, causing a loss, not a gain."

Thomas was unsure what the master was saying. Wisely he said nothing and contemplated what he had been told. First, Yeshua said he was not a master, *no, what he said was he was not MY master*, he corrected his thoughts. Then the door to understanding opened and he saw the plain truth, no one is the master of another, only of the self.

"How do I attain mastery, my teacher?" he asked.

Yeshua looked at him with pools for eyes, deep in the knowing of the Lord. "Now you ask wisely, now you begin to see. The journey to the Lord is made within, not through anything without. But, even as I say this, to scale the fears that hold us, we need a hand to reach down and help. I am a helping hand, Thomas, the right hand of the Lord. What you ask is how can you become the hand of the Lord.

"And this is both so easy and so hard. Have no thought for yourself but that you can know the Lord. Have no belief in anything any man holds dear, but respect all beliefs that nourish the heart. Like a musician singing a song, you will be guided to the next note by the invisible hand of harmony, and mastery is when you can sing from this harmony without hesitation or doubt. What is bubbling up in this present moment is the gift of the Lord. All you need do is serve this with a clear mind and a kind heart and you are the master of this moment."

When Thomas returned to his companions, they asked, "What did Yeshua say to you?"

Thomas went to speak, but held back, for he understood how siblings can be. "If I tell you one of the things which he told me, you will pick up stones and throw them at me; then a fire will come out of the stones and burn you up."

Peter laughed, saying, "You want Thomas to speak? Let me give you a rock, for you will get more from that if you wring it hard enough!"

Thomas said nothing, but sat and thought. Did the Master just say this to him, or was it dream walking? He knew the physical and spiritual reality could split when Yeshua was about, and you would not be certain in which world you stood. The more he considered it, the more he understood the words may have come from his spiritual self to his inner awareness, for Yeshua never spoke so openly and plainly about such things.

All knew, the master spoke in riddles and stories, offering no direct answer to a question but what you might divine from his words. He spoke plain enough to the people when talking about healing, so he COULD talk simply and directly, but he chose not to with his chosen ones. Why? The question lingered with Thomas for some time as he ate his bread and contemplated. Why did he come at all?

As if he had heard the question, Yeshua emerged from the shadows wherein he had been in contemplation, "Men think, perhaps, that it is peace which I have come to cast upon the world. They do not know that it is dissension that I give you: fire, sword, and war. If there are five in a house, three will be against two, two against three, the father against the son, and the son against the father. And they will stand solitary."

This seemed to surprise the fellows, normally Yeshua spoke of love. This seemed the opposite. But he did not stop to explain. He continued for the river of truth was flowing. "You wonder why I am here? I shall give you what no eye has seen and what no ear has heard and what no hand has touched and what has never occurred to the human mind. I will show you the path to the Lord but know it goes through your heart, and if your heart is troubled, this passage will stir the demons in your Soul. For man is born of trouble and lives in strife, so that when I reach my hand to pull you up, those creatures that beggar you will hold tight and scream for you to let go.

"And the uncertain man will be torn asunder, not knowing the path. The family will be torn, fearing their child is being taken by devils. The village shall fall into argument, not knowing that the darkness upon your heart is merely the moment before the dawn."

He paused, "That leper who came today, did you learn nothing? He raised himself out of misery and fear. He hoped for a better tomorrow to grow come from the ashes of his past. One out of ten it will be who hears my voice and follows. And from these, few will be chosen. Many seeds will be cast, most will fall onto rocky ground, some will find weak soil and sprout for a moment, but I say if but one in ten thousand finds deep soil and grows true to their spirit, then this is why I came."

Mathew asked, "Master, how does this end for all of us?"

Yeshua laughed, remembering the old sage in Persia when he asked of him what lay ahead. The old man had looked at him and suggested that maybe he should know where he was right now before he asked where he was going. "Have you discovered, then, the beginning, that you look for the end? For I tell you, in the seeds of the beginning there will the end be. An acorn will become nothing but an oak. First, know yourself, and after this, you may come to know God. Know the Lord, trust in him with all your heart, you will discover escape from the endless cycle and go past the angel of death.

"You are not the physical shell that is your body, you are a piece of the mirror that reflects the Lord. Blessed is he who came into being before he came into being. For those that become my disciples and listen to my words, these stones of truth will minister to you. For there are five trees for you in Paradise: Asiyah, Yetzirah, Beriah, Atzilut & Adam Kadmon. Their leaves do not fall, through summer and winter they blossom. Whoever becomes acquainted with them will not experience death."

"First is the Tree of Souls, whose fruit drops into the hand of the angel Gabrielle before he places it as a new life on Earth. From this wheel we learn patience. Second, the Tree of Good and Evil, the fruit of which Eve plucked before she was ready to receive this. From this we learn what the Indian calls Viveka, or discrimination. Third, the Tree of Beauty, upon which all that is wondrous and pure is wrought. This tree opens what the Indians call Chitta, the appreciation of beauty. Here is where we become free of tradition. Forth, The Tree of Light, that shines the truth of the Lord into all realms. This is where we gain what the Indian calls Vidya, or truthful visions. Know that all true knowledge in practice is wisdom. Fifth, the Tree of Man, that which anchors the heavens in the firmament for those that wander the earth. This tree is the ladder to all life in all realms of the Lord. It is the thread that connects you to all. This is where we learn to bring the gifts of the Lord into our heart and share them with any who call for it."

This made little sense, but as the master spoke of paradise, Andrew asked, "Tell us, what is the kingdom of heaven like?"

He said to them, knowing one day they would understand, "It is like a mustard seed. It is the smallest of all seeds. But when it falls on tilled soil, it produces a great plant and becomes a shelter for birds of the sky."

This puzzled the men completely. Surely paradise was a place? Yeshua said no more, for perhaps he had already poured more than their cups could hold. But when he looked to Thomas, that one understood, not completely, but he understood.

"Yeshua," Thomas asked, "tell us about dream walking."

The Master smiled, "You who ask about paradise forget that each night you have the chance to walk in it. The man ruled by greed, or fear, or lust in this world is still ruled by these demons in the next. His thoughts and feelings wrap around the things of this world, thinking he owns them, but truly they possess him, wholly and solely. His dreams are but echoes of his day and no divine truth comes down the corridors of his narrow mind and closed heart.

"But he who breathes in the day like it is a blossom, who delights in the play of children, and hears the song of life in the trees and rivers he passes when such a one closes his eyes, his truth can walk into the paradise of Eden. He who will know the joy of being in this world will find himself awake in the next. And then you will know, this world is the dream, not the next one.

"But to walk in Paradise is not enough for the man with the Lord singing in his heart. He must reach out and show others the path, so that they may share in the bounty. To such a one dedicated to the service of the Lord is given the grace by which they can step into the dreams of another and speak with them, guide their steps to a brighter place. This is what you call dream walking, where we move freely in the inner worlds and find those ready for the journey home."

"When I first met you, master, it was in a dream," said Peter, starting to grasp what he spoke of. "This is what you speak of?"

Yeshua laughed, "Yes, despite the brick-like head of yours, Peter, you were awake enough to know me, and this is why when I first saw you, I knew you. For to me, this world is a slow remembrance of the next. Here I am but one man, yet in the worlds of the Lord, I am many. I can walk with each of you as I do here, I can walk with a thousand, with ten thousand, with a whole nation if I must. And once you take my hand, once you trust my word, I am always with you."

John spoke, "I too saw you in a dream, standing with the Baptist. You showed me a flower and asked what I thought. The truth was, I thought very little of it, but you said, '*Smell this sweet perfume!*' and I did. It shocked me deeply, for it was so beautiful, so much so that I woke and wondered what it was. But when I met you, I knew you were that man."

Yeshua nodded, "This is the ancient truth, that when the student is ready, the master will appear. You smelled the blossom of Beriah, the Tree of Beauty of which I spoke. Its scent will drive you past your mind and intoxicate the heart with its serenity. John, your mind is like a trap, it gnaws the bone like a dog. But I ask, are you the dog or the bone? Do you have the Lord, or does the Lord have you? Let it go and trust that the breath of Spirit will fill you like the scent of that flower.

"Know this, as you find your center in the heart of the Lord, you too will do as I do, and more. You will reach out and touch the soul who calls, and comfort them, and give them a home. You will pick up the fallen, the lowly, the despised, and show them the mirror where their true self is reflected. You will pluck from the wisdom you have found and share it with all who call for truth. For this purpose you are here, and for you I am here."

The master paused, as if gathering the scent of the night air to his brow, drawing its moisture as inspiration. "The evening scent carries with it a remembrance of the day - we take this beauty into our dreaming. With the moon as our sun, our eyes shut, most welcome the sleep that brings our thoughts to a close. But not so for the chosen! At this hour they will stretch their limbs and begin to walk amongst men, spreading the bounty of love and wisdom they harvested through the day.

"For this is what it means to be chosen, not to be set apart from the common man, but given to serve him, with all our heart and soul. The chosen are plucked from the vine not to be harvested, but that the seeds within them can be planted afresh into the heart of the ones who wish to learn and grow into the wisdom of the Lord.

"The path of enlightenment is one of stones, for few come to the grace of the Lord easily. At first, you walk it in slumber, in the world of dreams, tripping over every root and rock. Then you start to focus and the path becomes more like your external world, and then you realize, that THIS path, it IS your world. Your physical life then becomes the dream as the dream becomes your truth."

The chirping of crickets met the silence that followed, as each man looked deep within, following the guidance of the teacher.

The Good Doctor

"I took my place in the midst of the world, and I appeared to them in flesh. I found all of them intoxicated; I found none of them thirsty. And my soul became afflicted for the sons of men, because they are blind in their hearts and do not have sight; for empty they came into the world, and empty too they seek to leave the world. But for the moment they are intoxicated. When they shake off their wine, then they will repent."
Gospel of Thomas, Saying 28

Some of the disciples had been asking about diet, as by this stage there were many cultures in the entourage, all of who observed different diets and faiths. Having the uncircumcised present was difficult enough for many of them, but to have people who thought nothing of eating cloven-hoofed animals was causing consternation and argument.

"We are defiled in the presence of such men," some of the followers complained to Peter, who thought the matter serious enough to raise it with Yeshua. He had suggested that as the master did not eat meat at all, that to him perhaps THEY were defiling HIS presence, which was an argument that brought some peace to the camp. But it was becoming a serious issue, and the matter needed to be clarified.

When the question was put to the master, he just looked to Peter, saying, "Whatever you put into your mouth does not defile your brother, but what you speak from your mouth can." Seeing that this was perhaps not enough to calm the angry spirits in the followers, he added, "If you do not fast as regards the world, you will not find the kingdom. If you do not observe the Sabbath as a Sabbath, you will not see the father."

Now this puzzled Peter, which he supposed was good for if he were not puzzled by the words of the master he was probably wrong. He stood there going over things, was the Master saying that you still had to be an observant Jew by obeying the Sabbath? "Shall I give these words to the camp, as you have said them, master?"

Yeshua smiled broadly, for he knew his fisherman well. "First give these words you hear in your mind to your heart, wherein perhaps you will understand what they mean!" He laughed at the poor man's confusion. "Woe comes to those who seek to find laws and rules that they must obey to find happiness. They are like a dog sleeping in the manger of oxen, for neither does he eat nor does he let the oxen eat."

Seeing none of this made sense to his master of the camp, he gathered people around, to speak to them of what was truth in the matter of diet and gentiles.

There was a man, an honest trader who observed the Sabbath. In his travels he had to cross distant seas and spend many months in countries far from his home. He suffered great loneliness but his spirit was fortified by the knowledge that his efforts would bring his family wealth and joy. In the weeks and months he traveled he had to go to many houses, deal with many men, and sit at many tables.

Now this man was not permitted impurity, and yet across the table from him sat a woman he knew to be a prostitute. He knew the fellow who owned the house was testing him, and should he walk out the door his journey would be wasted, so he chose not to see a woman who sold her flesh, but instead, he saw a woman in need of love. Because of his forbearance, he earned the respect of the man that ran that household, and his family profited greatly by his endeavors there.

At another time, he was invited to a great feast held by a prince who ruled the harbor wherein his ship was berthed. At this feast, the meat of the pig was served. He knew his law commanded him to leave, but he also knew this would anger the prince, who would impound his vessel, leaving him and his entire crew abandoned and poor in a far-off land. Wisely, he chose to see the meat of the pig as just another food that the Lord provided to his people. The prince understood what that man had done, and by his offer of respect the prince likewise welcomed him to their city and his family profited greatly from that trade.

Yet another time, he was in a castle far from home, and he had arrived just before the Sabbath. Grateful he and his men had found a place to observe the sacred day, he also knew that in that kingdom there was no day of rest. Men toiled every day, not giving their time to reflect on the greatness of God. He requested an audience with the prince who ruled that castle and asked if the man could be kind enough to allow them to observe their sacred day, which was to start at nightfall.

The prince was fascinated, a sacred day for the Lord? What a novel idea. So he asked, "Can you eat on this day?" The man said, "Oh we are EXPECTED to eat, but we must not cook." The prince hardly considered that a burden, so he asked, "Can you drink wine on this day?" The merchant said, "Oh we are EXPECTED to drink wine on this day, but we must not travel any great distance to get this wine!"

The prince is extremely interested, "So this day called Sabbath, what are you expected to do?" The merchant was happy to explain that they were expected to do nothing, but praise the lord and enjoy the presence of their family.

"But you have no family here?" The prince noted.

The merchant nodded, his loneliness and sadness evident on his face, then he brightened, and said, "Wherein we celebrate the Sabbath, my prince, this is our family."

The answer pleased the Prince, and the merchant intrigued him, along with his strange custom. "And if I ordered that we must conduct business tomorrow, what would you do?"

The merchant thought long and hard before answering. He had made many adjustments to his life in these far away countries. He had chosen to see a woman of sin as a woman needing love. He had chosen to see the meat of the pig as just meat provided by the Lord. But could he see the day of rest as anything but a day of rest? He was about to say, "Regretfully my prince, while I would not wish to put our customs above yours, every member of my entourage would feel the weight of sin on their hearts should they break our most sacred day. At the risk of abusing your kindness, we would have to move from your house, and live like animals in the forest outside your walls," but at that moment, an angel appeared behind the Prince, and the merchant knew what he must say. "My Lord, I would invite you to rest with us tomorrow, and tell us of the wonders of your kingdom, and the people who live here, and the crops you plant, and the greatness of your army, and the blessing that the Lord has bestowed on your wonderful country."

And this answer pleased the prince greatly, and he agreed that on the following day, no work was to be done and that all the people should go to their families, and spend the day reflecting on the wealth the good Lord has provided them. "For I see the truth of what you say," he explained, "that a day resting in gratitude for what we have is as important as six days working to achieve it."

It seemed that Peter and many there understood little of what the master had said in this story, but it was Thomas, the one who said very little, who laughed and explained. "Peter, as long as our fellows observe the Sabbath, we can overlook the differences between our cultures. The master is suggesting the best way to do this is to invite the gentiles in to celebrate the Sabbath with you."

And it was then that the fisherman understood, that we must allow differences, but give our truth in a way that lessens difference and increases understanding.

And when the men had left, Yeshua turned to Thomas, saying, "Come with me while I go to see an old friend." Yeshua then walked to a village, well out of the way, to see a man, an Essene who had been a healer his long life. "This man has been a doctor his whole life," he explained to his disciple, "and has learned much. He is the one who first taught me some of the ways to heal."

After some miles, they came to the home of this old doctor, and Yeshua called out, "Old man, may we enter?"

His wife answered the door and seeing Yeshua smiled broadly, recognizing him, "The Lord must have sent you!" she cried as she opened the door wide. "My husband is old and infirm now, and sad to his heart for he can do no more in this life," she explained.

They came to a room with a very aged man, lying on a bed, covered by a blanket. But when he saw the master he smiled, "You have come!" he called out and struggled to his feet. Thomas rushed to his side to help him up. "And you have brought strong, young arms to help me!" he called out in delight, all his misery gone.

Thomas helped him out into the sunlight, wherein the three sat and talked, with the old man speaking of the master when he was a child, "So mischievous he was!" he said laughing to Thomas. "Always asking questions, always reading through my scrolls, always wanting to know more. Never had I seen such a curiosity and so I gave him what truth I could and he used to help me with patients, and always after they left, so many questions. But I loved it, he was my best pupil."

Yeshua just smiled, sitting in the sun, enjoying the company of the old man in a way Thomas had never before seen. He seemed to relax deeply, knowing that here was a perfect place, a perfect moment. Having an interest in healing himself, Thomas asked the old doctor, "What is the most important thing you learned in all your long years of being a doctor, my friend?"

The old man bowed his head and laughed, "Oh I have learned much, so much and yet so little, for the search for truth never ends. But the one thing that truly brought me to an understanding of the path of healing was the truth that I heal nobody. Of myself, I can do nothing, but if my knowledge can find a pathway by which the Lord can come to visit the heart of the sick, then they can be healed. Not by my hand, but by the will of the Lord, and the will of the patient. The two must go together. And indeed, it is not two, but one - the diseased soul is the one who has broken his connection with the Lord, and by reconnecting them, the healing can come."

Yeshua finally spoke, "The master speaks of the Law of Three, Thomas. *Where there is two a third must appear*. When knowledge meets truth, wisdom is born. When wisdom meets love, courage is born.

When the healer meets the needy, the grace of the Lord is made manifest."

"Surely now I have seen my child grown to such a man that can I rest easy, knowing my life to be well spent," the old man sighed and fell into dreams.

As they left, his wife had tears in her eyes, "He had not left his bed for two years, master," she cried. "What a wonder and a joy you have brought to our house."

"What do you mean, woman! I tell you truly, every hour of every day your husband has walked with me, guiding my heart and whispering to me the secrets of healing."

The poor soul seemed confused, but Yeshua just smiled and held her shoulder, "It was a life well lived, woman. Do not regret its passing for your husband has laid a path for your whole family to follow, where you might all dwell in paradise."

As they made their way back to the camp, Yeshua spoke openly, as he would with this disciple, "Thomas, healing is a path that grows every hour of every day. What that man taught me was the first foot of a long snake that grew from his wisdom and love. In that humble house you saw the one who first cast the seeds of truth before me, and what grew from that became everything I am. This is how it must be, for no man came to the Lord's presence by his own two feet. We need those who part the waters and release us from the imprisonment of our past."

They went a long time in silence, Thomas not knowing what to say, so he said nothing. But in his mind's eye, he saw a snake, like the one on the staff of Asclepius used by the Greek healers. It traveled along the ground, eating up everything before it, growing larger and larger until it became a huge serpent that men feared. But then it came across the other snake, one still on the staff, yet when it ate that, it became small again.

He was puzzled by what this might mean. He knew it must be connected to the master saying that the old man gave him the first foot of a snake. He looked up to find the master smiling at him, "You have a question, silent one?"

Thomas described his vision, and Yeshua nodded, "The snake on the staff of Asclepius represents the messenger - the one who conveys the secret teachings from the Lord to man. Knowledge is the message, and with this knowledge comes power. But if power is all you want you may grow fat on knowledge, but it consumes itself. The staff represents the pathway Mercury travels on, and by following this path, the snake does not wind around to eat itself."

"The snake eating itself, this is the Egyptian symbol of eternal life, is it not? I had thought the dream was in some way relating to birth, growth, and rebirth, the cycle of becoming?" Thomas asked.

"It is, and in this way the rod also represents the finite nature of existence. The two are intertwined, the message from the Gods and the finite nature of man. These two symbolize the need for, and the practice of, healing." Yeshua noted. "In a higher sense, the only true healing comes when the endless wheel of becoming is brought to an end, when a Soul finds perfection in the Lord."

"Master, then what is perfection? It seems like an impossibility, for there is nothing perfect in this world where life and death chase each other."

Yeshua looked to the distance, "Perfection is not completion, it is balance. It is a momentary state of being in the chaos of the world, and when you learn to hold this in every waking moment, this is perfection. Here is the secret: For man to grow in peace and harmony, both sides of his nature must mature. The righteous man hides his fear and ignorance, which in time becomes a weapon to beat him down. The hedonist hides his fear of the Lord, which in time becomes an arrow through his heart. Neither can know the peace of the Lord, but if both should go to a performance of song, each will find their hearts filled with joy from the self-same spring.

"When two men sing in perfect harmony, the third note is created, and it is that divine creation that emerges from true harmony wherein perfection is to be found. Not in man, not in his actions, not in his works, but in the song that he joins as a perfect harmony with the Lord within. For then his truth becomes a note that sings pure and true in the world without. And that perfect note contains three, the man, the Lord, and the Spirit of his being."

The master stopped speaking and silence was between them as they made their way to the followers. And when they asked Thomas where they had been, he said little other than, "To pray." For while he knew how the petitioners and those who went with the train of souls that followed the master would swallow every inch of Yeshua they could, he also knew he had not the words for what he had seen.

The Cup

It was not long before the third Passover. Many had come to the banner of Yeshua, and behind him a small army of souls had formed. They came for many reasons, one of them being the words of the Baptist proclaiming him Messiah. However, mostly it was because this was a fascination. The healing was one thing, the miracles another, but more than anything, life was dull in those parts. Here was a vibrant streak of color all could enjoy, for the camp of the prophet was full of extraordinary sights and sounds.

It was a circus in the truest sense, with a parade of curiosity following the entourage. While it was known that the core group remained aloof and Distant, what did such a thing matter when there was song and dance and merriment with so many diverse peoples, for there were Parsi and Egyptian alongside Greek and even the odd Roman. It made the bias against the Samaritan seem slight, as even such ones as they were also present and smiling.

This was a camp of joy. Perhaps it was the presence of the master, perhaps it was the ready supply of food and drink, or perhaps even the lack of intoxication to be found in the wine, for what was provided was Essene fair. There was nothing from an animal in the soup, nor alcohol in the wine, nor even yeast in their bread, but it filled the belly and the heart, and none found the provisions wanting.

The disciples of the Master would go to the various section of this wandering tribe each day and spread the news the master had given them the night before, answering questions as they could, and if they couldn't They promised to bring the query to the ears of the master. If these talks were seen as a burden to be endured to receive the free food, so it was, but for most, it was a matter of interest and part of the reason they came.

But there were such absurd notions, such as loving your enemy! It seemed completely strange, yet when an apostle came and inquired of each individual about what created an enemy, when the comb was passed through each individual's situation and the reason for the enmity uncovered, it was almost always a small thing that had grown large.

There were many examples: A man who was at odds with his sister discovered the source of their hatred was himself, for she used to tease him as a boy and he had wanted to prove himself greater. He had thought she hated him but as he came to understand his own bitterness he saw that THIS was what had tainted the waters between them.

"Let it go," Luke urged the man. "I have had much trouble in my family over inheritance, but I chose to value family over gold, and went at length to understand why my brother was so aggrieved. It too came to small things, for he truly believed my father preferred me as the eldest to him as the youngest. He believed only the settlement of a greater sum on his part would balance this iniquity. But I chose not to see him as the enemy, even though he attacked me with words and fists. I chose not to enact judgment against him, even though he broke the law. I chose love, a constant blessing, and spoke with those around him to discover his plaint. And when we sat without anger, he understood his hate was misplaced love, and we embraced"

"Hate is misplaced love!" another snorted, finding this notion enormously funny.

Mathew, who went with Luke, assured the man this was truth, "Everything comes from the seed we plant. A seed of anger planted in childhood can grow to the spear of hate in the adult. A seed of mistrust given to a soul as a youth can grow into fear and loathing in later years. The soil the seed is planted in can color the crop that is grown. A seed planted in misunderstanding will grow confusion. A seed planted in loss can only grow a lack. As the master has said many times: No baby born of a woman hates. It is something we grow into from a seed that has been planted."

Luke continued, "I can harvest the weeds from my garden, but if I leave their seed behind, what do I get? More weeds. If I argue with my brother, unless I discover the root of it, tomorrow I have another argument. When we hate, we never uncover the root, and we always hold to our heart the problem. It is not a notion of foolishness the master speaks, but common sense. We do not love the problem or the cause of the problem, we love the soul suffering under the illusion of hate so that we might help them uncover the seed that grew it. For no baby was born to hate, and no man finds happiness with a bitter heart."

Mathew took up the message as he saw the thought start to penetrate the dense fog of misunderstanding around the minds of these followers. "And what does returning hate for hate give you? Your own heart becomes poisoned, this is the only gift hate brings you."

A voice calls out, "So you have become pure and undefiled and have no ounce of hatred in you, is this what you claim?"

"We pass on the message of the master, does this mean I have no hate in me?" Mathew asked. "Not at all. In truth, when I remind myself to NOT hate my enemy, this is when I discover the hatred buried deep inside. The master has given us his words not because we are angels, but because we are human. He is here to help us get past our bitterness and loss, and to find a greater love within, the love of the Lord."

Luke took a simple clay cup as the Master had done last night. He holds it up for all to see, "A simple cup, do you see?" (the crowd mutters agreement) "Can you see if needs cleaning when I hold it up over my head like this? Of course you cannot - you have to bring the cup to your eyes and inspect it. And if you find dirt, you wash it away, for surely the finest wine becomes tainted in a dirty cup. This cup is your heart, hatred and fear are dirt that sullies the taste of the wine poured into it. It is this simple, by returning hate for hate, all you do is dirty your cup. By returning love for hate, you clean your cup."

The people gave the notion thought, while a man spoke up, "The law says a tooth for a tooth. If a man kills my son, I must kill his, this is the Law. How can I love a man like this?"

Luke nodded, for all knew the law. "Did you know WHY that law was written? As a solicitor, I studied this, and the Law of Moses was not brought about for vengeance, but to STOP vengeance. It meant the judge you took your plaint to was authorized to give the value of a tooth back for any tooth taken. It is an instrument of law that allows fair compensation for loss, this is what it truly means: That you receive fair recompense for a wrong done to you. But the Master went further than this, when he said in his sermon on the mount, *wash each day in forgiveness of those who have trespassed against you, then you will know the Lord, and the Lord will know you."*

"Clean your cup with forgiveness, this is what stopping the hate will do. This is what allows the Lord into your heart." Luke ended.

Mathew explained, "You do not love the man who killed your son, you do not love what he did, but when you stop hatred in your own heart, then your eyes will see more clearly. You will then be able to see your own heart, and in seeing this truth so too will you begin to understand his. There is a reason for everything, there is a reason why he killed another, why he was taken to a place of hatred, but knowing this will not cure the pain you suffer. Only forgiveness will clear your heart of pain, only letting go will heal the broken cup inside you."

Perhaps one in a hundred truly heard, but as the Master said, many are called, few are chosen. He concluded, "On the morrow, we cross to Jerusalem by the Way of Blood. Be mindful and stay with the train, for we know the bandits lurk in the shadows."

A voice called, "So we should love the bandits as well?"

Luke looked up, saying, "A man steals from another because of the lack within himself. If you fill your heart with love, if you fill your world with love, then all he can steal from you is your love. And by stealing this he will lose all that he lacks and come into the grace of the Lord, and be a bandit no more."

As they walked back to the main camp, Mathew noted, "Almost as good as Yeshua, that last bit."

Luke nodded, "Yeah, wasn't me, it just came through. Just as Yeshua said it would. It is amazing, it felt fantastic." And as they walked, the pair felt that perhaps there was a future for them in this business of the prophet. For as they gave of the truth of the master, it became embedded more deeply into their own hearts.

Mathew notes, "I saw and felt it, the cleaning of the cup parable he spoke of us last night. But by speaking of it myself, it made the whole thing far more real to me. I felt it in my bones, the reason to forgive was not for the wrong done, but to heal the hurt inside. I do not forgive them their paucity of love, I forgive myself for momentarily failing in being a servant of the Lord."

As they walked they saw how large had become the preparations for the journey to Jerusalem. This was now a small army of followers. They felt the change, this whole show had taken off, and people were coming from all over to be a part of it. Their hearts were full of the love they had found as they made their way back to the tent of the master.

Part Three - Jerusalem

The Final Days

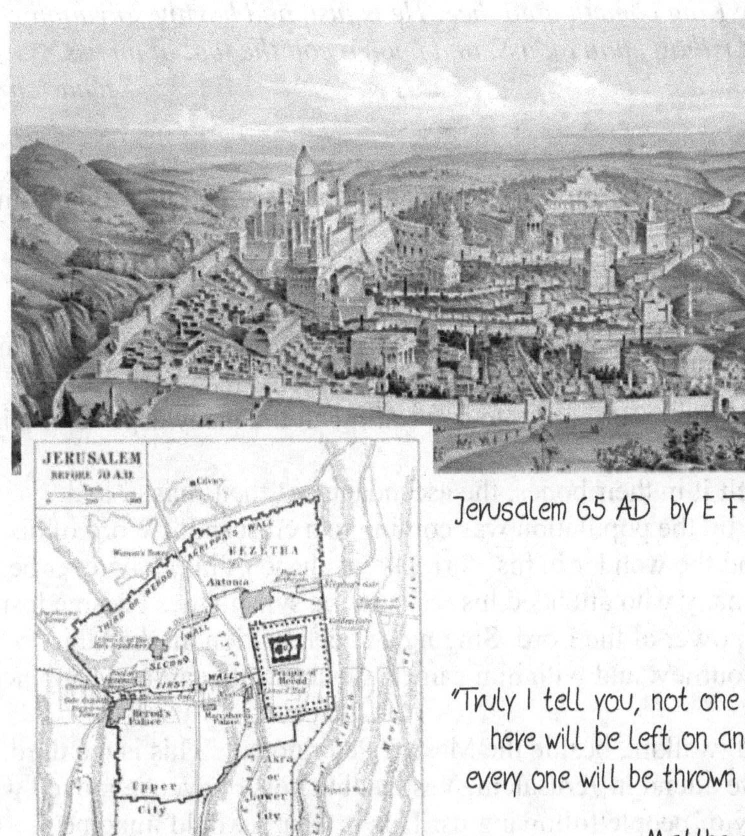

The city of Jerusalem as it was in the time of Herod the Great and before its destruction in A.D. 70 by Titus

Jerusalem 65 AD by E F Townsend

"Truly I tell you, not one stone
here will be left on another;
every one will be thrown down"

Matthew 24:2

A New Contract

Rejoice greatly, O daughter of Zion; Shout, O daughter of Jerusalem: Behold, thy King cometh unto thee: He is just, and having salvation; Lowly, and riding upon an ass, and upon a colt the foal of an ass.
Zechariah 9:9

The disciples had prepared for the week of Passover, traveling from Capernaum via Jericho and then up the Ascent of Adumim to the city of Jerusalem by donkey, carrying with them the healing tools and herbs, stalls for food preparation, as well as the gifts for the house of James. The entourage was great, with some thousand followers now in train. The treasurer, Judas Iscariot, had managed a feat worthy of a Roman Army in mobilizing and controlling all the many aspects of this campaign.

Many felt it in their bones, the ascendancy of their master and acceptance by the population was coming to a crescendo. Word of his miracles and the wonder in his stories went ahead of him wherever he went, and many who attended his visits to the synagogues became lost in the joyous power of the Lord. Singing and celebration marked this Messiah's journey, and with him came a gladness of heart and happiness of spirit.

Up front, walking beside the Master, Peter noted, "This is the third Passover we attend in Jerusalem, Yeshua, but never have we moved with such a body of people following us. This is what I would imagine a Roman Triumph would look like!"

The journey would take but ten hours from Jericho, where the entourage had been camped for a few days, teaching, baptizing, and healing beside the Jordan. They had met some followers of the Baptist who were also going to Jerusalem, and combined it was quite an impressive sight. With the joyous blowing of trumpets, it was a human river streaming over the desert road that lead to the East Gate.

There were special water carts pulled by donkeys that carried small casts of water that were freely available to all who were thirsty. Peter continued, "The plan is to camp outside the city walls this evening, where we will stop to respect the Sabbath day. It is close enough for people to obey the law yet go to the city and ensure lodging is prepared, or they can go to the campground of the followers. On the following morning, we make our way into the city. We will stop and pay respects at the Temple, but after this we cannot bring all these people to the Essene quarter, your brother's house will certainly be unable to cope, so I have organized for those without relatives in the holy city to go to Beth Zatha, where there is water and campgrounds."

He spoke the words knowing the master had little interest in such small details, but he liked to keep Yeshua informed with the general goings on of their day-to-day business. "Donations are up, so we have a little spare money. Will you question them on the payment of coin? We can afford it and you know this will stir up the priests horribly."

Yeshua smiled a little with this, "Do you think? The Temple Tax is a covenant, an agreement between Yahweh and the people. If it is paid, the plague will not come, that is the bargain struck. Yet it was not struck with silver, but the fruits of the land. It is merely convenient for the priests to have a half Shekel of equal value where the proof of worth is known. But do you truly believe the Lord wants greed and avarice on his door? A pestilence has already walked through and now stands in the Temple grounds disguised as the money changers."

Peter argued, "But a poor woman can throw some coppers into the well and not be struck off the lists."

"Would they accept coppers from many thousands? This is the question. Of course they will not take it, for then they are saying the money changers are no longer needed. Remember, they have struck a bargain with the men in the Court of the Gentiles!" He laughed at the irony. "Imagine a world where the money changers would no longer have a role to play, and the Temple itself could go back to being a house of the Lord." They both laughed.

Then Yeshua asked, "How are things going with the wife?"

Peter smiled broadly, "You know, this is proof you are the Chosen One in my eyes. She is happy, she even smiles when she sees me. She NEVER smiled, not even when we were first married, now she laughs. Master, I do not know how it happened, but from hating me with every fiber of her being, she now adores the ground I walk on."

"It is not so hard to understand, Peter, and it is no miracle. She was forced into a marriage with a fisherman, it was a contract she abided by, but not happily. Did you not notice, but you used to stink of fish? She had to put up with that, bear your children, and suffer the indignity of going to her parent's house as a peasant. The fact her family fell on hard times and married her off cheaply was salt in the wound of all her hopes and dreams that would never come to light." Yeshua looked off into the haze of the desert heat.

"Then it changed, you gave her the dignity of freedom without penalty, plus you stopped stinking of fish. People do not understand just how much their noses control their emotions, and when she saw you next, you were the leader of a group of men and you smelled nice. That gave her the chance to think again of her feelings towards you, and being a woman of a kind nature, the hate subsided and the love she always wanted to give emerged."

"When you gave me the advice that I could leave her, I thought you were mad. I thought everyone would look at me as a betrayer of trust, a man without standing. Now I understand you saw a longer game being played - But how could you have known that only by my leaving would love soften her heart?" Peter had never asked before, but it was truly the miracle of miracles. That hard-hearted woman was made of stone from the day he met her, and now she was soft and pliable as a newborn calf.

"I knew nothing, Peter. I know nothing but what the Lord whispers. You were deeply unhappy, she was deeply unhappy, why pursue misery? Why does a dog stay with a cruel master? We say it is love, but a dog will love anyone. The truth is the dog doesn't know it can leave. In like wise, many have written contracts and signed their life to them, not even understanding what they have done. The imprisonment most men suffer is all to do with the invisible agreements they have made. Just as a lawyer will draw up a contract that creates obligation, the unwritten contract obligates you to specific things."

"Master, what is an unwritten contract? How could this be binding?" Peter asked.

"Imagine if you will that the air is full of thousands of strings. They are strings of light, and when you desire something, it is like you lasso a string around the object of your desire. You are connected, and that is the unwritten contract," Yeshua noted.

"Surely it is not binding? I could cut that string and walk away." Peter protested.

Yeshua nodded, "You could, if you could but see it. But most men are blind to the obvious, let alone to the invisible!" he joked.

"And written contracts, can they also be broken this easily?" Peter asked.

"Everything can be renegotiated when you bring the Lord in as your master and guide. You felt you were in prison, I pointed out you can both fulfill your marriage contract and be free. You wisely chose this path, and as a result, your wife became free as well. With freedom of choice, we rarely choose misery, so her life became better, just as yours became lighter. Did you realize you never smiled for the first year I knew you? You would laugh, of a sort, but you never smiled. Now it is all you do!"

Peter laughed and smiled, it was true. He had been so bound up in his misery, blaming his father and his cruelty, blaming his wife and her bitterness, but when he let it all go, joy returned to his heart. "Was it true that I stank of fish?"

Yeshua laughed, "Oh yes, I used to hold my breath when you first turned up. Took quite some getting used to, especially for an Essene."

"Well, there is proof of the love you talk about!" They both laughed, happy to be on the road and traveling to the celebrations in Jerusalem. "Tell me more about contracts, and how they bind us."

Yeshua sighed, the cause of all misery. "You wish to catch a fish, so you take a line, add a hook, and to that hook you place some bait - you want to draw the fish to you. An insecure man might fish for compliments, a grieving man might fish for consolation. Every little thing we desire is like a string that connects us to the object of want.

“A man full of lust sees a woman and feels his need for her, but he cannot complete it. Yet even so, he has written a contract! He has drawn tics that bind him to his passion, so in isolation he finds pleasure, pretending he is with the object of his desire. Eventually, he gets married and wants his wife to fulfill his needs but in her heart she senses the contract he has written does not contain her signature. She feels more like a prostitute than a wife, and some women like that arrangement. Most do not, and so the marriage is destined for unhappiness, all because of a contract made with lust.

"But the real question is, when did the man make the contract with lust? We think that no child makes this contract, they have no physical need for sex, but this is not true. A child needs love, and needing love is the basis of lust. When the child matures and has the normal urges, this need for love combines with the fear that they are unlovable, and the result of this union is lust. Yet when such a man is given pure, deep kindness, it shakes the foundation on which that passion resides.

"This is how I sign a new contract with my followers. I will give them deep, abiding kindness, and I will exchange this for the contracts that have undertaken with their passions and needs. By writing this new contract, I free them from the past."

Peter looks at the master for quite some time, digesting what he has been told. "You usually speak in riddles, Master. I am very unused to the plain speak from your lips. So what happens with the old contract? Sin is sin, and must be paid for - As you have said, as we sew we shall reap."

"Let us say that sin is old Peter, a man where the air around him stank of fish," he jested, "when the person no longer smells of fish, where has the sin gone?"

"Much better, back to riddles I can't understand. For a moment there I felt intelligent!" Peter joked. "But seriously, are you saying it is just gone? Are you saying that by writing a new contract with you, one of kindness, we loosen the burden of all that has gone before? That sounds like a very good deal!"

Yeshua paused, wondering how to say this is a way it will be understood. “The pictures in our head, the things we believe, this is the basis of every contract we hold. When a man takes the image of unworthiness and replaces it with trust in the Lord, where does the unworthiness go? The answer is that no man is unworthy - it was a lie that evaporated in the light of the truth.

"Peter, my rock, I say this to you so that you might print it on your heart. When you sign a new contract, it is not with me. I am but a messenger of the Lord. I deliver the message of freedom, and when you sign that you agree with this, you write a contract with the Lord." He paused and looked directly at his follower, "It is the Lord who enters your heart and liberates your Soul. The chaff of desire will be burned, and the seeds of love will sprout. The past will be removed like an old cloak and by discarding this you will be born anew. When we cast off the night, the dawn will come. This is the Law of Love, the greatest contract of all for it binds you to the Lord."

Peter sat there absorbing this, watching the donkeys rocking as they moved up the long incline towards the high point of the pass. "What happens when someone writes a new contract but falls back into lust, or any of the passions that bind us to sin?"

Yeshua nodded, that was the real question. "The Lord will come again. He will knock on the door and all you need do is open it. He will come again and again and again - in a thousand ways he will return to your heart, knocking to be let in."

"But WHY?" Peter was feeling exasperated. "Why does the Lord bother with us at all? Yeshua, you speak fine words that make my heart sing, but I know what the priests in that temple are like. They will spit in your face when you offer them truth."

"This is the hardest thing to understand or forgive. These priests have a contract with evil, yet they earnestly think it is good. The song that we sing becomes the life we live, Peter, and the song of evil does strange things to the mind. Yet know it is a dance a person has arrived at from the seeds of upbringing and the need for survival.

"Here is the truth: When a pure man approaches a man who sings a contract with evil, the pure man will look sullied and out of tune to them, but when a sinful man comes he will look harmonious and pure."

Yeshua sighed, "But what you say is true, some will refuse the Lord all this life, all the next one, for thousand lifetimes they will curse his name. But what does this matter to the Lord? Peter, the Lord is love. Love will call on you in a thousand ways, for a thousand lifetimes, and you may fail it a thousand, thousand times, yet still it will come because this is what love will do. Love is a faithful dog that follows the heart of its beloved. The water of this love, shown in tears and tempest, will one day wear down the rock of ignorance, even if it takes ten thousand lives to do so."

Peter just nodded, a comforting thought, but there was so much of this world that was the opposite of love, and it too comes knocking. "So how do I know if it is the Lord, or a pretender at the door?"

"You will know only as much as you will know," Yeshua explained. "This is why the cup of the heart must be made deeper. This is why each day we must praise the Lord, not for his sake, but to deepen the well of understanding in ourselves. But there is one sure sign, the Lord never whispers harm against another, so if by your actions you cause harm, it is not the Lord."

"You whipped the money changers out of the temple?"

"A mother might strap a child, to teach it. To heal a deep wound you need to burn the flesh. To throw an interloper from your house is a kindness to those who live there."

Peter smiled, he had finally beaten the master in the game. "So, then you WILL cast the Romans out of Jerusalem!"

Yeshua laughed, "As many would wish, but do you forget that the Romans were invited in? I might ask a quarrelsome guest to leave, but it is against the Law to beat them out once they are invited in. This is the law of hospitality, and is one of the agreements Judea has made. Only when she turns to the Lord will she be forgiven this sin."

They walked on some way before Yeshua spoke again, "What holds sin in place more than any other evil is an inability to let go. The Lord receives all we offer, he will accept our lowest crime as easily as our highest praise. I say to you, give him your lowest ebb and he will return to you a king tide. When the waves of life threaten to overturn you, to drown you in their complication, give in to him, let it go, and he will give you a heart that cannot sink even in the greatest of tragedy and turmoil. This is the contract of the Lord, that as you give up your foolish self, he gives you your truth.

"Those priests who hold the people to ransom, their sin is pride. If they could let go of the finery and forget the need for praise, so many other sins would leave them." At this point the entourage had finally crested a rise on the Way of Blood and paused by a well for the stragglers to catch up. This was a dangerous road for individuals to travel, with many bandits.

Some people came to the well and saw the Master talking with his disciples. One man, a lawyer and a sceptic who came with his wife, asked him, "Rabbi, what shall I do to inherit eternal life?"

Yeshua looked up from where he was talking with his people, "What is written in the law? How do you read it?"

The man smiled, for the Messiah was walking into his next question. "You shall love the Lord your God with all your heart, with all your soul, with all your strength, and with all your mind; and your neighbor as yourself."

Yeshua knew the man's heart was not seeking truth, but argument. "Even so," he replied. "You have answered correctly. Do this, and you will live."

The man smiled, "Ah, but who is my neighbor?"

Yeshua laughed, "On this very road a man came, and he fell amongst robbers who stripped and beat him, leaving him for dead by this very well where we talk. By chance, a Sadducee was walking an hour later and saw the man. He had no obligation to help a stranger, so he walked to the other side of the road and kept on his way. Next, a man from the tribe of Levi came, and he too passed by the man, ignoring him. But when a Samaritan came by and saw the distressed Soul, he found compassion in his heart. He bound up his wounds, pouring on oil to heal, and then gave him some wine to recover. Finally, he covered him with his clothes and put him onto his donkey, to take care of him.

"He made his way to the nearest inn, just this side of Jericho, and gave the innkeeper some money, instructing the fellow to care for the beaten man. Any shortcomings he would make good on his return in a few days. You tell me, who followed the law?"

The lawyer forgot his game, and in understanding said, "He who showed mercy."

Yeshua nodded, "Go and do likewise."

As he departed, Peter spoke, "Was that a true story?" It did seem somewhat convenient.

Yeshua just looked at him, "If a dying man emerges from the desert and you give him water, does he ask where the water came from?"

ooo0000oo

In Jerusalem word had reached the house of James that large numbers were to be expected. In an already crowded city, the only option was to settle the multitudes into campgrounds outside the city walls, and many had taken the area around Beth Zatha. He had organized camp kitchens, latrines, and all manner of small necessities for the travelers to find rest.

Given the growing acidity against Yeshua, he had sent a messenger some days ago, suggesting he stay in a different area where he would be less recognizable. Especially now that a small army of pilgrims was descending from Jericho, it was the sort of thing that unsettled the Romans. He had asked the brother of Joseph at Mount Zion to care for his immediate entourage and sent provisions and gifts to cover their expected costs. So much had to be done that every day James blessed the foresight of his father in buying this house, which had become the central point for Essene worshippers in Jerusalem.

He contemplated his blessings on the small porch outside his bedroom window. Everyone had always known his brother was special and for a time he had been jealous. It was one of the reasons he came to Jerusalem, to escape the desert, but also to have a role of importance. He used to laugh about the small-minded world he used to live in on the Qumran, everyone knowing each other's business, but now he cherished it. The small gifts left by neighbors, the kindness shown all, nothing like this city, where bitterness and competition ruled the hearts of many.

But his brother worried him, he had drawn so much attention to himself, it was becoming dangerous to all. The Sadducee did not just hate Yeshua, but because he had been so vocal the priests now hated everything the Essene stood for. They were making life difficult for any persons they believed were connected to the new teacher, including himself. But for the present, all that could be done had been done. It was time for contemplation and rest.

The children were abuzz when he went to bid them good night, for they knew their uncle would soon be visiting, and were disappointed when their father explained the best uncle in the world was not staying with them that Passover.

ooo0000ooo

At the Temple, all was chaotic. Tens of thousands would be there in the coming days and already many thousands had gone through. So many beasts had to be procured, delivered, and housed, and the situation only got worse every year. Now, Roman tourists were making their way through the town, despite Pilate's recommendation for them to stay away. They mostly stayed at Caesarea and traveled down, feeling they were safe with a bodyguard - even so, they were a plump target for thieves. Which was a problem for the priests, as they were expected to make good any losses. It was all part of the secret deals made to have peace in the city.

Caiaphas swore at some workman for being too slow and beat him with his staff. He always did this to the slowest, to spur the others on. As he walked with his small entourage, he asked detailed questions on preparations, making sure nothing was amiss. A good part of their yearly income would arrive in the coming week. (Note: estimated yearly revenue for the Temple was $150 million in today's currency)

Some peasants turned up with copper coins, an insult. He kicked one of them, to ensure they understood their status. The traders all bowed their heads as he passed, and he scowled back at them, knowing they were cheating him out of every shekel they could. And THEN he gets the news that this Yeshua, who he detested, was now so popular he would be arriving at the temple with a small army in tow. This could become a serious problem, one that needed watching.

He pulled some of his trusted associates aside and asked that they bring him some learned men not directly associated with the priests. They found some lawyers known to support Herod who were willing to accept a small job.

He said to them, "When the carpenter's son arrives, the one that caused all the trouble two years ago, I want you to publicly embarrass him." Therein he detailed the questions he wanted asked. He would trap this Messiah in front of all his followers, forcing him to declare either for or against Rome. If he favors Rome, he loses most of his followers, if he goes against her, they will have him arrested for sedition. Caiaphas now thought it was good he was turning up with a mass of followers, all of whom would be shamed in public.

ooo0000ooo

When word reached the people that the Messiah had arrived on the outskirts of the city walls with a small army to overthrow the Romans, the people rejoiced. "The King is here, at last!" they cried. The day of deliverance was at hand, for the followers of the Baptist who had traveled ahead stoked the flame of rebellion, in the sure belief that the

Baptist was finally to be proved right, and that his chosen Messiah had indeed come.

Did it matter that this Yeshua had said again and again that he was not here to overthrow them? Not a whit did it deter them, for it was obvious that the Messiah WOULD say this until he had his army in tow. But now the force of thousands was descending on the city, they were certain the day had finally arrived. "Celebrate your freedom!" they shouted, "The day of Judgment is at hand!"

They told all who had ears, and this was a great many of the pilgrims, that the Messiah had arrived and was setting up camp outside the city walls, preparing to make his triumphal entry, where he would take over the Temple and clear out the Romans. The people cheered and were happy, at last, the day had come, and they were there to witness it!

The whisper was that the Romans AND the Sadducee would be cleared out of Judea. This meant free rent, for the priests owned much of the city. With Jerusalem full of tens of thousands of pilgrims there was much commotion about what the next day would bring.

Pilate sat in his office in Caesarea reading the reports from his people and laughed, he found the entire story fascinating. The would-be King of the Jews had arrived, but his spies told him that the 'army' was just peasants and country people who had traveled along the Way of Blood in greater numbers for safety. Not exactly a liberating army, still there could be trouble, so he ordered the group to be watched.

He shook his head, this place was completely insane. He had been governor for over five years and in that time there had been no less than twenty so-called rebellions to cast off the Roman yolk. None had come to fruition, partly because his network of informants was so effective at tracking down the culprits at the center of these things, partly because the people themselves were so bad at keeping secrets. They were the most gossip-prone race he had ever encountered and coming from Rome, that was saying something.

Jerusalem had a small population that grew on feast days to be very significant. But it was a city with walls to defend it and because of the safety this offered, trade and commerce followed - but in truth, it was like a large village, one where everyone knew the other's business. Even so, he had come to genuinely love the place and didn't miss Rome at all. However, his situation was now precarious, for Sejanus had been overthrown and Tiberius was back in charge.

The Emperor had little love for Pilate but seemed to like the Jews. The Proconsul had to stall his antics at irritating the priests for they now seemed to have half his ear. It was the Temple Tax, that vast sum of money the Jews accrued each year, that paid off several important persons in the Senate. Pilate found himself itching to get a hold of that cash. All the various holders of office in a vast number of territories also wanted to get their hands on what was passing from their Provence and pouring into the hands of the Sadducee, for Jews all over the world would send their silver back as tribute.

It had taken a couple of years for him to grasp, but this is what Sejanus wanted, the vast pool of money that poured in every year. He dressed his motivation up as hatred, but it was simple greed. A man who controlled a Parabellum so vast as the yearly Temple Tax stood to rule the world. If he had been able to achieve his aim, of discrediting the Sadducee, Sejanus would have installed his own High Priest to run the Temple and through this revenue attain absolute domination of the empire. Unfortunately, he lost his head and Pilate was left wondering if Tiberius had not planned it the whole time.

He now suspected Tiberius just used an unloved knight to topple the ruling families without any blood on his own hands. Patrician versus patrician was a war that lasted generations - As it was, he returned to an unchallenged seat of power, with all the knife work done and himself being held blameless. And what was Pilate but yet another unloved knight of the realm? The Equestrians had been achieving greater power throughout the Empire, so much so that the Patricians were certain to react and deal with the usurpers to the throne.

There was little he could do but see what dice were cast. Iacta Alea Est, as the great Caesar had said when crossing the Rubicon, *let the dice fly high*. Well, they were rolling now and the stakes were high. But this so-called 'army' on the door was just pilgrims. "Have this fellow and his people watched," he said to his lieutenant, "but take no action unless public order is threatened."

It was going to be a week of high tension until Passover was done, but at least one of his most serious concerns had been solved, they finally had the rebel leader, Barabas, in hand. The Zealots were the real threat in this city, with their assassinations of Roman supporters being a significant problem for him back in Rome. But with the head chopped off, the chicken will run around in circles and eventually die.

ooo0000ooo

The Sabbath was spent gazing out over the walls of Jerusalem. There was not a Jew who did not feel pride to see the city rebuilt, with the Temple and the city walls a tribute to the energy and commitment of the people. Most hated Herod for his burden of tax and his ruthless nature, but the city was far better off because of his kingship.

The wandering band of tribes - they had lasted as a people for well over a thousand years. They had kept the faith of Moses and Jacob, and the devout believers doubt they were core to the power of God in this world. This day at the start of Passover represented a glorious return by the people to the city that was the beating heart of Judaism, and tomorrow the celebrations would begin.

It was the day of rest, a time to greet your neighbor and ask about events in the last year as you supped tea, and ate fruits and bread, indeed any food not cooked on that day. A sense of celebration permeated the air. Soon the year would be behind them and they would sit with family and friends to enjoy the festivities.

Few understood how core it was to the faith that people stopped on the Sabbath, and cherished family and friends. This simple action bound the entire race into a unified whole and was the reason they survived.

Yeshua sat with his disciples over breakfast. He said little but listened to the happy murmur of content souls chatting away in the background. But peace was not to be had, for that day there were streams of visitors coming out from the city to see the new Messiah. The campsite had been chosen to be within one mile of the city walls, so not a technical breach of the Sabbath, but not a thing to be encouraged. He saw them not and retreated from the crowds.

In the hills near Gethsemane, he came across a black man, one of those from the Southern races, a Nubian. In Egyptian, he spoke words of welcome and was delighted to see that very large and dangerous looking man smile warmly in return. "Blessing to you," he responded.

They chatted for a time, about nothings, such as the pleasantries of the day, when Yeshua, noting his regal bearing, asked why he was in Judea. "I am one who delivers the coins to the Temple," the man explained.

"A dangerous journey, many pirates are seeking such ships as what you have taken to reach Caesarea, and even more who would plunder a caravan traveling South by the road."

The huge man laughed with a rich, deep voice. "This is why your priests pay me so well. But to answer your true question, I am the Captain of the Guard. We have no slaves on oars, only free men, for a slave will betray a confidence in the hope of escape. We are well organized and well defended, so we travel with little argument from brigands or thieves."

"You are far from home?" Yeshua noted as a question.

"My home is where my feet take me, my friend. Right here, I am home. If I go back to my father's house, I am home. If I go to Egypt to work in the Royal Guard, I am home," he answered with a smile and a look as to why this stranger was asking.

The man had the bearing of one who commands others. Yeshua was curious for he knew a little of the Nubians, how proud a race they were, and how many important military positions they held in Egypt. "Still it strikes me you do not travel far from your father's home just for money."

"This is truth. I enjoy the adventure of new lands, new people, new food, and new women! But you speak Egyptian, so it must be that you have traveled far as well?"

"I have my friend, from Egypt I went to Persia, and from there to India. It is a place I will one day return, the Lord willing." Yeshua noted.

"You must be a very wealthy man!" exclaimed the Nubian, surprised for he seemed a very humble fellow.

"I am a carpenter, I worked my passage repairing the ships and doing what was necessary to make my way."

"Well then, this is good news for me! In a few weeks, I am returning to Egypt and from there I take a ship delivering coin to Persia. I will be needing a carpenter and a person who speaks the language if you would care to come along?"

"Give me the name of your ship, my friend, and perhaps I will come with you. I can make no promise for on this day the future is uncertain." Yeshua concluded, understanding this to be a sign from the Lord.

They exchanged details of where the ship was birthed, and Yeshua invited the man back to his camp, to celebrate the Sabbath day, which he gratefully accepted.

ooo0000ooo

The following morning as day broke the camp was packed, ready to move to Beth Zatha. With Yeshua and his fellows leading the train they headed into the city. It was here that a vast surprise awaited the entourage, for multitudes had come out to welcome them, shouting Hosanna to the Son of David. Palms were laid at their feet as the crowds welcomed the one they called a King.

The disciples were ecstatic, at last their master had been recognized, but Yeshua was not so certain. He did not need this amount of attention, but it will be as the Lord wills. In the meantime, while he has this massive amount of support, it was a good time to go to the Temple. And so they made their way to the Court of the Gentiles, where Yeshua promised to speak and teach.

His people went out and spoke to the citizens, explaining where he was going. They, of course, had all heard of how he had cleared the temple of the money changers and came along expecting some fine entertainment at the expense of the Sadducee. Only two things in Jerusalem were a thing the majority agreed upon, the first was the hatred of the Romans, followed close on the heels by an almost equal hatred for the priests.

For the Sadducee were cruel landlords who were as extortionate with their rents as the Romans were with their taxes. They walked about in fine clothes, looking down on the locals whom they considered no more than landless peasants. If you did work for them, they were slow to pay and fussy about the result. If you charged a shekel more than they considered fair, they wailed and moaned, claiming you were stealing from their mother.

And the whole population knew, the father of Yeshua was one of the few men who regarded them as unimportant, but because of the fineness of his work, they kept bringing him back to the temple. Only those of the royal line could treat the priests like that. Combined with the words of the Baptist, all believed Yeshua had come to finish his father's work!

Such certainty in an uncertain world is a precious commodity.

Jesus entering Jerusalem on a Donkey - Palm Sunday

Palm Sunday

They came to the Temple as a great throng of followers, those of Yeshua as well as those of the Baptist. The Temple guards were on alert for this one who had caused so much trouble, and they sent word to the priests that he had returned, at the head of a great number of followers. And so it was that as Yeshua came to pay his Temple Tax, he was approached by a lawyer with some friends, "Rabbi," they called out, "A small question for you if you could be so kind?"

Yeshua looked and saw them for what they were, but let it play out. "Master they continued, you speak with such authority, but by WHOSE authority do you speak?"

He smiled at them, "First, can you tell me? I was baptized by John, as you know. But John's baptism - where did it come from? Was it from heaven, or of human origin?

They realized that they themselves had been trapped and discussed it among themselves, saying, "If we say, 'From heaven,' he will ask, 'Then why didn't you believe him?' But if we say, 'Of human origin' - we will upset the people, for they all hold that John was a prophet."

So they answered Jesus, "We don't know."

Yeshua shrugged and said, "Then how can you understand by whose authority I am doing these things?" When they appeared confused, "But as you seem to respect the Baptist, let me ask a simpler question of you. What do you think? There was a man who had two sons. He went to the first and said, *'Son, go and work today in the vineyard.'*

" '*I will not,*' he answered, but later he changed his mind and went.

"Then the father went to the other son and said the same thing. He answered, '*I will, sir,*' but he did not go. The question is this, "Which of the two did what his father wanted?"

"The first," they answered.

Jesus said to them, "Then it would seem that the tax collectors and the prostitutes are entering the kingdom of God ahead of you. For John came to you to show you the way of righteousness, and you did not believe him, but tax collectors and prostitutes did. Unless you think the Baptist was false?"

Yeshua was laughing now at their confusion, as were many of the followers, who were indeed a small army behind him now. Many of the lawyers were not even sure what he said and did not know how to respond. "Very well, let us pose an even easier question, one I am sure you will be able to answer. There was a landowner who planted a vineyard. He put a wall around it, dug a winepress in it, and built a watchtower. Then he rented the vineyard to some farmers and moved to another place. When harvest time approached, he sent his servants to the tenants to collect his fruit.

"Well, these tenants seized his servants; they beat one, killed another, and stoned a third. So he sent other servants to them, more than the first time, and the tenants treated them the same way. Last of all, he sent his son to them. 'They will respect my son,' he said.

"But when the tenants saw the son, they said to each other, 'This is the heir. Come, let's kill him and take his inheritance.' So they took him and killed him. the question is this: What do you imagine happened when the owner of the vineyard came? What will he do to those tenants?"

"He will bring them to a wretched end," they replied, "and he will rent the vineyard to other tenants, who will give him his share of the crop at harvest time."

Yeshua shook his head and said to them, "By your own words I tell you that the kingdom of God will be taken away from you and given to a people who will produce fruit for the Lord."

When Caiaphas and Annas were brought word of how the lawyers they paid had failed so badly, they were angry and berated them. But they had not gotten to their position by giving up, and so they sent some more men out to question the would-be Messiah.

Yeshua's people half filled the Court of the Gentiles now, the priests understood they had to be careful. They had one of Herod's men, a clever lawyer, who went up to the master as he spoke with the people, "Teacher," he said, "we know that you are a man of integrity and that you teach the way of God in accordance with the truth. You aren't swayed by others, because you pay no attention to who they are. Tell me then, what is your opinion? Is it right to pay the imperial tax to Caesar or not?"

Yeshua looked at the hypocrite, and asked, "Why are you trying to trap me? But please, show me the coin used for paying the tax." The man brought out a Roman coin and Yeshua asked him, "Whose image is this? And whose inscription?"

"Caesar's," the man replied, stating the obvious.

Yeshua looked at him, "Then the answer is simple. Give back to Caesar what is Caesar's!" With this, he held up one of the half-shekel silver coins used for the temple tax, and tapped the face of Heracles imprinted upon it, "But we are expected to give to the priest's a Greek God? The covenant was to give to the Lord what is due to the Lord, was it not?"

The people behind Yeshua laughed at the foolishness of that man and the cleverness of Yeshua, calling the priests Greeks like that. He said nothing further but left to report back to the priests.

Annas was angry. "He is making us look like fools," he snapped.

Caiaphas urged caution, "He has a thousand men behind him. He can overrun us easily, and there is nothing we could do to stop them. Do you want the Romans in here, during our most sacred of times?"

"He is insulting us with every breath he takes," Annas fumed with the indignity of the position he was being forced into. "Do you forget that we have controlled the crowds for a hundred years? Look here, he stands ruling over the people. Pay heed to me, Joseph ben Caiaphas! What comes next is an attack on US, I promise you!"

The words of his father-in-law rang true. All this Yeshua need do is unleash those people on the priests and the Sadducee were done. Everyone of importance was here, they could all be killed with a single stroke and what would Pilate do? He would install Nicodemus as High Priest and steal the Temple coin for himself. And what would the senate in Rome do? Nothing, for the flow of bribes from the Temple Treasury will have ceased and the clients who paid them would be dead. He had never realized the fragility by which they held power until that moment, looking over to the Rabbi, who was laughing at them. "I will take care of this," was all Caiaphas said in response.

He went over to some of his most promising young priests and whispered to them the question they needed to ask. All they need do was force this prophet to speak words against the Law of Moses, and they could have him on charges before the Sanhedrin. The priests, bustling with self-importance at being chosen, as well as at the wisdom of their leader, went up to Yeshua and asked, "Master, If a man's brother dies and leaves his wife behind him, but has no children, then the Law is that his brother should take his wife, and raise children for his brother. But what if there were seven brothers: the first took a wife, and died without children? And the second took her, and died without issue, then the third likewise, unto the seventh who married her, yet he too died without a heir."

They smiled, for herein lay the trap. "If there is a resurrection of the dead, when they rise, whose wife shall she be?" He must now either reject his Essene belief in the resurrection or deny the word of Moses.

The master looked at the sad creatures sent to trap him, knowing it was Caiaphas who engineered this sad excuse for cleverness. "Do you truly not know the scriptures, nor the power of God? When they rise from the dead, they neither marry nor are given in marriage; but are as the angels which are in heaven."

The priests looked shocked. For one, this wandering Rabbi is claiming an intimate, first-hand knowledge of the resurrection they do not believe in, claiming people turn into angels. How absurd! Yet the followers they hoped to disenfranchise loved his words. This was having the opposite effect of what they wanted. Yet neither could they find words with which to respond, though one shouted, "You are saying a chicken could die and rise up as an eagle? That is madness."

Yeshua was not finished, "Have you not read in the book of Moses, how in the bush God spoke to him, saying, I am the God of Abraham, and the God of Isaac, and the God of Jacob? I AM, he said in your book. I AM! He is not the God of the dead, but the God of the living."

One of the men, a priest who was a scribe at the temple and knew the texts well, was deeply moved. He had never even imagined such a thing, but it was true. I am that I am, the greatest words ever written, and up till this moment, he had not understood them. The Lord God was present with them NOW, and he shone through this one before him. Humbled, he asked. "Master, in the books there are many commandments, some say ten, some say twelve, some say seventeen. What is the greatest commandment we must follow?"

Yeshua smiled warmly at the fellow. "We all have heard the first of all the commandments. The Law of Moses commands us to have no other God before the Lord. But what does this mean? It means that we must love the Lord with all our heart, with all our soul, with all our mind, and with all our strength: This is the meaning of the first commandment.

"From this flows the second, the hidden commandment that occurs when one truly obeys the first, which is that we must love our neighbor as ourselves. Think dear Soul, if you love the Lord with all your heart, then you must love his creation. Why then do you wish to harm the creatures of the Lord? Would you harm your brother? Would you steal from him? Would you covet his wife if you truly loved the Lord?"

He then holds up once more the temple coin showing the face of Heracles upon it. "The first commandment says you shall have no other gods before the Lord. What is on this coin you take for your tax?"

The priest who was a scribe bowed his head. This man spoke the truth. Their trap had closed on them, not Yeshua. "It is a false God, Master," he acknowledged. And in his heart he saw, he saw clearly for the first time in his life. He repeated the scripture, "We must have no god but the Lord, and to love him with all the heart, and with all the understanding, and with all the soul, and with all the strength, and to love his neighbor as ourselves, this is more than all the burnt offerings and sacrifices." He broke down in tears.

Yeshua put his hand on the man's shoulder, "You art not far from the kingdom of God, brother."

The other priests were in a panic. They did not understand what had just happened. "Are you saying the temple Tax is false, because of the coin of Tyre?" they demanded.

Yeshua looked at their dull and foolish minds, "Beware the scribes, who love to dress well, who adore people bowing to them in the marketplaces. Beware those who look for the chief seats in the synagogues and the uppermost rooms at feasts. For it is they who devour the houses of the widows, living a life of pretense that they do this obeying the first commandment. I tell you, these people shall receive only damnation from the Lord."

At that moment, a little old lady, one of the widows that shall soon have her house eaten up by these same Sadducee, went to the Temple treasury and threw in a couple of coppers. "I say to you, to ALL of you, that this poor old soul has just now cast in more than the whole of the offerings of this day. For she has NOTHING, yet she still gives what she can with her heart!"

The berated priests scrabbled back to their master, while the scribe remained, with tears still flowing down his face. Everything this man had said, it was the pure truth of the Lord. Everything he said destroyed every piece of his faith in the path of the Sadducee. How could he have not known? And then he understood, his pride had forced him not to see the obvious, but before this man his pride had been destroyed and he had been set free.

That was it for Caiaphas, he ordered the Temple guards in to arrest this interloper, this troublemaker. Peter tapped the master on the shoulder, whispering, "The temple guards are moving in our direction, shall we block them so you can escape?"

"Go do as we have already done, loosen the bindings of the animals and set them free, then meet me on the Mount of Olives." And as the disciples went to pretend to buy animals, insisting they be loosened so they can inspect that they are a perfect offering, Yeshua once more took cord and wound it to a whip. Looking over to where he knew the High Priest was watching in the shadows, he raised his hand as if in salute, then laughed, and shouted and whipped and drove the animals into a panic so that they ran over the tables and broke open the cages of the money lenders, setting free doves and pigeons while scattering their precious coin all over the ground.

The people there shouted in delight and scooped up the ill-gotten gains of the merchants, and ran from that place of iniquity. Once more Yeshua ruined the marketplace, once more the temple guards were unable to find him in the melee, once more he walked from there leaving a trail of destruction behind. Mark caught up, laughing, "Well, they will most surely love you now, those who dwell in that fine building of stone."

Yeshua, in a trace, said simply, "I say to you, soon not one stone shall sit atop the other."

As they made their way back to the others, they found them laughing. As the master came up, they cheered him, knowing that they had struck a blow against the nest of vipers, as Yeshua called the priests. But the teacher was in another world, and his outworldly presence silenced them, until you could hear a bird chirp in the distance. "This land is a place of war," he said softly. "But do not be troubled, for it is as it must be and the end is not yet here. Yet soon, nation shall rise against nation, there will be earthquakes, famines, and many sorrows. Within a generation that Temple shall fall. Know I am with you, when dangers reach out to take you, know I am with you."

Peter told the followers who were going to Beth Zatha to depart. They had to be less of a target for surely the priests would now demand Pilate arrest them all. He then gathered up the chosen band, the disciples, and they made their way to the house of James.

ooo0000ooo

Indeed, Caiaphas was already sending riders up to Caesarea, demanding something be done about the renegade Rabbi who insisted on destroying the temple grounds. Later that day, as Pilate read through the shrieking missives, he laughed. He liked this Yeshua more and more, for one, he was making Rome look good. The priests could not control their own people and even better, were now in fear of a man who went around preaching loving god and loving your neighbor.

The irony was too much - There were an awful lot of Romans who loved God while they loved their neighbor! But not in the way the rabbi intended, he was sure. Still, it would make an entertaining report to the Senate, so he set his mind to writing and called in some scribes.

Wondering where to start, he realized, of course - begin just as Caesar would.

"In Judea, there are three parties of note, the Sadducee, the Pharisee, and the Zealots. The Sadducee are few, they are the wealthy citizens who control the Temple, the Pharisee are many, they control the bulk of the people, and the Zealots are madmen intent on destroying Rome and her holdings. Each party hates the other, and of late, a fourth group has come into focus, the little known agricultural community of scribes and farmers called the Essene.

"Entering into the fray of the Judean politics one of these Essenes at the Jerusalem Temple this day berated the Sadducee. They asked him if the Jew should pay tax to Rome, and he very cleverly held up a Roman coin, asking them whose face they saw upon it. When they said 'Caesar' he laughed at them and said, 'Give unto Caesar what is Caesars'."

He paused in his thoughts, no, there would be no mention of God or Gods. That was a nice touch - just telling the senate that a large portion of Judean society were accepting of Rome, and telling them in such a way as to get them laughing. It was a very clever turn of phrase, worthy of a Cicero. Now he had to put the nail into the coffin of all the complaints that would flood in from the good Senators clients here in Judea.

"This greatly upset the Priests, and an uproar of considerable note erupted, with all the sacrificial animals in the Temple grounds panicking, and causing a stampede that inflicted significant damage. It must be noted that the priests were the ones bringing up the question of taxation, therefore I would request of the senate permission to inspect their financial records, to ensure they are paying the correct taxation."

That should do it, he has painted the picture that the rich people here might be evading their taxes, which they were. Without Sejanus behind him, he could no longer barge into anyone's house and demand accounting, so in this way he would remind the Senate of the real reason he was proconsul, to rake in the money and to keep the place in order.

He then finished the report outlining the general events, monies raised, and any grievance of note, solved or otherwise. As always, he ended with a request for more funds and more troops. He certainly saw no reason to rush down a day ahead of schedule to sort out a problem for the priests, nor did he issue orders for this Yeshua fellow to be arrested as Caiaphas had demanded.

The High Priest was increasingly getting above himself, demanding Rome do his bidding like this. The job at Passover was to stop riots in the streets, not protect the Sadducee in their own temple. Pilate also looked over the report from his garrison situated overlooking the temple grounds and noted that the commotion settled down soon enough.

ooo0000ooo

John had arrived at the house of James and immediately sent out spies into the streets, looking for guards or soldiers who might approach. He was worried they had not much time before some official would call by, looking for the troublemakers. But Yeshua seemed unhurried and unconcerned, spending time embracing and being welcomed by his brother and wife as well as the children. James had expected them and had put before them a banquet of delightful morsels, as befitted the holiday.

When all had had their fill, the master was asked for a story by the children who had gathered around (as they always did once their father permitted it). He looked at them, and said, "A different story today, for many ears are listening and many eyes are watching."

A young man had a fine horse, a stallion of which he was very proud. It would carry him to war, and all the people that saw him on it were awed, such a fine beast, such a great warrior. In time, the man grew tired of the parades and pageantry demanded of his station, and he left that place for his curiosity bade him to see what the world had to offer.

He left the horse in a field, by a creek, so it would want for nothing, and traveled. He sailed the seas for many years, so long that when he came back home, no one knew him, for his teeth were long and his fine clothes were worn. So he went to find his horse, but he could barely remember where the field was where he had been left. Find it he does, yet when he approaches the horse rears as if to strike him.

He sees that he has been away so long that his horse no longer knows him, and has gone wild once more. He resolves to put things to rights, so he goes to see his father, but alas, both his father and his mother had died. Worse, they died without an heir, it was believed, so the family lands had been sold.

'Woe is me,' called the youth, 'does no one know I have returned?' But in passing by a mirror, he sees his reflection and is shocked. He is an old man with no hair, dressed in rags, and he moans, 'I have wasted my youth and my life, now I have nothing.'

The disciples lean forward, looking to what the ending of the story might be, what twist Yeshua would find in the tail, but there is no more. The master is in a far-off place and does not seem to notice his friends wanting a better end to the tale. "And so, what happens to the young man who wasted his life?" Peter asked.

Yeshua looked up, "The young man is the life you are given, his horse are the talents you receive, and his inheritance is the ground of possibility underneath your feet. You tell me how your story ends."

The children just laughed at the madness of the thing, imagine a person so old they lost their hair? Such a thing was as far away from their thoughts as Rome.

But each one of the disciples is shocked, has the master accused them of wasting their lives by following him? They all left home and family, brothers and sisters, fathers and mothers behind to hear his words and follow his ways. He did not seek to allay their fears.

ooo0000ooo

They left the house of James, greatly concerned that the Romans would arrest them, for the actions of their master at the temple would not be overlooked this time, they felt certain. Yeshua was unperturbed and went North beyond the city walls to see the people who had followed them to Jerusalem and ensure they were made comfortable.

It was in a place called Beth Zatha, where there were healing and cleansing pools, and the master bade the men to be cleansed of their travels. As they performed the rituals, he saw an old man sitting alone, and went to speak with him.

"Why are you alone? Where are your friends and family?" he asked.

The old man was weary and troubled, "Family I have none, none that I know of who care to know me, at least. As to friends, well they love the taverns, and I am too poor and too disinterested in their prattle."

"So, old man, why do you sit here?"

"I sit hoping to be able to be the first in to the healing pool, and have my affliction lifted. But I am too old and too tired and too slow, after which I am too sad to even move. And if I leave, where will I go? I have a sister, but her husband makes it clear I am unwelcome, calling me a sad old fool." The man sat there on the stone steps, looking utterly helpless.

"Try this healing herb," Yeshua took a small parcel from his healing belt, and gave it to the man.

"What does it do?" he asked.

"Your heart is heavy, your mind bears a weight you can no longer carry, these herbs will open you to the stars and you will see a bright future. That is all you need my friend, to understand you have a life worth living."

The man took the herb, and inside a short time, his eyes filled with love, followed by tears. "At last I see the mysteries I had always sought!" With this, he stood up, though he had looked infirm, and thanked the master for his gift.

"Where do you go?" Yeshua asked of him.

"To my sister, to apologize. I see now that I had become lost in misery, that my happiness had departed. My conversation, once speaking of the stars has fallen into complaints about the world and how unfair it was. I have been the author of my own misery. But master, you have shown to me the stars once more and set my heart free to roam, so I thank you."

The man left and James was amazed, "I had thought him a cripple, sitting there helpless. But I see now he was healthy."

Yeshua shook his head, "Crippled in the mind, is the same as crippled in the world. A man trapped in his thoughts needs the light of understanding to dawn, for he is lost in darkness. But give this man the light and he will lean towards it more surely than a child runs to play."

And Peter smiled, and was greatly relieved, for he saw THIS is what the story of the horse was about. It was a warning, though, of this he felt sure.

After this Yeshua went to visit his people, giving them words of kindness and encouragement for many were fearful of what would come of them after his episode at the temple. And when the guards of the Sadducee were looking about and demanding where this Yeshua, the carpenter's son, might be, he quietly made his way back to Mount Zion, where they had a house belonging to a Pharisee waiting for them.

This man called Simon bad them welcome, he was the brother of Joseph the tin merchant, and like many of the Pharisee felt happy that this man had come and disturbed the peace of the Sadducee. He brought them in, and amidst the amazement of his children that their father would bring Essenes and Zealots into their home, he welcomed them and gave Yeshua a place of honor at his table.

"You are all most welcome, I promise this is the very last house the Sadducee will look for you!" he said with delight. "Now tell me what happened at the Temple, you pointed out the false god on the temple coin, I am told? This is true?"

Much laughter ensued as the tales were retold, mostly by John and Peter, who acted out the looks on the faces of the priests as Yeshua confounded them. All present were amazed at how the divisions between the men of Judea were healed that night, and they thought even a Samaritan would be made welcome in this house of the Lord.

Raising the Dead

The Essene had come to the house of the Pharisee bearing water on his shoulder, to show all his faith. He explained the room over the tomb of David had been prepared for Passover and that James had furnished all that would be required. They need bring nothing but themselves, and so in small groups, the followers of Yeshua made their way to this hidden place near to where they had been staying. This was the early morning, before the light of day fully revealed itself.

With the scent of dew still in the air, the master made his way to the house of ceremony.

Once settled into the quiet upper room, Yeshua felt the energy shifting. Like a spider existing in the middle of a web, the filaments of his light stretched out across the land, feeling all that moved and shifted. He had once met an ancient people that spoke only in dreams. They had come to him in dreams, showing how the land itself speaks to you, and that the web of life is entwined through all places, people, and things.

He gazed into the distance at the Mount of Olives, a slight shiver running up his spine. Hundreds of years of cultivation had shaped the hills all around the Mount of Zion where he stood looking out the window, thousands of lives had toiled away to carve and create the lands about them. He was so tempted at that moment, to just walk away. It was so easy, just leave, go back to Kashmir, to his house and all he had left behind. Go to the Qumran, collect tools, and work his passage as he had done before.

The haze of dreaming permeated his thoughts. He remembered the smallest of details, arising as they did like ghosts from his past. It had been over three years since he first stepped foot back in Judea. He had traveled the length and breadth of the land, speaking to all who had ears, giving the message of the Lord. He had trained up men capable of understanding a little of what he needed to give to the ordinary man so that all might have the chance to rise about the humdrum and embrace their spiritual self.

It was the most extraordinary thing - the people calling him the King of the Jews. He smiled, the humble carpenter had been raised above the Tetrarchs. That was crazy, but he knew it was a bell that rang out only trouble. Just as he knew bringing Lazarus back would threaten the Sadducee. 'King of the Jews', this title loomed in the air, threatening to strike like a snake. In the distance, birds flew above the trials of human existence. All they wanted were a few morsels to survive, a pure and clean example of the spirit of the Lord.

He felt it, the drawing of threat coming from the hatred of the priests. The poison they spat into the heart of the people, this was the curse that had to be lifted, but was it his yoke to bear? Was the burden of healing Judea his alone to carry? He could walk out that door, down those stairs, and go South, catch a ship to Persia, then on to India. But he knew he would not. Lazarus had failed, the cup was his and he must drink it. He felt the power of the Lord wrap around him, that which rendered him invisible to enemies. There must be soldiers about, looking for him.

His so-called invisibility was really finding a perfect affinity with his present moment, allowing all that was not in harmony with this to move around him. It was all about finding that pure state. For more than three years now he had been training up his people in this one simple truth, finding the state of transparency to the divine impulse. He slowly taught them the subtle arts, giving them small tasks until they perfected one, then giving them another, moving them on to greater things.

This was to be the third Passover since he had joined John and the first since he had been taken by Herod, but John's people carried on the work of Baptism he had taught them, releasing the downtrodden from their fear, and giving them hope.

His own Master, the Zadoc, had passed to the higher plane only months ago, but the people of the Qumran carried on the work, knowing another would take his place. Like the hills in the distance that had given Jerusalem food and wine for centuries, the internal cultivation of man's heart by the Lord within would continue, ever onwards and upwards. But to provide spiritual sustenance here in the physical, there had to be a master present in the body to carry the current into this world. He sighed for what was to come.

The human was such a wonder clothed in rags, the heart of every person was a bright sun surrounded by clouds. It was time to part the mist of unknowing, to speak the plain truth, and to trust the courage of his disciples would carry them through. They were all there together, preparing for the Passover ceremony, but were they ready to break with the death shroud of tradition?

Just as he felt the pain and suffering of the people, he also saw the pointless murder of thousands upon thousands of innocent creatures. A world cannot move forward in harmony while it destroys creation for no gain and to no purpose. It was so utterly stupid, imagining the Lord needs blood to be content, it was a thing that must change.

For so many reasons, it must change. It was not just the cost to the and getting nothing of their true worth in return. For those involved with the slaughter, the foolishness of them imagining they were chosen by God for their barbarous act, it was so stupid. The utter absurdity that a person could believe the Lord would somehow pay more attention to their prayers because blood was spilled - Not one person benefited from this idiocy.

As he sat in contemplation an image formed in his mind's eye. He saw a cube, a perfect die, and he laughed to himself. The world is so set, so convinced it is the correct structure. The Romans truly believe they should rule, the Sadducee truly believed they are the only ones worthy of being priests. They were all absolutely certain that the God or Gods must be appeased and that traditions must be upheld.

He opened his eyes and saw some of the disciples anxiously watching their master. Peter, as always the practical one, was making tea. He too had been concerned, for Yeshua had seemed so distant of late. In another room, Peter's wife slept happily, quite pleased with the Essene habit of the men doing the work. It was one of those great joys, that Peter's wife had come back to him, blessed with the understanding of how the madness that fell upon her husband was, in truth, the grace of the Lord.

Yeshua, who saw the heart of all, was happy for his oldest disciple. More than this, Peter would need her support in what was to come.

"Can anyone tell me what is beyond a cube?"

Peter looked over, and laughed, relieved their master had come back to them. He seemed so distant all the time now. "Another riddle? I know nothing of such things. Tell us, what is beyond a cube?"

"Think Peter. What is BEFORE a cube? From what is a cube born?"

"A square?" he suggests.

"This is truth, simple unadorned truth. No one can argue that the Cube came from any place other than the square. But what is the destiny of a Cube? What does it beget?"

Andrew considers the notion, "Should you cleave it in two, cleanly, it becomes two pyramids. Such as what you saw in Egypt."

"We get closer to the truth. We gain two things from one." Yeshua laughed.

"Does the soul within the cube rise to become a greater self, like we do when we travel from our bodies?" Mathew asked.

"This also is truth, but does a cube have a soul, or is it the Soul of its maker that gives it life?"

Judas suggested, "Perhaps you speak of the Temple, that is one cube upon another until, with many working together, a greater purpose is created from the stone."

"Why, I do believe you have all started discovering your imagination!" Yeshua exclaimed. He was delighted, a few years ago all he got were blank stares from uncomprehending faces. *"There was a man, a Pharisee, who walked upright in the knowledge of the Law. He appraised every situation that came into his life in accordance with this understanding and he felt himself rooted and strong in the garden of his people. Another man, his neighbor, was a Sadducee. He too was firm and strong in his beliefs. He had made a good life, he was comfortable, and he had surrounded himself with beautiful things. He too felt secure and deeply rooted in the garden of his people.*

"Beside them lived another, a poor man who had no proper house but sticks and rope, and his soil was so barren he could barely grow sufficient to survive. But he loved the Lord and offered praise to his glory despite his wretchedness. And the people that walked down that street would look at the fine houses of the Pharisee and the Sadducee with their beautiful gardens. It was clear that God favored them, unlike the poor fool living in the dirt.

"But then the earth buckled, the world shook off the houses of the Pharisee and the Sadducee. Made of squared stones as they were, they rocked and fell to the ground, killing all inside. But the poor man with nothing? He survived, for there were no stones to fall upon him."

Peter spoke, "There is nothing past the cube, then?"

Yeshua looked upon them, his chosen few, the ones with whom he had entrusted everything he had built. "I say to you, every story I have told, everything I have done, every miracle you have witnessed, THESE are the stones of truth upon which you will build a Temple far greater than the house of the Pharisee and the Sadducee. You will cleave these stones in two, you will stack them one on the other, you will write them onto scrolls, turning stones of truth into lines of wisdom, all these things you will do. But remember, the spirit of the craftsman lies behind each stone of truth, and no matter WHAT becomes of the stones, his spirit is within them, yearning to be set free. And as you set the truth free, it will set your heart to fly. My warning is to take no glory in this, and do not root your life into this world as the rich will do. Be like the poor man and live only in the worship of the Lord."

He paused, looking directly at Judas, "Those who preach the law live in a box of certainty, stacked one on top of the other with careful balance. These pillars of law are built from the stones of truth and those who live within them know their shape is true. The man of logic builds his house with one certain piece of stone at a time and lives with the confidence of his truth. Yet I say to you, the Lord shall soon strike down this house of vanity. (he paused, allowing the message to sink in) But do not weep, for your loss will set you free."

Thomas, as usual, said nothing. But he gazed at the Master, wondering why the others did not seem to hear what he had just said.

"Today we travel to the tomb of Lazarus. I know you wondered why, if he was such a close friend, I did not attend when I first heard. The reason is that he has attempted the ritual of death, necessary to achieve the role of the Zadoc. It appears he has failed to bring himself back, which is of grave concern to my people, for we have no High Priest."

Thomas finally spoke, "Is this part of the story of the stones that fall, Master?"

Yeshua smiled, this one would do great things for he had both purity of heart and doubt in his mind. You need both if you are to survive the whispers and rise up into the ether of the Lord. "The Essene cannot continue without a High Priest, he is the pillar upon which their house is built. For another to take this role, they must undergo the ritual of death and resurrection, which is undertaken in a number of ways. Usually, as was the case with Lazarus, a concoction of bitter herbs is ingested that slows the heart. This drives the Soul from the body, as unto death. Then you accept the vinegar, another herbal mixture that triggers the release of poisons. From this point, you heart virtually stops and you must find your way back from outside your house of flesh. You must heal yourself from the toxins and come back to your body."

Peter whistled, "That's pretty harsh, but I wish Caiaphas would give it a go!"

They laughed, and Yeshua smiled. He loved their rough ways, their simple natures. "All over the world, for a man to ascend to a spiritual height and become one with divinity, there are rituals of death and rebirth. It is one way to remain absolutely certain that the spiritual guardian is true."

The entourage had their breakfast and made their way to the tomb of Lazarus, at Bethany, where they found many members of the Essene faith wailing and calling out to their brother. Yeshua explained, "This is how it is done, the person undertakes the ritual, and the love of his people calls him back. It would seem simple, but you do not know how blessed a virtuous life becomes when we pass from this world. It is so peaceful and calm. Soul wishes never to leave, but if you hear the voices of loved ones calling you back, you can make the choice to return."

With these words, he indicates for the men to roll aside the stone to the tomb, and calls out, "Lazarus, I come to call you back. Awaken in your body, and come to Passover with your loved ones." There was nothing, only the echo of the words returning. Yeshua is unperturbed and asks for a container of herbs. "Lazarus, I bring to your lips the herbs of awakening. I ask that you do not refuse this gift and that you return to us."

Yeshua goes into the tomb and comes out a few minutes later carrying the emancipated body of Lazarus, but he is breathing, and there is a tear from his eye. "He lives!" shouts Peter, and a great cheer arises from the people.

What they did not hear was the whisper of the one who undertook the ritual, "I have failed, Master. Who shall be the Zadoc now?"

Yeshua choked slightly on the words, "I shall take your place, brother, until you are strong enough to carry the burden. Rest now, eat, drink, let your body gather its power once more. You have not failed, you have stepped into the breach before your time, that is all."

Following the entourage were some Pharisee who saw the miracle. They confirmed with others in the town that it was true - Lazarus had been in the tomb for three days and, as a result, they were in shock. How can this be? At the same time, they smiled for this would destroy the belief of the Sadducee. When next they claim there is no resurrection of the body, they can now say: *What about Lazarus?* The scribes went back to report to their master what had transpired. This morning's episode upended everything, perhaps this wandering Rabbi WAS the Messiah?

Van Gogh's interpretation of the Raising of Lazarus

The Passion Begins

"Then the chief priests and the Pharisees gathered a council and said, "What shall we do? For this Man works many signs. If we let Him alone like this, everyone will believe in Him, and the Romans will come and take away both our place and nation." And one of them, Caiaphas, being high priest that year, said to them, "You know nothing at all, nor do you consider that it is expedient for us that one man should die for the people, and not that the whole nation should perish." Now this he did not say on his own authority; but being high priest that year he prophesied that Jesus would die for the nation, and not for that nation only, but also that He would gather together in one the children of God who were scattered abroad. Then, from that day on, they plotted to put Him to death." *John 11:47-54*

There had been a great commotion that day, emerging from the place where Lazarus had been reborn. Had a man done the impossible? Arguments and debate raged: Had the Messiah come? How could it not be the Messiah? Who is this Messiah? Sadducee attacked Pharisee, Pharisee attacked Zealot, Zealot attacked Sadducee, and all were either ridiculing or praising the Essene known as Yeshua.

Gossip raged like a wildfire and the very ground on which people stood was shaken by the inconceivable notion of a man rising from the dead. Was this man Yeshua a demon? Was he the Messiah? What would he do next?

ooo0000ooo

The master had not said a word since returning to the upper room with the disciples. All had been deeply moved to see a man rise from the dead, even though the master had explained it was an Essene ritual that had gone wrong. They went about the business of the day, lost in the wonder of all they had seen these last few years, preparing for the evening celebration, and leaving the master alone to his thoughts.

It had been a day since Lazarus had risen, and word came that he was recovering well, which pleased the Master greatly. But the Zadoc must continue, his people must have one they call High Priest, and he had accepted the burden. It needed a great deal of thought, for nothing would be the same once this course was set.

Yeshua came out of contemplation, his terrible vision still hanging in the air. He had seen the Tree of Life, in all its majesty, towering above him. But a rumbling had shaken the Earth, causing buildings to fall and people to cry out. A huge stone wheel was rolling towards the tree, destroying everything in its path, grinding all before it like the mill wheel grinds the wheat. He knew that soon it would smash into the tree and tear it apart. That wheel was tradition, the blind observance of the way things must be done.

The murder of the animals screamed in his ears. The brutality of man towards his brothers, the husband beating the wife, the wife shouting at the children, cruelty that passed from one generation to the next, it formed a cacophony of dread. The grief of the widows whose husbands had been lost in yet another pointless war rang out like the trumpets that brought down the walls of Jericho. The pride of the rulers, standing on the dead bodies of those they rule while they built yet another monument to their personal greatness. And the wheel kept rolling, crushing all.

The Awagawan the scholars in India called it, the inevitable rush of the images that fill people's heads. It would stream forth from the untrained mind, the Santana and Samsara of life, excluding all kindness from the heart, causing people to run mindlessly to the cliff of their oblivion. Yet it was all just pictures in the mind, all of it. All the pain and suffering, all the loss and fear, all the shame and misery - all of it, just pictures, but these images controlled the populace.

So, how do you change the image in someone's mind? People guard against change, they resist any effort made to lift their heads up to see a brighter day. He could go up to any man and point out the cause of his suffering, but would he change? No, he would take up the sword and attack the one who pointed out a better tomorrow that awaited him. Change is feared, and any who brings it becomes the monster that would tear down their world.

So he told stories, he posed riddles, for these were a bait to draw the consciousness of the trapped soul out from its hiding place and into the light of the day. Slowly, he drew out the poison of tradition and the toxins of fear that kept them in place, showing one after another the release from all fear and self-loathing that came with the Jivan Mukti, the spiritual liberation.

In Kashmir, he had thought he had found the perfect society. A place where the ideals of his people were the norm - a place where the notion of a man returning to Earth again and again until he reaches perfection was accepted. It was a place where the concept of what you sew is what you reap was universally accepted. And you might have thought this would have brought spiritual understanding and freedom to all - but no.

Tradition ruled. It did not matter that the people believed in reincarnation and karma, cruel men still ruled them, arrogant scholars still held sway in the courts of opinion, and foolish priests still paraded about in finery, presuming they were better than their fellows. God was an image on a pedestal, not a flower in your heart. The wheel of tradition had to be broken if man was to look up and see a new day dawn.

A man had to be born again in Spirit to rise above the weight of his past. A man had to release his shame and guilt, and replace it with compassion and kindness if he were to walk the narrow path into the kingdom of the Lord. Only then would he be pulled aside from the relentless grinding of the wheel of becoming.

The people needed a symbol to instigate change, a shining light on a hill that would take their attention from their internal woes. They believed this would come in the form of a Messiah, but what they truly needed was the courage inside their own heart to break with the past.

Today there would be no stories. Today there would only be the cold, hard truth, for his time was short. He felt a shiver, the premonition of what was to come. He reached for the cup and noticed his hands shaking. "Lord, would you let this cup pass me by?" he asked. It was not too late, he did not have to touch the poison. He could leave now, but that stone would roll down and crush the tree. Why he had been chosen for this, he did not know, but in releasing Lazarus, the burden became his.

He took the bitter herbs and drank them in one gulp. Mary said nothing. She sat quietly beside him, holding his other hand, knowing the pain her man was now to go through. Finally, she spoke, "It is done, Raboni. I will see you on the other side of this journey." The Essene way must continue, the ritual must be observed, the consciousness of the Zadoc must arise from the death of the old, a symbol of the wheel of rebirth all must traverse until they reach the perfection of being.

She left him to his contemplations, going to the house of Joseph, the tin merchant, to announce the ritual had begun, and to prepare the oils for anointing and the vinegar for the last stage. She walked from that place in silence. The Essenes who protected this sacred place nodding solemnly to the Lady of Herbs and Healing as she passed.

For countless decades the protectors had lived above the tomb of David. Perhaps they knew what was buried in the catacombs underneath, it was not known. Yet this was less important than the symbology of this place to the Essene and why it was called the house of resurrection.

Mary the Magdalene was the chief healer, a task she undertook because priesthood was barred to her. She had such fury in her early days; her knowledge of the Torah was second to none, her grasp of the dream state unsurpassed, but she was a woman. Her presence would tempt the scribes, distract them from their labor, she had been told.

Her wild and wilful ways drove her, she protested and complained, and railed against the injustice. She had gone to her father on the Qumran, declaring her intention to claim a rightful post in the ancient citadel, but he had shaken his head. The best he could do was to bring her scrolls and documents, which she devoured, looking for a pathway into the priesthood of the Essene. Instead, she found ancient herbal lore for the preparation and administration of healing herbs, as well as how to create the poisons needed for the ritual of rebirth.

By her own hands, she had brewed the cup for her husband. In twelve hours it would take hold, he would go deep into the world bordering death, and when it was time, she would administer the vinegar that would complete the task, and he would be taken to the tomb. There he would either live or die, and their contract would be fulfilled.

If he lived, he would become the Zadoc, the living vision quest of her people. He would become the channel through which the truth would flow down from the high worlds of the Lord and into the heart of the Essene. She did not know what she would do after that, but for now, she would do what she must.

ooo0000ooo

Thomas had heard the inner call, and went to see the master. He did not speak, as usual, but sat in silence, observing the fluttering of the eyelids that indicated Yeshua was traveling in other worlds. He was not an Essene, but he understood their ways and respected their truths. It made sense, this one life did not determine your eternity. The soul within the body would return again and again until it found the wisdom and perfection of the Lord, and then it could shine like the sun.

He, too, saw the pointlessness of sacrificing dumb animals to a hidden God, as if blood being spilled made a difference to your prayers for enlightenment. But mostly, he saw the patience and kindness of his Master as the cure for his own angry heart. He hated the unfairness of this world, he detested his weakness and impatience, but this man made all that go away. There was something that happened just sitting with him, a better self emerged, a kinder self.

Yeshua opened his eyes and smiled. "You have heard the call. Good, I have things to say, and time is short. Tonight we will celebrate the Passover, all the disciples must be here, if you could ensure this it would be appreciated. Tell no one, but I have taken the place of Lazarus and accepted the bitter herbs. I have read the signs, a time of great change is coming, and I may return to India. I have seen you there, Thomas. For now, the Essene brothers will prepare for the evening meal."

With this, the master closed his eyes. India? How strange, Thomas had been having dreams of walking in that far-off land with Yeshua. Thomas said little, as always, and went to bring the chosen to the feasting hall. There was so much about the strange religion of Yeshua he did not know, but he spoke of Lazarus taking the bitter herbs, which he knew from his studies meant undertaking the ritual of death and rebirth. He had hoped he heard that wrong.

ooo0000ooo

There was little that could dim the joy of the brotherhood when they all gathered, especially for so joyous an occasion as Passover. Normally there would be many present, the people who had helped as the troupe of healers moved around the country, but while the actions at the Temple had made things difficult, the raising of Lazarus had everyone at a fever pitch. On this Passover, there were only the apostles and their immediate families present.

According to the Essene tradition, red wine had been fermented with beets until it had the consistency of blood, which would be painted on the door as tradition required. It had taken time, but the disciples had gradually come around to understanding that the Lord did not desire the death of animals, though many of them still ate meat.

As evening now approached it came time to paint the doorway with blood, and Yeshua took a brush along with the special Essene mix and performed the ritual.

"Sacrifice your frailty, your anger, your fears to the Lord," Yeshua told them as he painted the ritual blood over the door. "In this wine, I have placed my shortcomings. In this wine, I have begged forgiveness of the Lord for any transgressions I have made. Such a thing has meaning and purpose, for in giving up these things you open the door for the Lord."

Simon asked, "Why then did the Lord command the sacrifice of a perfect animal to him?"

Yeshua responded, "How does the death of a lamb help the Lord to enter your heart? The world of the Israelites was bound up in their animals, they were everything, their food, their milk, their clothing. The sacrifice of an animal was significant to that household and it forced the greed and pride in ownership to depart, for in offering your wealth to the Lord you removed the blockage of anger and avarice from your heart.

"But today, we earn our way in the world in many ways. Very few Jews base their entire life around the flock anymore. For a rich man to offer up a lamb he bought from a local farmer, it means nothing. It is merely beating the hollow drum of tradition. Ask the rich man to cast half his gold over a cliff into the sea, and you will hear the pain it causes him as his wealth is torn from his grasp. It is the pain and suffering that opens the door, not the blood.

"This is why the Essene do not sacrifice a dove at the temple, we pay the tax, but we do not shed the blood of innocence. This is why I drove the animals from the courtyard, not just for the greed of the merchants, but because they are innocent of the payment demanded of them. I say to you, the time of blood is passing. The Lord calls for a more meaningful sacrifice from us."

Peter laughed, "A few more half shekels, you mean?"

The master smiled, "The Temple Priests are as disconnected from the truth of the Lord as a fish is from the land. They have created a pool of sin in which to swim, one where they are entirely comfortable."

Thomas asked, "What IS sin? We hear everyone talk about it, how it needs to be forgiven, but is it the act of corruption, the thought of corruption, or the remembrance of being corrupted?"

Yeshua looked to the far distance, once more the core question, but how do you answer in such a way as people will understand? "Perhaps a story?" he asked. They all leaned forward in expectation.

A man had been banished by the Emperor and now stayed in a foreign land. The people there did not understand nor respect his ways, for their customs were very different. They thought him strange that he must bathe every day, and when they asked him why, he explained it was for reasons of purity.

Well, they thought this very humorous. To them, bathing was a thing you did to stop you smelling, and as it was a cold climate they did not sweat as we do in this country. But they accepted his ways. The man was far from home and was unable to celebrate feast days with his family and indeed, their calendar was different from his, so he did not even know what days he must practice them.

This went on for many years, until one day his son arrived, saying that a new emperor had come, and his banishment was at an end. The man thanked those who had been kind enough to look after him, and made his way back home. But now, back with his family, he realized to his shock and dismay that he had performed the wrong rituals on the wrong days.

The disciples laugh at the absurdity of the story, but Yeshua asks them, "Tell me, has the Lord convicted this man of a sin?"

Peter said, "He tried to obey the law, so his heart is true."

Yeshua sighed, "But he did not pay the Temple Tax, how can you even call him a Jew? Surely he is an outcast from Paradise, as surely as Adam and Eve were cast from Eden?"

John suggested, "But his family should have paid it for him."

Phillip, a relative of Yeshua said, "He was banished, by Roman Law, he was dead. No one would have ever believed he could return, so why would they pay the tax?"

Peter reminded them, "The question was, what was sin? How does this story tell us about sin?"

Yeshua fuelled the debate, "It was said in Isaiah: *To what purpose is the multitude of your sacrifices unto me? saith the LORD: I am full of the burnt offerings of rams, and the fat of fed beasts; and I delight not in the blood of bullocks, or of lambs, or of he goats.*"

All knew of the conflicting texts in the Torah, but what it meant in regard sin, they were uncertain. Yeshua continued, "And following this in Isaiah, it is written, *When you come to appear before me, who has required this at your hand, to tread my courts? Bring no more vain oblations; incense is an abomination to me; the new moons and Sabbaths, the calling of assemblies, I cannot away with; it is iniquity, even the solemn meeting. Your new moons and your appointed feasts my soul hates: they are a trouble unto me; I am weary to bear them. And when you spread forth your hands, I will hide mine eyes from you: When you make many prayers, I will not hear them: for your hands are full of blood.* "

Mathew said, "Which we all know directly opposes Leviticus - again, what is sin? What is wrong in the eyes of the lord?"

Yeshua explained, "Perhaps what is right is easier to grasp? The scholars of the Qumran explain that in the time of Solomon there were two opposing groups, the northern Israelites, and the Southern. Each had their own beliefs, but in order to unite the tribes, Solomon in his wisdom first had to unite their beliefs. So too does the opposition we encounter in our lives force us to choose what is right for us. Here I will give you a solution with the simple truth: *What is a sin for a Roman is not a sin for a Gaul, that is the nature of things*."

Andrew understood, "When the man was in a different culture, he followed the ways of that culture. He did not sin, for in that place he lived a blameless life."

"And you who would follow the word of the Lord will come to many cultures and beliefs. Many will call you false, and many will claim you follow a charlatan and a liar, but what matters is that in your own heart you are settled and true. I say to you this is the truth: If you are divided within yourself, you live in sin. If you lie to yourself, you live in sin. If you chastise another before your own heart is pure, you live in sin. If you blindly live in the traditions of the past, I say truly, you also live in sin."

Yeshua felt the herbs taking hold, deeper and deeper his thoughts feel into his dreaming. "But who am I to make this claim? Who am I to teach you wisdom? Who am I to make any claim of greatness or truth? I have no authority but that the Lord speaks through me. I have no power but that the Lord gives me strength. But I say to you, once you have given yourself to the Lord, you become his right arm. He will use you to fulfill his prophecy and guide you to be a beacon of his light.

"I say to you, to be less than your true self is the only lasting sin. All else can be forgiven."

With this, the Master closed his eyes and fell into contemplation. The disciples knew this day was different from the others, for the master rarely spoke so plainly. They did not yet know what it meant.

ooo0000ooo

In a gathering of the Sadducee, held in the palace of the High Priest, Annas summed up their situation, "Brothers, this must not stand. This so-called prophet is spitting in our face, not only attacking the temple for a second time, but this raising from the dead business - it is an attack on US. We know what the court magicians do in Persia and other places, performing their pretend miracles to make the people gasp. But they are harmless, and only want some coin for their dance.

"This one, however, wants to bring us down. He hates us, he has said so many times in so many words, and he had predicted our end. The Pharisee do not raise a hand against him, which is their job, to arrest false prophets. He has not been tried, he has not been weighed as to the veracity of his words, and I say we MUST arrest him. We MUST put him on trial. If we do not, then his actions will stand, and we will look like fools in the eyes of the people. Soon Nicodemus will make a move, challenging our role as priests of the temple, and we will be cast out."

His ancient voice raised in pitch, betraying his fear, "But it won't be by the hand of the people, he will appeal to PILATE! He will use the logic that our basic principles have been proven wrong, and that the Sadducee do not deserve the role of High Priest, and Pilate will agree with the Pharisee. Pilate will agree purely because it will cause us grief, and give him greater control over our state."

A general stamping of feet showed the agreement amongst the brotherhood. Caiaphas rose to speak, "I say this only to you who were invited here, our most trusted fellows. I have a plan to arrest this pretender to the throne, this one the people call the King of the Jews - But I need your help, this day you must go amongst your most trusted fellows. Pay them to attend the courtyard this dawn, and say that the only name on their lips shall be the Zealot Barabas. We will pay Roman soldiers to stand guard, to let no one in who does not say this name.

"We will stand your costs in arranging this, and when you all have at least fifty fellows that you are certain of, return here without an entourage. Draw little attention to yourselves, we will have rooms and food enough for all, you need bring nothing. When we have the pretender, we will bring him here to be judged, and then on to Pilate, as we will be demanding death. Pilate will choose to offer clemency but the courtyard must be full of people who will shout Barabas. Further, instruct your guards to ask all who they see what man they support, and if any say Yeshua, have them beaten and cowed into silence.

"We will end this scourge before Passover, and rest easy. We will not fail, we cannot fail, for if we do not act, within months we will be thrown from the Temple grounds. And when we object to this, Pilate would use this as an excuse to plunder our wealth and call US a threat to peace. Be not distracted from this purpose we give you, fill that courtyard with the word Barabas. We will do the rest to protect the brotherhood."

Caiaphas then sent the businessmen and wealthy people of Jerusalem out to do the business of their survival, while he and Annas turned their attention to the Zealot leaders gathered in secret in a room off the main hall. "You have heard, and you have seen. We will work together to free your man. You too must fill the courtyard with those who will unfailingly support the release of Barabas, plus harass any and all followers of this Yeshua. This poison is infecting the whole of Judea.

When they were gone, Annas asked, "Have you yet managed to get a worm into the ranks of this false messiah?"

"I am working on it, Annas. There is a weak link that we can exploit."

Anointing the Feet

Anoint them just as you anointed their father, so that they may also serve Me as priests. *Exodus 40:15*

Mary returned from meeting Joseph. She needed to prepare her husband for what was to come. With her she brought the jars of oil that would stimulate the circulation and give him a better chance of passing through the trial. In ritual dress, covered head to foot with a veil drawn over her face, she ceremoniously demonstrated the nature of the Lord - Unseen yet present.

The other disciples had gathered, she could sense the growing unease amongst them, for they felt the change in their master. It was good, she supposed, that they were not blind, deaf, and dumb as so many other men were. The bitter herbs were starting to take effect, she could see the dullness in his eyes as he looked up, smiling warmly towards her.

She set up the utensils, the pins for sharpening the nerves, the combs for easing the fluids in the body, and the anointing oils. She put on him the ceremonial robes, and wrapped him in the garb of office as if to say "Here is the one born anew in spirit". For to become the Zadoc, to enter into the ministry of the High Priest, the ritual of rebirth must be completed. With all preparations done, she started working at the top of the legs, using the oils of revitalization, and combing them down whilst working them into the skin.

These rare oils would be absorbed by the blood, giving it air and sustenance that it would surely need in the trial to come. In truth, she would have preferred not to have the men around, for they had no grasp on what this ritual was for, nor the importance it had with the survival of Yeshua. Then she took the fragrant oils, with a scent so sharp it would puncture the layers between the worlds, to reach out to him, to call him home.

As she worked down to the feet, she undid her braids and cut the end of her hair to work it into a brush, which she then gently used to massage the oil into the skin. She was so deeply connected to this man, all her life they had known each other, they had played together as children, always enjoying each other's company. Who could have imagined the paths they would take in adulthood, him traveling to far-off lands, her becoming the healer of her people?

She wept as she worked, so cherished was this one. He barely noticed, for the herbs were talking hold - soon he would be completely on the other side, just peering back into this room. Another reason for the oils, the strong sweetness of their scent would keep him wanting to be here, to stay with them.

She heard the annoyance of one of the men, saying this was an expensive indulgence and that the money spent on these things would have helped the poor. Yeshua lifted up his distant eyes, laughing, saying to this Judas Iscariot, "Why are you bothering this woman? Mary has done a beautiful thing for me. The poor you will always have with you, but you will not always have me. When she pours this oil on my body, she does it to prepare me for burial."

There was a shock across the faces of the men, but none more so than Judas. Burial? But no more words did Yeshua say that hour, for his eyes closed and he went to other worlds.

Judas went outside, not just for the sickening scent of the Spikenard oil that nauseated him, but for the weird behavior. This was such a strange thing the master did, receiving wealth and indolence like he was a priest. And the robes? They were embroidered ceremonial robes, such as priests would wear. Had he deceived them in some way, was he not just a humble Rabbi servicing the poor and needy?

Confusion descended on his brow, and he wondered about the conversation he had with the Sadducee the other day, about how his former master, Barabas had been caught by the Romans and sentenced to death. He made his way to the household, for it was not far, just inside the city walls.

ooo0000ooo

"Yes," the priest said blandly, "They did catch Barabas. Nasty business, he will be crucified after Passover. You used to work for him?"

"I did," responded Judas. "Do you know where they are holding him?"

"Of course, you wanted to visit, to give your last respects?"

"I would, he was a great man." Judas nodded his head, thinking he should go, for he never apologized to Barabas for leaving him without warning. It was a strange thing, when he first went to the house of James, being told that Caiaphas and the Sadducee supported his former master. It seemed a terrible thing at the time, but now it made sense. Everyone just wanted to be rid of the Romans.

"He still is a great man, Judas Iscariot. As you know, normally we do not get on with the Zealots, but in times like these, bridges must be built to unite the people, and so Caiaphas tore down the walls between us and welcomed Barabas as a brother. He saw that the removal of the Romans was a greater purpose than old enmities, and he persuaded us all to support the Zealot cause."

Judas did not know what to say, a thing that had seemed so awful a couple of years ago seemed now to be perfectly reasonable and good. The priest continued, "Perhaps if you are visiting you could take some clean clothes and a little food? I am sure he would appreciate it. I, of course, cannot go into an unclean area where there is so much death, but as you are going I wonder if you could deliver a small gift?"

"Of course," said Judas, then eyes narrowing, "As long as there is nothing incriminating in there." It was so strange to him that a high-born priest would be speaking with a peasant like himself, but at the same time, Yeshua had preached acceptance of the gifts.

The priest smiled, "Please feel free to look through it. Oh, and here are a few shekels, because the guard will want to charge you for a torch."

ooo0000ooo

The house of the Tin Merchant was abuzz. He had contacted James, the brother of Yeshua, and arranged for all that would be needed. He contacted Nicodemus and spoke at length about what was planned. "We need to keep him safe and in a secure place until the ritual is done," he had explained.

The Pharisee had agreed to do nothing, but the word was the Sadducee were very active. Spies told him that Caiaphas had been to the palace of the governor many times, but Pilate remained in Caesarea.

The Zealots were focused on getting Barabas out of prison and were talking about attacking the Roman forces head-on. Suicide for most of them, but they may just succeed, which was even worse for Judea. Outright rebellion would result in the Roman Legions turning up, and countless lives would be lost. Why anger Rome? The truth was, Judea was running better than it had in centuries.

Mary had told him what Yeshua had committed to, well, if anyone could survive to become the Zadoc, it was he. Even as she knew this meant an end to their marriage, she spoke the words without flinching and took the oils of consecration with no complaint. He had long admired her spirit, now he felt an overwhelming love for them both.

He thought of sending a rider to Pilate, but he never enjoyed the parry and thrust of the Judaic politics, so better to let Nicodemus speak in private when he was here, which would not be long as the Sadducee Passover was in a few days. The Essene one was tonight, of course, so he made preparations. Indeed, he prepared for those now sitting above David's tomb as well, for if Yeshua has indeed taken the bitter herbs, he will be in no condition to organize anything.

For now, all he could do was wait, and seize what opportunity as would present itself.

ooo0000ooo

Judas Iscariot carried the parcel of food and clothes provided to him by the Sadducee. The priest had explained he could not be seen talking to a convicted criminal, but a true patriot should not suffer alone and in darkness, waiting for his death. This much was true. Out of the compassion his master taught, and a little because of the guilt he felt, he agreed to go down into the Roman dungeons. When stopped at a gate by a guard, he explained, "I am the cousin of Barabas, one of your prisoners. I am bringing him provisions."

The Guard laughed, "Bit of a waste, boy. You know he is up the mountain carrying a cross soon? He was sentenced a few days ago."

Judas knew when a bribe was being demanded, "Well, perhaps you would like the sweetmeats then, and I will just take him some bread and cheese?"

The guard looked through, took what he wanted, and ensured no weapons were in the carry bag. "On you go then, down two floors, bit dark down there and you would be pushed to find him. But I can sell you a torch for a couple of shekels."

Judas paid, he had expected as much, and the Sadducee had paid, after all. The man had been adamant Judas needed to speak with his former friend. It was true, he had not left on the best of terms, and given the short time the poor man had left, it was the smallest of mercies to bring him a little kindness before he passed from this world. To think, he had once held Barabas up as the best of men, a courageous fighter for Judea, a man who would rid the Jews of the Roman plague. It was the same reason why he had taken up with Yeshua: he had thought the Messiah had come, the one who would bring an end to the incursion by foreigners.

Yeshua just told stories, yes, there was great love, but it was just stories. He seemed to have little interest in changing the world let alone being a Messiah, and even less interest in throwing the Romans out of Jerusalem. And that anointing with oil, it was confusing. The man was an Essene. They were meant to share everything, not indulge in expensive luxuries. It was difficult, he felt this tremendous love for that man, yet he refused to act in ways becoming of the Messiah.

The torch was worth the few shekels because down in the second dungeon, where all the criminals sentenced to death were kept, it was pitch back. All around him, desperate faces shone in the torchlight, and he had to push back quite a few before he found Barabas, snoring away and apparently perfectly at ease. "Wake up Barabas, I have some things for you."

He opened an eye, "I know that voice. How are you Judas - long time no see. What brings you down here, tourism? Curiosity?"

Judas laughed, the man's legendary humor was intact. He propped the torch into a slot in the wall and brought out the food and clothing. "A Sadducee asked me to bring this down to you, to make your life a little easier."

Feet in the background started shuffling over to the food, the smell being released with the bag unwrapped. "Piss off!" Barabas shouted. His reputation ensured they did exactly that. "So, come to say goodbye then?"

"Pretty much. We didn't leave on good terms. Yeshua tells us we must not leave a scent for evil to follow, which I think means we should make amends for any we have wronged. I felt as a disciple that I should do what I can to leave us both on better terms."

"Five men died because you left your post and followed that carpenter, Judas. You going to bring them back to life?" A tense moment lingered, "But fair enough - done is done. Thank you for coming, I appreciate the gesture. How is it with the new guy?"

Judas didn't say all that was on his mind, "All good. Things are pretty hot up there right now, the Romans are stamping their feet over everyone."

"Pity I am down here, hey? I could be DOING something about the fucking Romans instead of rotting in a dungeon." Barabas snorted.

"Yeah, well, I don't see a lot of your followers down here breaking you out. Is there anything you want me to pass on to people? I am not part of the crew anymore, but if I can help, I will."

Barabas stared at Judas while he ate some bread and cheese. "You know, there might be a way we can help each other. The Passover is coming up, yeah? Well, not a lot of people know this, but the funding for our little revolution was coming from the Sadducee. I have a little bird whispering that they are going to try and get me out of here with the yearly pardon offered by the governor."

Judas laughed, two years ago Yeshua had told him the priests funded the Zealots in their fight against Rome. "Well, that would be great - but Pilate seems to be quite happy to have caught you. I doubt he will let you go, or even if he will continue that little offer."

"Got to say, with you turning up like this, it has got me thinking. You know the Sanhedrin are chasing down all the Messiahs about town, and while your guy seems to have avoided them, it is only a matter of time before he is hooked and jailed. I know all about rich-boy Simon with his seat at the table and how he would never let an Essene go to trial, but what if he WERE brought to trial - I mean, he IS guilty of being the Messiah, isn't he?"

"Well, yeah," Judas agreed, but not knowing where this is going.

"We know Pilate doesn't give a death sentence to Messiahs, lucky if they even get whipped. He likes the fact they stir up trouble and that the Pharisee and Sadducee both hate them. But here is the thing I was thinking, you could kill two birds with one stone here."

"What do you mean?" Judas is deeply confused now.

"Suppose, just suppose, we get your Yeshua to trial. He is guilty of being a Messiah, so the Sadducee hands him over to Pilate for sentencing, demanding the death penalty. What is he going to do? I tell you what he will do, he is going to stick it up their noses. Let's face it, the guy rode into town on a donkey with people throwing palms at his feet calling out "Messiah!" And what did the Romans do? Nothing, because they just don't care.

"So tell me this, when the inevitable happens and Pilate gets Mr. Popular for sentencing, what will he do? He will let him go, most likely. Now, just suppose that this business were to happen THIS Passover? Pilate will do what he does, and go out and offer up the usual pardon, knowing that the people love this Yeshua of yours. So he goes free by popular vote. Full pardon, he can't be tried by the Sanhedrin ever again. That could work in his favor, yeah?"

"How would that help you in here?"

"Well, just suppose I stack the courtyard with my people. Pilate offers the pardon, he asks the crowd who they want freed, and they say to his vast surprise, 'BARABAS!' Well, what can he do, he has given his word. So they release me."

"Yeah, but now MY guy is stuck in jail. How is that good for anyone?" Judas laughs at the absurdity of the notion.

Barabas smiles like a fox that found the chicken coop door open. "Well, I know you Judas Iscariot. I know you have a few niggling doubts, yeah? I know how you think. And honestly, this is the SMART way to go. But are you really working this through to a logical end? Here we get a chance to prove things, because if he IS the Messiah, well prison walls won't keep him nailed down, will they? If his destiny is to save Judea from the Romans, then God will open the side of the prison and he will just walk out of there. And if he doesn't? Well, there is your proof he is not really the Messiah.

"It is hard to argue against the simple truth. If he stays in prison, he isn't the messiah and your doubts are proven. If he walks, they are answered. Win-Win. In the meantime, I get to live another day, and I promise you - I won't be sitting around waiting for God to do something. I am going right back to making weapons and killing Romans." Barabas laughs, seeing the confused face of his former accomplice.

"You are crazy, Barabas. I can't willing betray the Messiah, just to get you out of prison."

"Absolutely correct, Judas Iscariot. Whatever way this goes down, you cannot betray the Messiah. Yeshua is either the guy, or he isn't. He either walks free of the Romans, or he doesn't. But consider this, if he isn't what you think - then HE is the one betraying YOU. Now, I will be honest, I expect the guy to be stuck in jail, because I don't think he is the prophet at all. He tells nice stories, a lovely guy I am sure, but do you see any flaming sword of righteousness in his hand? Do you see him doing ANYTHING to get the Romans out of here? For fucks sake, they park soldiers in the temple fucking grounds! Pilate put up fucking posters of Tiberius inside the sacred precincts of the Temple where only Jews are allowed.

"And here's another thing, Judas. The other niggling doubt I have over your guy - Yeshua went in and chased the money changers out. OK, weird, but I like it. This makes a good statement. Yet what has he done about the paintings of Tiberius? Is he saying that it is OK by NOT doing anything about this? I don't get that. You and every other fucking Jew knows it is wrong, dead wrong, just as we all know the only good Roman is a dead one. My problem is not your Messiah, my problem is what the fuck is wrong with YOU that you don't see this?"

"I'll think about it. I can talk with the priest," was all Judas could muster. The confusion was that everything Barabas said made sense. His master DID chase out the money changers, but ignored the other insults. It was very confounding, like that expensive oil, a crazy thing, saying it was for his burial.

"Look, I know you are the loyal type. I am not asking you to be disloyal, I am asking you to think clearly. Do that for me, please, think about things, and talk to the priest. Go knock on the door of the Sadducee who sent you here, and he will get you a meeting with the High Priest. You know, not to put too fine a point to it, but he has money, and he wants me out of here - Add up the facts and go see what is on offer. You could set yourself up with this opportunity."

As Judas went to leave, disorientated and not understanding why he was so confused, Barabas called out, "And it IS an opportunity, Judas. This IS the answer to all your doubts! You KNOW this, get over your quibbles and get the ONE fucking person who can do something useful out of this shit box."

The departing torch left only gloom and darkness behind. Barabas had thrown the dice, now they would rattle around in Iscariot's head for a bit. The boy wasn't an idiot, he would see the sense of it, but would he act? He will know soon enough.

ooo0000ooo

The guard came down shortly after Judas had left, his torch lighting up the darkness far more fully than the feeble one of Judas. He just stood there, Barabas got up and went towards him. The fellow was a mute, paid by the priests. The others knew well enough to not approach.

Barabas was taken to a washing pool, where fresh linen was provided as well as olives and bread. After he was cleansed of sin, a thing he found outrageously funny, he was taken back to his private cell where his visitor awaited.

"So?" the High Priest of the Temple had one arched eyebrow.

"I think he will." Barabas nodded to Caiaphas, his protector and patron. What he thought was, *Judas was always a sucker for logic, having so little of it himself.* What he said, was, "Your plan is excellent. It made sense to Iscariot."

Caiaphas noted the lack of formal address from the rebel. He did not doubt that if this rebel were truly successful in removing the Romans, his head would be the next one on the block. However, there was little chance of that rabble defeating the greatest army on the planet. "What matters is that you and your people continue to harass Pilate. Now that Tiberius is back in charge, the Proconsul has lost his power base in Rome, as has Herod. The tribes are one step closer to autonomy because of your efforts."

What he did not say was that talks were advanced in Rome about the Jews having their own army once more and that, with a favorable Governor, the power of the Sanhedrin will be restored. Already the influence of the Tetrarchs was all but broken which left just Rome and the Sanhedrin, and Rome will not be able to govern the province without them. People like Barabas made sure of that.

"You risk being called unclean, visiting my cell like this," Barabas noted, cynically smiling at the two-faced nature of his High Priest.

"All of Jerusalem is unclean with Pilate and Herod running the show. You are the bath that will clean them from our streets. But once I get you out of here we need to take a different tack, no more killing Romans, we want no animosity from Tiberius. What we need to do is start assassinating Jews who cooperate with them." Caiaphas looked carefully for a reaction.

"Pharisees, you mean?" Barabas laughed. He knew what Caiaphas was, a man with no Soul, but he was useful to the movement, and a master of negotiating with Pilate.

"Well, we both know this war between our people must end, and the only ones fit to rule are the Sadducee. However, sadly, some of our own are complicit with the Romans. I will give you a list."

"And I am to presume your name is not on it, despite you being the MOST complicit Jew working with the Romans?" Barabas smiled.

"That is the risk I take with you, Barabas. But I am sure the supply of money is important to your people, otherwise, god forbid, you might have to start doing some WORK to support yourself. It goes without saying that no man who has contributed to our mutual cause will be on the list." Caiaphas knew the fellow was just baiting him and enjoyed the spectacle of sitting as an equal with the High Priest. But he will play his part *because* Caiaphas humiliated himself enough to sit with him, thereby acknowledging him as an equal. "But tell me more about Iscariot, and why you believe he will give up his teacher."

"Judas is a pie-eyed fool. He was a Sikrin, a follower of the Oral Law, who fervently believe the Messiah would come and cast off the yoke the Romans have placed upon us. But like all Zealots he needed money, so he came to me asking for employment. As per your instructions to gather followers, I gave him work which he gratefully accepted. He was the man out in the street watching for patrols and distracting soldiers looking for our weapon making facilities.

"Then the fool got talking to one of the disciples of this Messiah of yours that you hate so much. He left his post and followed the new guy, still does. Got himself into the inner circle. But Judas loves one thing more than anything, money. He is always broke, he is always needing cash. Right now he is very disappointed in his Messiah having no apparent interest in evicting the Romans, so the logic of testing the claim by the carpenter, that he is the Son of God, made sense. I reckon he will come to see you. Play it sweet, offer him a bit of silver, and he will hand over that Messiah of his. Then it is up to you." Barabas knew this game was a long shot, but it was his only chance of getting out alive.

"Why do all you Zealots even want a Messiah? What God is coming down from heaven to save us? We have to save ourselves and right now that means saving YOU, Barabas. You can organize things, you can create the army, and take control. Together we CAN eliminate the Roman threat - Tiberius has thinned the ranks here in Judea, and right now they have nothing like the soldiers needed to save their skins. But let's be smart and avoid all-out confrontation. If we work carefully, Tiberius will simply recall Pilate, admonish Herod, and THEN I will be able to convince the Romans that a Jewish army is a benefit to Rome, not a threat.

"You run the army, I run the government. Once we are strong enough we can forcibly boot the Romans from Judea. After that, they have to take stock of the cost to get it back. Their supply lines are thin, the cost of war is high, and their Empire is fading. All we have to do is get a deal, then in a few years make it too expensive for them to want re-take Judea."

A messenger knocked at the door. Caiaphas took the note, then looked up at Barabas and smiled. "Well, that didn't take long. He will meet me at the place I arranged. We will have you out of here by tomorrow."

ooo0000ooo

Nicodemus was concerned. His spies had reported Caiaphas visiting the dungeons, they were planning something, and it had to do with this Yeshua, for one of his disciples was seen going in there. He knew in his bones that Simon was right - there was no good to be had pursuing the Nazarene. The man had raised the dead, after all! And while he could not accept he was the Messiah, this Yeshua was completely different from John. He offered no preaching to get rid of the Romans, just the priests, but there was no inciting the crowds to violence.

Despite his Essene roots, THIS Messiah was entirely amenable to reason. He had sidestepped every trap, had managed to elude his pursers, and stirred no discontent. Wherever he went the people cheered. They loved him, and the Pharisee was beginning to see why. The whole throwing of the thieves out of the Temple for the second time was a very positive sign. It told the Pharisee Yeshua wasn't after the Romans, what he wanted was to end the hypocrisy of the Sadducee.

What could you say? His thoughts exactly. In private he admired this prophet from the wilderness. Despite the fact he was an Essene, the man supported the sanctity of marriage, preached that people should uphold the law, and his notion of just two laws was not an affront. Yes, it was foolish, to imagine the people would drop their hatred and pettiness and love each other, but it was well-intentioned. If people loved God and Loved their neighbor as themselves, you wouldn't need ANY laws.

However, here was where the logic was missing - The Law existed BECAUSE man was a flawed and sinful creature, and to suppose that this Soul inherent in man could ascend to perfection, that it could rise about the mire of misery that was Judea - Well, that was as solid as the dreams the Essenes recorded their writings from. It would be nice if everyone could get along. We all dream of such pleasantries, but the best you could hope for was a united front against the Roman occupation.

But Caiaphas must be insane - planning outright rebellion? He may have been able to work Pilate around his little finger, but if the Syrian Legate turned up it would be a slaughter. The Legate was a brutal, uncompromising dog faithful only to the Emperor. If he marched down, Jerusalem would be bathed in the blood of Jews, and all the treasures of his people would be taken. The fact was that when Sejanus was removed the High Priest should have stopped this business of supporting the Zealots. Tiberius was a fair ruler, they could have gained greater freedom from the yoke using diplomacy and bribes. But no, Caiaphas was power mad. He wanted to say he was the one who defeated the Romans, to be the High Priest whose name will be forever remembered.

It seemed that he wanted the paving stones painted with the blood of martyrs. But Nicodemus knew, once you unleash the madness, there is no stopping it. No good will come from loosening the insanity of the Zealots onto the streets.

ooo0000ooo

It was a quiet place, away from observing eyes. Out of the East Gate near the cemetery was a sheltered grove where no one could approach unseen. Caiaphas was there, in disguise, waiting for the follower of Yeshua to arrive. The priest had brought an armed guard with him, though they were dressed as priests. If this Iscariot failed to act as promised, then the good news was that he would shortly get to ask God if Yeshua was his Messiah!

Judas was not a large man, unlike so many others in the close circle of the prophet. He was a wiry thing with a beak for a nose and brooding dark eyes - shiftless and lazy, the priest was informed. He would sell his mother for a few Shekels, was the general summation. Exactly what they needed.

Whatever it was about this prophet, he was impossible to find. He had noted it while watching the first time he attacked the money changers, he seemed to be invisible. Well, at the time he considered that if this Yeshua were the Messiah the truth would soon out, he would either walk into one of the traps set to catch him, or he would cast out the Romans. Either way, they won. However, the raising of this Lazarus from the dead ended any thought of compromise. Even some of his own people were agitating to have the High Priest speak and explain how such a thing could be.

They were ignorant fools. He had seen the Persian magicians. They could make things vanish, make things appear, and even supposedly raise the dead, but he knew it was a trick. But because of these tricks, soon this Yeshua would be in a position of power, with the people behind him doing whatever he asked - and it was very clear to him this would-be Messiah had every intention of ridding Jerusalem of the Sadducee rulers. Not the Romans. The Sadducee would all be murdered in their sleep and Pilate would do nothing to stop them - in truth, he would laugh. Who knows, he might even have this Yeshua on his payroll.

The father, Joseph, had been a surly and unpleasant man, but he did excellent work and knew his place. The son witnessed how Joseph treated the priests, with virtual contempt, and so he believes the same. Like father like son, typical lower class rubbish. The guards indicated an approaching figure, it looked like an old woman, hobbling towards the grove. She walked in, cast off the disguise, and there was Judas.

He stood there for some time, saying nothing, not prostrating himself or declaring the names of the High Priest. *Fair enough,* thought Caiaphas. Their business of assassination was not something anyone would be recording in the Mishnah. "Welcome Judas Iscariot," he nodded.

"High Priest," Judas returned a small bow of acknowledgment.

Caiaphas held out the bag of silver, "You will take us to Yeshua, identify him and make sure he can be seen. In return, you will receive this bag of silver." He took out one of the coins and flipped it towards the Zealot. "This is to seal the deal, agreed?"

Judas bent down, inspected the coin, and nodded, "It is agreed. He will be in the Garden of Gethsemane this evening. Keep your soldiers here and I will fetch them when the time is right. They will have payment?"

"Do you think I would leave this amount of silver in the hands of soldiers? They will play dice and gamble it away before you see them. No, come to the Temple and we will conclude the bargain."

Judas looked at him suspiciously. "I think I will have full payment here and now, and I will not be responsible if your men fail to act or if he gets away." Of course, he is thinking they won't be able to hold Yeshua, no one ever has. But if they do, then the logic of Barabas is sound - He kills two birds with one stone, as well as feathering his nest.

Caiaphas wondered why he bothered. Everywhere he suffered small suspicious minds with no view of the larger plan. Yet he would have paid gold coin for this troublemaker to be put into prison, so a bit of silver was a bargain. He threw the bag to the traitor and left, saying, "You know what happens should you fail to fulfill your bargain?"

Judas did indeed know that the High Priest was little more than a thug, who would be happy to see him dead and thrown onto the dung heap. It was done.

ooo0000ooo

Yeshua was almost in a trance, the disciples had seen him distant, that was normal - but this day he seemed so far away that he was barely here at all. Peter was his most familiar friend, and asked, "Master, you seem to be walking in distant lands. Can you tell us what you see?"

It was the right question, for the master returned to them, laughing. "What I see is a dream to you all, but in my eyes, what YOU see is the dream."

Peter relaxed, he was back to riddles, all was good with the world.

Yeshua just looked at the small band around him, "A story then?" They all cheered. They were like children, finally.

A man prayed to the Gods for riches. He prayed earnestly, devoting himself to the quest, knowing that if there were a god in the sky he would answer him. Just as God gave fruits to trees, so would he give wealth to this poor man who prostrated himself and begged for his mercy. For many days he prayed, his wife thinking him mad. For many months he prayed, his children certain he had lost his mind. For years he prayed, and finally God answered him, 'You who have prayed for wealth, I have heard and will bestow this upon you!' A great voice shook the night sky where the man was crouched, praying to the moon.

He came out of his trance, at least he had been heard! He blessed the world, he blessed his family, for soon he would be a wealthy man. His children and wife would no longer think he was insane. And as God had promised, pearls began to fall from the heavens like rain. Exquisite pearls of astounding value dropped all around the man, and with joy he gathered them up until he had a bucket of pearls, enough to buy a mansion and servants and all manner of good things.

He had thought to stop, but how could he? After all these years of praying, he got another bucket, and another, filling them to the brim with glorious pearls. His family would never go hungry and he would finally be given a place worthy of his devotion to God. He gathered his pearls till the morning light came over the horizon, then he took a cart laden with his buckets of treasure into the nearest town, to house of the trader.

Yet when he got there, a hundred people were already at the door of the pearl merchant. They were shouting and angry, pushing each other out of the way, trying to get in the door with their bucket of pearls. 'Well,' the man thought to himself, 'God has been good to us all. One day they will thank me for all the prayers I gave to God that brought this about.'

However, when he finally got in the door, the pearl merchant looked at his buckets of pearls with disdain, 'More pearls?' he laughed. 'I had hoped you would have brought me apples, being a farmer as I know you are.'

It was then the poor farmer realized all his pearls were now worthless, and the simple harvest he had neglected was the true wealth. But the world was not yet done with him, for he announced, quite foolishly, 'To think, I prayed to God for years to bestow wealth upon me, and when he finally rained down pearls from heaven, the irony is that he gave me worthless wealth!'

The pearl merchant shouted, "What? YOU are the reason my good business has been ruined? You are a curse and a plague upon my house!" and with this, the merchant beat the man out the door. Then the people asked what he was doing, and he explained, 'This man's prayers brought all these worthless trinkets from the sky.'

And so the people also beat the man, for disrupting their lives so much, and raising their hopes only to find them dashed. At last, he made it back home, beaten and bruised, his cart still laden with worthless pearls, and he thought that he might pray to God to turn the pearls into apples. But when his wife saw him, she laughed when he told her what he thought to do. "If God turns all those pearls to apples, what will your apples be worth, fool?"

That is why the man stopped praying to God for wealth and went out to his untended orchard to start the slow task of trimming and preparing the fields for harvest.

Peter asked, "So, the message is not to pray to the Lord for wealth?"

Thomas was the one who answered, laughing, "Peter, the message is that true wealth comes from effort, not prayers. The good Lord gives equally to all, what we give to ourselves is the right to earn our fair portion with our labor."

Yeshua looked up out of his daze and smiled. They were as ready as any could be. "I say to you, while miracles pave the path of the Lord, they are but stepping stones to him. So pray not for miracles, pray not for wealth, pray not for any thing. Pray only for the path the Lord wants you to walk be revealed. Then pray for the courage to walk it."

His thoughts wandered to the future, to the past, and back to the present. There was one more thing they must know before he left this body, hc must show them the ritual of renewal. "Is the Passover prepared?" he asked.

"It is master," Peter replied. "The sun is setting, do you need help getting to the table?"

A curious effect of the herbs was that, in his vision, color was barely present. The world looked to be black and white and shades of grey. He did not need assistance to walk, indeed, walking helped restore clarity and strength. He got up and went to the stone table in that ancient room set over the Tomb of David. The Essene had cared for it for hundreds of years, the strange paradox being that because of the Babylonian exile many of what were to become the Essene were given the vineyards and olive groves to care for.

His people, for so long under the heel of the rich and powerful, THANKED Nebuchadnezzar for taking away the landlords and rulers, and willingly paid him the tax required for the land they were given to till. Without trade and without merchants all Judea regressed to an agricultural community, without name and without purpose. Yet his people flourished in this world, they had wealth and happiness that lasted up till the rebuilding of the temple. That was when the rich and powerful began to take charge once more. Even so, they all coexisted until the rise of the Sadducee. That was when the Zadoc moved to the Qumran. Rather than witness the false claims to truth from the wealthy, the High Priest took the religious community to the plateau, a place of no value to anyone, and made it fertile.

Of course, those who became the Sadducee, those who made wealth on the backs of others, they slowly took back all that his people had worked for and gave them nothing in return. Thieves, all of them, parroting righteousness while breaking the most basic laws of hospitality.

"Do you remember, those of you who were with me in the first year of my teaching, when the people on the Terrace of Solomon wanted to stone me, saying I blasphemed and called myself the equal to God?" he asked.

John nodded, "I remember, you said you were the doorway to the pastures of the Lord. You spoke of thieves coming to steal the sheep, and how a hireling shepherd will run from wolves who come to hunt them, but that the good shepherd will stay to defend the flock, even unto death."

He laughed, "And we had to hide with the Baptist's followers! They were good times. Do you remember, you asked me why I came? I said that I came to give you life, but you did not grasp what this meant at the time. Those priests in the Temple, they are brigands who seek to steal the sheep from the Lord. They have attacked the good shepherd with gossip, they have accused him of falsehood, and they have told all in the village that he is the thief, not them. And soon they will attack again, not for what he is, but because they want the flock he protects."

Yeshua was in India, at the feet of a Savant, a wise man. He had asked him, *"How does one Soul lift another into the love of the Lord?"*

The old man had smiled, "You speak of being awake and how to awaken another who slumbers. I ask you: *What brought you here? What raised the question in your heart*? The answer is only that we have woken up to the delight of the spirit within. Only when we dance this truth do we come to true Consciousness. As we delight in the Lord, as we learn to trust his guidance, he learns to trust us. We then take up all our learning, all our pain, all our suffering, and we use these stones to build in our hearts a doorway to the divinity within. This is not something we can give another, but it is part of the gift of life that flows through us, and with this another might ask, *'How do I catch this joy I see in that man?'* This is your answer: You must be the giver of life, for only life can awaken the sleeping soul."

He looked at the fish loaves on the table, the ancient ceremonial bread of his people. He looked at the Essene wine, rich in nourishment. A man could live on just these two things alone. As the last rays of the sun fell away, the heart of Yeshua was illumined, and in that moment he knew what he must teach.

He took the bread, and breaking it, said, "This is the feast of the unleavened bread. As you know, the Essene bread is made from sprouted grains, and without yeast - for we celebrate with unleavened bread every day of the year. This too you will do. This bread I give to you, it is my body. It is everything I am, everything I stand for. Not one thing cried out in pain during its making, it is pure and nutritious. A man can live on this bread.

"But a body cannot exist without blood, so take this wine also, the Essene wine made from fruits and herbs. A man can live on this wine. I was raised on it, the herbs purify the water, the fruits fortify the soul. This wine is my blood, this bread is my body, take it and eat, knowing you are taking a part of me into your soul as you do so." Yeshua poured the wine into the prepared cups, and broke off some of the bread to share it amongst the disciples and those of their families that were present.

"I shall not eat again until the time of trial has passed, so while I enjoy this last meal with you, know that by partaking of this simple ritual, I am with you. By this act, you will bring me into your hearts and be renewed. This is my covenant with you, that as you accept me into your heart, I will hold you dear in mine. As you welcome me into your life, so too will you bring the Lord, for he and I are as one. Affirm my covenant and you will know the water of life everlasting.

"I say to you this, whenever two or more of you are gathered in my name, I am with you as surely as you see me here today."

It was at this point Judas returned, making his apologies for his lateness. Yeshua laughed, seeing the truth behind the mask, "And I wonder what the cause of such delay might be? I say to you all, in this time of testing many shall find their hearts wanting."

"Not I," said Peter stoutly. He would never fail to support his master.

Yeshua laughed again, and in a seeming trance spoke, "Peter, I say to you that before the cock crows, you will have denied me three times." Without waiting for a response, and enjoying the look of shock and confusion on the faces of his fellows, he sang one of the psalms:

"I love the Lord, he has heard my voice and prayers. He has listened to me, therefore will I call upon him as long as I live. The sorrows of death have surrounded me, and the pains of hell gotten hold of my heart: I found trouble and sorrow. Then called I upon the name of the Lord; O Lord, I pray, deliver my soul. Gracious is the Lord, and righteous. Our God is merciful. The Lord preserves the simple: I was brought low, and he helped me. My soul rests easy for the Lord's bounty is upon my heart.

He has delivered my soul from death, my eyes from tears, and my feet from falling. I will walk before the Lord in the land of the living."

The men, knowing the psalms well, sang along, feeling the love and presence of the Lord reach down and enter into their hearts.

And after this ritual, they all went to the Mount of Olives.

ooo0000ooo

As he made ready to go to the Mount of Olives, Caiaphas was called over by Annas. "You are certain of this Iscariot? Much weight is being placed on him."

Caiaphas shrugged, "No, I have no faith in any Zealot, especially one who is a follower of Yeshua. But he has been paid to hand over their master, and if he reneges, we know the general whereabouts of the followers. We will butcher any and all we see should he fail to deliver, which if nothing else, will cause his followers to depart the city. I have already whispered in Pilate's ear that the people are ready for uprising and he knows he no longer has the soldiers to deal with this." He brightened up, coming out of that face of grim determination to what was almost a smile. "We should write a letter to Tiberius, thanking him for making Pilate so vulnerable!"

Annas nodded, "His life hangs by a thread. May we be the ones that assist the fates in snipping it."

"Soon, my dear father-in-law, soon we will be done with the curse of both prophets and Romans."

The Kiss of Judas by Ary Scheffer

The Arrest

Then Pilate entered the headquarters again, summoned Jesus, and asked him, "Are you the King of the Jews?"

Jesus answered, "Do you ask this on your own, or did others tell you about me?"

Pilate replied, "I am not a Jew, am I? Your own nation and the chief priests have handed you over to me. What have you done?"

Jesus answered, "My kingdom is not from this world. If my kingdom were from this world, my followers would be fighting to keep me from being handed over to the Jews. But as it is, my kingdom is not from here."

Pilate asked him, "So you are a king?"

Jesus answered, "You say that I am a king. For this I was born, and for this I came into the world, to testify to the truth. Everyone who belongs to the truth listens to my voice."

John 18:33-37

The assistant to Caiaphas was a man called Malchus. He organized mercenaries to be present and had the audacity to allow the men to remain in their Roman battle dress. "He is NOT to be killed, I don't care about his followers, but we need this Yeshua alive. He doesn't carry weapons that we know of, so it won't be difficult."

"Zealots can be a little crazy. We can't be blamed if this Messiah dies. How do we know who he is, anyway? These prophets and followers all look much alike," the captain of the guard queried.

"We have an informant who will point him out to us. We are waiting here for his signal. When this is done, we want the apostate at the palace of the High Priest, for trial and sentencing. We NEED to have him there, he is part of a bigger plan." Malchus did not like this end of the business, but his uncle had to be catered to. He wanted to keep his position and salary, and HIS opinion about what was decided higher up the chain was not required, nor ever asked for.

All the same, he hated it.

"My missus reckons this Yeshua guy is alright. Is he getting the chop 'cause he embarrassed you lot, or what?" one of the Romans asked.

"Shut up Marcus," his Captain responded. "We get paid to do a job, not think."

"He raised a guy from the dead, boss! Everyone is talking about it, not your normal Messiah. That's not the normal 'lame people walking' business which they set up, the guy was in the fucking tomb for days!"

The Captain looked at Malchus, "That true?"

"And if it was?" Malchus sneered back.

"I don't want no curses on me or the boys."

The Sadducee hated the superstitious nature of the Romans. "Caiaphas wants the guy off the streets, reckons it is brewing to a full-on revolt and this guy is at the heart of it. So we either collect him now or you will be dealing with mobs in the streets shouting death to Romans?"

The Captain smiled, looking at the lads, "Could be fun! A little sword chopping exercise is good for you."

"Well, the Temple doesn't want this. You are getting double the usual rate, that should cover the cost of your superstition." Malchus hated every inch of this job. Dealing with the Romans, out in the dead of night like some thief - He came from a noble family. He should be at home with a nice little fat wife and be popping out babies, not sulking about on covert missions for Caiaphas.

A child turned up, coming through the trees and catching everyone by surprise. Malchus waved to let him through, but the boy said nothing, just indicated the direction they must go in. "You have been sent by Judas Iscariot?" Malchus confirmed. The boy just nodded. Probably a mute, he thought. "Show us to the way, then."

Shortly they came to a place where Iscariot stood, holding a bag of robes. "Put these on, you will look like followers turning up to hear the words of the master. When I touch him, you will know who to arrest. Now walk silently behind me and do not speak lest you scare the rabbit away."

ooo0000ooo

Pilate sat with his wife that evening entirely unaware of the shift in the tide of men that was about to occur, where fate was drawing its bow. The moon was soft and coming to fullness, tinged with a red from the dust storms of the last few days. It was a moment of beauty, the fleet of Herod below, the lapping of the waters against them beating a rhythm that echoed the power of the Romans in this place. Their time in this province had not been without difficulty, but Claudia and he had adjusted, found new friends, and now genuinely enjoyed the place, much to his surprise.

They had created a comfortable world in Judea, far wealthier and more luxurious than they could have dreamed of in Rome. Judea had made the family rich, and when they went back to Rome it will be to a house on the Palatine, laden with stunning fabrics from India and intricately carved furniture from Persia. Nothing so ostentatious as that ridiculous gold leaf that Crassus used, their house would be seen as the epitome of modern elegance. Presuming they escaped the cloud of Sejanus that hung over his appointment here, their future was bright.

His thoughts were now on what was coming next. No word from Tiberius was a good thing, but how much longer before the senate voted in a new proconsul? Still, there was nothing to do but soak up the unique beauty of this desert country. Claudia was there with him, she was happy to permit a lack of conversation, her husband had many things on his mind, and his wife was content to sit with her man, knowing he felt the same about her. It was the only security she needed, for after all, it was not her throat that would be throttled should things turn bad.

Wives of powerful men in Rome had influence, not direct power, but they shaped things in the background, carving the pedestal on which their husbands stood. The wise men knew this and gave their women every respect. Claudia Procula would have been called a witch in some cultures, for she had a deep understanding of herbs and healing, plus she worshipped the ancient mysteries, having a fascination with the mystic Greek teachings in particular. She knew her husband was far too practical a man for such things, but he knew she had a connection to The spirits and listened to her. It was she who advised him to follow Sejanus, it was also she who advised him to write to the senate as much as he did his sponsor. In both cases, wise advice.

The stillness of the evening was permeated with the soft song of their nightingale, strangely answered with the wood chopping *Chonk Chonk Chonk* of the nightjar in the distance. The depth of peace was beguiling, but Pilate knew the crest of the wave was about to strike: the trouble in the streets, the murmuring of revolt, it had grown to a crescendo, so opposite to this place where they sat.

Claudia may have had some inkling of what was to come, for she mentioned the new Messiah, "This one seems much better than the others, dear," she noted as they sipped the watered down wine on the balcony at the *Caesarea* home. The marble tiles, simple and clean in Grecian white, contrasted against the fruit wood tables laden with fruits and morsels - everything expressed their wealth and unhurried sophistication.

He knew who she was talking about, everyone was talking about this Yeshua. The Son of God, many had declared. "Herod likes him but is worried. He attracts large crowds and while he offers no word of agitation or uprising against Rome, the same cannot be said about his words about the Sadducee. He tears into them, you know. Caiaphas is always at my door when we are in Jerusalem, arguing that the man is dangerous. Was it true he raised someone from the dead?" Pilate asked.

"Word is yes, he did. The fellow was in the tomb for more than three days, and the wandering prophet just knocked on the door, rolled the stone aside, and told him to get up, as you would do with a lazy child. This Lazarus fellow DID get up, not in great shape, but he is alive."

Pilate shook his head. He had no way of being able to write this in a report without him being called crazy and relieved of his post. "Well, as this directly opposes everything the Sadducee teach I am thinking he set this up, specifically to goad Caiaphas, for whatever reason. Nicodemus likes him, especially as he rubbed the priests' noses in it with another round at the Temple, and now this Lazarus thing. I am of the mind he has done a deal with the Pharisee for them to take over the Temple. We will find out tomorrow, I will be away early to Jerusalem for the Passover celebrations, the official ones."

Claudia knew better than to argue with her husband. She had made discrete inquiries, and it didn't look like a setup as he suggested, but of course, that is what would be in the report to the Senate. "Why do they seem to have more than one Passover? The Pharisee have theirs, then the Sadducee have a different day for it."

"The Essene have another yet day for their Passover, can you believe? Depends on what calendar you follow. Another reason for the great wisdom of Caesar, when he adjusted our calendar to make sense. They would have been exciting times, my dear, but we won't see the like of a Pompey or a Caesar again." Pilate yawned and stretched, it had been a long day.

"Check in on the children before you sleep, darling," his wife urged. "They stay up for you, and there is nothing the nurse can do to settle them when they know you are home."

He nodded, such a fine woman. His house was in perfect order, no one ever questioned her chastity, and the children were adorable. He was a bit of an idiot over them, he knew, but she and the children were the one constant pool of love in his life. He embraced her, kissing her cheek with tenderness.

This time, she held him close, whispering, "I have had a vision. Take care with this Messiah. Whenever someone stirs up political turmoil, only trouble will follow. He must have known how this would have challenged the Sadducee, and they will be angry. That means mobs on the street, looting, blood being spilled, and all that goes back to Rome via the spies the Senate has in place. You need to be very circumspect in your dealing with him, not a toe out of place."

He nodded, she was never wrong in these sorts of things. "We will find out soon enough my darling, but as you say, absolutely by the law. It will only be a threat for a few days. When Passover is done, the crowds will clear the city and we can breathe more easily. Hopefully it will have settled down enough that I don't have to be there in the middle of their damn squabbles. By the gods, I have never seen any race more argumentative and pernickety that the Jews."

"Too long away from attending to the Senate, my dear?" she laughed.

He smiled. Point taken, they were worse. He took his leave, going to see the kids. As he walked, still fit and lean, she sighed. Claudia should have been perfectly happy, but something was amiss. It was nothing inside the family circle, she felt her husbands trust and love like a warm blanket around her. No - her unease was to do with this Messiah.

She had seen his face, clear as a bell, looking at her. It was not threatening, he just gazed at her as a dislocated face, those eyes peering into her. It was a message from the Gods, but how could she be certain of what they were saying?

ooo0000ooo

A small group had come with Yeshua to Gethsemane. He was passing on information about the nature of spirit but not in stories, this time he spoke as a direct teaching, a thing that was exceedingly rare for him to do. "The nature of existence is like a large house with many rooms. Our physical world is but one room, all of Judea is a tiny corner of this room, and we are floating seeds waiting to strike good soil. This house has many floors, each one higher and finer than the one below it. In dreams we can visit these higher rooms, and gain insight and wisdom from the teachers who care for those who come to them.

"No one owns this house, for though it is the house of the Lord, he gives it freely for all to share. You may come and go to these higher floors at anytime your heart is open to them. There are laws that govern all worlds, things that give rules for this play, this game of life.

"Understanding these laws will allow you to pass unhindered through any room.

"But first you must have a key! You must have the special gift that unlocks the doors to my father's house. I say to you, this key is a quality of the Lord inherent in your heart. It is mercy, and the practice of mercy opens the door to the house of the Lord, for only a compassionate heart can enter the kingdom within. When men revile you for your simple faith, take their hatred and put it into the fire of your mercy. It will soften and bend to your will. For no man can hate a humble soul and not suffer for it. No man can detest a kind heart and not suffer for it. Have mercy on them, for they do not understand what it is that they do, and only mercy will provide the fire in which their arrogance and foolish dreams can be reformed."

Peter scratched his head, the concept of mercy being a fire baffled him, like so much of what the master would say. Yet it made sense and he didn't even know why.

It was Thomas, the quiet one who spoke, "Who built the house?" he asked.

Yeshua looked at him, "You will, Thomas." He paused, "You all will be builders of the mansion wherein the Lord shall reside. In this world, you will create a path, brick by brick, that will lead to the house of the holy. But you cannot build the Lord's House with physical things, you build it with faith, hope, and charity. Just as Herod built the Temple knowing he would not live to see the end, so too will you build a house for those that follow you. I have given you the stones of truth that will form the foundation of all that comes, but it will be you who builds the house."

At this point a small crowd of new people were coming to the garden. Mary knew it was amiss and grabbed Yeshua's arm to lead him away, but he put it from him, saying, "Woman, I will accept the cup."

She looked at him questioningly, "Raboni?" she asked, using the formal form of Aramaic only used by the wife of a Rabbi. As such, she was bound to obey him in religious matters, but he was saying he would undertake the death ritual and become the Zadoc in prison? She could sense the priests were behind a plot to catch him, he needed to leave, and leave now. He must have a quiet, sacred space to prepare. "You must do this in the space under the upper room, my husband," she protested. "It is all prepared, the task is hard enough without an added burden!" Then she understood, and stepped back to the shadows, unwilling to see or be a part of what was to come.

Judas came up, with a crooked smile, "Master," he said, taking his hand and kissing it.

"And by this you do what you came here to do," Yeshua sighed. The touch of another's hand disturbed the flow around the Master, and that which protected him from profane eyes fell away.

Suddenly the soldiers who had come in disguise could see the man they had been hunting. How they had missed him, they knew not, but now they moved forward to seize Yeshua. Peter drew his fishing knife, a thing that never left his side, and quickly going to the Sadducee who was in charge, put it to his ear, ready to plunge it in to his brain should the man refuse to order the mercenaries away, but Yeshua spoke loudly, "Do not, Peter. Those who live by the sword die by the sword."

He looked confused, but withdrew the knife, leaving the ear bleeding and cut. But then, from his own hand, he felt a flow of power and he watched the cut heal. This was the healing power the Master spoke of, but it could not be him, it must have been Yeshua. He was the worker of miracles.

The soldiers had weapons drawn, expecting a bitter fight, but no one raised an arm to help their teacher. The Romans snorted, what a useless pack of pricks, and hauled away the one Judas identified, off to the Palace of the High Priest.

ooo0000ooo

Claudia woke choking in fear. The moon streamed through into her room and painted the walls with ghosts. It was the dead of night, the shifting tide of night whispers from the hills about them sang a weird, haunting song, such as cows wail on the full of the moon. But this is not what had unnerved her, for she had a dream and in it, a silhouette of the old woman appeared, one of the Fates. She knew in her bones great change was being wrought in the inner worlds.

You never saw one of the Fates without the tide of destiny being turned. She saw the maiden in her youth, just before Pilate proposed marriage. She did not even like the arrogant knight that he was, and he was far below her station - but she knew, the Fates had decreed it must be so. She saw the mother just before coming to Rome, where her husband was introduced to Sejanus. She knew then this was also destiny playing out, even before the man who ran the Praetorian guard found his meteoric rise in public office. That was why she had advised Pilate to accept him as a Patron, which he wisely did.

And now came the third, the old woman, the hag. The end of the cycle was upon them. Her heart was bitten with fear, but she took charge of her emotions, cleared her mind, and asked for guidance from the

Gods. This is all you could do when presented with Fate, ask for their assistance and with their power, you can turn Fate into Destiny.

She knew it had been written in the Stars that her husband come to this place. Her sisters in Rome had laughed, calling it a barbaric place she sailed to. They advised her to stay with the children, to keep the house and servants, "It is a proconsul position, he will be removed within the year!" they said. No one believed Sejanus could usurp the senate and command them with his will, and everyone knew Pilate was not the choice of the old men. "You are sailing into trouble and more trouble," they advised.

Unlike them, she loved her husband. Not at first, but he was a rare one, he listened. He took her quiet words of advice and put them to good use, and had provided well for the family not only without complaint but with never even a hint of anger towards her. She had grown not just to love him, but to cherish him, even his faults. His arrogance was the worst, it caused him no end of umbrage from clients and those in his circle, but she supposed it was the necessary arrogance of Rome he carried with him. That was his way: Pushing through obstacles, laughing at difficulty, and more than happy to gamble with the gods on whatever dice they threw.

But it was his way with the children that had completely won her over. They adored him, and it was mutual. Not just the boy, but the girls as well, he loved them equally. No mother could resist this charm. As a result of her natural love, he had little time for mistresses and prostitutes, unlike so many other men. She was lucky to have him, but the old woman had shown her face, yet in profile? What did that mean?

Another vision! A raven flies past with a streak of blood on it. Change is coming, a storm so vast it will shake the world. She got up and called the old woman Herod had sent to her, to help raise the children and teach them the ways of the Jews, so they would fit in. She came in wrapped in a gown she had hastily put on, "My lady?" she asked.

"Rebecca, I have seen a vision of change. I would ask what it means to your people." With this, she explained the vision of the Fates, and the red-streaked raven.

The old woman was very serious, "This is connected to someone. Have you had a vision of any person in the last few days?"

"Yes, the new prophet, the one who raises people from the dead!" she exclaimed and KNEW it was part of this.

The old girl smiled her toothless smile, "Ah, yes. I met him at my house in Galilee. He came seeking shelter from a storm with some of his followers, fishermen all, like my dead husband. He is the wisest man I have ever met. He told me a story, about a man who went mad for the love of his brother who was dying. He knew me, he knew my life, though I had never met him. People sneered at me when my husband died in madness, saying I was tainted and had caused it. I was avoided by all until this Yeshua came from out the blue and asked me a riddle. He knew what pain I had in my heart, and without a word, without doing anything, he took it away. Because of him I could face the world again.

"As soon as he was done, the storm outside ceased, and he went on his way. That was just before you asked Pilate for a woman who knew the herbs and healing magic of our people, so indirectly, Yeshua is the reason I am here today. He is the one your visions are about."

"In what way?"

"I know not, my Lady. But the blood-stained Raven indicates an ancient sacrifice, and the third Fate indicates the end of a cycle, but this only ever means the start of the new once the winter is done. It is both promising and fearful, and wrapped around the prophet."

"Do you believe he is the Son of a God, as the people say?" Claudia found that sort of arrogance too bitter a pill to swallow. Who did they think he was, Heracles?

"I know of no son of man who can command storms, raise the dead, and give sight to the blind, my Lady. But I have followed his travels, I go to hear him when I can, which is not often but I can tell you, every time he is asked if he is the Messiah, the chosen one, he laughs, and says, *'We are all chosen by the Lord'*. He does not deny it, he does not affirm it. He speaks of us ALL being the children of the Lord, every one of us has a pearl inside our hearts, and we just have to open the oyster of ignorance to find it there."

"Yes, but do YOU believe he is the Messiah, the one the Jews believe will throw us out of Judea?"

The old woman smiled, "Perhaps if you understood the Essene path he follows it would make more sense. They believe that ALL men go through lifetime after lifetime, coming here to this world again and again, to find perfection. The Essene does not hold that this world is worthy of anything but sacrifice, but if a man can find harmony with the Lord and dwell in his spirit, then his life is one of peace and understanding. So if THAT sort of evolved Soul is a Messiah, then yes, he is.

"Keep in mind, my Lady - Yeshua says not one word against the Romans. My understanding is that he is not particularly interested in THIS world, but in showing people how to ascend to a higher place. So no, I do not think he is the Messiah of the Jews, I think he is something better than that. Any man who, with a few words, can unload the burden of pain and suffering I have lived under my whole life, is worthy of my love and trust." The old lady stands there, wondering what else this high-born woman will want of her. Living here with the Governor and his wife had been a revelation to her, seeing the love each had for the other, and the delight they took in their children. It was so very unlike what the people thought Romans were like.

"Rebecca, look after the children while I am away. I will go to Jerusalem with my husband." Claudia now knew the storm to come was about this new prophet, and it was certain he would be in Jerusalem for the Passover, like all the other observant Jews.

The old lady bowed and went to her duties, which included tying a note to a pigeon that would inform Herod of events.

Claudia packed and ran to her husband, catching him up before his entourage left the house in the early hours. "I come with you today my darling, if I may?"

Pilate looked up, his wife despised the day-to-day nonsense of Jerusalem. He had a question in his eyes, "Of course you may come, woman. I am surprised, I thought you could not stand by and watch the goings on of the mad Jews."

She confessed, "I have had visions, my husband. I must see if they are true."

He had long learned to respect the otherworldly side of his wife. After all, every oracle was a woman, so the wise man understood how the Gods would always speak through that gender. His job was deciphering what was paranoia and what was genuine insight.

ooo0000ooo

Peter followed Malchus, not knowing what else to do. A few of the disciples came with him, and when it was clear he had been taken to the palace of Caiaphas, not the Temple, he got Andrew to hurry to the house of Joseph of Arimathea to seek his assistance.

Yeshua was arraigned before the jury of priests, not the proper Sanhedrin, too many would have objected. No, this was a small cadre of trusted allies, all committed to removing this pestilence from their midst. The charges were clear: Violating the Sabbath law, threatening to destroy the Temple, practicing sorcery, exorcising people by the power of demons, and claiming to be the Messiah.

However, just as the charges were agreed upon, Joseph burst in, demanding that the proper procedure be followed. There was a roaring commotion as he was shouted down, and his points of order were ignored. He stayed as a witness.

Yeshua was brought in, bound and gagged, while being hissed and booed at by the priests. The charges were read by Malchus. "You stand accused of violating Sabbath Law. You have publicly stated you will seek to destroy the Temple. You are accused of the practice of sorcery, and of partnering with demons to perform false miracles. Worst of all, you have claimed to be the Son of God, the Messiah. How do you plead?"

Yeshua said nothing. It was Joseph who spoke up, "This is absurd. I read your list of accusations, and you say this man violated the Sabbath by HEALING people on that day? Next you will be accusing mothers of daring to feed their children on the Sabbath. And if one man can destroy the Temple I would be mightily impressed, as it has taken thousands of men decades to create it. I mean, if he could do what you are accusing him of, then he would be the Son of God, wouldn't he? Heracles would be pushed to equal this."

Joseph was ignored, while Yeshua stood there in silence, even when onc of thc priests came up and slapped him, then spat in his face, saying, "Son of God, the arrogance, the PRIDE!"

Yeshua smiled at the irony of the arrogance and pride before him that made the accusation, which only annoyed the man further. "Look at him," he called out to his fellows, "He thinks he is better than us, you who call yourself the son of GOD."

He replied quietly, "Are we not all the children of the Lord?"

Another shouted, "Child of some demon from the desert, more like it!"

In his mind, he is twelve years old again, his father had been working at the temple, and on this day the whole family had come. Some priests were having an argument over what it meant to work on the Sabbath, and the young boy had gone up and asked them if a fisherman fishing on the Sabbath was forbidden.

They laughed, "Of course," they all snorted in agreement.

"Then if a poor man fishes to feed his family who is starving, if HE fishes on that day, then he also sins, this is what you say?" He already knew how impractical these rich men who called themselves priests were. They had never done a days work in their life.

"Well, no, but he cannot cook the fish, therefore there is no point to him fishing."

"So the Lord wishes his people to go hungry?"

Another laughed, "Foolish child, this is expressly forbidden. No, he must eat! At least three meals that day he must eat."

Yeshua had smiled that smile of the mouse caught in the trap, "But he is poor. On the best of days, he can barely give his family one meal, let alone three, and now you are telling me he is not even permitted to be poor?"

The men started arguing amongst each other, which caused the young boy great delight. He posed question after question: Surely a boy was allowed to fish for enjoyment? Which they all agreed was a fine thing to do. But then he was killing for the sake of killing, on the Sabbath Day? How could this be right? And it was illegal to cook food on the Sabbath, but if a man left a fish on a metal plate in the sun, and the LORD cooked the fish, was this OK? He had done this for almost an hour before his mother found him, and rightly accused him of arrogance. But his father laughed when hearing the tale and stood up for him, just as this Joseph does. He looked up at the only truthful man in the room, sending him his love.

Joseph looked back at the accused, a cousin of his wife. A good, pure soul who only ever helped those around him. All this was so wrong, men shouting, Caiaphas stacking the room with all of his own people, but as he gazed at the helpless Yeshua, he saw him pick up an empty cup, and run his finger around the rim three times before some guard snatched it from him, smashing it to the ground.

He sighed, this is what his wife did at the beginning of many of the Essene rituals. She explained she was inviting the Lord in to fill the cup with his wisdom, and she would sup on the water three times, asking for his blessing. At this point, John the disciple had arrived and touched his robe. Joseph was exceedingly grateful for this show of support. "Peter and some others are outside, but we cannot break in here and free him without bloodshed, which the Master has expressly forbidden. What must we do?"

Joseph whispers, "He has indicated to me this is part of an Essene ritual. Please send someone to speak with James and ask why he would take a cup and rub his finger on it three times."

John nodded. The Master had done exactly this with the cup, saying he was turning the Essene wine into his blood. He had asked years ago why the Essene did not drink alcohol or eat meat and he had answered it was because the Lord does not seek blood, rather a man should die daily for his sake, and become a risen Soul in every moment.

So many things he had said that he had not grasped, but now he was beginning to see. "He said after he brought Lazarus out from the Grave that he must undertake the task of becoming the Zadoc for his people. I am given to understand this means a death ritual. I will send a man to see James and see what we must do if this is the case."

Joseph just nodded, helpless before the weight of lies and hypocrisy that was before him. "Yes, Mary told me, but he cannot undertake it here, in the prison of the Sadducee. He will most surely die."

An angry accusation cut through. "You lead the people astray, Yeshua. You are *kakopoios* - a magician!" The voice of Caiaphas broke up the general dissension and argument in the room. "It is this simple, you practice magic and create what appear as miracles in order to deceive the people, to have them believe you are the Son of God, the Messiah. Your presence disturbs the foundation of our faith, and for this we will demand of Pilate the death penalty."

Then arose the voice of Annas, the oldest of the priests. "I quote the law in Deuteronomy - *'If there arise among you a prophet, or a dreamer of dreams, and he gives you signs and wonders, and the sign or the wonder come to pass, after which he says, Let us go after other gods, then this prophet, or that dreamer of dreams, shall be put to death'.* What do you say against this?"

There is a general cheering from the priests. That was the way to do this, the legal way. Pilate cannot refute the pure logic of this argument.

Most still considered Annas to be the real High Priest. He came from the shadows, his evil eyes gleaming with triumph. "In Exodus, it is made clear, *'Thou shalt not suffer a witch [either male or female] to live.'* This man practices witchcraft, therefore the law decrees this man must die!"

His voice took on a shrill note, "This man says he can bring down the temple, Joseph says this is absurd, and I would agree with him - but this man has already caused storms to cease, and instructed nature herself how it must behave. Perhaps he CAN speak with the elemental forces, perhaps he CAN ask them to create earthquakes to attack us, and to bring down our Temple? How far will this Yeshua go in his hatred of us? We have all seen how he despises our existence, how he has flogged our money changers on TWO occasions. TWICE he has attacked our sacred Temple, TWICE. We must not permit him the third attempt."

There is a roaring from the priests, the blood is stirred and there is no doubt in any of them that they must have this man put to death.

Caiaphas smiled, "What say you, are you this so-called Messiah?"

Yeshua looked at the creature before him, a man crawling in the dust of power, begging for scraps from the Romans while parading himself as an Emperor amongst his people. "I spoke openly to all. I taught in the synagogue, and in the temple, and in secret have I said nothing. What do you ask me to answer? Surely you must ask those that heard me speak and ask them what they believe?"

Annas snorts, "We HAVE asked the people, they proclaim you as the Messiah, the King of the Jews! So we ask you, are you the King of the Jews?"

Yeshua sighed at the falseness of the creature. "Whatever I say to you, you will not believe. If I asked you for truth, you could not answer. But from this day forward, the Son of Man will be seated at the right hand of the Lord."

Caiaphas slaps his chair, "His arrogant mouth confesses. Take him before Pilate!"

There is a general roaring of agreement, and Yeshua is taken away into a back room, where temple guards blindfolded and then beat him, saying, "Tell us prophet, which one of us hit you?" They did this for some hours, laughing while they awaited taking him to the place of judgment.

ooo0000ooo

Outside, sentries around the house noted that a gathering of people has occurred. There seemed to be one man organizing things, never a good look. They go up to him and demand, "Are you a follower of the magician inside?"

Peter looks up earnestly, saying, "I know of no magician."

"Then why are you here in the early hours of the morning, with all these people?"

The fisherman weighs his words carefully, if he is arrested, who will take charge of the proceedings to find some way to get Yeshua out of their clutches? "I say to you, I know nothing of what you speak. Am I on private property such as you are charged to protect? No? Then leave us."

He then said to the followers, "We must disperse, they will soon send Romans out to drag us in. However, we know they will try to have him executed, so get to the courts at dawn, where Pilate will be sitting for the days' proceedings. The rest, get to James' house and gather up everything. Caiaphas will be looking for witnesses to justify his actions, so make sure no one is home when the soldiers call. We may need to get out of Jerusalem."

Mathew and John were with him as they made their way to the courts. John described the events in the High Priest's house. "They are going to try him not on blasphemy, but on being a witch," he explained.

Mathew snorted, "That is nonsense. Pilate will throw them out."

John was not so sure, "The one significant area of overlap between Roman Law and Jewish Law is that witchcraft is forbidden and punishable by death. They are very superstitious, the Romans, and they live in fear of someone placing the evil eye on them. This can be used as the justification to carry out a death sentence."

Peter was weeping, "But Pilate has freed all the Messiahs sent to him. Surely scourging is the worst we can expect." Even that was too much for him.

John was more pessimistic. "Yeshua raised a man from the dead, Peter. This openly defies the Sadducee and everything they preach. If they let him live they believe he will destroy them not with a war, but with his word and actions. Everything he says and does is anathema to them. Our best bet is to fill the courtyard of judgment, and hope that Pilate enacts the Passover peace offering of letting the people choose who they want released from prison."

Peter nodded, "I agree. Let us get everyone in there and make a show of support. They can't arrest thousands before Passover, they don't have the room in their jails."

But when they get there, the entrance is ringed by Roman guards, asking all who wish to enter what their purpose was."What is this?" asked Mathew. "Why are the Romans questioning everyone?"

John was almost white, "Because they have been paid to do so. This is the work of Caiaphas, he has something planned,"

Dawn was almost breaking, Peter had to act, "I will see what they want."

He strides up to the portal of the courtyard but is stopped by a guard. "Why are you here?" he demands.

"Just coming to see the day's proceedings," he answered nonchalantly.

"Are you a follower of Yeshua?" The guard demanded.

"No, never heard of him."

But still he was not allowed inside, "Who do you follow?" the guard questioned.

Peter was surprised. What sort of question was this? Then he heard a ruffian speaking beside him, answering the same question with, "Barabas!"

As he heard this, the Cock crowed. Peter bowed his head, three times he had denied knowing his master, just as he had predicted. But in his heart he could not say he followed Barabas, nor would he expect any of the other disciples and followers to do this. He knew what this was now, it wasn't about Yeshua at all, but about getting Caiaphas' chosen one out of prison. And of course, who delivered the master up to them? None other than Judas Iscariot, the former follower of Barabas.

When Peter didn't respond, the guard just pushed him back and kept on with the job he had been paid to do, to only let in the followers of Barabas.

He left that place, sick to his belly and wanting to throw up. He had thought with the arrest warrant being issued that they wanted Yeshua but in the end, his master was just a piece in a larger game. He felt the violence of his father raging inside, he knew at that moment how easy it was to murder, to beat a person to a pulp, to harm another and not even think about it.

The storm that took his father and his older brothers still raged in him and he had not the power to silence it. The Baptist had brought him forgiveness, but it was Yeshua who had truly given him peace, and now this peace was to be sacrificed. In a rage of righteous anger, he went to find a weapon, until a voice in his thoughts reminded him, "He who lives by the sword shall die by the sword."

But how could he sit by, doing nothing?

ooo0000ooo

The morning proceedings started with the usual declarations to the Roman Gods, a thing that invariably caused the priests and petitioners to wrinkle their noses. Which was why Pilate made them extra long, for he enjoyed that part of the day.

First order of business, a beaten man is brought before him, blindfolded with hands tied. The court scribe read out the request, "The Sanhedrin has declared this man a witch, they say he has admitted to this, by his actions and words, and that the sentence must be death."

"Step forward and explain to me why the man is here," said Pilate, fairly bored already.

Caiaphas himself stepped up, "This is the Nazarene known as Yeshua. He has created quite a stir, disturbing the peace at the temple, while making promises to the people to lure them to follow a false god, himself. We say his so-called miracles such as raising people from the dead are the work of a devil, and that he is a witch."

"Not the usual Messiah claim, Caiaphas?"

"Indeed, people also make this claim, and further they are saying this man is the rightful King of the Jews. He admitted as much to me at a trail we just held." The priest bows, and steps back. He then signals his scribe to take the written testimony up to Pilate, which he reads through.

Watching from behind the curtains, Claudia gasps. This is the man in her vision. She hastily scribes a note on some papyrus, *"Please husband, do not have anything to do with this man for I have suffered a great deal today in a dream because of him"* He looks up from the prosecuting documents to the letter delivered to him from a scribe. He reads it, arches his eyebrow, and thinks carefully.

He then calls Caiaphas over. "What is this really about?"

The High Priest bows and grovels, "Governor, there is much anger and disturbance in the streets over this man. Wherever he goes, large crowds gather. To be fair, maybe he is a magician, maybe he is just a smooth and careful man with many tricks, maybe he is even innocent, but I have it on certain knowledge that if he is out in the streets this Passover there is going to be a riot so large your soldiers will not be able to quell it. He has declared to me that he is the Son of God, and the people want him as their new King. As you are well aware, I would personally be very happy to see the end of your good friend Herod, but the result of letting this one walk will be bloodshed and rioting."

Pilate just grunts, and wonders what the old fox is really up to. "You have tried and judged him according to your laws, why is he here?"

Caiaphas holds his hands open in helplessness, "Why, because the sentence was death, and as you have assumed that role of final arbiter in these matters we Sadducee can no longer maintain the order of our society as we see fit."

Pilate looks over to Yeshua, "So, do you claim to be King of the Jews?"

Yeshua looks up, "Are you asking for yourself, or because others make this claim?"

"Do I look like a Jew? Obviously, the priests have brought you to me and made this accusation, if this is what it is. What have you done that is so upsetting to them?" Pilate was impressed by the man's courage and left it very open for this Yeshua to clear his name.

"My kingdom is not of this world. If this WERE my kingdom, would my servants allow me to be delivered to these Jews?" Yeshua indicates the priests.

Pilate had to stop his face from smiling. Excellent answer. "So, are you a King?"

The man before him paused, looking briefly at his accusers. Yeshua then looked Pilate squarely in the eye, saying, "As you say. To this end was I born, and for this cause came I into the world, that I should bear witness to the truth. Every one that is of the truth hears my voice."

Pilate smiled openly, what a nice swipe at the priests, calling them deaf and dumb to the individual right of a man to be the ruler of their own world. This was a basic Roman belief, that in your own house, you were as a King. He could execute his wife, the granddaughter of Octavius, and not be brought before any court, but only if he did it within the walls of his own home."So, what is truth?" he asked, rhetorically.

The courtyard below was full of people calling and shouting. Pilate imagined it must be the followers of this man, so he smiled as he found a way to heed the advice of his wife. He went out onto the balcony, calling for silence. As the crowd settled he made his intention clear, "I find no basis for a charge against this man brought before me. As it is a custom for me to release to you one prisoner at the time of the Passover, I ask you. Do you want me to release 'the King of the Jews'?"

To his surprise, the crowd roared back, "No, we want Barabas! Free Barabas!"

Pilate almost flinched, he had been trapped. This was what the old fox was up to, tricking him into releasing a real criminal. He turned and went back inside, saying to the priests, "I find no fault with this man."

Bilibus shouted out, "But he stirs the people, he creates trouble, and has done so ever since he left Galilee!"

Pilate smiled, "From Galilee you say? He is Herod's problem, my friends."

And with this he walked inside, indicating an ending of proceedings. Behind him, furious faces erupted into argument, until Caiaphas settled them down. "We take him to Herod, then."

"We cannot go into his palace, it is unclean!" exclaimed another of his people.

"Then you can wait OUTSIDE! He is in Jerusalem for Passover anyway. Get this man to Herod." Caiaphas wheeled about and went to speak to Pilate. He didn't overly care what happened to the Rabbi anymore, he had just gotten what he wanted.

He walked in, Pilate was angry, saying, "That was nasty, even by your standards. Why do you want Barabas out?"

"Governor," he groveled, "everything I said today was true. But releasing Barabas is all part of keeping the city calm and peaceful. This Yeshua IS a problem, he is causing great rifts even in the Sanhedrin itself, and the Zealots hate the fact that all their messiahs are being ignored for this new one. Everywhere I look, trouble brews. Handing Barabas back to his people will settle them down. This is one thing sorted, there will be no riots from that quarter. But remember, only days ago the people were throwing palms at the feet of this Yeshua, calling him the King of the Jews, shouting Hosanna! The next step, we all know it, they get excited and start agitating for change, asking for their man to be recognized. They will soon be running up to Tiberias to attack Herod's palace, demanding he quit. But to be perfectly blunt, if this Yeshua is dead, they won't be."

Now, it just needed some Roman logic. "Surely, one man's life has less value that the lives of the hundreds, possibly thousands that will die if he lives?"

"Get out of here, it is Herod's problem now."

Caiaphas bowed, then wheeled about, leaving the governor to stew.

As soon as he left, Claudia came out from where she had been watching. She went to her man, understanding the difficulty of the situation. Jerusalem was a pot boiling over, everyone could feel the tension.

In a rare moment of complete trust and intimacy, Pilate explained, "It was all a ploy for the priest to get his boy out of prison. I have to let this Barabas go now, but if I release this Yeshua as well, even though I judged him to be blameless, the crowd will tear him apart. I did the next best thing and sent him to Herod. Herod likes his prophets, despite him beheading the last one, so I expect he will hold him for a bit then let him go. That also means no one will be rioting, trying to get him out of prison here. Plus Herod hates the priests, so my guess is he will release him in Galilee, so no reports go to the Senate about Roman tourists getting killed by insane Jews. Because THIS is what would happen. We have a lot of rich Romans in the city right now, and they are the ones who will be targeted by angry mobs, as the palace is too hard a target."

She nods, her man knew how to juggle the complexity of politics. "I saw his face clearly in a dream. I saw the Old Woman. I saw a Raven streaked with blood. This Yeshua is a pivot, the axle to all this, and it seems you found the way to remove us from the wheel."

He looked at her, this granddaughter of greatness. "Breakfast?"

ooo0000ooo

The Tetrarch of Middle Judea was in Jerusalem for Passover, along with all the other Jews in the country. It did not take long to reach his house, nor long for Yeshua to be ushered in.

Herod could not believe it, he had been wanting to meet this new Messiah for over a year, and only more so since he heard he had raised someone from the dead! The priests thought they would have had to press him for an appointment, but he welcomed them, asking them to bring him this King of the Jews everyone was talking about.

Yeshua was not the strapping fellow he had expected, not like John, and he had been beaten by the Sadducee. Crude bastards, without even the decency to clean him up before presenting him. "And why does Pilate send this man to me?" he asked.

"He resides in Galilee, the Governor said it was your problem. He is accused of many crimes, but specifically that of witchcraft, which requires the death penalty." the priest said, delivering the sealed message sent by Pilate.

Herod's wife was also present, "The Proconsul sent him, you mean. Get this poor lad some wine. Looks like he needs a drink." She knew he was an Essene and bound to refuse alcohol. Unlike her husband, she considered this Yeshua a threat to the stability of the house. "And after all, he is a king, so he stands above us, darling. Perhaps we should give him a palace as well?"

Herod knew her whiles, "Get the boy some water and kindly remove my darling wife from the court if she opens her mouth again." He smiled pleasantly at her. "Now Yeshua, if I may call you this. I must apologize for the awful treatment, but what can you expect from a Sadducee?" He looked at the priest, and smiled.

"He is accused of being a witch, he has admitted as much," the priest ignored the barb but wished Caiaphas was here instead of getting Barabas out of jail.

The note from Pilate asked for him to deal with this King of the Jews. Herod Antipas knew why he was seeing this Yeshua, the whole city was ripe for rebellion and Pilate wanted him shipped him up to his palace. Maybe, as long as he wasn't another fun killer like the Baptist. He might even be entertaining. "Oh, well I would love to see one of these magician miracles. Show me something amazing, Yeshua, and we can ignore everything these priests are saying." Herod was all smiles, this promised to be an excellent distraction.

But Yeshua said nothing.

"Come on now, no need to sulk. I didn't do anything to you, after all. Give the priests the silent treatment, not me." Herod loved these barbarous Messiahs, though he had always deeply regretted the incident with John. "You were a friend of the Baptist and he told people you were the Messiah. Of course, he also insulted my wife, which was regrettable. I assure you, I would have preferred to let him live, but he refused to reconsider his position."

Still Yeshua said nothing.

"They DO say you are the new King, Yeshua. Imagine that? I am a mere tetrarch, but YOU are the KING! All these people believe in you, and I want to as well. I just need a little proof, a small miracle, like turn that water we gave you into wine, as you do - or some other bit of cleverness!"

Yeshua was a rock. He did not even look up to the Tetrarch of Galilee.

He stood like this for many minutes, with Herod waiting for him to do something, but it seemed like he was drugged. That was possible, the priests might have wanted his silence. Still, a proper Messiah would have done SOMETHING.

"Well this is disappointing," Herod muttered. There was nothing worse than a boring prophet. "But at least this much is clear, I can't stand judgment over a man who will not speak, priest. I cannot find him guilty nor can I find him innocent. Sadly, I must rely on the greater wisdom of Rome's governor, and send him back."

Herod ordered a Tyrion Purple robe to be brought, to cover up the blood-stained shirt, and sent him back to Pilate, dressed as was more befitting the King of the Jews. He knew Pilate would appreciate the joke.

After they left, Herodias sneered, "You should have had HIS head off as well."

Herod was left thinking, given the imminent defeat of his army due to King Aretas, the father of the wife he cast off for this vulgar cow, that perhaps the Baptist WAS correct.

"I miss the Baptist. He was far more entertaining than this one." He glance back to Zachariah, who nodded his agreement. His man had spoken to the Sadducee, they had warned him of what would happen if Herod let this Yeshua go. The riots would start, Pilate would be overwhelmed, and then King Aretas of the Nabateans would swarm in to the Roman lands, looting and pillaging. And that meant the Legate in Syria would come down and sort everyone out. The survival of Judea was at stake, and they could not afford to look vulnerable.

Even so, if the man had performed one genuine miracle, one clear sign he was the one John had said he was, he would have risked keeping him in Tiberias until the heat of the Passover blew past.

The Trial of Jesus

Pilate's wife had returned to Caesarea, thinking the matter was sorted, but now Herod returns the problem to him. He stood there in the purple robe, looking at the floor like he was drugged. He responded to nothing, not even the scourging, not even the joke of the crown of thorns placed on his head.

Even so, this Yeshua would recover from that humiliation and the reputation of Roman Law would be held intact. Pilate had presumed that by parading this sad spectacle in front of the crowd it would have satiated their blood lust, but it did not. Now they called for crucifixion. This was madness. All the boy need do was to say the correct words and avoid his fate. He MUST know this was a setup by the Sadducee? He indicates for his guards to bring the accused to his private chambers behind the courtroom. Once there he looks at the sorry mess before him.

"Let it go, Yeshua. There is nothing more to prove. Speak to me, tell me you are not what they accuse you of. Just say the words."

Still the man stood there in silence. Pilate was beside himself, why should he care about these insane Jews and their petty little quarrels, and yet he did. He had come to love this place, despite its madness, or perhaps because of it. Did it have the strict regulation of Rome, no. Did it have order, no. But it had spirit, the place was ALIVE.

"Yeshua, you know I have the power to free you, or the power to have you crucified. Speak to me, tell me you are innocent, as I know you are of these accusations, and I can set you free." Pilate almost pleaded with the fellow to see reason.

Yeshua finally looked up, and staring the governor squarely in the eye, he said, "You have no power at all over my fate, except it were given you from above. The ones that delivered me to you? They bear the greater sin."

"We all know the Sadducee are corrupt to the core. It is no secret. We know this whole show with you was a charade they performed, to get Barabas out, as well as to remove a threat to themselves. This is all they see when they look at you, a threat to their rule." Pilate paused, he had to make sure his Aramaic was clear and well voiced - it was not as clear and clinical language as Latin, but he was perhaps the first governor of this province to bother to learn the language of the people. One of the reasons the Sadducee gained ascendancy with the former Governors was because they all spoke Greek and could communicate. Did the man understand him? He wanted to let him go.

Yeshua looked at the poor fool before him, one who had no concept of what was to come, or what had truly been the purpose of all this. He said, not unkindly, "If I asked you what is the first casualty of war, innocence or truth, what would you say?" Without waiting for a reply, "I say to you, both die in the heart of the aggressor at the very moment the intention to draw blood from another is formed in their mind."

Pilate looked at him, "Don't you understand, it is not enough to find you innocent. If I just let you go you will be killed by this rabble. You can end this war, but you MUST say publicly that you are not the Messiah, the returned King come to guide the Jews out of darkness. After this, I can get you out of Jerusalem and that will be the end of it."

Yeshua smiled, "I say to you, if you sacrifice the dove of peace with either a word or a knife, it makes no difference. It dies the same death as the love in your heart when it is murdered by anger, selfishness, or fear."

The Governor brought forward his translator and made sure he had understood the Aramaic correctly. He just shook his head, why do these people get so stubborn over such tiny details and miss the bigger picture?

Pilate felt that old anger rising, why these pointless puzzles? The man just has to declare himself innocent of the charges, give the undertaking to keep it quiet for a bit, and it will all blow over. "Does not your survival matter to you, man? Do you demand the weeping of women over your dead body so much that you will not just refute the charges, and declare you are not the King come to save Judea from the Romans? Your reputation is not worth anything when you are dead and these people will most surely see you dead otherwise!"

It infuriated Pilate that this innocent man, set up by that power-mad priest to get his boy out of trouble, would not just say the words that needed to be said. "If you will not speak for yourself, is there no one else to speak for you?" Every Roman had the right to representation, this was Roman Law. He could extend this protection to Yeshua, if only he would ASK for it. Already Nicodemus and Joseph the tin merchant had seen him privately, saying they would post bond and keep him out of sight until it all cooled down.

But Yeshua would not say the words that would save him. With regret, Pilate stepped out onto the pavement, where all had gathered to hear his proclamation. "I find no fault in this man," he stated.

They shouted at him then, they booed, they hissed - they blatantly abused his good nature and kindness. "Crucify him!" they screamed with a passion that told the Roman that Caiaphas was indeed correct. This

Yeshua had angered the wealthy of the city so much with his talk of no rich man going to the grace of the Lord, with all his talk of Samaritans being better than Jews, that if he let him walk, they would tear him to pieces in public.

The practical side of his nature returned. It must be as it must be, if the man will not save himself, and he had been given every opportunity, there was nothing more he could do. He went to a ceremonial purification bowl, and washed his hands, saying, "Then take him away to be crucified, but I say to you, I find no fault in this man."

He bitterly turned his back and left them standing. He did not know what he would say to Claudia but the one present and certain reality was that if they tore this prophet to pieces in the street, Roman Law would have been broken. He would then have had to send out soldiers to arrest so many people that insanity would be unleashed, and the streets would run with blood. All because of one man's stubborn dignity. But by the Gods, what courage he had, foolish though it was.

A large riot in Jerusalem would overwhelm the guard here, now that Tiberius had greatly reduced it. Losing to this rabble would mean his ability to govern the province would be brought into question and he would be recalled to Rome, to answer why he allowed such madness to erupt. He knew Caiaphas had his friends in the Senate, people he paid to whisper against him. All they needed was the smallest excuse to petition the emperor for his head and Tiberius would give it to them. Now it was about personal survival and if the prophet will not save himself, it was not his job to do so.

He instructed the centurion to put a sign over the man's cross, saying "King of the Jews". For he WAS a King in bearing and courage. This man they would kill was better than ALL of the damn priests that accused him. Plus, the sign would get up the nose of Caiaphas.

Joseph and Nicodemus looked on in sorrow as the crowd got what they wanted, cheering as if they had won a great game. Nicodemus could not understand it, "All he had to do was refute the claims and say he would leave the city and not return. He would have lived, that was the deal. Pilate was happy about it, it solved all the concerns. Why?"

Joseph sighed, "The man he raised from the dead, Lazarus? He had undertaken an Essene ritual, one where you brought yourself back from the dead. Without someone undertaking this ritual, the high priest, called Zadoc after the original high priest of the Israelites, cannot be replaced. Without a Zadoc, the entire religion fails, for it is crucial to them. It seems our Yeshua has agreed to this ritual, though it is nothing like what the Essene would normally do. But yes, madness indeed."

"What can we do?" Nicodemus had come to genuinely care for this strange prophet.

"I will ask my wife for the herbs of somnambulance and organize for him to receive them. He will look to all as if he is dead. I have a prepared tomb for the ritual, he can use that, and see if he survives."

Nicodemus shook his head, "No one survives crucifixion, Joseph. No one!"

A tear welled in the merchant's eyes, "I know, old friend. But we will do what we can."

ooo0000ooo

Yeshua went through the streets on his journey to Golgotha carrying the crossbar. The people who were laying palms at his feet mere days ago were now hurling insults. The priests had been busy, applying the logic that if this were truly the Messiah, then he would not have been held and captured by the Romans, so this Yeshua had lied to the people.

Crowds are gullible, they swing to the loudest voice, and many voices were calling out that he was a fraud, deserving of crucifixion. Yeshua himself barely noticed for he was well past the hour he should have had the vinegar that would tip him into the other worlds. The bitter herbs push you out of your body, and the pain, humiliation, the struggle with the crossbar, all of this seemed incidental.

Why the casting of the dice had to fall this way, who could say? But the will of the Lord was what it was, and despite the savagery of the circumstances, the master was not moved from his center. He had to keep the focus, hold to the path, and be whatever it was he must be. He was surprised he was still on his feet, in truth.

His thoughts were not in Jerusalem, they were in Kashmir and the lovely house he had by the lake. The flowers that bloomed around it were full of scent, so sweet they carried away any burdens you might have. So different to Judea, with its soft lush forests, the rain, the people who laughed so easily. Compared to this desert, this house of ruin waiting to fall, this place filled with bitter hearts and angry men, India was heaven.

The place called Golgotha came up before long, and soon he was pinioned to the cross beam and hauled up onto the already fixed stake. The ropes ran through a pulley on the top and he was easily hefted up by the Roman guards. They then notched the crossbar into its place and the final dance of this madness started to play.

If he saw his mother or his wife looking at him sorrowfully he gave no hint. His thoughts were with the elephants he had ridden, the places he had seen, and the scholars and wise men he had spoken to in his life.

The Roman soldier looked with boredom at the woman with the bucket and sponge coming to visit the rebels on the cross. "What do you want woman?"

"I am a relative of that one, I have some wine for him, give him a little peace before his last moment. I have a stick with a sponge, as you can see, so may I offer him some to drink before he dies?"

The soldiers may be cold and heartless to most, but an old mother showing kindness was something all understood. The sergeant sniffed the bucket, just a cheap wine. "Go on then, old one. It is the last kindness he will know."

She soaked a sponge in the herbs that would simulate his death and tying it to a stick, pushed it up to his lips, speaking in Aramaic so the soldiers would not understand, "Yeshua, drink - these are Essene herbs to help you pass over." But he did not seem to hear or understand.

A Roman took the pole from the old soul, "I do this a lot, woman." and he pushed the sponge hard against his lips, forcing them open as he did so. And with this, Yeshua drank the vinegar.

It took but a moment, and he said, "It is done!" and his head fell forward as in death. And it was so, for when the soldiers went to break the legs of the other two, to ensure they were dead before the Sabbath, Yeshua was already gone. It was the one thing Roman soldiers understood well, death.

ooo0000ooo

Pilate did not want to receive late supplications but in this case, he made an exception. Nicodemus personally had intervened on behalf of that poor soul he sent to die and had asked to take the body from the cross and bury him as per Jewish custom, before the Sabbath. He waved his hand as if to say they could do as they will. His scribe wrote out a permission.

They arrived before nightfall with the approval, and the guards took down the crossbar, though why these foolish men wanted to let down gently they had no idea. Still, you don't argue with rich men. "Why do you care? He is dead!" the sergeant asked.

"It is our custom," replied Nicodemus, giving them some coin for the trouble.

Well, if the man was paying he got extra service, so they let the cross beam down carefully and removed the pinions, allowing the body to be placed onto the cart the workmen had brought with the rich fellows. As soon as they had him, they started administering herbs, saying it was part of the cleansing rituals.

The Romans cared not a whit and were happy to see them gone. Sitting there guarding dead bodies was a waste of their time.

The cart made its way to the ceremonial tomb of Joseph, with the Essene healers sitting on the cart beside the body, working in the herbs of revitalization. "Will it work?" Nicodemus asked, truly not seeing how a dead man could come back to life.

Joseph sighed, "I am told it can, but this is normally done in a controlled environment, with a body not subject to the cruelty that this soul has been put through. However, the vinegar puts the system into shock, it appears to shut down, and it does - but with the application of these herbs and the binding they are doing, it can bring the body back to a semblance of life. Of course, the person still has to wake up, and if they don't the tomb will be their end. Or so I am told, these healers know far more, but the Essene healers rarely speak."

"So what do we do now?"

Joseph looked at his old friend, "The healers will stay with him, as a precaution. For ourselves, we wait for the prescribed three days and see if he wakes up. Did you know, I have seen the druids do similar in Britain? Their way is different from the Essene, but the principle is the same. Over there, they put a wine and bitter herb mixture into a green stone cup, and there is some sort of reaction between the stone and the wine that causes the simulation of death. If a druid wished to become a High Druid, a man of real power, they have to undertake the ritual."

Nicodemus shook his head, "A thing I will never understand, nor wish to. All I feel is sadness and the desire to drink wine, a lot of it!"

Joseph laughed for the first time all day, "I know how you feel, but this is done now, and just in time before the Sabbath. You can come to my place and my wife will help lessen the sorrow with stories of the Essene path if you wish, or I can go to yours and we can just drink?"

"My place then! I don't want to be alone when I tell my wife what I have done."

The two men bade farewells to the Essenes who had prepared the tomb and made their way to the home of Nicodemus. "It was a noble thing, you did my old friend. Might I ask why?"

The Pharisee shook his head, "Madness would explain it better than my words. I was galled by the cruelty of the Sadducee, and if there is a chance he will live, well, we had to try. I doubt if anyone but myself could have gotten permission from Pilate."

Joseph smiled, and wanted to say, *"But anyone could have helped."* The Nazarene had gotten to the Pharisee and broken down that hard heart of his in some way. "If there is a chance our Yeshua can survive this, I want to see the face of Caiaphas when you tell him."

They grimly laughed at that thought.

Resurrection

Great misery and sadness had gripped the disciples. Nothing would shake them from the cloud of deep uncertainty, for all their plans, all their dreams, had been crushed with the death of their master. Not having anywhere else to go, they stayed in the meeting hall that was above the tomb of David, with Peter struggling to contain his own emotions let alone deal with his fellows.

The pall of uncertainty was one thing, but the blow to their cause was immeasurable. He knew he should go to Beth Zatha, to talk to the followers, to console them, but he had no heart to speak anything to anyone that morning. Silence haunted the shadows and even the sound of the birds seemed vacant. The world appeared to mourn the loss of the purest light it had ever seen.

At the time of his crucifixion, there had been a small earthquake and the night that followed seemed full of an awful darkness. All knew a great soul had passed from this place. Peter tried to recall the words of compassion his master had spoken, but all he felt was emptiness and rage - they had been so utterly helpless to change things. Right now his fury was at the priests, for he knew the Sadducee had wanted his master dead, and finally had managed it, thanks to that worthless worm called Judas.

The coward had vanished and for the sake of the community, it was good that he had, for all the words of love and kindness would have departed if he had shown himself. They would have taken him and stoned him in public view for what he had done. Which, sadly, only told Peter how little they had truly taken in of the master's teaching. With these thoughts, tears began to fall once more, and he found a quiet spot to gaze out of a window to the fields and forests beyond.

There was not a thing to cheer a single soul in that house all that day. No uplifting words, no stories, no song. Just a deep, indescribable sadness that seeped into the texture of life. As he sat there in grief, united with all in the household over the loss, he could not even wonder what he might do now. Nothing made sense, the last three years, four if he included the Baptist, they were for what?

Like an empty drum, his thoughts beat out a dirge that sang of what might have been with a life cut so terribly short. It was such a waste, and the paucity of truth in the coffers of a State that could kill a man so clearly innocent of any blame - It shocked him. Even the ROMAN governor said that Yeshua was blameless, yet still he was murdered under the guise of law.

Bitterness and regret swelled in his heart. He hated everything, everyone: the lies, the deception, the pretense. And at that moment, like a clear and lonely sound of a distant trumpet, it struck him - this was his father. Somewhere, somehow he too suffered this grief and it marked his heart with a cut so deep he could not surpass it. At that moment, he finally understood it. Peter felt submerged, drowning in that self-same murderous hatred of his father - the same hatred his master had spoken against so often.

But Yeshua was no longer here to help him rise above it. He had foolishly thought it gone, but no, it had just submerged like a beast in the water, waiting for him to come to the edge where it might grab him and take him into its depths once more. Yet in his abject loss, he remembered a story, one of the first the master had told - of his ship being under water, surrounded by a bubble, and a monster comes.

You must accept the monster, for it is change. You must let it breathe life into you, lift you up, and bring you back to the sunlight. Despite his need to lash out, to destroy the falsehood that submerged him, Peter stopped. Yes, this was what the master had warned him of. He now had a choice, repeat the pattern of the past, or learn to accept change.

In acceptance, he prayed. He prayed for guidance, he prayed for forgiveness, he prayed that he could find mercy in his torn heart. And he felt it, the wings of spirit, flowing into him. A kindness washed over his grief and he felt the lead weight of guilt drop behind him. His heart blossomed with a deep love and appreciation for all he had been given. It was not just the Master, it was his life, his wife, and his children. Every little thing in every part of his world had become better because of Yeshua. One word, *GRATITUDE*, whispered like a song bird in the distance. He understood, in the midst of his pain he must practice the simple exercise the master had given him so long ago.

In his mind's eye, he saw the parade of every single person he had met in his life. The wonderful grandfather, who taught him how to sew a net, that one was easy to love. He placed him there at the front of his thoughts, sending out gratitude for all he had been and done. Then his mother, long suffering, raising boys in such difficulty. It was so easy to have gratitude for her. And the brothers he lost, their petty squabbles seemed so small compared to the loss created without them, but he blessed them, one by one. He even blessed the storm that took them.

But then it came to his father, the scowling, ugly man full of bitterness. How could you be grateful for one such as him? But even as he thought it, he released the hatred and blessed his father. He was the greatest lesson in what not to become, he realized. He was the symbol of how not to live a life, and yet, he provided for the family, gave them food if not comfort, gave them shelter if not love. It was no easy thing to thank such a man, but Peter understood, by forgiving the past we release ourselves in the present.

The master had said, "Do not find fault in the splinter of the eye of another man while you carry a log in your own!" He laughed then, it was true, everything he hated about his father was in him, and he forgave him, deeply and without reserve - he forgave him for any slight, real or imagined. And then the real challenge presented itself, Caiaphas came into his mind's eye, the man responsible for the death of Yeshua.

How can you forgive such a one? How can you release your righteous anger of one so poisonous? He was a snake, ready to bite all who crossed his path. And in this image, Peter understood, the man was helpless before his demons. The master had said it over and over in a thousand ways, no baby comes into this world hating - it is a thing we learn. To blame Caiaphas for what he is, why this was to blame a snake for being a snake.

The master knew what he was, and made it clear what all the priests were. "It is harder for a rich man to find the grace of the Lord in paradise than it was for a camel to go through the eye of the needle." the words rang true, to get a camel through the needle gate it had to be unloaded, all that it carried, even its saddle had to be taken from its back, and then it could be led through. Even one such as the High Priest, should he put down his trinkets of power, his arrogance, his disdain, even he could pass into the grace of the Lord.

Peter nodded in humble acceptance, the wisdom of the master was still with him, still teaching him. What he must do was listen for that still and certain voice within his heart. He released his hatred of the priest and all the man stood for. He released his hatred of the last day, and all the injury done to himself and his people, but mostly, he released his pain and accepted the love he now felt flowing deep inside.

As he did so, the grief and suffering began to wash away. Tears fell, sadness still clung to the walls, but he felt his heart breathe once more. *Accept the change*, the words came through. There was nothing else he COULD do, and despite the need for justice, Peter bowed his head and allowed the Lord into his heart. *Stop asking why,* a voice seemed to echo in the distance, *and start asking what next!*

This made little sense, what could come next? And then he almost laughed, for he had spent all that day asking that very question.

Perhaps the master was with him still, tricking his stubborn heart in the right way to go? A small glimmer of hope began to enter, a small opening where the spirit of the Lord might find purchase. He started thinking of how the others were coping, for surely they were in grief as much as he was. Picking himself up, he understood his task. It did not matter how heavy the burden he felt, his job right now was to help raise the spirit of the brothers, to lift them out of the pointlessness he had almost been submerged in.

"Brothers!" he called out. Slowly there was a movement in the tide of grief that had swept through the house, "We must pray for guidance. Just as the followers of John suffered grief at the loss of their master, so do we. We must now pray for what we must do next. Come into the sunlight with me, and let us ask the Lord for guidance."

One by one they got up and followed Peter into the sunlight. Thomas was already there and smiled thinly as the brothers emerged from the shadows. He spoke few words at the best of times, and right now his silence was a welcome balm to the hearts of all.

ooo0000ooo

The house of the Governor was despondent. Pilate was still in Jerusalem, but Claudia was inconsolable, as was her nanny. Together they watched the children playing on the balcony overlooking the sea, saying nothing. She held the note from her husband, explaining why he had to act as he had. She understood, but it didn't make things easier.

What could she have done more to save that man? What did his death mean to them? She did not know, but she felt it in her bones, the shifting of the tide. Finally, she asked the old woman that Herod had sent them, "Rebecca, tell me what he taught."

The old woman smiled for the first time that day. She dried her tears, and said, "I have no idea! He always talked in stories and didn't seem to teach anything, but whenever I left his people I felt better. But from the moment he first came, you knew there was something special, though what it is I cannot say."

Claudia considered things deeply. She had done all she could, given her situation. What could she do now? "Rebecca, I feel this man needs to be remembered. Can you make special note of finding out the words he said and the deeds he did, and describe these to a scribe back here? I feel we should put into writing a little of his life."

The old woman was glad enough to do this, but she had doubts, "I cannot imagine that the followers will still be about. Once the leader is gone, these groups vanish like the wind. But I will ask people what they know and do as you request, my Lady. One thing is certain, it seems that he would speak to people in dreams, so perhaps they would speak of these things."

Claudia nodded. Indeed, that was how he had appeared to her. "The Gods have their ways, Rebecca. Let us find out what ripples that particular pebble in the pond of life has created, it is the least we can do."

ooo0000ooo

Great celebrations were to be had at the palace of the High Priest. Annas praised Caiaphas for his magnificent handling of the matters before them, being the release of Barabas, and the removal of the temple pest, Yeshua. "Adroit and masterful handling of the matter, beautifully executed, and we secure our position at the cost of Pilate. What could be better?"

Much laughter ensued. "Pilate, saying the rabbi was blameless yet STILL handing him over to be crucified - well done Caiaphas," the voice of some priest called out.

The man himself stood to accept the applause of his peers. "A long road to go, brothers. We have weakened the Romans, but we still have them on our doorstep. This is all just a painful reminder that every day we must renew our efforts to rid ourselves of unwelcome guests. More importantly, we have put the Pharisee back in their box, and let me assure you, we have a plan to sort out any who oppose us. Opposition to the Sadducee is effectively supporting Rome, and I put it to you that any Jew who supports Rome is a traitor. And as a traitor, they should receive the death penalty!"

A rousing chorus of voices calls back, "Here here!"

The High Priest smiled, then settled down to cover the business of the day, happy in the knowledge that his covert plan to eliminate opposition had just been approved by the Sanhedrin, or at least, that is what the official book would note.

ooo0000ooo

Perhaps it was the warmth of the sunlight, perhaps the closeness of the fellows, but all the disciples in the courtyard of the meeting place found themselves feeling very drowsy. Then, to their vast surprise and great delight, Yeshua walked in and stood amidst their sad and sorry faces, bringing them joy and happiness they never thought they would see again, "A story?" he asked.

Eagerly they leaned forward, strangely forgetting he had died.

There was a ship that had to face a tremendous gale. It loomed dark and menacing on the horizon, and the sails strained to catch the wind, but the Captain knew they would not escape it. "We must lash what we can to the ship to increase her buoyancy. Every empty barrel must be brought up from below and tied to the gunwale - The more the better, we must do what we can to stop her from keeling over," he called out, and the crew responded.

Despite their efforts, the storm rode them down and forced the ship onto a reef, breaking it up, however, the empty barrels now served as a life raft to float the men to the nearby island that the reef surrounded. The ship itself was a shattered wreck, with planks breaking off and being carried away, however, the men survived.

When the storm was done they looked about and found food and water to suffice, but as to their ship, it lay broken and battered, with little chance of repair. "Create some shelter fellows, see what food and water you can find. And look for trees we can use, for we need to piece together some sort of ship to be able to get back to our homes and families!" the Captain encouraged them.

The island was a paradise of flowers and there were fruit trees of a sort the men were unfamiliar with, but they tasted good. It was easy to catch a fish, and soon the men forgot all about their families and their friends, and even their home. "This is home now," the men said to themselves, for the peril of crossing the open waters was clear, and this island offered security and peace.

They grew to resent the Captain for urging them on, to try and find a solution to their exile, It was easier here, just lying in the sun, letting the days pass by. And soon, the sense of forgetting grew strong, and for many of the men their former life was now just a dream they woke from. But not so for the Captain, he knew their home awaited, loved ones were shedding tears, and children would need their fathers, so with the few men who were with him, they found trees to fell, and plants that could be wound to rope.

A high tide came, lifting the wreckage off the reef, and the men were able to get her afloat. The ship could now be repaired enough to find home - every day the small crew worked hard, patching holes, repairing sail, making the ship seaworthy as best they could, until in a week they were ready to get underway.

"Ho men," the Captain called to those who laid about in leisure, "we are making to sail home, get yourself aboard!" But they laid there in the sun ignoring him. "Your wives and families cry for you, get up, it is time to go home!" he called, but still they ignored him.

The casks they had floated to shore were now being filled with fresh water from the one spring they had found, and the men who wanted to go home were storing it on board. They had also gathered what fruits they could, and whatever seemed edible that would survive the journey. And still, the lazy men who had done nothing laid about in their paradise.

Not knowing what else to do, the Captain called out, "We leave on the next tide, men. Get yourself up and come aboard, or we must leave you behind." But even this did not stir the hearts of the men, who saw the ship as dangerous and the land they had left one of trial and woe. Better to stay in paradise.

And so the Captain sailed on, leaving them behind. He understood why they stayed, but would their wives, or children? So he talked with the other men with him, and they decided it were better for all to say the men died in the storm, for indeed, what men they had been did indeed die that night of the shipwreck. All that was left of them was a shadow lost in dreams.

Peter woke with a start to find the sun low in the sky. It had just been a dream, but as he got to rise, the other men were also waking, rubbing the slumber from their eyes. "What a strange dream," one said, "I saw the Master and he told a tale about shipwrecked sailors!" And one by one, they all agreed that they too had the same dream.

Peter knew not what to make of it, but the meaning was clear. In some way, Yeshua still lived. They must call him back as the women did at the tomb of Lazarus. "Tonight we will speak of Yeshua, all he did for us, all we learned from him. We first must remember his voice and what he gave, and from there we will come to an understanding of what we must do, for we are the shipwrecked sailors, men. We must bind together to find our purpose, or we shall waste our days in what has been.

ooo0000ooo

Mary the Magdalene sat with the mother of Yeshua and other Essene women, readying themselves for the vigil outside the cave where they would call his name, to bring him back. So many familiar faces from Galilee and the Qumran had come, knowing that the ritual of resurrection needed their presence, as it had done for countless generations.

As they had called for Lazarus, now they would call for Yeshua, hoping he would hear their voice. "The Sabbath will be done soon," said Mary the Mother. "We must prepare." So it was the women gathered water and bread and dried fruits to sustain them during the time of calling. Those ignorant of the tradition thought it was women wailing for a dead one, but theirs was a song of lament not for the dead but for the living.

As they made ready for the journey, the mother of Yeshua asked his wife, "What now Magdalena? You know even if successful, your husband has ascended to a new world, and your contract with him is canceled - what are your plans?"

The Magdalene nodded, "Not the Qumran, that is certain. Mother, all I can say is that this society is a wheel running down a road going to a destination I do not belong to. I will give my future heed when the vision of what it must be will come, but I know it will not be here, fighting the stupidity of men."

"Where would you go, daughter?"

"I heard a calling to the North, past Rome, to a place known as Gaul. There a woman is not secondary to a man, but an equal, in law and practice. I feel the calling to set up a surgery, to be a doctor to the people." she paused, looking at the kind woman whom she had known her whole life, "But mother, I do not see your son remaining here either."

She seemed confused, he would be the Zadoc, he must live in the cave. "Do you think he will go with you?" she asked.

"No mother, I feel his heart calling him to distant lands."

"But who will be the High Priest to the Essene?" she seemed at a loss.

"It remains to be seen, but he said to Lazarus that he would fill the breach until he was ready, so perhaps in due time that one will take over the role."

The mother of Yeshua nodded. These were strange times, unlike any that had gone before. "Well, soon I will be past caring for all of it, my daughter, and be with my husband again."

"The grace of the Lord will surely see you ascend to his side," Mary nodded, kindness in her eyes. So much would change from this day forward, she felt it in her bones. But only if they forged the links to make this new day dawn. One such as her husband was a gift to be cherished and to be spoken of; that a man can find perfection and sit at the right hand of the Lord was a message all must hear.

The women were now ready and made their way to the tomb for the calling of his name.

You can imagine their surprise when they arrive and find the entrance stone already rolled to one side. They were shocked, nothing like this has happened in their history. Who could have done this? There was a guard, but while guards will sleep, they could not sleep through a stone being rolled to one side. Mary goes to see the confused fellow, who is completely without explanation, and without memory of what happened.

He could have been drugged, but by who? And why? The Magdalene goes in with another woman, a healer, not knowing what to expect. The binding bandages the healers wrapped him in are to one side, the spiced water from the recovery font has been drunk, and there is no body lying on the stone, but the blanket it was laid on still holds the blood from Yeshua, stiff and dry.

The Magdalene comes back out and explains what she has seen. Mary the mother collapses in a mixture of shock, confusion, and relief, for he has either somehow survived that which cannot be survived, or someone has come and stolen the body. The fear is that the Sadducee, in their bitter hatred, have taken the body and cast it on a dung heap.

The Magdalene went to voice her deep concerns to the calling women, but from them there was silence, for a stranger had come into their midst. He seemed so familiar, but she could not recognize who it was, and she was not sure who or how this could be. Perhaps he was one of those who had taken the body? "What are you doing here?" she asked.

"Capio Vale'," the stranger said as he walked up to the women, but they did not speak Latin enough to understand, so they asked the Roman guard what it meant. He seemed pale and confused, disorientated as he stammered out, "He is saying that he has taken hold, or captured, something but that he is also saying farewell."

Mary will have none of this, and demands to know who the stranger is, "Why are you here? Why do you approach women like this?" It was known a stranger should never come up to women in public unless they are a relative or introduced by a husband. But then she softens, he is possibly a gardener, and may know where the body of her husband has been taken, "Sir," she asked more kindly, "Someone has taken the body of my husband. If you have carried him away, or know where he has been taken, tell me and I will get him."

The man just smiles, nods to her with warmth and affection, then speaks in Aramaic, "Mary." Just that, he speaks her name, but in a voice so familiar it was like her own heartbeat. And as he speaks this is like a funnel of light poured down and into her, and she saw this was no stranger.

She bowed her head, tears flowing from her eyes, saying, "Raboni!" Her husband had returned, though the body seemed different, it was him. There was no question it was her Yeshua, and yet, it was not. She went to hold him, but he held up his hand. "I have grasped the Lord, the Lord has taken me, but the process is not yet done."

And she understood, he was in the turning, the time when the body was still infused with the healing power of the Lord and had to be left to proceed. He had not yet completed the transformation into the Zadoc. But was he just an astral projection, coming from the dream worlds?

He laughed at her thought, for now these things he heard as clearly as if she spoke to him. "Woman, tell my brothers I have returned. Explain to them I am in the Interregnum, the place of transition, but that I have risen in my body."

The Magdalene, for all her years studying the healing and medicine scrolls of her people did not fully grasp what was happening, but the Mother of Yeshua came up, beaming. "It as I was told by Gabrielle, Mary. Fear not, he is risen from the tomb and walks amongst us." She beamed at her wonderful boy, embracing him inwardly with all the love only a mother can raise. "Born of man and risen to the divine."

Yeshua was with the wind, the keen high note of a distant flute played through him, feeding him both life and joy. His breath was that of spirit, and he understood. The cruelty and deceit that went into his suffering were the lowest elements of man, which he had now subsumed and transformed. Every evil thing done to him was now transformed into a greater truth. But he needed some days to let the energy settle, for at this moment he was more of a projection than a reality.

As he felt the power of the Lord flowing, he smiled at them all, at the astonished faces, the tears of joy, the confusion, and wonderment. The human being was the most marvelous thing in all creation, capable of so much and yet so fearful of their capability. He saw into their hearts, into every small choice each person had made that led them to where they were, and he knew that the master Pythagoras was right, there are no coincidences. Everything comes to its own place and its own time by the path of the choices a person will make.

All he wanted to tell people was that, given the choice between love and hate, choose love. That was all. He left the tearful women and the shocked guard, and made his way to a place of contemplation so that he could complete the task that the women had called him away from. He had to allow the Lord time to rebuild this body, revitalize it, reconstruct it, and transform it. Soon he would go to see the Nubian, but for now, his people had their Zadoc returned.

In truth, he had not understood what a power it was, this transformation. He had entered into the dark worlds between the planes, the pain and suffering of his crucifixion driving him away from his body, yet the faint hint of the Spikenard oil Mary had worked into his skin reminded him he was still alive. Then the vinegar, that which shut him from consciousness of the physical world entirely, separating his spirit from his body so that he soared into the angelic realms. It was so beautiful, so gloriously free of care, that all he desired was to walk in those angelic fields of flower and birdsong.

He was unaware he had been taken from the cross and that Essene healers were working oils and preparations into his body, bringing the nerves and muscles back to a semblance of life. He was completely ignorant of everything but the beauty that surrounded him, until his old master, the Zadoc appeared, smiling and embracing him.

It was he who pointed out the body lying on that stone in the tomb, asking him if he wished to complete the task he started. All of him wanted to reject it, to turn away, to say enough of the pain and the misery and the ignorance. All of him wanted to stay in the harmony he had found, but as his master gazed loving at his student, the student understood. The task was not complete.

But the body was ruined and damaged, he could not just step back into it. This was when the other Zadocs came forward, the masters who had held the baton of his faith for hundreds of years. They all stepped forward as angels, and placed their etheric hands over his body. He could feel them pouring in their love and their power, healing it, uplifting it, transforming it.

He felt the whirling of the current connecting him to his heart, he felt it beating once more, and he opened his eyes to where the Essene healers had waited patiently for him. They still said not a word, but gently assisted him to drink of the healing water they had prepared, smiling with warmth and kindness, a thing he had seen so little of these last few days.

Over the next few hours, while his body started to heal, to come back to some semblance of life, he had wandered in the dream worlds. He saw his disciples, lost and fearful. He saw the Sadducee, arrogant and proud. He saw all who had played their part in this theatre that was Judea. And he saw the future unfold, and the purpose of the Lord for putting him through the awful test of his faith.

All was well, he had chosen love over hate, so all would be well.

ooo0000ooo

When the women went to the meeting room to give the news of Yeshua risen, no one truly believed them. Or more correctly, they wanted to, but could not bear the sense of loss should it prove false. Peter, though, knew in his heart the truth of it, and he had to go and see.

He rushed to the tomb, forgetting any fear of Romans of Sadducee guards, to see if what Mary had said was true. He could barely contain his excitement, but neither could he believe his ears. When he got there, with some of the younger men running excitedly ahead, it was as she said. The death shroud had been removed, the bandages lay beside it, and there was no trace of the master.

Of course, it could have been an hallucination by the women, hysteria can do this, and wishful thinking, but the Magdalene was not prone to such things. And the mother was so calm and certain, this was as clear a sign that the master had indeed risen from the dead, just as he had lifted up Lazarus. But how could a body survive the cruelty of the Roman crucifixion? Surely it had simply been stolen?

The guard was gone, the tomb empty, and not a soul was to be seen. He ordered the men to gather up the wrappings and implements that had been placed there, for he knew that the tin merchant had arranged for all of this. "Take all this to the house of Joseph of Arimathea, and tell him that it appears that Yeshua has indeed done the impossible. And thank him for all he has done, for I know he and the Pharisee took him from the cross personally."

That of itself was a miracle, that the highest ranking Pharisee in the land would have helped take the dead body of an Essene from the cross and risk being called impure. What wonders this master had wrought in the cold heart of such a one as Nicodemus for this to be so. At that moment he understood what his master would want, "I will go to thank Nicodemus personally for all he did to help us," he said to Andrew.

And he made his way to the fine house of the leader of the Pharisee, thinking of the story Yeshua spoke before his torture, that the house of the Pharisee and the Sadducee would fall, killing them all. But that was because of their pride, perhaps such a one as Nicodemus could be redeemed in the eyes of the Lord?

Soon thereafter he found himself calling out at the door of the Pharisee, to have a servant appear, asking what he wanted. "I have come with a message from the tomb of Yeshua. I have come to give Nicodemus praise and thanks, and to tell him the good news."

At this point, the bloodshot eyes and very drunk form of the Pharisee appeared, "What is this? What possible good news could you bring?"

Peter bowed in acknowledgment of the man's status, "First, I thank you for all you have done, risking your privilege as you have. The good news, Yeshua is not in the tomb and witnesses say they have spoken with him. It appears he has indeed risen from the dead."

Nicodemus stood there slack jawed, not really comprehending what he had just been told, "Could it be?" he wondered out aloud. He had thought his entire position in Judean society was done, for Caiaphas would never have allowed a man who had touched the body of the dead back into the Sanhedrin. "It is so? Yeshua has been seen alive?"

"It is so, Nicodemus, in no small part due to your kindness," Peter replied.

He smiled for the first time in days, "Well, this is indeed good news!" the Pharisee brightened up. "Thank you Peter," for he knew who the close followers of Yeshua were, having spied on them for this last three years. "Would you come in and celebrate with my family?"

Peter was indeed shocked, a fisherman invited into the highest house of the Pharisee, but there were many things to do and good news to pass on. "I thank you for the kindness, master," he said, "but there is so much to do this day. Perhaps you would grace us with your presence on a day of celebration for the return of Yeshua?"

The Pharisee nodded and giving his thanks once more, went in to dress and tell his fellows. Once inside the cool of his bedroom, he looked at the robes he had thought he would never wear again, and put them on. When his wife came in and asked what he was doing, "It appears I did not touch a dead body, woman, as Yeshua has been seen walking about and talking to people!"

His dear wife was both shocked and relieved. She had nagged him horribly over what he had done, blaming him for everything they were going to lose, demanding to know why he helped out a miserable Essene and ruined his station like that. Nicodemus smiled to see the look on her face, "No need to apologize woman, all is mended, and the good news needs to be spread! Not that Caiaphas will enjoy hearing it," he laughed as he made his way out to speak to all and sundry.

"You should check first if it is truth," she called out.

He just kept laughing, ignoring her. After all, it really didn't matter if it were true or not, the fact was there was no proof he had touched a dead body now, so it no longer mattered what Caiaphas would seek to prosecute - he had no evidence, no witnesses, and no dead body, therefore no standing to prosecute the matter.

ooo0000oo

Peter arrived back to the upper room of the meeting hall to hear sounds of happiness, but nothing prepared him for what he saw, there in front of the men was Yeshua. He was not sure if this was a dream, but the master looked up and smiled, so what did it matter if it WERE a dream!

"A story then?" he asked the cheering men and their families, all who had gathered to mourn but who now were laughing with happiness.

Once there was a house where many different people lived, but not just people, things from the dream world, creatures of myth also lived there. What this meant was that a man was fearful to leave his room lest he meets some monster and so, while he would brave the risk to find food and drink for his family, he forbade them from stepping out from where they lived.

Slowly, the man found other men, and despite their differences, they were not so great as between man and monster, so they made peace with each other and formed into a tribe. But of course, one man's rule is another's blame, and so there was argument as to what was right and wrong, and what path the law between them must take. And it came to blows, before the women stepped forward and told their men this was nonsense - their only problem were the monsters that lived in the house, and that they should go out and slay them.

This made sense, so the men organized a leader who could take them into battle and they all agreed that, for the sake of the families they protected, they would follow his rules to slay the beasts that threatened them.

But a child was curious, for he had heard of monsters, but having never seen one, he asked, "How many people have these awful monsters killed?"

"Oh, many," a man replied.

"But HOW many?" the boy insisted.

As this was a good question, the men got together and compared stories, arguing once more as to what monster killed who and when and where, until finally they had to admit, no monster appeared to have ever killed anyone in the house. That was when they saw the truth, that the child must be a monster in disguise, sent to lull them into a sense of safety - because all knew monsters lay outside in the house, waiting to fall on any of them, and eat them.

So they killed the child, and said to the grieving women, "See! We have caught and killed a monster already! Now, are there any more questions?"

Of course, there were no more questions, and so the men through the child out of their room and went about creating the laws by which their world would operate, and thus keep the tribe safe from evil.

Even Peter laughed at the absurdity, for it was clear, Yeshua was back to poking fun at the Sadducee. Finally a story he understood without needing an explanation, Yeshua was the innocent child they put to death for asking too many questions which they had no answer for. But the story was not yet over ...

However, the child they thought they had killed by beating him and throwing him out the door was not yet dead, but lay there, battered and bruised. He stayed in that spot until one of the monsters came and took pity on the poor thing, taking him up to the upper rooms of his house, for this monster was the one who owned that place.

He cared for him, fed him, and helped heal him from his wounds, until the child grew strong and turned into a fine, strapping young man. The fact that the person who looked after him had the head of an eagle, the body of a lion, and the tail of a snake did not bother the child, for he loved this monster who loved him. And in the course of time, he came to meet all the other monsters that did indeed live in the house.

He could see no reason why the men feared them so much, so he asked one day, when a group of them were visiting, "Why do men fear you?"

This green slimy thing was more of a moss than a thing, but it answered, "My name is disease, and man fears me greatly for I can enter into his world and destroy him utterly."

Another thing that looked like an ancient tree spoke, "My name is old age, and man fears how I will wear him down and break his spirit."

There was a thin, wispy thing, barely a reed that spoke next, "I am loneliness. Man fears me most of all, for when he sees my face he runs screaming in terror."

"And father, what is your name, and why do men fear you?" the child asked of the Chimera.

The monster that saved him spoke, "I am called Fear, my boy. I live inside every heart, and I cause men to do the most abominable things to each other."

"Like killing me?" the boy asked, at last understanding. "But tell me father, what is my name, and my purpose?"

The monster of fear smiled broadly, "Your name is Truth, and your purpose is to kill me!" he laughed.

"Then why did you save me, show me love, and bring me up to be so strong and healthy?" he could not understand why his foster father could possibly want to be killed.

"You have already conquered me, my beautiful boy. Your love and your truth has beaten the fear from fear, cured disease from disease, defeated death and loneliness. Now it is time for you to leave this house, and teach others to do the same."

There was not a dry eye in the room, for it was true. This was no story, it was the simple unadorned truth. Yeshua spoke, "Now it is time, for you have learned all I have to give you, to spread this message of love to all who have ears to hear, my brothers. As he held up his hand in blessing, they all felt it, a fire in their hearts, a love for all things. "As the Lord has sent me, so I send you out into the world to spread this message of hope. Let your love first conquer the fear in your heart, and by your example you will allow the fear in another to leave. In this way they will be shown the path to freedom."

But when they went to thank him, he was no longer there. The disciples sat there in wonderment at the mystery they had been shown, feeling the love he had shared with them all. And all through the room, a thin, biting wind blew - yet not a hint of a breeze stirred.

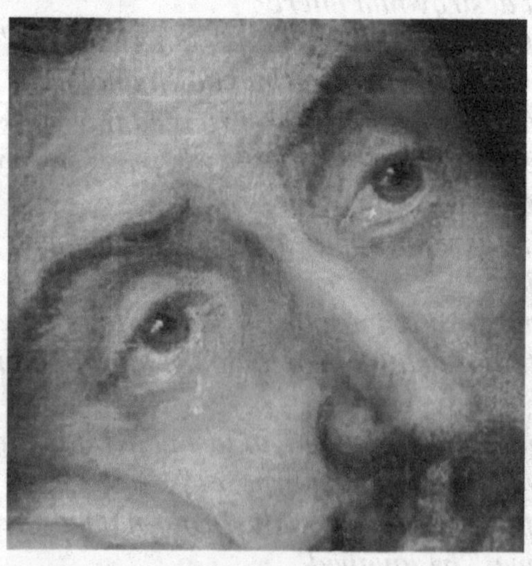

Peter the Apostle

The Departure

Peter shook his head at Thomas. "How can you doubt, Thomas? We all saw him, the Magdalene saw him, his mother saw him. He is risen, as surely as I rise each day to greet the dawn, he is risen!"

Thomas smiled, he knew and understood how Yeshua could project his being into the physical world from the dream place. For one such as Yeshua, it was not difficult to put forth an image of himself that people would see, hear and know. But in truth, his body could be asleep or dead, and what they saw was his dream body walking and talking amongst them. Certainly, by the mysterious way he vanished, that was a pretty clear clue as to what had happened.

At the same time, if Yeshua can wake up and create the illusion of a body in the physical while he had crossed over to the other side, this alone was indeed a miracle and proof of his divinity, "I do not mean to demean your faith, Peter, or appear to doubt what you believe what you say. But I have seen Yeshua dream walking in what seems this physical world, speaking to me like he was present, but he was in truth elsewhere."

Peter was too wrapped up in the joy of knowing his master lived to hear any of it, "He is back, Thomas. Despite the Sadducee and the Romans, he is back!"

Thomas drifted in his thought, floating over the last day as if it were a dream he watched

Thomas had gone with the tin merchant to the Temple and heard firsthand the many furious arguments by Caiaphas as he sought to unseat Nicodemus from his role in the council. The Pharisee had laughed at him, saying there were many independent eyewitness accounts saying they had spoken to Yeshua, therefore he was not dead.

He had also gone with Joseph the tin merchant to a meeting in Caesarea to meet personally with the wife of Pilate. They gave her the gossip on Yeshua somehow surviving the crucifixion and discovered her extraordinary interest in the Rabbi. She wanted to know all about him, where he had been, what he had said, and even asked what teaching he gave.

Thomas, as a follower, had been forced to speak for hours all about the master, a task that was extremely difficult for one who far preferred to listen than talk. She seemed delighted by what he said and wanted to know more and more, having her scribes note down all that he offered. "I will tell everything you have said to my husband," she explained as they were leaving as honored guests. "He will be relieved, for as he said, it was clear that your master was entirely blameless of the accusations made of him."

Thomas had to risk offending his host, "But he sent him to crucifixion?"

She smiled, "It is difficult being the ruler of a country where so many argue over everything," she explained. "If my husband had released your master, the crowd would have torn him to pieces, and there would have been riots all through the city. Thousands would have died. I am also given to understand, my husband tried to get your master to say he was not the King of the Jews in public, but he would not. In fact, your Yeshua berated him, can you believe it! Told Pilate he had no authority."

Thomas noted dryly, "If the rumor is true that he is risen again, then perhaps Yeshua spoke the truth. But in all honesty, I am not certain if he dream walks or if he is really here with us."

She smiled even as she shed a tear, "My husband was placed into a position he did not want to be in, but it seems to me that if this whisper is true, all is forgiven for our Yeshua has done the impossible and survived. But tell me what this dream walking is?"

Thomas was in disbelief, the wife of the Roman Governor is saying 'our' Yeshua. "The master could present as a physical person, speak with you, discuss things in a conversation - but later I would discover he was somewhere else entirely. I am not sure how he did this, but he did indeed appear in two places at the one time. I accepted this as a proof of his divinity."

Claudia was vastly impressed by this man's knowledge and wisdom. Plus he was so circumspect, he was almost Roman. She felt that no matter what he said, she understood what he MEANT - not just the words he spoke, but what they meant underneath the language. It was as if he spoke in Latin to her. "I must know more, I must know everything about this remarkable messiah of yours, so please, when you have time come back."

They were escorted from the palace to their carriage, where the horses had been groomed and watered. Joseph could not believe this, no Jew was ever this well received in the past. In somewhat a state of shock, Joseph said to Thomas, "I had always thought you were a bit dull-witted, for you never spoke. Now I see you understand more than any of us. Do you not know how well you speak, and how clearly you explain things? It was like Yeshua himself was standing there with you!"

How could Thomas explain, Yeshua WAS standing there, guiding his words, explaining that the Romans, more than any other people, needed to hear the truth he spoke.

With a start, he came back to the present, looking at the curious face of Peter before him once more. "Peter," he said softly, "Yeshua is always with me. I do not need his physical body to be here to understand what he wants, for he is with me even now."

Peter laughed, "Well maybe, who am I to naysay the master or what he wishes for us. But I am telling you, he is here!"

Thomas shook his head, "Have you touched him? Have you felt his flesh like you can feel mine?" he asked.

"Well no, but I didn't need to. He was here I am telling you!"

Thomas just laughed. He loved the old fisherman's enthusiasm and had no complaint, for this was so much better than the despondent pile of misery he had on his hands on the day of the crucifixion. "We will no doubt see soon enough," he responded. For the present, he was being regularly called up to see the wife of the governor, who also was asking if the rumor were true, as she wanted to meet Yeshua personally.

He laughed as, in his mind's eye, he saw the man Pilate crucified being invited to dinner. Not to say that Judea was crazy, but it was.

ooo0000ooo

The Governor looked incredulously at his wife, "You had one of his followers here? By the gods, woman, I put their master to death! Did you not fear repercussions? You know how insane these Jews are."

Claudia just smiled and put her arm around his as they walked out to the terrace. "I took precautions, for the scribes I had with me also had weapons, but darling, the two could not have been more pleasant, and that follower of his, I felt like his master were in the room talking to me. I was very moved, and he has no animosity towards us at all - a thing that proved to me beyond doubt that they truly practice what this Yeshua taught."

"And what was that?" Pilate asked cryptically.

"Many things, my husband, they speak of love over hate, of course. Everyone does that, but they speak with a certainty that love will guide them. They have an understanding like our Oracles, that life has an intelligence that guides us. They call it the Lord, but I understood what they meant, that the deeper wisdom of life itself whispers to us if we have the ears to hear."

"Hardly seems to be what the Sadducee think, they said he was a rabble-rouser who they believed would turn the crowd against them." he snorted.

"Darling, the people ALREADY are against the priests. I know you don't want to hear this, but Sejanus was right in wanting to be rid of them, for they do not represent the people at all. They are like the worst of our arrogant Patricians in Rome. Born of a single bloodline, believing that their heritage in some way makes them better than their fellows." she soothed.

That got him laughing, "Well my darling, as you are one of those arrogant Patricians who married far below her station, you should know. I am still amazed you grew to love me. I am grateful every day, but amazed. We both know the only reason our marriage was contrived was because your family did not have the dowry for a better match, but I am not complaining."

"We did well, all things considered, husband." she smiled and kissed his cheek. "I am the one who is most surprised, to find that arrogant young whelp turn into the faithful old dog that you are!"

He knew an invitation when he heard it, so he scooped her up and took her to their private chambers, with Claudia squealing, "Oh no, he's going to ravish me!" and laughing all the way.

ooo0000ooo

The huge black man smiled as he met the carpenter, "So you are a God? Coming back from the dead as you have, perhaps I should bow before you?"

Yeshua greeted him warmly, "My time here will soon be done, my friend. I realized that I do not even know your name?"

The captain smiled, "They call me Simon in this country, it is easier to adopt a familiar name. You need no introduction, of course, the famous Yeshua, the one who rose from the dead. That is quite a trick! But yes, despite your self-evident divinity I gather you have not yet sprouted wings and still need passage?"

"I do Simon, and as to divinity, what I am is what you are. My purpose is to be transparent to the will of the Lord, and when I am glass, then I am divine, as all of us will be when we attain this - if this makes sense to you?" Yeshua explained. He did not want people feeling uncomfortable around him, which was why the Zadoc always lived alone in a cave.

He was understanding it fully now, where he walked the emanations of Spirit flowed out and touched all around him. It upset many, they did not know why, but he could feel spirit moving out, touching and changing their lives. Most preferred to have a life without change.

Plus, having people worship him like they did the Zadoc on the Qumran? He found deeply offensive. To imagine he was somehow a God was false. All he was, all he could ever be from this day forward, was a vessel for the Lord. But to remain here and be the Zadoc? Living in a cave in the desert, that was not a life. Let Lazarus pass the test when he is ready and take over the mantle from him, for this is what he wanted. But there were other reasons, he could not stay in this country where the priests would still want to hunt him down and kill him. He knew this with certainty, that if his death pleased Caiaphas, his resurrection angered him beyond comprehension. Going to the Qumran would put everyone there in danger, so it was best he move on.

Simon laughed, he liked this fellow, a lot. "You know my little friend, I have served Pharaohs who were quite certain they were Gods. I have served High Priests, who truly believed they were the next best thing to a God, but I have never served a God who proclaimed himself a man. It is a refreshing change. They say you can also calm storms, that is a very useful god to have on a boat!"

"Despite the priests that you serve wanting me dead, you are still happy for me to sail with you to Persia? I have a friend who will be sailing with me, so we will need a cabin for two." Yeshua asked.

"Your own cabin, hey? Well, as a God I guess you qualify. Your wife?"

Yeshua smiled, "No, a friend. My wife will be going in the other direction."

"Oh, she feels uncomfortable being with a god?" Simon laughed, not meaning to pry, but at the same time, he needed to understand why people were on board and what their purpose might be. A ship needed harmony.

"The ritual I undertook, Simon, it changes you. All that was in the past is now gone, and all contracts are fulfilled. My wife will travel to Gaul, where she can work as a healer and teach the people as a priest, which has always been her calling," he explained.

"This I understand, my friend. My own dear wife is a priestess, but here she would be called a witch and killed for her knowledge. She prefers me to be sailing anywhere but her backyard! I haven't seen her for years, but she sends a note to say she is well and that the children are growing. I will be having the oldest with me next year, it seems, as he wishes to learn the trade of a soldier." Simon grasped so easily what few seemed to understand, that when a person lives in a spiritual realm, they have a sense of disconnection from people, despite a deep connection and love for them.

"You are not the ordinary soldier, Simon." Yeshua laughed.

"This is true my friend, for in my country I too would be called a King, except that we already have a King and he is not particularly keen to have another!" They both laughed, for Simon had heard of Yeshua being called the King of the Jews, with that being the reason they crucified him.

ooo0000ooo

Back in Tiberias, Herod looked out over the waters. Could it be true that this Yeshua he ridiculed actually rose from the dead? He was still haunted by nightmares of the Baptist, coming and looking at him, accusingly. Even worse than this, he had also heard that Pilate's wife was looking into the fellow, asking questions, finding out facts.

It seemed to him there was a plot in the background, but he had no idea what it might be, which drove him crazy. His coffers were being drained in that stupid war, created because he ditched the Petrian princess for his current wife. He still regretted every inch of that decision, Herodias was a cow that treated him like dirt. Plus all the kindness he had shown the locals didn't seem to count for so much as a free fish. They bitched and moaned at the slightest tax.

Worse, that damn brother-in-law, Agrippa, was getting up his nose, wanting money all the time to cover his debts. He was such an arrogant little pup he wanted him flogged, but his nasty little wife seemed to oppose him beating her brother for some reason.

The truth was, the damn Baptist was right. Everything started going sour the moment he took that bitch to bed.

ooo0000ooo

It had taken a week, but the transformation was finally done. The old Masters in India had spoken of the Keya Kalp, the rejuvenation of the body to maintain a longer life, but those herbs were not available in Judea. Yeshua had been directing the spiritual currents to flow through his body, to repair the organs and restore the blood to vitality, but also the tremendous loss of fluids had left him depleted.

The healers had stayed with him in the tomb, chanting the songs of awakening, channeling the power of the Lord into his ruined body, and together they had done what was thought impossible, survived crucifixion. He then stayed in a different cave with these men, away from all society, finding the silence to help with the healing. All week he had projected outwards to speak with his people, to help them keep faith. He knew now, the Lord had used him as a symbol, one these men could hold onto while he was gone.

It was strange, being doctored to by another, with himself the cripple. But he also ministered to his own body, as if he were a doctor visiting himself, and indeed, he was! Standing outside that suffering pain that was still his physical form was the only way to get through this. But he knew, it was the last of his earthly debts being burned, the final step to a true union with the Lord.

It was not as he imagined, no great thing at all, in many ways. He felt the extraordinary flow of divinity, one that was undeniable - the ancient current of the savior poured through him in an unquenchable river, a cornucopia of love. Yet it was also power, raw power. But the two were in harmony. It was beyond age, and yet new. It was vast, yet tiny. In this state, all things were one, even as they were many, and at last, he truly understood the phrase he had been given, "From the one to the many to return to the one".

Now the last stage of the journey for Judea was beginning, where he would seek to convey the power of the Law of Three to the men, and trust they will carry the torch when he is gone. That was the hard part, not being able to stay, but he knew wherever he went he would be hunted like never before. But he would be with them inwardly, and his dream self could assist in a thousand ways he could not even imagine here in his physical body.

That was what so few grasped, that this world was but a blink of time and that our true existence lay only in the eternal realms of the Lord. Man must come again and again to this place, to perfect his union with the divine, and finally, it joins with him - he becomes as Pythagoras had said, as a God.

When Socrates repeated this, they put the Greek to death for saying a man could become divine. It is an inherent fear of men, that another will rise so far above you that you cannot hope to attain their position. But it was not a position at all, it was a state of grace. And you do not rise to it, it unfolds within you. The whole purpose of his teaching was to help people accept that they already had divinity within their heart, they just had to understand what got in the way of receiving this gift.

They called him Messiah, they called him a King, they called him a miracle worker, but in truth he was a doctor, healing their broken hearts, mending their bruised and frightened child within. All he had ever wanted was to heal the hate and the suffering he saw, and to teach people the spiritual truth that one plus one equals two.

His thoughts were now in the foothills of Kashmir, where he met the ancient one, that nameless saint who had lived in his body for countless years. Some said over a thousand years, but who would know? His wisdom was truly ageless and when he had asked of that saint how to educate a man so that he understood the Lord, he laughed, and said, "First you must teach him mathematics - and the first lesson is One plus One equals Two. THEN he can learn how One plus One equals Three."

Yeshua had contemplated that strange wisdom for years, rolling it around in his thoughts, trying to see how the impossible was possible. How can one plus one equal three? He had grasped the first bit, all children know only love, they are one - they are pure and undefiled. But then they learn a new thing, it might the mother teaching the child to share, and this addition of Love plus Sharing equals a Heart of Giving. Or they might learn loss, and so Love plus Loss equals Need, and they grow into need as their basis in this life.

The seeds planted in the heart of the young create the society of the future. If you want harmony in Judea, teach the children to all get along, to love their country, and to respect their fellows, which was pretty much the opposite of what they were taught - and so, sadly, the country will be broken up once more. The arguments will cleave the tribes apart and they will wander lost and alone until they chose the path of harmony and forgiveness.

It was listening to music that he grasped the second part, for if two musicians play two perfect notes in resonance, then a third note just appears in the air. It comes from nowhere, which is to say, from the Lord. He watches and waits for perfect harmony, and therein makes himself manifest. So first, we must learn to be in harmony with our life, and then life will sing with us and create a chorus of angels to carry us into the heart of truth. This is the Law of Three.

Sitting in this vast current of harmony of opposites, he saw it all so clearly. The pain and suffering, the joy and laughter, the fear and loathing, and the confident sprouting of new grain, it was all part of the same oneness. We were all a drop in an ocean of love and mercy, where some believed they were drowning while others believed they were swimming, while others believed they were flying. It was all in how you saw, not what you saw, that created your reality.

If your heart sang in a harmony with your fellows, if your Soul was clothed in humility and justice, if your thoughts were only filled with goodwill to all, then you walked with the Lord in paradise, even when your body hung in agony on a cross. This he knew now, this he knew with such certainty for his heart had wedded the Lord. He had become the Zadoc.

And yet he was still human, as fragile as a flower, even as his heart was strong as a lion.

It was time for the journey. The healers, his angels from the Lord, had known what he had intended without him needing to say a word, for they had fetched his father's tools and packed them into a case that they loaded onto a wagon. Finally, he would be able to practice the work he loved so dearly, fashioning wood into beauty and form.

But first, he must say his farewells. Farewell to his friends, farewell to his past, farewell to his wife, to his mother, to his entire history. A part of him wanted to stay, to just go to his father's workshop, with his wife, and settle there, but the itch in his palm would never go away, and the Sadducee would never forgive. Plus the people, beloved though they might be, were so enmeshed in their traditions of what the Zadoc must be, that he doubted they would have permitted it. No, let Lazarus take the burden of his people when he was well and able to survive the test.

His first farewell was to the men that saved him. They just nodded and would soon go back to the deep desert, to collect the herbs and prepare their tinctures. One thing that had surprised him was how powerful adding crushed garlic to honey was for wound healing, all knew honey disinfected, all knew garlic healed, why he had not put the two together he did not know, but all infection fled from it. He must mention it to Mary.

He pulled a hood over his head so no one would recognize him, and made his way down to where the disciples would be waiting.

ooo0000ooo

The Temple was full of dissent and shouting, as accusations were flung at the Pharisee, who in turn responded with accusations of corruption against the Sadducee. "And why in the name of all that is holy was Caiaphas seen entering the prison, a place of death, where we knew Barabas was being held? He who accuses ME swims in corruption up to his EARS!" Nicodemus shouted across the way at the High Priest.

"Baseless accusations!" shouted Bilibis, looking worn and tired now. "Not like the clear report in the writing of the Roman speaking of one Nicodemus pulling a dead body from a cross!"

Joseph the tin merchant laughed, "And yet, so many eyewitness reports that that so-called dead man is walking and breathing. Maybe we should call in LAZARUS to ask what he thinks of this?" And on and on it went for many hours, the not-so-subtle to and fro of power politics. There was not a man there who did not understand what the Sadducee were fighting for, the money from the Temple Taxes.

The Sadducee knew they were the only ones with the connections in Rome to ensure peace and a degree of autonomy in Jerusalem, and that the money was needed for bribes and for purchasing favor. Who knew what the idiot Pharisee would do if they got their hands on it? Only one thing was certain, it would not be put to paying the bribes necessary for the ongoing independence of Judea.

The real problem was the assassinations that had started. All knew it was Barabas, all knew Caiaphas supported him, so there was no doubt who was really to blame. The Sanhedrin had devolved into outright warfare between the tribes, the very thing it had been contrived to eliminate.

"Despite the loudness of the debate, the real question is one of law. The Sadducee knowingly and wilfully broke the law of gathering by convening an illegal court that sentenced an innocent man to death," Nicodemus stood so his voice could be heard by all, especially those listening outside of the court where they sat. "The Roman Proconsul himself found the man blameless, but only relented to the crucifixion due to the pressure of the crowd, which we KNOW was funded by the Sadducee for we have eyewitness accounts of the priests sending people to that courtyard, for this reason."

A great deal of shouting and booing came from the other side of the aisle, with shouts of 'sit down' and 'shut up' from the priests. "My question is a simple one, how can such men who ignore the law so blatantly continue to pretend they have a right to sit on this council?"

There was, of course, no answer nor any resolution, and the assassinations kept adding to the death toll in Jerusalem.

ooo0000ooo

The Master walked into the meeting room, went to the table, and took bread and wine, breaking it and handing it out as a reminder of his blessing to all. Peter was overjoyed, Yeshua had returned and THIS time

Thomas was here to verify it! And indeed, he did! With great reverence, he went to the master, and inspected the cut and abrasions, noting how remarkably well they had healed. "Honey and crushed garlic, can you believe? I knew of garlic, we all knew of honey, I had never thought to mix them. All infection was chased away, and the wounds healed rapidly after that," Yeshua shared.

At the same time, he whispered, "Passage for both of us is booked to Persia. I leave in three days, I will send you a message when I know our meeting place."

Thomas nodded, and went to sit down, with Peter shouting happily, "See! Did I not tell you truly, our master is ALIVE!"

Yeshua settled the crowd down with his hand in the air, "I must speak with you all of the future, for soon I will no longer be here with you..." a pin could have dropped and sounded like a bell with these words. "If I remain, the Sadducee will hunt us down and murder us, for they see me as their most deadly enemy, and by association yourselves as well. With me gone, they will let the sleeping dog lie, and you will be able to quietly go about the work I have taught you.

"Do not despair or be discomforted, it is as it must be. I have given you knowledge of healing, and an understanding of the power of the Lord. You have been initiated into the rite of Spirit, and baptized by the holy fire, you are ready. So too, as we meet here today, must you continue to do. To share, to teach, to heal the heart and soul of all who need your help.

"Know that I am with you. If you are assailed by doubt, look within and you will find me there. I say to you, the Lord will work through you and pave your way. Do not doubt his blessings, do not flinch from the tasks he sets you, which will be many and difficult. Men will blame you, forgive them for they live in ignorance. Men will revile you, forgive them for they know not the love of the Lord. As you share this bread and wine as I do today, remember, it is ME you are handing out, for I am with you in all truthful and loving actions you do.

"Know that where I go, spirit prepares the place for yourself to reside. In the home of many mansions that you will build, always leave a place aside for my presence, and I will be with you then as surely as I am with you now. In your hearts, the plans are already laid by the Lord. You need only read your truest, deepest intention to know how to build my house, the house that is open to all, that offers hospitality to the lowest as it does the highest."

Phillip called out, "Master, show us the father, show us the one we must seek counsel from in your absence!"

Yeshua smiled, "Do you know me not? How can you say '*show us the father*' when he and I are now one? What you see before you is a man united with the Lord, heart, and soul. You may think of yourself as less than this, as a son who needs the guidance of the father, but truly I say to you the Lord resides in YOU. Trust this, and know that all I have done is to show you to the place within where you can do greater work. Just ask for humility and guidance, and the way will open before you.

"This is so because you have been given the gift of the Spirit of the Lord. It resides in your heart, and it will bring you whatever you need, just ask with humility for guidance. Spirit will come, it will be the right hand of the Lord, reaching through you into this world."

Thomas asked, "Lord, what you were accused of, being a witch and a magician, how do we avoid that fate? How can we thread the path through the Needle?"

"Do all in my name. Men will accuse you, but do all in my name so that in your heart there is certainty. Let no doubt assail your faith. Men, I have said over and over again, it is not me, but the father that moves through. He does the miracles, he heals the lost and the diseased, he finds the path to a righteous life. The Lord is here now, in our hearts, know this, trust this, be worthy of his presence, and the path will be made clear."

Yeshua felt the spirit of the Lord stepping forward, willing to reach out and touch each man personally, "Know this, I have shown you the way, the truth, the light. Trust in me." Then Yeshua returns to himself, laughing, for this is what being the Zadoc felt like. "Know this, those who come to the father through me will find my outstretched hand, guiding, helping, offering succor. Whatever truthful and kind thing you ask in my name, the Lord within shall provide to you.

"The Lord sent me here, to you, to give you the words of truth, love, and charity, and to show you the path to the Lord within. Now you know, I was not killed on the cross, but consecrated to the Lord. Whatever comes in your path, as you act in my name, know that all is part of this consecration to the higher purpose of the Lord.

"Because I know you, because I love you, the pathway to the house of the Lord is formed. And so too must you find ones you love and cherish, and by your love, you too will show them to the house of the Lord. With these words, I send you as emissaries of the Lord out to the world, so that you might find those who are ready for the words and stories I have shared with you. Use these Stones of Truth to build a house wherein the soul can reside."

Yeshua paused, for he knew, should the people of Judea accept this kindness he offered, their world would change. Yet he knew they will react with malcontent and ferment rebellion against his simple truth. All he has ever said was that love is the doorway to happiness. He prayed for them, that they would find the way through to freedom. "The fire of the Lord is with you, let it burn down the obstacles before you, let it warm you at night, let it flow out as love to all who cherish you, and kindness to all that do not. For all I have done, all I have said, all I have given you comes down to this simple, clear truth: *The Lord is within your heart*. Knock, and the door shall be opened to you."

The men ate and drank, and laughed, and told stories, and remembered the wise things, the foolish things, and the crazy things they had done over the last few years. They were deeply saddened Yeshua must go away, but it was obvious that Caiaphas would not release his hate any time soon. However, his time as High Priest would end one day, and they were sure that after a few years passed, things would settle down, and he would return.

ooo0000ooo

Visiting the children of his brother James, Yeshua scooped them up, delighting in their joy and happiness. They laughed and sang and told him all about what had happened since he had last seen them, which was but days ago, yet to the children it could have been a year.

James had walked with him from the meeting room, sad but understanding, "This has become a dangerous place, brother. Essenes used to be ignored, but your politics has changed many things. Where will you go from here?"

Yeshua put the children down, "Back home," was all he said.

James knew better than to quiz him on technical things, like what that might mean. "Our father's wisdom in buying this house has proved to be beyond measure. Do you miss him?"

"What, miss the taciturn frowning and the critical look of nothing ever being quite good enough? (James laughed) Yes, I do. Now that I understand him, I miss him greatly."

"Unless we understand something, we are not able to appreciate what it is, and until something is gone, we have no idea what it truly means to us," James sighed.

Yeshua laughed, "Not like you to be so cryptic - I thought that was my job!"

James smiled, weary and tired from the last week, but content. His brother lived and had done the impossible. But as the Zadoc now, he felt the change in him. "And I thought politics mine - the Magdalene?"

"You know my life is wholly of God, but that is not the reason for our parting. The forefathers insisting on celibacy with the monks on the Qumran made that choice for many reasons. For one the land was harsh and unsuited to raising children, and if you are married, well, that is what will happen. This affected their thinking until they came to believe that purity of thought required a life of abstinence. How can a lack of love and kindness make a man better, I ask you? It cannot.

"Mary needs to teach, to be a priest as I have been, and that is not possible here. Her heart tells her to go to Gaul and I have seen her path, which is glorious but not one I must walk. My time is done, brother, and from here I slip into the shadows, teaching only in the dream worlds." The children had been gathered by their mother and were happily buzzing about as she made them ready for sleep.

"A story for them, to help them sleep?" she asked her brother-in-law.

They all went to the nursery when the children piled like kittens into their bed and Yeshua gave them one last tale to take them across into the world of dreams.

In a place far away and high in the mountains, so high as if to touch the clouds, there was a lake, a calm, peaceful lake. On that lake, there were wonderful boats, large boats, filled with fabrics and made of wood from enormous trees. And in those boats lived people, all their lives they lived there. They were born on the boat, they fished food from their boat, and they made fabrics that they sold to visitors to the lake.

Not surprisingly, they were called the boat people! They were happy and had few cares other than trading for what they needed. Of course, there was the odd storm, but these were large boats, owned by families for generations, and they were used to weathering those. If such a thing approached, they all sailed to the safe harbor of the town that was on that lake so far away and so high in the mountains, and instead of fearing the storms, it was an opportunity for them all to get together and laugh and play.

Like here, they had a king, who had soldiers, and who had laws that must be obeyed, but what did this matter to the boat people? He could hardly march out over the water and say, "You are sailing this the wrong way!" could he? (the children all laugh) They paid their taxes, but they had so little that few taxes were required, yet they also had everything, for to these people the sun, the moon, the wind, and the water were their wealth.

For in this world, the fish would come, which gave the men useful work, and this work provided the threads the women wove, which gave them useful work. And the fabrics they made were prized throughout the land, which gave them all that they needed to live. But they were wise, in their way, for they told the people, when the storms blew and they were in harbor, that they lived with great fear - for monsters patrolled the waters of the deep, and they had to watch day and night.

But they were just telling a story to keep other people off their lake, for there were no monsters but those that lived in the imagination of the townspeople. And around that lake were huge mountains, capped with white - a cold thing called snow. And there were green trees and gardens and fertile fields, for even the land people were happy in that place, so far away and so high in the mountains, as if to touch the clouds.

As he told the story of so far away and so high in the mountains as if to touch the clouds, the children all fell into dreams. Yeshua smiled, if his brother now understood where he was going, then it was well. If he didn't, this also was fine.

ooo0000ooo

It was far more difficult than he realized, saying farewell to his wife, to his life in Judea. Back in time, as a youth, when he had first ventured into the unknown on the ship sailing down the straights to Persia, he felt weak and confused, not knowing why he was leaving all he had known behind. But at that time the thirst for adventure rose over any fears that might have held him back.

He no longer had a thirst for anything but the Lord, and fear no longer lived in his heart. He could not give himself a good reason for leaving, but neither could he find a reason to stay. Then he had the vision of Thomas with him in India, and he knew, even before the cross and the awakening, he knew his path was leading him to return to the East.

The one disciple he could speak directly to was Thomas, perhaps because he preferred to listen than speak, perhaps because his heart was ready, but in this one he saw greatness, a model for the future. "Do you understand, Thomas, that we go to a culture as old as ours, but with very different views on the world?" Thomas said nothing, of course, but he knew they would go past Egypt, and he wondered why the Lord was so cruel to the Egyptians. He had always wondered about that.

The bracing wind as they made their way down the gulf carried salt and freshness with every breath they took. For Yeshua, it was a joy to be underway, to have completed the task, and to return to his home.

Perhaps he heard the thoughts of his disciple. Yeshua laughed, and said, "We celebrate Passover every year, but do you wonder why we do not curse the Egyptians? More to the point, why did a loving God hate the Egyptians so much? To understand this, we need to understand that the Hebrew faith in that distant time was a tribal faith, and every tribe believes their God loves them, but obviously, if he loves them, he cannot love their enemies."

Thomas did finally speak, "I too have wondered how the Lord could have been so cruel to the Egyptians. I asked as a child and was beaten for my efforts."

“What happened, Thomas, is that the faith grew up. It was like a child back then, prone to tantrums, and not understanding its place in the world. But the prophets came and saved us. They are the ones that lifted the Jews from savagery. Men illuminated by the divine light of the Lord came to help us, to lift our understanding of the world and our place in it. They cast off the yolk of ignorance and brought us the burden of love.

"Hosea taught us that Love is God in action, that forgiveness and kindness are the path of the Lord. Amos taught us that God is justice, and that to worship god is to respect and practice justice to all. More than any, he molded my faith and understanding when he said, *'You worship God, yet you do not even see the poor'*.

"And Jonah, what a story that was. It came from just after the exile in Babylon, when men were casting about for reasons why the Lord had betrayed them, and given them to captivity. They had decided that it was because the race was no longer pure, and they started to purge the gentiles, killing or exiling them, even though they may be married to a Jew. Jonah is a story that opened the heart and enabled the people to resist that cruelty when he asked, *'Do you not know that God's love is greater than your own?'*

"Malachi forced us to question our self-centered belief that the Lord was OUR god, for he brought to our nation that the Lord was a universal God, a God to all men, regardless of their faith. This was one of the greatest steps of all, for it allowed us to extend love and justice to all. he asked, *'Are we all not all from the one father? Has not God created us all?'*

"But when I teach this in the synagogues, they want to stone me. Tradition, the clinging to the past, this is what imprisons the heart. As fear creates the prison, tradition forges the links of the chains that bind us in place. The job of the teachers is to break the chains and open the door, but we cannot force a man to leave the darkness, they must want the light with all their being if they are to leave their past behind.

Sometimes Yeshua felt he was talking to himself, people so rarely saw the obvious in what was before them. "Let me tell you a secret - if we can see through the illusions that dance before our eyes, the pretense, the dreams, the notions of greatness that control the hearts of most men, then all things are made clear. But to do this, you have to leave your prison, to walk into the sunlight of the Lord's grace, just as a child does. It is so simple, the whole message I give is so simple, be free!

"But to be truly free our heart must be full of curiosity and love, for this gives us the power to keep moving forward."

And silence flowed deeply upon the waters of their faith as they sailed to the next adventure.

The End?

We all know, this was
where the story began

Acknowledgment

This is a story I had wanted to write some forty years ago, but in truth I did not hold the wisdom in my heart at that time to give it a proper voice. There are many to thank for bringing me to the point of understanding, not the least being my father, who was unfailingly kind and humble.

My spiritual grandfathers, Ken Littlehawk and Erwin Baudzus, both who guided me with wisdom enough to not say a word, but to simply show me love.

My mother, of course, who asked nothing of me but to find happiness and who only knew to love her children. Her deep love for Jesus is part of the fabric of this book.

To Professor George Cockcroft who, through quiet instruction, taught me the power of saying more with less, and whose quiet approval of the "Gatherer of the Flax" convinced me this was a book that was worthy to be Written.

Bishop Spong offered tremendous clarification on so many points, and I viewed his videos and read his books with gratitude. May he rest in peace.

This is not even mentioning the spiritual guides, they who spoke through dreams and placed understandings into my heart. To all I say thanks, but in truth the true offer of my thanks is this book, which I give to you as my masters and teachers and mentors have given to me.

Cudgen, Australia
22 Oct 2022

Book of Yeshua

Author: Ecallaw Leachim
ISBN: 978-0-6452723-1-4

All enquiries via Email to: qrcaustralia@gmail.com
Published by Ladder to the Moon Publications.

Hunters of the Mist

Author: Ecallaw Leachim

ISBN: 978-0-6452723-0-7

Was this planet even Earth? Some sort of cataclysm has descended and the sun itself no longer shines upon the land. The crew of the Canter return after an extended away time to find a suffocating mist covers most of the land, a mist that houses creatures of horror who seek to dominate all that come near them.

Small pockets of humanity remain, but it is like the stone age. Jack Blake undertakes an arduous program, one that runs for decades, slowly educating the primitive people to perform the most basic tasks of civilization. And through it all, the Gregorians, the witch hunters track into the mist and free the land from control by the aliens that have taken residence in it.

Publisher: Ladder to the Moon Productions
Email: qrcaustralia@gmail.com
Web: laddertothemoon.com.au

Planet Aqua

Home for the Hated

Author: Ecallaw Leachim

A new world is discovered, one where Humans cannot go!

The Earth is ruined - Plastic Particulate has corrupted the eco-system, creating a world-wide desert. Humanity must subsist on synthetic food and live indoors as the atmosphere and climate have become hostile. Only the rich can afford fresh food, decent housing and a private eco-system. Then a miracle, a new planet is discovered, one where nature is vital and food is plentiful - The problem, it has a toxic atmosphere making it uninhabitable by humans. The solution is to create a race of hated clones, manufactured humans who will be built to function on that world, and become the farmers for earth.

... If only things were this simple

About the Author

Ecallaw Leachim is considered by many to be a polymath. He is accomplished in many diverse fields, as a Master Musician, Master Body Worker, Master Numerologist, Dice Master, Recording Artist, Songwriter, and Publisher. He is also a prolific Author with over twenty four titles in print.

The concept for the Gospel of Yeshua came out of inner experiences he had in his Twenties and, forty years later, he wrote it down.

www.laddertothemoon.com.au

Aiming for the Stars is much easier if we stop off at the Moon. We are then out of the atmosphere of our past, and can see things more clearly. We are lighter, can jump higher and further than ever before, and it takes far less energy to start each journey.

The hard part is climbing that Ladder to the Moon.

www.ingramcontent.com/pod-product-compliance
Lightning Source LLC
Chambersburg PA
CBHW010456100726
47904CB00010B/2563

* 9 7 8 0 6 4 5 2 7 2 3 1 4 *